Humankind's ultimate betrayal
will come from within . . .

THE JUDAS STRAIN

○—○

By James Rollins

ALTAR OF EDEN
THE DOOMSDAY KEY
THE LAST ORACLE
THE JUDAS STRAIN
BLACK ORDER
MAP OF BONES
SANDSTORM
ICE HUNT
AMAZONIA
DEEP FATHOM
EXCAVATION
SUBTERRANEAN

Coming Soon in Hardcover

THE DEVIL COLONY

JAMES ROLLINS

THE JUDAS STRAIN

A Σ SIGMA FORCE THRILLER

HARPER

An Imprint of HarperCollinsPublishers

HARPER

An Imprint of HarperCollins *Publishers*
10 East 53rd Street
New York, New York 10022-5299

Copyright © 2007 by Jim Czajkowski
Excerpt from *The Last Oracle* copyright © 2008 by Jim Czajkowski
ISBN 978-0-06-202236-3

First Harper paperback international printing: June 2010
First Harper paperback printing: June 2008
First Harper special paperback printing: May 2008
First William Morrow special trade paperback printing: July 2007
First William Morrow hardcover printing: July 2007

10 9 8 7 6 5 4 3 2 1

TO CAROLYN MCCRAY
*who read all my earliest scribblings
and didn't laugh too much*

ACKNOWLEDGMENTS

TOO MANY PEOPLE, not enough space.

First, to everyone at HarperCollins, I owe you all a long-overdue acknowledgment for the past decade of guidance, hard work, and expertise:

To the big guns, Michael Morrison and Lisa Gallagher, thanks for all the support and confidence. Past, present, and future.

To the art directors, Richard Aquan and Thomas Egner, thanks for making the books stand out so handsomely. I could not be prouder.

To the marketing directors, Adrienne DiPietro and Tavia Kowalchuk, thanks for your ongoing leadership in getting the books out there . . . and noticed!

To the best PR team in the world, Pam Spengler-Jaffee and Buzzy Porter, thanks for not making me jump out of a bush plane in Alaska.

To a trio of women who put me on the map and in bookstores—Lynn Grady, Liate Stehlik, and Debbie Stier—a huge thank-you (and I'm writing this on bended knee).

To the indomitable force behind national sales and accounts—Carla Parker, Brian Grogan, Brian McSharry, and Mark Gustafson—thanks for all your extra efforts and energies to elbow the novels into stores and onto shelves.

To Mike Spradlin, thanks for both sales and zombies (in no particular order).

And to the hundred and one others whom I've failed to mention, but whom I appreciate no less—THANKS!

Moving closer to home, I must acknowledge my dark cabal who tear apart each chapter and reconstruct it into something better: Penny Hill, Steve and Judy Prey, Chris Crowe, Lee Garrett, Michael Gallowglas, Leonard Little, Kathy L'Ecluse, Debbie Nelson, Rita Rippetoe, Dave Murray, Dennis Grayson, Jane O'Riva, and Caroline Williams. And I'd like to give a special shout-out to Steve Prey for the book's map and Penny Hill for all the working lunches. To Cherei McCarter for the great series of articles featuring advanced weaponry. And to David Sylvian for listening ad nauseam as I read sections out loud (your ears will stop bleeding).

And once again, to the four people instrumental at all levels of production: my fantastic editor, Lyssa Keusch, and her stalwart colleague May Chen, and my indomitable agents, Russ Galen and Danny Baror. You all rock . . . big-time!

And lastly, I must stress any and all errors of fact or detail fall squarely on my own shoulders.

NOTE FROM THE HISTORICAL RECORD

HEREIN LIES A MYSTERY. In the year 1271, a young seventeen-year-old Venetian named Marco Polo left with his father and uncle on a voyage to the palaces of Kublai Khan in China. It was a journey that would last twenty-four years and bring forth stories of the exotic lands that lay to the east of the known world: wondrous tales of endless deserts and jade-rich rivers, of teeming cities and vast sailing fleets, of black stones that burned and money made of paper, of impossible beasts and bizarre plants, of cannibals and mystic shamans.

After serving seventeen years in the courts of Kublai Khan, Marco returned to Venice in 1295, where his story was recorded by a French romanticist named Rustichello, in a book titled in Old French *Le Divisament dou Monde* (or *The Description of the World*). The text swept Europe. Even Christopher Columbus carried a copy of Marco's book on his journey to the New World.

But there is one story of this journey that Marco refused to ever tell, referring only obliquely to it in his text. When Marco Polo had left China, Kublai Khan had granted the Venetian fourteen immense ships and six hundred men. But when Marco finally reached port after two years at sea, there remained but two ships and only eighteen men.

The fate of the other ships and men remain a mystery to this day. Was it shipwreck, storms, piracy? He never told. In fact, on his deathbed, when asked to elaborate or recant his story, Marco answered cryptically: "I have not told half of what I saw."

Return Journey of Marco Polo (1292–1295)

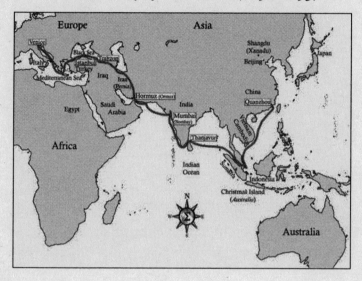

The pestilence came first to the town of Kaffa on the Black Sea. There the mighty Mongolian Tartars waged siege upon the Italian Genoese, merchants and traders. Plague struck the Mongol armies with burning boils and bloody expulsions. Struck with great malice, the Mongol lords used their siege catapults to cast their diseased dead over the Genoese walls, and spread plague in a litter of bodies and ruin. In the year of the incarnation of the Son of God 1347, the Genoese fled under sail in twelve galleys back to Italy, to the port of Messina, bringing the Black Death to our shores.

—Duke M. Giovanni (1356),
trans. by Reinhold Sebastien in *Il Apocalypse*
(Milan: A. Mondadori, 1924), 34–35

Why the bubonic plague suddenly arose out of China's Gobi desert during the Middle Ages and slew a third of the world's population remains unknown. In fact, no one knows why so many plagues and influenzas of the last century—SARS, the Avian Flu—have arisen out of Asia. But what is known with fair certainty: the next great pandemic will arise again out of the East.

—United States Centers for
Disease Control and Prevention,
Compendium of Infectious Diseases,
May 2006

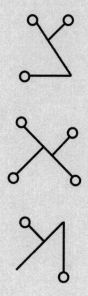

1293

Midnight

Island of Sumatra
Southeast Asia

THE SCREAMS HAD finally ceased.

Twelve bonfires blazed out in the midnight harbor.

"Il dio, li perdona . . ." his father whispered at his side, but Marco knew the Lord would not forgive them this sin.

A handful of men waited beside the two beached long-boats, the only witnesses to the funeral pyres out upon the dark lagoon. As the moon had risen, all twelve ships, mighty wooden galleys, had been set to torch with all hands still aboard, both the dead and those cursed few who still lived. The ships' masts pointed fiery fingers of accusation toward the heavens. Flakes of burning ash rained down upon the beach and those few who bore witness. The night reeked of burned flesh.

"Twelve ships," his uncle Masseo mumbled, clutching the silver crucifix in one fist, "the same number as the Lord's Apostles."

At least the screams of the tortured had ended. Only the crackle and low roar of the flames reached the sandy shore now. Marco wanted to turn from the sight. Others were not as stout of heart and knelt on the sand, backs to the water, faces as pale as bone.

All were stripped naked. Each had searched his neighbor for any sign of the mark. Even the great Khan's princess, who stood behind a screen of sailcloth for modesty, wore only her jeweled headpiece. Marco noted her lithe form through the cloth, lit from behind by the fires. Her maids, naked themselves, had searched their mistress. Her name was Kokejin, the Blue Princess, a maiden of seventeen, the same age as Marco had been when he started the journey from Venice. The Polos had been assigned by the Great Khan to safely deliver her to her betrothed, the Khan of Persia, the grandson of Kublai Khan's brother.

That had been in another lifetime.

Had it been only four months since the first of the galley crew had become sick, showing welts on groin and beneath the arm? The illness spread like burning oil, unmanning the galleys of able men and stranding them here on this island of cannibals and strange beasts.

Even now drums sounded in the dark jungle. But the savages knew better than to approach the encampment, like the wolf shunning diseased sheep, smelling the rot and corruption. The only signs of their encroachment were the skulls, twined through the eye sockets with vines and hung from tree branches, warding against deeper trespass or foraging.

The sickness had kept the savages at bay.

But no longer.

With the cruel fire the disease was at last vanquished, leaving only this small handful of survivors.

Those clear of the red welts.

Seven nights ago the remaining sick had been taken in chains to the moored boats, left with water and food. The others remained on shore, wary of any sign among them of fresh affliction. All the while, those banished to the ships called out across the waters, pleading, crying, praying, cursing, and screaming. But the worst was the occasional laughter, bright with madness.

Better to have slit their throats with a kind and swift blade, but all feared touching the blood of the sick. So they had been sent to the boats, imprisoned with the dead already there.

Then as the sun sank this night, a strange glow appeared in the water, pooled around the keels of two of the boats, spreading like spilled milk upon the still black waters. They had seen the glow before, in the pools and canals beneath the stone towers of the cursed city they had fled.

The disease sought to escape its wooden prison.

It had left them no choice.

The boats—all the galleys, except for the one preserved for their departure—had been torched.

Marco's uncle Masseo moved among the remaining men. He waved for them to again cloak their nakedness, but simple cloth and woven wool could not mask their deeper shame.

"What we did . . ." Marco said.

"We must not speak of it," his father said, and held forth a robe toward Marco. "Breathe a word of pestilence and all lands will shun us. No port will let us enter their waters. But now we've burned away the last of the disease with a cleansing fire, from our fleet, from the waters. We have only to return home."

As Marco slipped the robe over his head, his father noted what the son had drawn earlier in the sand with a stick. With a tightening of his lips, his father quickly ground it away der a heel and stared up at his son. A beseeching lo upon his visage. "Never, Marco . . . never . . ."

But the memory could not be so easily ground aw had served the Great Khan, as scholar, emissary, eve tographer, mapping his many conquered kingdoms.

His father spoke again. "None must ever know what found . . . it is cursed."

Marco nodded and did not comment on what he had drawn. He only whispered. *"Città dei Morti."*

His father's countenance, already pale, blanched further. But Marco knew it wasn't just plague that frightened his father.

"Swear to me, Marco," he insisted.

Marco glanced up into the lined face of his father. He

had aged as much during these past four months as he had during the decades spent with the Khan in Shangdu.

"Swear to me on your mother's blessed spirit that you'll never speak again of what we found, what we did."

Marco hesitated.

A hand gripped his shoulder, squeezing to the bone. "Swear to me, my son. For your own sake."

He recognized the terror reflected in his fire-lit eyes . . . and the pleading. Marco could not refuse.

"I will keep silent," he finally promised. "To my death-bed and beyond. I so swear, Father."

Marco's uncle finally joined them, overhearing the younger man's oath. "We should never have trespassed there, Niccolò," he scolded his brother, but his accusing words were truly intended for Marco.

Silence settled between the three, heavy with shared secrets.

His uncle was right.

Marco pictured the river delta from four months back. The black stream had emptied into the sea, fringed by heavy leaf and vine. They had only sought to renew their stores of fresh water while repairs were made to two ships. They ~~ld~~ never have ventured farther, but Marco had heard ~~s~~ of a great city beyond the low mountains. And as ten days were set for repairs, he had ventured with twoscore of the Khan's men to climb the low mountains and see what lay beyond. From a crest, Marco had spotted a stone tower deep within the forest, thrusting high, brilliant in the dawn's light. It drew him like a beacon, ever curious.

Still, the silence as they hiked through the forest toward the tower should have warned him. There had been no drums, like now. No birdcalls, no scream of monkeys. The city of the dead had simply waited for them.

It was a dreadful mistake to trespass.

And it cost them more than just blood.

The three stared out as the galleys smoldered down to the waterlines. One of the masts toppled like a felled tree. Two decades ago, father, son, and uncle had left Italian soil, under the seal of Pope Gregory X, to venture forth into the Mongol lands, all the way to the Khan's palaces and gardens in Shangdu, where they had roosted far too long, like caged partridges. As favorites of the court, the three Polos had found themselves trapped—not by chains, but by the Khan's immense and smothering friendship, unable to leave without insulting their benefactor. So at long last, they thought themselves lucky to be returning home to Venice, released from service to the great Kublai Khan to act as escorts for the lady Kokejin to her Persian betrothed.

Would that their fleet had never left Shangdu . . .

"The sun will rise soon," his father said. "Let us be gone. It is time we went home."

"And if we reach those blessed shores, what do we tell Teobaldo?" Masseo asked, using the original name of the man, once a friend and advocate of the Polo family, now styled as Pope Gregory X.

"We don't know he still lives," his father answered. "We've been gone so long."

"But if he does, Niccolò?" his uncle pressed.

"We will tell him all we know about the Mongols and their customs and their strengths. As we were directed under his edict so long ago. But of the plague here . . . there remains nothing to speak of. It is over."

Masseo sighed, but there was little relief in his exhalation. Marco read the words behind his deep glower.

Plague had not claimed all of those who were lost.

His father repeated more firmly, as if saying would make it so. "It is over."

Marco glanced up at the two older men, his father and his uncle, framed in fiery ash and smoke against the night sky. It would never be over, not as long as they remembered.

Marco glanced to his toes. Though the mark was scuffed off the sand, it burned brightly still behind his eyes. He had stolen a map painted on beaten bark. Painted in blood. Temples and spires spread in the jungle.

All empty.

Except for the dead.

The ground had been littered with birds, fallen to the stone plazas as if struck out of the skies in flight. Nothing was spared. Men and women and children. Oxen and beasts of the field. Even great snakes had hung limp from tree limbs, their flesh boiling from beneath their scales.

The only living inhabitants were the ants.

Of every size and color.

Teeming across stones and bodies, slowly picking apart the dead.

But he was wrong . . . something still waited for the sun to fall.

Marco shunned those memories.

Upon discovering what Marco had stolen from one of the temples, his father had burned the map and spread the ashes into the sea. He did this even before the first man aboard their own ships had become sick.

"Let it be forgotten," his father had warned then. "It has nothing to do with us. Let it be swallowed away by history."

Marco would honor his word, his oath. This was one tale he would never speak. Still, he touched one of the marks in the sand. He who had chronicled so much . . . was it right to destroy such knowledge?

If there was another way to preserve it . . .

As if reading Marco's thoughts, his uncle Masseo spoke aloud all their fears. "And if the horror should rise again, Niccolò, should someday reach our shores?"

"Then it will mean the end of man's tyranny of this world," his father answered bitterly. He tapped the crucifix resting on Masseo's bare chest. "The friar knew better than all. His sacrifice . . ."

The cross had once belonged to Friar Agreer. Back in the cursed city, the Dominican had given his life to save theirs. A dark pact had been struck. They had left him back there, abandoned him, at his own bidding.

The nephew of Pope Gregory X.

Marco whispered as the last of the flames died into the dark waters. "What God will save us next time?"

MAY 22, 6:32 P.M.
Indian Ocean
10° 44'07.87"s | 105° 11'56.52"E

"WHO WANTS ANOTHER bottle of Foster's while I'm down here?" Gregg Tunis called from belowdecks.

Dr. Susan Tunis smiled at her husband's voice as she pushed off the dive ladder and onto the open stern deck. She skinned out of her BC vest and hauled the scuba gear to the rack behind the research yacht's pilothouse. Her tanks clanked as she racked them alongside the others.

Free of the weight, she grabbed the towel from her shoulder and dried her blond hair, bleached almost white by sun and salt. Once done, she unzipped her wet suit with a single long tug.

"Boom-badaboom . . . badaboom . . ." erupted from a lounge chair behind her.

She didn't even glance back. Plainly someone had spent too much time in Sydney's strip clubs. "Professor Applegate, must you always do that when I'm climbing out of my gear?"

The gray-haired geologist balanced a pair of reading glasses on his nose, an open text on maritime history on his lap. "It would be ungentlemanly not to acknowledge the presence of a buxom young woman relieving herself of too much attire."

She shouldered out of the wet suit and stripped it down to her waist. She wore a one-piece swimsuit beneath. She had learned the hard way that a bikini top had the tendency to strip away with a wet suit. And while she didn't mind the retired professor, thirty years her senior, ogling her, she wasn't going to give him that much of a free show.

Her husband climbed up with three perspiring bottles of lager, pinching them all between the fingers of one hand. He grinned broadly upon seeing her. "Thought I heard you bumping about up here."

He climbed topside, stretching his tall frame. He wore only a pair of white Quicksilver trunks and a loose shirt, unbuttoned. Employed as a boat mechanic in Darwin Harbor, he and Susan had met during one of the dry-dock repairs on another of the University of Sydney's boats. That had been eight years ago. Just three days ago, they had celebrated their fifth anniversary aboard the yacht, moored a hundred nautical miles off Kiritimati Atoll, better known as Christmas Island.

He passed her a bottle. "Any luck with the soundings?"

She took a long pull on the beer, appreciating the moisture. Sucking on a salty mouthpiece all afternoon had turned her mouth pasty. "Not so far. Still can't find a source for the beachings."

Ten days ago eighty dolphins, *Tursiops aduncus,* an Indian Ocean species, had beached themselves along the coast of Java. Her research study centered on the long-term effects of sonar interference on cetacean species, the source of many suicidal beachings in the past. She usually had a team of research assistants with her, a mix of postgrads and undergrads, but the trip up here had been for a vacation with her old mentor. It was pure happenstance that such a massive beaching occurred in the region—hence the protracted stay here.

"Could it be something other than man-made sonar?" Applegate pondered, drawing circles with his fingertip in the condensation on his beer bottle. "Microquakes are constantly rattling the region. Perhaps a deep-sea subduction quake struck the right tonal note to drive them into a suicidal panic."

"There was that bonzer quake a few months back," her husband said. He settled into a lounge beside the professor and patted the seat for her to sit with him. "Maybe some aftershocks?"

Susan couldn't argue against their assessments. Between the series of deadly quakes over the past two years and the major tsunami in the area, the seabed was greatly disturbed. It was enough to spook anyone. But she wasn't convinced. Something else was happening. The reef below was oddly deserted. What little life was down there seemed to have retreated into rocky niches, shells, and sandy holes. It was almost as if the sea life here was holding its breath.

Maybe the sensitive creatures *were* responding to microquakes.

She frowned and joined her husband. She would radio over to Christmas Island to see if they'd picked up any unusual seismic activity. Until then, she had news that would definitely get her husband in the water in the morning.

"I did find what looked like the remnants of an old wreck."

"No bloody way." He sat up straighter. Back at Darwin Harbor, Gregg offered tours of sunken WWII warships that littered the seas around the northern coast of Australia. He had an avid interest in such discoveries. "Where?"

She pointed absently behind her, beyond the yacht's far side. "About a hundred meters starboard of us. A few beams, black and sticking straight out of the sand. Probably shaken free during that last big quake or perhaps even exposed when the silt had been sucked off of it by the passing tsunami. I didn't have much time to explore. Thought I'd leave it to an expert." She pinched him in the ribs, then leaned back into his chest.

As a group, they watched the sun vanish with a last coy wink into the sea. It was their ritual. Barring a storm, they never missed a sunset while at sea. The ship rocked gently. In the far distance, a passing tanker winked a few lights. But they were otherwise alone.

A sharp bark startled Susan, causing her to jump. She had not known she was still a bit tense. Apparently the strange, wary behavior of the reef life below had infected her.

"Oy! Oscar!" the professor called.

Only now did Susan notice the lack of their fourth crew-mate on the yacht. The dog barked again. The pudgy Queensland heeler belonged to the professor. Getting on in age and a tad arthritic, the dog was usually found sprawled in any patch of sunlight it could find.

"I'll see to him," Applegate said. "I'll leave you two love-birds all cozied up. Besides, I could use a trip to the head. Make a bit more room for another Foster's before I find my bed."

The professor gained his feet with a groan and headed to-ward the bow, intending to circle to the far side—but he stopped, staring off toward the east, toward the darker skies.

Oscar barked again.

Applegate did not scold him this time. Instead, he called over to Susan and Gregg, his voice low and serious. "You should come see this."

Susan scooted up and onto her feet. Gregg followed. They joined the professor.

"Bloody hell . . ." her husband mumbled.

"I think you may have found what drove those dolphins out of the seas," Applegate said.

To the east, a wide swath of the ocean glowed with a ghostly luminescence, rising and falling with the waves. The silvery sheen rolled and eddied. The old dog stood at the starboard rail and barked, trailing into a low growl at the sight.

"What the hell is that?" Gregg asked.

Susan answered as she crossed closer. "I've heard of such manifestations. They're called *milky seas*. Ships have re-ported glows like this in the Indian Ocean, going all the way back to Jules Verne. In 1995, a satellite even picked up one of the blooms, covering hundreds of square miles. This is a small one."

"Small, my ass," her husband grunted. "But what exactly is it? Some type of red tide?"

She shook her head. "Not exactly. Red tides are algal blooms. These glows are caused by bioluminescent bacteria, probably feeding off algae or some other substrate. There's no danger. But I'd like to—"

A sudden knock sounded beneath the boat, as if something large had struck it from below. Oscar's barking became more heated. The dog danced back and forth along the rails, trying to poke his head through the posts.

All three of them joined the dog and looked below.

The glowing edge of the milky sea lapped at the yacht's keel. From the depths below, a large shape rolled into view, belly up, but still squirming, teeth gnashing. It was a massive tiger shark, over six meters. The glowing waters frothed over its form, bubbling and turning the milky water into red wine.

Susan realized it wasn't *water* that was bubbling over the shark's belly, but its own *flesh*, boiling off in wide patches. The horrible sight sank away. But across the milky seas, other shapes rolled to the surface, thrashing or already dead: porpoises, sea turtles, fish by the hundreds.

Applegate took a step away from the rail. "It seems *these* bacteria have found more than just algae to feed on."

Gregg turned to stare at her. "Susan . . ."

She could not look away from the deadly vista. Despite the horror, she could not deny a twinge of scientific curiosity.

"Susan . . ."

She finally turned to him, slightly irritated.

"You were diving," he explained, and pointed. "In that water. All day."

"So? We were all in the water at least some time. Even Oscar did some dog-paddling."

Her husband would not meet her gaze. He remained focused on where she was scratching her forearm. The wet suit sometimes chafed her limbs. But the worry in his tight face drew her attention to her forearm. Her skin was pebbled in a severe rash, made worse by her scratching.

As she stared, bruising red welts bloomed on her skin.

"Susan . . ."

She gaped in disbelief. "Dear God . . ."

But she also knew the horrible truth.

"It's . . . it's *in* me."

EXPOSURE

I

Dark Madonna

JULY 1, 10:34 A.M.
Venice, Italy

HE WAS BEING HUNTED.

Stefano Gallo hurried across the open plaza square. The morning sun already baked the stones of the piazza, and the usual throng of tourists sought shady spots or crowded the gelato shop that lay within the shadow of St. Mark's Basilica. But this most lofty of all of Venice's landmarks, with its towering Byzantine facade, massive bronze horses, and domed cupolas, was not his goal.

Not even such a blessed sanctuary could offer him protection.

There was only one hope.

His steps became more rushed as he passed by the basilica. The piazza's pigeons scattered from his path as he stumbled through them, heedless of their flapping flight. He was beyond stealth. He had already been discovered. He had spotted the young Egyptian with the black eyes and trimmed beard as he'd entered the far side of the square. Their gazes had locked. The man was now dressed in a dark suit that flowed like oil from his wide, sharp shoulders. The first time the man had approached Stefano he had claimed to be an archaeology student out of Budapest, representing an old friend and colleague from the University of Athens.

The Egyptian had come to the Museo Archeologico searching for a specific bit of antiquity. A minor treasure. An obelisk from his country. The Egyptian, financed by his government, wished it returned to his homeland. He had come with a sizable payment, bonded cashier notes. Stefano, one of the museum's curators, was not above accepting such a bribe; his wife's escalating medical bills threatened to evict them from their small apartment. To collect such secret payment was not untoward; for the past two decades the Egyptian government had been buying back national treasures out of private collections and pressuring museums to return what rightfully belonged in Egypt.

So Stefano had agreed, promising at first to deliver it up. What was one small nondescript stone obelisk? The object had remained crated for almost a full century according to the manifest. And its terse description probably explained why: *Unmarked marble obelisk, excavated in Tanis, dated to the late dynastic period (26th Dynasty, 615 B.C.).* There was nothing unusual or particularly intriguing, unless one looked closer, followed its trail of provenance. It had come out of a collection that graced one of the Musei Vaticani in Rome: the Gregorian Egyptian Museum.

How it ended up in the vaults here in Venice was unknown.

Then yesterday morning, Stefano had received a newspaper clipping, sent by private courier in an envelope with a single symbol stamped into a wax seal.

$$\Sigma$$

The Greek letter sigma.

He still did not understand the significance of the seal, but he did understand the import of the enclosed clipping. A single article, dated three days prior, reported news of a man's body found on an Aegean beach, his throat slashed, his body bloated and nested with feasting eels. An especially fierce storm surge had returned the body from its watery grave. Dental records identified the body as that of his university colleague, the one who had reportedly sent the Egyptian.

The man had been dead for weeks.

Shock had caused Stefano to act rashly. He clutched the heavy object to his bosom, wrapped in sackcloth and still prickling with packing hay.

Stefano had stolen the obelisk from the vault, knowing the act would put him, his wife, his whole family, at risk.

He'd had no choice. Along with the dire article, the sealed envelope had contained a single message, unsigned, but plainly scrawled in a hurry, in a woman's hand, a warning. What the note contended seemed impossible, incredible, but he had tested the claim himself. It had proved true.

Tears threatened as he ran, a sob choked his throat.

No choice.

The obelisk must not fall into the hands of the Egyptian. Still, it was a burden he refused to shoulder any longer than necessary. His wife, his daughter . . . he pictured the bloated body of his colleague. Would the same befall his family?

Oh, Maria, what have I done?

There was only one who could take this burden from him. The one who had sent the envelope, a warning sealed with a Greek letter. At the end of her note, a place had been named, along with a time.

He was already late.

Somehow the Egyptian had discovered his theft, must have sensed Stefano was going to betray him. So he had come for it at dawn. Stefano had barely escaped his offices. He had fled on foot.

But not fast enough.

He checked over his shoulder. The Egyptian had vanished into the milling crowd of tourists.

Turning back around, Stefano stumbled through the shadow of the square's bell tower, the Campanile di San

Marco. Once the brick tower had served as the city's watch-tower, overlooking the nearby docks and guarding the port. Would that it could protect him now.

His goal lay across a small piazzetta. Ahead rose the Palazzo Ducal, the fourteenth-century palace of Venice's former dukes. Its two levels of Gothic arches beckoned, offering salvation in Istrian stone and rosy Veronese marble.

Clutching his prize, he stumbled across the street.

Was she still there? Would she take the burden?

He rushed toward the sheltering shadows, escaping the blaze of the sun and the glare off the neighboring sea. He needed to be lost in the maze of the palace. Besides housing the duke's personal residence, the Palazzo Ducal also served as a governmental office building, a courthouse, a council chamber, even an old prison. A newer prison rose across the canal behind the palace, connected by an arched bridge, the infamous Bridge of Sighs, over which Casanova had once made his escape, the only prisoner ever to break out of the palace's cells.

As Stefano ducked under the overhanging stretch of loggia, he prayed to the ghost of Casanova to protect his own flight. He even allowed himself a small breath of relief as he sank into the shadows. He knew the palace well. It was easy to get lost in its maze of corridors, a ready place for a clandestine rendezvous.

Or so he placed his faith.

He entered the palace through the western archway, flowing in with a few tourists. Ahead opened the palace's courtyard with its two ancient wells and the magnificent marble staircase, the Scala dei Giganti, the Giant's Stairs. Stefano skirted the courtyard, avoiding the sun now that he had escaped it. He pushed through a small, private door and followed a series of administrative rooms. They ended at the old inquisitor's office, where many poor souls had suffered interrogations of the most pained and brutal sort. Not stopping, Stefano continued into the neighboring stone torture chamber.

A door slammed somewhere behind him, causing him to jump.

He clutched his prize even tighter.

The instructions had been specific.

Taking a narrow back stairway, he wended down into the palace's deepest dungeons, the Pozzi, or Wells. It was here the most notorious prisoners had been held.

It was also where he was to make his rendezvous.

Stefano pictured the Greek sigil.

Σ

What did it mean?

He entered the dank hall, broken by black stone cells, too low for a prisoner to stand erect. Here the imprisoned froze during winter or died of thirst during the long Venetian summers, many forgotten by all except the rats.

Stefano clicked on a small penlight.

This lowest level of the Pozzi appeared deserted. As he continued deeper, Stefano's steps echoed off the stone walls, sounding like someone following him. His chest squeezed with the fear. He slowed. Was he too late? He found himself holding his breath, suddenly wishing for the sunlight he had fled.

He stopped, a tremble quaking through him.

As if sensing his hesitation, a light flared, coming from the last cell.

"Who?" he asked. *"Chi è là?"*

A scrape of heel on stone, followed by a soft voice, in Italian, accented subtly.

"I sent you the note, Signore Gallo."

A lithe figure stepped out into the corridor, a small flashlight in her hand. The glare made it hard to discern her features, even when she lowered her flashlight. She was dressed all in black leather, hugging tight to hips and breast. Her features were further obscured by a head scarf, wrapped in a bedouin style, obscuring her features fully, except her eyes that reflected a glint of her light. She moved with an unhurried grace that helped calm the thudding of his heart.

She appeared out of the shadows like some dark Madonna.

"You have the artifact?" she asked.

"I . . . I do," he stammered, and took a step toward her. He held out the obelisk, letting the sackcloth fall away. "I want nothing more to do with it. You said you could take it somewhere safe."

"I can." She motioned for him to set it down on the floor.

He crouched and rested the Egyptian stone spire on the floor, glad to be rid of it. The obelisk, carved of black marble, rose from a square base, ten centimeters per side, and tapered to a pyramidal point forty centimeters tall.

The woman crouched across from him, balancing on the toes of her black boots. She ran her light over its drab surface. The marble was badly chipped, poorly preserved. A long crack jagged through it. It was plain why it had been forgotten.

Still, blood had been spilled for it.

And he knew why.

She reached across to Stefano and pushed his penlight down. With a flick of her thumb, she switched on her flashlight. The white light dimmed to a rich purple. Every bit of dust on his slacks lit up. The white stripes of his shirt blazed.

Ultraviolet.

The glow bathed the obelisk.

Stefano had done the same earlier, testing the woman's claim and witnessing the miracle for himself. He leaned closer with her now, examining the four sides of the obelisk.

The surfaces were no longer blank. Lines of script glowed in blue-white sigils down all four sides.

It was not hieroglyphics. It was a language that predated the ancient Egyptians.

Stefano could not keep the awe from his voice. "Could it truly be the writing of the—"

Behind him, whispered words echoed down from the floor above. A skitter of loose rock trickled down the back stairs.

He swung around, fearful, his blood icing.

He recognized the calm, clipped cadence of the whisper in the dark.

The Egyptian.

They'd been discovered.

Perhaps sensing the same, the woman clicked off her lamp, dousing the violet light. Darkness collapsed around them.

Stefano lifted his penlight, seeking some hope in the face of this dark Madonna. Instead, he discovered a black pistol, elongated with a silencer, aimed at his face, held in the woman's other hand. He understood and despaired. Fooled yet again.

"Grazie, Stefano."

Between the sharp cough and the spat of muzzle flash, only one thought squeezed through the fatal gap.

Maria, forgive me.

JULY 3, 1:16 P.M.
Vatican City

MONSIGNOR VIGOR VERONA climbed the stairs with great reluctance, haunted by memories of flame and smoke. His heart was too heavy for such a long climb. He felt a decade older than his sixty years. Stopping at a landing, he craned upward, one hand supporting his lower back.

Above, the circular stairwell was a choked maze of scaffolding, crisscrossed with platforms. Knowing it was bad luck, Vigor ducked under a painter's ladder and continued higher up the dark stairs that climbed the Torre dei Venti, the Tower of Winds.

Fumes of fresh paint threatened to burn tears from his eyes. But other smells also intruded, phantoms from a past he preferred to forget.

Charred flesh, acrid smoke, burning ash.

Two years ago an explosion and fire had ignited the tower into a blazing torch within the heart of the Vatican. But after much work, the tower was returning to its former glory. Vigor had looked forward to next month, when the tower would be reopened, the ribbon cut by His Eminence himself.

But mostly he looked forward to finally putting the past to rest.

Even the famous Meridian Room at the very top of the tower, where Galileo had sought to prove that the earth revolved around the sun, was almost fully restored. It had taken eighteen months, under the care and expertise of a score of artisans and art historians, to painstakingly reclaim the room's frescoes from soot and ash.

Would that all could be so recovered with brush and paint.

As the new prefect of the Archivio Segretto Vaticano, Vigor knew how much of the Vatican's Secret Archives had been lost forever to flame, smoke, and water. Thousands of ancient books, illuminated texts, and archival *regestra*—leather-bound packets of parchments and papers. Over the past century, the rooms of the tower had served as overflow from the *carbonile,* the main bunker of the archives far below.

Now sadly, the library had much more room.

"Prefetto Verona!"

Vigor startled back to the present, almost wincing, hearing an echo of another's voice. But it was only his assistant, a young seminary student named Claudio, calling down from the top of the stairs. He awaited Vigor in the Meridian Room, having reached the destination well ahead of his older superior. The young man held back a drape of clear plastic tarp that separated the stair from the upper room.

An hour ago Vigor had been summoned to the tower by the head of the restoration team. The man's message had been as urgent as it was cryptic. *Come quickly. A most horrible and wonderful discovery has been made.*

So Vigor had left his offices for the long trek to the top of the freshly painted tower. He had not even changed out of his black cassock, donned for an earlier meeting with the Vatican's secretary of state. He regretted his choice of garment, too heavy and warm for the arduous climb. But finally he reached his assistant and wiped his damp forehead with a handkerchief.

"This way, *prefetto.*" Claudio held the drape aside.

"Grazie, Claudio."

Beyond the tarp, the upper chamber was oven-hot, as if the stones of the tower still retained heat from the two-year-old fire. But it was just the midday sun baking the tallest tower of the Vatican. Rome was going through an especially scorching heat wave. Vigor prayed for a bit of a breeze, for the Torre dei Venti to prove its namesake with a gust of wind.

But Vigor also knew most of the sweat from his brow had nothing to do with the heat or the long climb in a cassock. Since the fires, he had avoided coming all the way up here, directing from afar. Even now he kept his back to one of the chambers off to the side.

He once had had another assistant, before Claudio.

Jakob.

It hadn't been only books that had been lost to the flames here.

"There you are!" a voice boomed.

Dr. Balthazar Pinosso, overseer of the Meridian Room's restoration project, strode across the circular chamber. The man was a giant, nearly seven feet tall, dressed almost like a surgeon in white with paper-booted feet. He had a respirator pushed to the top of his head. Vigor knew him well. Balthazar was dean of the art history department at the Gregorian University, where Vigor had once served as the head of the Pontifical Institute of Christian Archaeology.

"Prefect Verona, thank you for coming so promptly." The large man glanced at his wristwatch and rolled his eyes, silently and amusingly commenting on his slow climb.

Vigor appreciated his gentle teasing. After he'd assumed the high mantle of the archives, few dared to speak to him beyond reverential tones. "If I was as long-legged as you, Balthazar, I could have taken two stairs at a time and gotten here well ahead of poor Claudio."

"Then best we finish here so you can return for your usual afternoon nap. I'd hate to disturb such diligent labors."

Despite the man's joviality, Vigor recognized a bit of tension in his eyes. He also noted that Balthazar had dismissed all the men and women who worked alongside him on the restoration. Recognizing this, Vigor waved Claudio back toward the stair.

"Could you give us a few moments of privacy, Claudio?"

"Certainly, *prefetto*."

Once his assistant had retreated back to the stairs and vanished through the drape of plastic tarp, Vigor returned his attention to his former colleague. "Balthazar, why this urgency?"

"Come. I'll show you."

As the man stepped toward the far side of the chamber, Vigor saw that the room's restorations were nearing comple-

tion. All along the circular walls and ceilings, Nicolò Cir-
cignani's famous frescoes depicted scenes from the Bible,
with cherubs and clouds above. A few scenes were still
crisscrossed with silk grids, awaiting further work. But most
of the repairs were already complete. Even the carving of
the zodiac on the floor had been cleaned and polished down
to its bare marble. Off to the side, a single spear of light
pierced a quarter-size hole in the wall, spiking down atop
the room's slab floor, illuminating the white marble meridian line that ran across the dark floor, turning the chamber
into a sixteenth-century solar observatory.

On the far side, Balthazar parted a drape to reveal a
small side closet. It even looked like the original stout door
was still intact, evident from the charring on its thick
wooden surface.

The tall historian tapped one of the bronze bolts that
pegged the door. "We discovered the door has a bronze core.
Lucky for that. It preserved what was in this room."

Despite Vigor's trepidation at being here, his curiosity
was piqued. "What was in there?"

Balthazar pulled the door open. It was a cramped, win-
dowless space, stone-walled, barely room for two people to
stand abreast. Two shelves rose on either side, floor to ceiling, crowded with leather-bound books. Despite the reek of
fresh paint, the mustiness of the chamber wafted out, proving the power of antiquity over human effort.

"The contents were inventoried when we first took over
here and cleared the closet," Balthazar explained. "But nothing of great significance was found. Mostly crumbling historical texts of an astronomical and nautical nature." He
sighed loudly and a tad apologetically as he stepped inside.
"I'm afraid I should have been more careful, what with all
the day laborers. But I was focused on the Meridian. We
kept one of the Swiss guards posted up here at night. I
thought all was secure."

Vigor followed the larger man into the closet.

"We also used the room to store some of our tools." Balthazar waved to the bottom shelf of one rack. "To keep them from getting underfoot."

Vigor shook his head, growing tired from the heat and the heaviness of his heart. "I don't understand. Why then was I summoned?"

Something like a grumble echoed from the man's chest. "A week ago," he said, "one of the guards chased away someone snooping about." Balthazar waved a hand to encompass the closet. "In here."

"Why wasn't I informed?" Vigor asked. "Was anything stolen?"

"No, that's just it. You were in Milan, and the guard scared off the stranger. I just assumed it was a common thief, taking advantage of the confusion here, with the comings and goings of work crews. Afterward, I posted a second guard up here, just in case."

Vigor waved for him to continue.

"But this morning one of the art restorers was returning a lamp to the closet. He had it still switched on when he entered."

Balthazar reached behind Vigor and shifted the door closed, shutting out the light from the other room. He then clicked on a small hand lamp. It bathed the room in purple, lighting up his white coveralls. "We use ultraviolet light during art restoration projects. It can help bring forth details the naked eye can miss."

Balthazar pointed to the marble floor.

But Vigor had already noted what had appeared under the lamp's glow. A shape, painted crudely, shone on the center of the floor.

A curled dragon, nearly turned upon its own tail.

Vigor's breath choked in his throat. He even stumbled back a step, trapped between horror and disbelief. His ears roared with the memory of blood and screams.

Balthazar placed a hand on his shoulder, steadying him. "Are you all right? Maybe I should have better prepared you."

Vigor stepped out of the man's grip. "I . . . I'm fine."

To prove this, he knelt closer to inspect the glowing mark, a mark he knew too well. The sigil of Ordinis Draconis. The Imperial Royal Dragon Court.

Balthazar met his eye, the whites glowing under the ultraviolet. It was the Dragon Court that had burned this tower two years ago, aided by the traitorous former prefect of the Secret Archives, Prefetto Alberto, now dead. It was a story Vigor had thought long ended, finally put to rest, especially now with the tower's phoenix-like rise from the smoke and ashes.

What was the mark doing here?

Vigor knelt with a crick of his left knee. The mark looked hastily sketched. Just a crude approximation.

Balthazar hovered at his shoulder. "I studied it with a magnifying loupe. I found a drop of restoration paste *beneath* the fluorescent paint, indicating it had been recently drawn. Within the week, I'd guess."

"The thief . . ." Vigor mumbled, remembering the start of the story.

"Perhaps not just a common thief after all."

Vigor massaged his knee. The mark could only be of dire import. *A threat or warning, maybe a message to another Dragon Court mole in the Vatican.* He remembered Balthazar's message: *A most horrible and wonderful discovery has been made.* Staring at the dragon, Vigor now understood the *horrible* nature of that message.

Vigor glanced over his shoulder. "You also mentioned discovering something *wonderful* in your note."

Balthazar nodded. He reached behind and opened the closet's door, allowing in a flood of light from the outer room. With the brightness, the phosphorescent dragon vanished off the floor, as if shunning the light.

And Vigor allowed a long breath to escape with it.

"Come see this." Balthazar knelt beside Vigor. "We would have missed this if not for the dragon painting on the floor."

He leaned forward on a palm and reached out with his other hand. His fingers brushed across the bare stone. "It took the loupe to reveal this. I caught sight of it when examining the fluorescent paint. While I waited for you, I cleared some of the centuries of grime and dirt from the carving."

Vigor studied the stone floor. "What carving?"

"Lean closer. Feel here."

Concentrating, Vigor obeyed. He felt more than saw, with his fingertips, like a blind man reading Braille. There was a faint inscription in the stone.

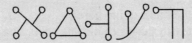

Vigor didn't even need Balthazar's assessment to know the carving was ancient. The symbols were as crisp as scientific notation, but this was no physicist's scrawl. As the former head of the Pontifical Institute of Christian Archaeology, Vigor recognized the significance.

Balthazar must have read his reaction. His voice lowered to a conspiratorial whisper. "Is it truly what I think it is?"

Vigor sat back and rubbed the dust from his fingertips. "A script older than Hebrew," he mumbled. "The first language if you were to believe the stories."

"Why was it drawn here? What does it signify?"

Vigor shook his head and studied the floor, another question growing. Again the dragon sigil appeared, but only in his mind's eye, lit by his worry rather than the glow of ultraviolet. Upon the stone, the dragon had coiled around the inscription, as if protecting it.

His friend's earlier words returned to Vigor. *We would have missed this if not for the dragon painting on the floor.* Maybe the dragon was not so much protecting the ancient carving as meant to *illuminate* it, to cast a spotlight upon it.

But whose eyes was it meant for?

As Vigor pictured the twisted dragon, he again felt the weight of Jakob's body in his arms, smoking and charred.

In that moment Vigor knew the truth. The message was *not* meant for another Dragon Court operative, another traitor like Prefect Alberto. It was meant to draw someone intimately tied to the history of the Dragon Court, someone who would know its significance.

The message had been left for him.

But why? What was its meaning?

Vigor slowly stood. He knew someone who might be able to help, someone he had avoided calling for the past year. Until now, there had been no need to keep in touch, especially after the man had broken up with Vigor's niece. But Vigor knew a part of his reticence rested not just with broken hearts. The man, as much as this tower, reminded Vigor of the bloody past here, a past he wanted to forget.

But now he had no choice.

The dragon sigil glowed before his mind's eye, full of dread warning.

He needed help.

JULY 4, 11:44 P.M.
Takoma Park, Maryland

"GRAY, CAN YOU empty the kitchen trash?"

"Be right there, Mom."

In the living room, Commander Gray Pierce picked up another empty bottle of Sam Adams, another dead soldier of his parents' July Fourth celebration, and chucked it into the plastic bin under his arm. At least the party was winding down.

He checked his watch. Almost midnight.

Gray gathered another two beer bottles off the front entry table and paused before the open doorway, appreciating a bit of breeze through the screen door. The night smelled of jasmine, along with a lingering hint of smoke from fireworks exploded by the block party. Off in the distance, a few whistles and crackles continued to punctuate the night.

A dog howled from the yard behind his mother, aggravated by the noise.

Only a few guests remained on the front porch of his parents' Craftsman bungalow, lazing about on the porch swing or leaning on the railing, enjoying the cool night after the usual swelter of a Maryland summer. They had watched the fireworks from the perch there hours earlier. Afterward, the partygoers had slowly dwindled away into the night. Only the most diehard remained.

Like Gray's boss.

Director Painter Crowe leaned against a post, bent next to the teaching assistant who worked for Gray's mother. He was a dour young man from the Congo who attended George Washington University on a scholarship. Painter Crowe had been inquiring about the state of hostilities in the man's homeland. It seemed even at a party, the director of Sigma Force kept a finger on the world's pulse.

It was also why he made such a great director.

Sigma Force functioned as the covert field arm for DARPA, the Department of Defense's research and development division. Members were sent out to safeguard or neutralize technologies vital to U.S. security. The team consisted of ex–Special Forces soldiers who had been hand-picked in secret and placed into rigorous doctoral programs, forming a militarized team of technically trained operatives. Or as Monk, Gray's friend and team member, liked to joke: *killer scientists.*

With such responsibility, Director Crowe's only relaxation this night seemed to be the single-malt scotch resting on the porch rail. He'd been nursing it all evening. As if sensing the scrutiny, Painter nodded to Gray through the door.

In the wan illumination of a few candlelit lanterns, the director cast a stony figure, dressed in dark slacks and a pressed linen shirt. His half–Native American heritage could be read in the hard planes of his face.

Gray studied those planes, searching for any cracks in

his demeanor, knowing the pressure he must be under. Sigma's organizational structure had been undergoing a comprehensive NSA and DARPA internal audit, and now a medical crisis was brewing in Southeast Asia. So it was good to see the man out of Sigma's subterranean offices.

If only for this one night.

Still, duty was never far from the director's mind.

Proving this, Painter stretched, pushed off the rail, and stepped to the door. "I should head off," he called to Gray, and checked his wristwatch. "Thought I'd stop by the office and check to see if Lisa and Monk have arrived safely."

The pair of scientists, Drs. Lisa Cummings and Monk Kokkalis, had been sent to investigate a medical crisis among the Indonesian islands. The pair, traveling as adjuncts to the World Health Organization, had left this morning.

Gray pushed through the swinging screen door and shook his boss's hand. He knew Painter's interest in the pair's itinerary stretched beyond his role as field ops director. He read the worry of a man in love.

"I'm sure Lisa is fine," Gray assured him, knowing Lisa and Painter had barely been apart of late. "That is, as long as she packed her earplugs. Monk's snoring could rattle the engine off a jet's wing. And speaking of the one-man bugle corps, if you hear any news, you'll let Kat know—"

Painter raised a hand. "She's already buzzed my Black-Berry twice this evening, checking if I'd heard any word." He downed his scotch. "I'll call her immediately once I hear."

"I suspect Monk will beat you to that call, what with *two* women to answer to now."

Painter smiled, if a bit tiredly.

Three months ago Kat and Monk had brought home a new baby girl, six pounds and three ounces, christened Penelope Anne. After being assigned this current field op, Monk had joked about escaping diapers and midnight feedings, but Gray recognized how it tore a little hole in his friend's heart to leave behind his wife and baby girl.

"Thanks for coming over, Director. I'll see you in the morning."

"Please pass on my thanks to your folks."

Reminded, Gray glanced to the flood of light along the left side of the house, coming from the detached garage around back. His father had retreated there some time ago. Not all the fireworks this evening had been out on the streets. Lately, his father was finding social situations more and more difficult as his Alzheimer's progressed, forgetting names, repeating questions already answered. His frustration led to a private flare-up between father and son. Afterward, his father had stomped off to the garage and his shop.

More and more his father could be found holed up back there. Gray suspected he was not so much hiding from the world as circling the wagons, seeking a solitary place to protect what remained of his faculties, finding solace in the curl of oak from his wood planer or turn of a well-seated screw. Yet, despite this manner of meditation, Gray recognized the growing fear behind his father's eyes.

"I'll let them know," Gray mumbled.

As Painter departed, the last of the straggling partygoers followed in his wake. Some stopped inside to wish his mother well while Gray said his good-byes to the others. Soon he had the porch to himself.

"Gray!" his mother called from inside. "The trash!"

With a sigh, he bent and recollected the bin with empty bottles, cans, and plastic cups. He would help his mother clean up, then bicycle the short way back across town to his apartment. As he let the screen door clap behind him, he switched off the porch light and headed across the wood floor toward the kitchen. He heard the dishwasher humming, and the clatter of pans in the sink.

"Mom, I'll finish up," he said as he entered the kitchen. "Go rest."

His mother turned from the sink. She wore navy cotton slacks, a white silk blouse, and a damp checkered apron. At moments like this, harried as she was from an evening of entertaining, his mother's advancing age suddenly struck him. Who was this gray-haired old woman in his mother's kitchen?

Then she snapped a wet towel at him and broke the delusion.

"Just get the trash. I'm almost finished here. And tell your father to get inside. The Edelmanns do not appreciate his nocturnal woodworking. Oh, and I've wrapped up the leftover barbecued chicken. Could you take that to the re-frigerator in the garage?"

"I'll have to make a second trip." He hauled up the two plastic sacks of garbage in one hand and cradled the bin of empty bottles under his arm. "Be right back."

He used his hip to push through the rear door and out into the shadowy backyard. Carefully climbing down the two back steps, he crossed toward the garage and the line of garbage cans along its flank. He found himself moving with a soft tread, attempting to keep the clink of bottles silenced. A Rainbird water sprinkler betrayed him.

He tripped and the bin of bottles rattled as he caught his balance. The back neighbor's Scottish terrier barked a com-plaint.

Crap . . .

His father swore sharply from the garage. "Gray? If that's you . . . gimme a goddamn hand in here!"

Gray hesitated. After one near shouting match with his father this evening, he didn't want a midnight encore. Over the past couple years, the two had been getting along fairly well, finding common ground after a lifetime of estrange-ment. But the past month, as some of his father's cognitive tests began to slide downward again, an all-too-familiar and unwelcome brittle edge had returned to the taciturn man.

"Gray!"

"Hold on!" He dropped the garbage into one of the open cans and settled the bottle bin next to it. Girding himself, Gray crossed into the light flowing from the open garage.

The scent of sawdust and shop oil struck him, reminding

him of worse days. *Get the goddamn strap, you piece of . . . I'll make you think twice about using one of my tools . . . get your head out of your ass before I knock you clear to . . .*

His father knelt on the floor beside a spilled coffee can of sixpenny nails. He was brushing them up. Gray noted the streak of blood on the floor, from his father's left hand.

His father craned up as Gray stepped inside. Under the fluorescent lights, there was no denying their familial ties. His father's blue eyes held the same steel as Gray's. Their faces were both carved into the sharp angles and clefts, marking their Welsh heritage. There was no escaping it. He was becoming his father. And though Gray's hair was still coal black, he had a few gray hairs to prove it.

Spotting the bloodied hand, Gray crossed and motioned his father to the back sink. "Go wash that up."

"Don't tell me what to do."

Gray opened his mouth to argue, thought better, and bent down to help his father. "What happened?"

"Was looking for wood screws." His father waved his cut hand toward the workbench.

"But these are nails."

His father's eyes lit upon him. "No shit, Sherlock." There was a well of anger in his gaze, barely constrained, but Gray knew it wasn't directed at him for once.

Recognizing this, he remained silent and simply gathered the nails back into the coffee can. His father stared down at his hands, one bloody, one not.

"Dad?"

The large man shook his head, then finally said softly, "Goddamn it . . ."

Gray offered no argument.

When Gray was young, his father had worked the Texas oil fields until an industrial accident had disabled him, taking a leg off at the knee, turning an oilman into a housewife. Gray had found himself bearing the brunt of his frustration, always found wanting, never able to be the man his father wanted him to be.

Gray watched his father stare at his hands and recognized a hard truth. Maybe all along his old man's anger had been directed inward. Like now. Not so much frustration with a son as a father's anger at failing to be the man *he* wanted to be. And now once again, disability was slowly taking even that away.

Gray sought some words.

As he searched, the roar of a motorcycle sliced through any further contemplation. Down the street, tires squealed, vandalizing asphalt with rubber.

Gray straightened and placed the coffee can atop the bench. His father cursed the rude driver, probably a drunken reveler. Still, Gray swept an arm and doused the garage lights.

"What are you—?"

"Stay down," Gray ordered.

Something was wrong . . .

The cycle appeared, a black and muscular Yamaha V-max. It roared into view, skidding sideways. Its headlamp was off. That's what had set Gray's nerves jangling. No spear of light had blazed up the street, fleeing ahead of the engine's growl. The cycle was running dark.

Without slowing, it skidded sideways. Rear tires smoked as it tried to make the sharp turn into their driveway. It hesitated, balanced, then ripped forward.

"What the hell!" his father barked.

The rider overcompensated for the turn. The bike bobbled, then the bump of the curb sent the vehicle careening to the side. The rider fought for control, but the rear fender caught the edge of the porch step.

The bike went down in a showering skid of red sparks, becoming yet another Fourth of July display. Thrown, the rider shoulder-rolled end over end, landing in a sprawl not far from the open garage.

Farther down the drive, the bike's engine choked and died.

Sparks blew out.

Darkness descended.

"Jesus H. Christ!" his father exclaimed.

Gray held a hand back for his father to stay in the garage. His other hand pulled a 9mm Glock from an ankle holster. He crossed toward the prone figure, all dressed in black: leather, scarf, and helmet.

A soft groan revealed two things: The rider was still alive, and it was a woman. She lay curled on her side, leathers ripped.

Gray's mother appeared at the back door to the house, standing in the porchlight, drawn by the noise. "Gray . . . ?"

"Stay there!" he called to her.

As Gray approached the downed rider, he noticed something lying steps away from the bike, its black shape crisp against the white cement of the driveway. It looked like some stubby pillar of black stone, cracked from the impact. From its dark interior, the glint of a metallic core reflected the moonlight.

But it was the glint of another bit of silver that caught his eye as he stepped to the rider's side.

A small pendant around the woman's neck.

In the shape of a dragon.

Gray recognized it immediately. He wore the same around his own neck, a gift from an old enemy, a warning and a promise when next their paths crossed.

His grip on his pistol tightened.

She rolled from her shoulder to her back with another small groan. Blood streamed across the white cement, a black river forging toward the mowed back lawn. Gray recognized a raw exit wound.

Shot from behind.

A hand reached up and pulled back the helmet. A familiar face, tight with agony, stared up at him, framed in black hair. Tanned skin and almond eyes revealed her Eurasian descent and her identity.

"Seichan . . ." he said.

A hand reached to him, scrabbling. "Commander Pierce . . . help me . . ."

He heard the pain in her words—but also something he'd thought he'd never hear from this cold enemy.

Terror.

2

Bloody Christmas

JUST ANOTHER LAZY DAY at the beach . . .

Monk Kokkalis followed his guide along the narrow strand. Both men wore identical Bio-3 contamination suits. Not the best choice of apparel for strolling along a tropical beach. Under his suit, Monk had stripped to a pair of boxer trunks. Still, he felt overdressed as he slowly baked inside the sealed plastic. Shading his eyes against the midday glare, he stared out at the nearby horror.

The western bay of Christmas Island frothed and churned with the dead, as if hell itself had washed up out of the deep. Mounds of fish carcasses marked last night's high tide. Larger hillocks of shark, dolphin, turtle, even a pygmy whale, dotted the beach—though it remained hard to tell where one began and the other ended, flesh and scale melted into a reeking mass of bone and rotting tissue. There were also scores of seabirds, contorted and dead, on the beach and in the water, perhaps attracted by the slaughter only to succumb to the same poisoning.

A nearby blowhole in the rock spewed a fountain of sludgy seawater with a ringing bellow, as if the ocean itself were gasping its last breath.

Ducking under the spray, the pair of men worked north along the beach, traversing a narrow trail of clear sand between the foulness of the tidal zone and steep jungle-shrouded cliffs.

"Remind me to skip the seafood buffet back on the ship," Monk mumbled through the rasp of his respirator. He was glad for his suit's canned air. He could only imagine the reek that must accompany this tidal graveyard.

He was also relieved his partner, Dr. Lisa Cummings, had remained back aboard the cruise ship on the other side of the island. The *Mistress of the Seas* floated in Flying Fish Cove, safely upwind of the sickening pall that wafted across the island from the toxic soup on its western side.

But others had not been as lucky.

Upon arriving at daybreak, Monk had witnessed the hundreds of men, women, and children being evacuated from the island, all in various states of contamination: some blind, others merely blistered, the worst with skin dying off in pustulant slides. And though the toxic readings were rapidly declining, the entire island was being cleared as a safety precaution.

The *Mistress of the Seas,* a giant luxury cruise ship out on its maiden voyage among the Indonesian islands, had been evacuated and diverted, turned into an emergency medical ship. It also served as the operations center for the World Health Organization's team, called in to discover the cause and source for the sudden poisoning of the surrounding seas.

It was also why Monk was out here this morning, seeking some answers in the aftermath of the tragedy. Back aboard the ship, Lisa's skill as a medical doctor was being put to hard use while Monk's training had him tromping through this cesspool. Because of his expertise in forensics—medical and biological—he had been handpicked for this particular Sigma assignment. The op had been classified as low risk—survey only—an operation to ease him back after taking three months off for family leave.

He shied away from that last thought. He didn't want to think of his little baby girl while slogging through the filth here. Still, it couldn't be helped. He flashed back to Penelope's blue eyes, pudding cheeks, and impossible corona of blond hair, so unlike her father's shaved head and craggy features. How could something so beautiful share his genes? Then again, his wife may have stacked the deck in that department. Even here, he could not dismiss the ache in his chest, a physical longing for them, as if a tether bound him as surely as any umbilical cord, a sharing of blood between the three of them. It seemed impossible he could be this happy.

Up ahead, his guide, Dr. Richard Graff, a salt-hardened oceanic researcher out of the University of Queensland, had dropped to one knee. He knew nothing of Monk's true identity, only that Monk had been recruited by the WHO for his expertise. Graff settled his plastic sample case atop a flat shelf of rock. Through the face shield, the man's bearded countenance was tight with worry and concentration.

It was time to get to work.

The pair had been dropped off in an inflatable rubber Zodiac. The pilot, a sailor from the Royal Australian Navy, remained at the boat, beached beyond the kill zone. An Australian Coast Guard cutter had arrived to oversee the island's evacuation.

The remote island, resting fifteen hundred miles northwest of Perth, was still Australian territory. First discovered on Christmas Day in 1643, the uninhabited island was eventually colonized by the British to take advantage of its phosphate deposits, setting up a major mine here, employing indentured workers from throughout the Indonesian islands. And though the mines were still in operation, the tropical island's main industry had turned to tourism. Three-quarters of the island's highlands, thick with rain forests, had been declared national parklands.

But no tourists would be flocking here anytime soon.

Monk joined Dr. Richard Graff.

The marine researcher noted his arrival and waved a gloved hand to encompass the massive die-off here. "It started a little over four weeks ago, according to reports of some local fishermen," explained Graff. "Lobster traps were found full of empty crustacean shells, the flesh dissolved away inside. Trawling nets blistered hands when pulled from the sea. And it only grew worse."

"What do you think happened here? A toxic spill of some sort?"

"No doubt it was a toxic assault, but it was no *spill*."

The scientist unfolded a black collection bag, emblazoned with a hazardous chemical warning, then pointed to the nearby surf. The waters frothed with a foamy yellowish slurry, a poisonous stew thick with meat and bones.

He waved an arm. "That is all Mother Nature's handiwork."

"What do you mean?"

"You're looking at slime mold, mate. Composed of *cyanobacteria,* an ancient predecessor of the modern bacterium and algae. Three billion years ago, such slime flourished throughout the world's oceans. And now it's on the rise again. It was why I was called in here. Such organisms are my primary area of expertise. I've been studying such blooms out near the Great Barrier Reef, specifically one called *fireweed*. A mix of algae and cyanobacteria that can cover a soccer field in less time than it would take you to eat lunch. The bloody creature releases ten different biotoxins, potent enough to blister skin. And when dried, it can aerosolize with the burning force of pepper spray."

Monk pictured the devastation back at The Settlement, the island's largest township. It lay not far from the bay here, in the path of the tradewinds. "Are you saying that's what happened here?"

"Or something like it. Fireweed and other cyanobacteria are blooming all across our oceans. From fjords of Norway to the Great Barrier Reef. Fish, coral, and marine mammals are dying off, while these ancient slimes, along with venomous jellyfish, are blooming. It's as if evolution were running in reverse, the oceans devolving into primordial seas. And we've only ourselves to blame. Runoff of fertilizers, industrial chemicals, and sewage have been poisoning deltas and estuaries. Overfishing of the past fifty years has driven the population of large fish down by ninety percent. And climate change is acidifying and warming the waters, lessening its ability to hold oxygen, suffocating marine life. We are rapidly killing the seas beyond the ability to heal."

With a shake of his head, he stared out at the dead pool. "In its wake, we are seeing the return of seas from a hundred million years ago, teeming with bacteria, toxic algae, and venomous jellyfish. Such dead spots are found all around the world."

"But what caused this one?"

That was the question that drew them all here.

Graff shook his head. "A new unidentified slime mold. Something we haven't seen yet. And that's what scares me. Marine biotoxins and neurotoxins are already the most potent poisons in the world. So nasty that they are beyond even man's ability to duplicate. Did you know saxitoxin, from bacteria in certain shellfish, has been classified by the United Nations as a weapon of mass destruction?"

Monk grimaced through his face shield at the seas here. "Mother Nature can be a nasty bitch."

"The greatest terrorist of them all, mate. Best not to piss her off."

Monk didn't argue.

With the biology lecture over, Monk bent down and helped organize the collection kits. He struggled, fighting the plastic gloves of his suit. He was further compromised by a numb left hand. Maimed after a previous mission, he now wore a five-fingered prosthesis, state-of-the-art, chocked full of the latest in DARPA gadgetry, but synthetics and bioelectronics were not flesh. He cursed a bit as he fumbled a syringe into the sand.

"Careful with that," Graff warned. "I don't think you want to puncture your suit. Not out here. Though the toxic readings are receding, we'd best be cautious."

Monk sighed. He would be glad to be out of this monkey suit, back aboard the ship, back to his own suite. En route to the island, Monk had pulled strings to have an entire forensics suite airlifted to the cruise ship. That's where he'd rather be.

But first they needed lab samples. And plenty of them. Blood, tissue, and bone. From fish, shark, squid, dolphin.

"That's odd," Graff mumbled. He stood and glanced up and down the beach.

Monk joined him. "What?"

"One of the most ubiquitous animals on the island is *Geocarcoidea natalis*."

"And in English, that would be . . . ?"

Graff stood up and glanced up and down the beach. "I'm referring to the Christmas Island red land crab."

Monk studied the fouled coastline. He had read up on the island's flora and fauna. The terrestrial red crab was the star of the island, growing to the size of dinner plates. Their annual migration was one of the wonders of the natural world. Each November, timed to lunar cycles, a hundred million crabs made a mad dash from jungle to sea, dodging seabirds and attempting to prove their right to mate by surviving this gauntlet.

Graff continued, "The crabs are notorious scavengers. You'd think all the carcasses out here would attract them. Like the seabirds. But I don't see a single one here, alive or dead."

"Maybe they sensed the toxin and kept to their jungles."

"If they did, such a factor might hold some clue to the origin of the toxin or the bacteria that produced it. Maybe they've encountered such a deadly bloom before. Maybe they're resistant. Either way, the faster we can isolate the source, all the better."

"To help the islanders . . ."

Graff shrugged. "Certainly that. But more importantly, to keep the organism from spreading." He studied the yellowish sluice, and his voice lowered with worry. "I fear this may be a harbinger of what all oceanic scientists have been dreading."

Monk glanced to him for elaboration.

"A bacterium that tips the scales, an agent so potent it sterilizes all life in the sea."

"And that can happen?"

Graff knelt to begin the work. "It may already be happening."

With that dour pronouncement, Monk spent the next hour collecting samples into vials, pouches, and plastic cups. All the while, the sun rose higher above the cliffs, glaring off the water, cooking him in his bio-suit. He began to fantasize about a cold shower and a frozen drink with an umbrella in it.

The pair slowly worked down the beach. Near the cliff face, Monk noted a cluster of charred incense sticks stuck in the sand. They formed a palisade in front of a small Buddhist shrine, no more than a faceless seated figure, long worn by sea and sand. It rested under a makeshift lean-to splattered with bird droppings. He imagined the incense sticks being lit to ward against the toxic pall, seeking some heavenly intervention.

He continued past, nettled with a sudden chill, wondering if their efforts here would prove any more useful.

The throttling growl of an approaching boat drew his gaze back out to sea. He glanced down the beach. While collecting samples, he and Graff had traveled past a spit of land. Their Zodiac lay beached beyond the rocky point, out of sight.

Monk shaded his eyes. Was their Aussie pilot moving the boat closer to them?

Graff joined him. "It's too early to go back."

The spat of rifle fire echoed over the water as a blue-hulled, scarred speedboat shot around the point. Monk spotted seven men in the rear, their heads wrapped in scarves. Sun glinted off assault rifles.

Graff gasped, backing into him. "Pirates . . ."

Monk shook his head. *Oh, that's just great . . .*

The boat turned toward them and skimmed through the chop.

Monk grabbed Graff by the collar and tugged him off the sunlit beach.

Piracy was on the rise worldwide, but the Indonesian waters had always been rife with such cutthroats. The many islands and small atolls, the thousand secret ports, the thick jungles. All of it created the perfect breeding ground. And after the recent tsunami in the region, the number of local pirates had boomed, taking advantage of the chaos and the thin stretch of policing resources.

It seemed this current tragedy proved no different.

Desperate times bred desperate men.

But who was desperate enough to risk these waters? Monk noted the gunmen were wrapped from head to toe in their own makeshift bio-suits. Had they heard the toxic levels were dropping here and decided to risk an assault?

As Monk retreated from the water's edge, he glanced in the direction of their beached boat. Among the islands, their Zodiac boat would fetch a pretty penny on the black market, not to mention all their expensive research equipment. Monk also noted the lack of return fire by their Zodiac's pilot. Caught by surprise, the Australian sailor must have been taken out in the first assault. He also had their only radio. Cut off, they were on their own.

Monk pictured Lisa aboard the cruise ship. The Australian Coast Guard cutter patrolled the waters around the tiny port. At least she should be safe.

Unlike them.

Cliffs cut off any retreat. To either side, empty beaches stretched.

Monk dragged Graff behind a tumbled boulder, the only shelter.

The speedboat aimed toward them. Gunfire chattered, pocking the sand in an arrow toward their hiding place.

Monk pulled them lower.

So much for that lazy day at the beach.

11:42 A.M.

DR. LISA CUMMINGS smeared the anesthetic cream across the back of the crying girl. Her mother held her hand. The woman was Malaysian and spoke in soft whispers, her almond eyes pinched in worry. The combination of lidocaine and prilocaine quickly soothed the burn across the child's back, dissolving the girl's pained cries into sobs and tears.

"She should be fine," Lisa said, knowing the mother was employed as a waitress at one of the local hotels and spoke English. "Make sure she takes the antibiotics three times a day."

The woman bowed her head. "*Terima kasih*. Thank you."

Lisa nodded her toward a group of men and women in blue-and-white uniforms, the staff of the *Mistress of the Seas*.

"One of the crew will find a cabin for you and your daughter."

Another bow of her head, but Lisa was already turning away, stripping off her gloves with a snap. The dining room on the Lido Deck of the *Mistress of the Seas* had become the major triage point for the entire ship. Each evacuee from the island was examined and divided into critical and noncritical cases. Lisa, with the least experience in crisis medicine, had been assigned to first aid. To assist her, she was given a nursing student from Sydney, a skinny young man of Indian descent named Jesspal, a volunteer from the WHO medical staff.

They made an odd couple: one blond and pale, the other dark-haired and coffee-skinned. But they operated like an experienced team.

"Jessie, how are we doing on the cephalexin?"

"Should last, Dr. Lisa." He shook the large bottle of antibiotics with one hand while filling out paperwork with the other. The young man knew how to multitask.

Snugging the green scrub pants higher on her hips, Lisa

glanced around her. No one waited for immediate care. The rest of the dining room remained in a state of subdued chaos, punctuated by cries and occasional shouts, but for the moment, their station was an island of calm.

"I think the bulk of the islanders have been evacuated," Jessie said. "I heard the last two tenders from the docks arrived only half full. I think we're seeing the dribs and drabs from the smaller outlying villages."

"Thank God for that."

She had treated over a hundred and fifty patients during the course of the interminable morning, cases of burns, blisters, racking coughs, dysentery, nausea, a wrist sprain from a fall at the docks. Yet she had only seen a fraction of all the cases. The cruise ship had arrived at the island last night, and the evacuation had been well under way by the time she arrived at daybreak, flown in by helicopter. It required her to hit the ground running. The tiny, remote island had held over two thousand inhabitants. Though quarters were tight, the ship should accommodate the entire populace, especially as the number of dead had tragically climbed past four hundred . . . and was still rising.

She stood for a moment, hugging her arms around herself, wishing it were Painter's strong arms instead, embracing her from behind, his cheek, rough with stubble at her neck. She closed her eyes, tired. Even though he was absent, she borrowed a bit of his steel.

While laboring, case after case, it had been easy to turn clinical, to detach, to simply treat and move on.

But now, in this moment of calm, the enormity of the disaster struck her. Over the past two weeks, the illnesses here had started small, a few burns from immediate exposure. Then in just two days, the seas had churned up a toxic cloud, erupting in a final volcanic expulsion of blistering gas that killed a fifth of the population and injured the rest.

And though the toxic cloud had blown itself out, secondary illnesses and infections had begun afflicting the sick: flus, burning fevers, meningitis, blindness. The rapidity was disturbing. The entire third deck had been designated a quarantine area.

What was she doing here?

When this medical crisis first arose, Lisa had petitioned Painter for this assignment, stating her case. Besides her medical degree, she held a PhD in human physiology, but more importantly, she had extensive field experience, especially in marine sciences. She had labored for half a decade aboard a salvage ship, the *Deep Fathom,* doing physiological research.

So she had a sound argument for her inclusion here.

But it was not the only one.

For the past year Lisa had been land-bound in Washington and found herself slowly being consumed by Painter's life. And while a part of her enjoyed the intimacy, the two becoming one, she also knew she needed this chance away, both for herself and for her relationship, a bit of distance to evaluate her life, out of Painter's shadow.

But maybe this was too much distance . . .

A sharp scream drew her attention toward the double doors into the dining room. Two sailors hauled in a man atop a stretcher. He writhed and cried, skin weeping, red as a lobster shell. It looked as if his entire body had been parboiled. His bearers rushed him toward the critical care station.

Reflexively, she ran the treatment through her head, going clinical again. *Diazepam and a morphine drip.* Still, deeper inside, she knew the truth. They all did. The suffering man's treatment would be merely palliative, to make him comfortable. The man on the stretcher was already dead.

"Here comes trouble," Jessie mumbled behind her.

Lisa turned and spotted Dr. Gene Lindholm striding toward her, an ostrich of a man, all legs and neck, with a shock of feathered white hair. The head of the WHO team nodded at her, indicating she was indeed his target.

What now?

She didn't particularly care for the Harvard-trained clinician. He came with an ego to match. Upon arriving, rather than helping here, he had sequestered himself with the owner of the cruise line, maverick Australian billionaire Ryder Blunt. The billionaire, notorious for his hands-on approach to business, had been aboard the ship for its maiden cruise. And while he could have left when the ship was commandeered, the billionaire had remained on-site, turning the rescue event into a marketing opportunity.

And Lindholm cooperated.

However, such cooperation did not extend to Monk and Lisa. The WHO leader resented the strings that were pulled to include the pair on his team. But he'd had no choice but to acquiesce—still, that didn't mean he had to be pleasant about it.

"Dr. Cummings, I'm glad to find you here idling with nothing to do."

Lisa bit back a retort.

Jessie snorted.

Lindholm glanced to the nursing student as if he'd been unaware of the man's presence—then just as quickly dismissed him and returned his focus to Lisa.

"I was instructed to include you and your partner in any findings related to the epidemiology for this disaster. And as Dr. Kokkalis is out in the field, I thought I should bring this to your attention."

He thrust out a thick medical folder. She recognized the logo for the small hospital that served Christmas Island. Staffed with only on-call doctors and a pair of full-time nurses, the hospital had been quickly swamped, requiring the more severe cases to be airlifted to Perth. But that became impractical after the full brunt of the biological meltdown struck the island. Once the cruise ship had arrived, the hospital had been the first to be evacuated.

Lisa flipped open the folder and saw the patient's name listed as John Doe. She quickly scanned the history, the little that there was. The patient, a man in his late sixties, had been found five weeks ago wandering naked through the rain forest, clearly suffering from dementia and exposure. He could not speak and was severely dehydrated. He subsequently slipped into an infantile state, unable to care for himself, eating only if fed by hand. They sought to identify him by fingerprint and by searching through missing person records, but nothing had turned up. He remained a John Doe.

Lisa glanced up. "I don't understand . . . what does this have to do with what happened here?"

Sighing, Lindholm stepped next to her and tapped the chart. "Under the list of presenting symptoms and physical findings. At the bottom."

" 'Moderate to severe signs of exposure,' " she mumbled, reading down the list. The last line stated *deep dermal second-degree sunburn to calves, with resultant edema and severe blistering.*

She glanced up. She had treated similar symptoms all morning. "This wasn't just a sunburn."

"The island's clinicians jumped to that conclusion," Lindholm said with evident disgust.

Lisa could not blame the island's doctors or nurses. At that time, no one was aware of the environmental disaster brewing. She again checked the date.

Five weeks ago.

"I believe we may have found Patient Zero," Lindholm said pompously. "Or at least one of the earliest cases."

Lisa closed the folder. "Can I see him?"

He nodded. "That was the second reason I came down here." There was a grim waver in his voice at the end that disturbed Lisa. She waited for him to explain, but he simply turned on a heel and headed out. "Follow me."

The WHO leader crossed the dining room to one of the ship's elevators. He hit the button for the Promenade Deck, third level.

"The isolation ward?" she asked.

He shrugged.

A moment later the doors opened into a makeshift clean room. Lindholm waved for her to don one of the bio-suits, similar to the one Monk had taken to collect samples.

Lisa climbed into a suit, noting the slight body odor as she pulled the hood over her head and sealed her seams. Once both were ready, she was led down a passage to one of the cabins. The door was open and other clinicians were crowded at the entry.

Lindholm bellowed for the others to clear a path. They scattered, well trained by their leader. Lindholm led Lisa into the small room, an inside cabin, no windows. The only bed stood against the back wall.

A figure lay under a thin blanket. He looked more cadaverous than alive. But she noted the shallow rise and fall of the blanket, a panting weak breath. Intravenous lines ran to an exposed arm. The skin on the limb so wan and wasted as to the point of translucency.

She instinctively looked to his face. Someone had shaved him, but hastily. A few nicks still oozed. His hair was gray and wispy, like a chemo patient, but his eyes were open, meeting hers.

For a moment she thought she noted a flash of recognition, the barest startle. Even a hand lifted feebly toward her.

But Lindholm strode between them. Ignoring the patient, he peeled back the lower half of the blanket to expose the man's legs. She was expecting to see scabbed skin, healing from a second-degree burn, like she had been treating all day, but instead she saw that a strange purplish bruising stretched from the man's groin to toe, pebbled with black blisters.

"If you had read further into the report," Lindholm said, "you would have discovered these new symptoms arose four days ago. The hospital staff surmised tropical gangrene, secondary to the deep infection in the burns. But it's actually—"

"Necrotizing fasciitis," she finished.

Lindholm sniffed tightly and lowered the blanket. "Exactly. That's what we thought."

Necrotizing fasciitis, better known as *flesh-eating disease,* was caused by bacteria, usually beta-hemolytic streptococci.

"What's the assessment?" she asked. "A secondary infection through his earlier wounds?"

"I had our bacteriologist brought in. A quick gram stain last night revealed a massive proliferation of *Propionibacterium.*"

She frowned. "That makes no sense. That's just an ordinary epidermal bacterium. Nonpathogenic. Are you sure it wasn't just a contaminant?"

"Not in the numbers found in the blisters. The stains were repeated on other tissue samples. The same results. It was during these second studies that an odd necrosis was noted in the surrounding tissue. A pattern of decay sometimes seen locally. It can mimic necrotizing fasciitis."

"Caused by what?"

"The sting of a stonefish. Very toxic. The fish looks like a rock but bears stiff dorsal spines envenomed by poison glands. One of the nastiest venoms in the world. I brought Dr. Barnhardt in to test the tissue."

"The toxicologist?"

A nod.

Dr. Barnhardt had been flown here from Amsterdam, an expert in environmental poisons and toxins. Under the auspices of Sigma, Painter had personally requested the man's addition to the WHO team.

"The results came back this past hour. He found active poison in the patient's tissues."

"I don't understand. So the man was poisoned by a stonefish while wandering in delirium?"

A voice spoke behind her, answering her question. "No."

She turned. A tall figure filled the doorway, a bear of a man squeezed into a contamination suit too small for his girth. His grizzled and bearded face fit his size, but not the delicacy of his mind. Dr. Henrick Barnhardt pushed into the room.

"I don't believe the man was ever stung by a stonefish. But he is suffering from the venom."

"How is that possible?"

Barnhardt ignored her question for the moment and addressed the WHO leader. "It's what I suspected, Dr. Lindholm. I borrowed Dr. Miller's *Propionibacterium* cultures and had them analyzed. There is no doubt now."

Lindholm visibly blanched.

"What?" Lisa asked.

The toxicologist reached and gently straightened the blanket over the John Doe patient, a tender gesture for such a large man. "The bacteria," he said, "the *Propionibacterium* . . . is producing the equivalent of stonefish venom, pumping it out in quantities enough to dissolve this man's tissues."

"That's impossible."

Lindholm snorted. "That's what I said."

Lisa ignored him. "But *Propionibacterium* doesn't produce *any* toxins. It's benign."

"I can't explain how or why," Barnhardt said. "Even to begin any further assessment, I would need a scanning microscope at least. But I assure you, Dr. Cummings, this benign bacteria has somehow transformed into one of the nastiest bugs on the planet."

"How do you mean *transformed*?"

"I don't think the patient caught this bug. I think it was a part of his normal bacterial flora. Whatever the man was exposed to out there, it changed the bacterium's biochemistry, altered its basic genetic structure and made it virulent. Turned it into a flesh-eater."

Lisa still refused to believe it. Not without more proof. "My partner, Dr. Kokkalis, has a portable forensic lab assembled in our suite. If you could—"

Lisa felt something brush the back of her gloved hand. She almost jumped away, startled. But it was only the old man in the bed, reaching again for her. His eyes met hers, desperate. His lips, chapped and cracked, trembled with a dry breath.

"Sue . . . Susan . . ."

She turned and gripped the man's fingers. Plainly he was

still in a delirium, mistaking her for someone else. She squeezed reassurance.

"Susan . . . where's Oscar? I can hear him barking in the woods . . ." His eyes rolled back in his head. ". . . barking . . . help him . . . but don't . . . don't go in the water . . ." She felt his fingers go slack in her grip. His eyelids drifted closed, dragging away the brief moment of confused lucidity.

A nurse stepped forward and checked the man's vitals. He was out again.

Lisa tucked his hand back under his blanket.

Lindholm stepped forward, close, invading her space. "This forensics lab of Dr. Kokkalis's. We must gain access to it as soon as possible. In order to confirm or dismiss this wild conjecture by Dr. Barnhardt."

"I would prefer to wait for Monk's return," Lisa said, stepping back. "Some of the equipment is of special design. We will need his expertise to operate it without damage."

Lindholm scowled—not so much at her as life in general. "Fine." He swung away. "Your partner is due back in the next hour. Dr. Barnhardt, in the meantime collect whatever samples you'll need."

A nod by the Dutch toxicologist acknowledged the order—though Lisa noted the slight roll to Barnhardt's eyes as the WHO leader departed. Lisa followed Lindholm out of the room.

Barnhardt called after her. "You will page me when Dr. Kokkalis returns, *ja*?"

"Of course." She was as anxious as everyone else to discover the truth here. But she also feared they were still barely scratching the surface. Something dreadful was brewing here.

But what?

She hoped Monk would not be gone long.

As she left, she also remembered the patient's last words. *Don't . . . don't go in the water . . .*

11:53 A.M.

"WE'LL HAVE TO swim for it," Monk said.

"Are . . . are you crazy?" Graff answered as they cowered behind the rock.

Moments ago the pirates' speedboat had ground up against a submerged reef, one of the many that gave rise to the name for this section of island: Smithson's Blight. Out on the water, the gunfire had ended, replaced by the roar of the engine as the boat sought to drag itself free.

Monk had popped his head up to evaluate the scenario, only to almost lose an ear to a sniper's bullet. They were still pinned down, trapped, with nowhere to run—except into the face of the enemy.

Monk bent down and unzipped one of his suit's seals near his shin. He reached through the opening and removed the 9mm Glock from its ankle holster.

Graff's eyes widened as he pulled free the pistol. "Do you think you can take them all out? Hit the gas tank or something?"

Monk shook his head and zipped back up. "You've been watching too many Bruckheimer movies. This peashooter will only serve to get them to duck their heads. Perhaps long enough for us to hit the surf over there."

He pointed to a line of boulders that stretched out into the water. If they could get on the far side, keep the boulders between them and the boat, they might be able to make it around the next point. Then if they could reach the beach on the far side before the pirates freed their boat . . . and if there was some path that led into the island's interior . . .

Damn, that's a lot of ifs . . .

But there was only one certainty here.

They were dead if they stayed shivering like a pair of rabbits.

"We'll have to stay underwater as much as possible," Monk warned. "Maybe we could even take a breath or two if we keep air trapped in our contamination hoods."

Graff's face looked little comforted by this idea. Though the worst of the toxic event was over, the bay remained a poisonous cesspool. Even the gunmen knew better than to leave the safety of their boat. The masked men were using oars to pry the craft off the rocks, rather than climbing in themselves and lightening the load.

If even pirates refused to go into the water . . .

Monk suddenly began to question the wisdom of his own plan. Besides, he hated diving. He was a former Green Beret, not a friggin' Navy SEAL.

"What?" Graff asked, reading something in Monk's expression. "You don't think your plan is going to work, do you?"

"Let a man think already!"

Slumping down, Monk found himself staring back toward the worn Buddha statue under its lean-to, protected by its charred row of prayer sticks. He wasn't Buddhist, but he was not above praying to any god that would get him out of this scrape.

His eyes again settled to the burned prayer sticks. Without turning away, he spoke to Graff. "How did these worshippers get here?" he asked. "There's no village for miles along the coastline, the beach is protected by reefs, and the cliffs appear too sheer to climb."

Graff shook his head. "What difference does it make?"

"Someone lit those prayer sticks. Within the last day or so." Monk shifted up. "Look at the beach. No footsteps but our own. You can see where someone knelt to light their smudge sticks, but no steps head out to the water or along the beach. That means they had to come down from above. There must be a path."

"Or maybe someone just raised and lowered a rope."

Monk sighed, wishing for a more dim-witted companion, someone less able to poke holes in his reasoning.

"Water or Buddha?" Monk asked.

Graff visibly swallowed as the speedboat's engine throttled up. The pirates were almost free.

Graff turned to Monk. "Is . . . isn't it good luck to rub the belly of a Buddha?"

Monk nodded. "I think I read that on a fortune cookie somewhere. I hope that Buddha read the same cookie."

Monk shifted around, raising his pistol. "On my count, you haul ass. I'm going to be at your heels, blasting at the boat. You just concentrate on getting to that Buddha and finding that path."

"And I'll pray the worshippers didn't use a rope to—"

"Don't say it or you'll jinx us!"

Graff clammed up.

"Here we go." Monk braced himself, bouncing a bit to get circulation into his legs. He counted off. "Three . . . two . . . one . . . !"

Graff took off, bolting out like a jackrabbit. A bullet rang off the rock at the man's heels.

Monk cursed and jerked up. "You were supposed to wait for *go,*" he mumbled, squeezing the trigger and firing toward the trapped boat. "Civilians . . ."

He peppered the boat, driving the snipers onto their bellies. He watched one man throw his hands up and go toppling overboard. A lucky shot on Monk's part. Return fire consisted of a few wild blasts, fired in an angry panic.

Ahead, Graff reached the Buddha and skidded in the sand, slipping past the prayer sticks. Twisting around, he caught his balance and leapfrogged behind the lean-to.

Monk took a more direct route and crashed through a sandy thornbush. He landed next to Graff.

"We made it!" Graff gasped out with way too much surprise in his voice.

"And pissed them off damn good."

Monk pictured the man going overboard into the toxic soup.

Possibly in retribution, rifle blasts tore through the lean-to and exploded the vines and leaves draped along the cliff wall. Monk and Graff sheltered together, protected by Buddha's wide stone belly. Surely there was symbolism in this last act.

But that was about all Buddha had to offer.

Monk studied the cliffs behind the wooden shack.

Sheer and unscalable.

No path.

"Maybe one of us should have rubbed that belly when we ran up here," Monk said sourly.

"Your gun?" Graff asked.

Monk hefted it up. "One round. After that, I could always throw the pistol at them. That always works."

Behind them the boat finally freed itself with a roar of its engine. Worse yet, the boat was now on the *island* side of the reef, sidling toward the beach, sluicing through the bodies of the dead.

Before long there would be another two bodies to add to the soup.

A volley of shots peppered the Buddha and shattered through the lean-to. More vines were shredded. A ricochet sped past Monk's nose—but he didn't move. He watched one of the drapes of blasted vine fall away, revealing the mouth of a cave behind it.

Monk crawled forward, keeping the statue between him and the approaching pirates. He nudged open the vines. Sunlight revealed a step, then another . . .

"A tunnel! So much for your rope-ladder theory, Graff!"

Monk turned and saw the doctor slumped to one side, a hand pressed to his shoulder. Blood welled between his fingers.

Crap . . .

Monk hurried back to him. "C'mon. We've no time to dress it. Can you walk?"

Graff spoke between clenched teeth. "As long as they don't shoot me in the leg."

With some help, the two crawled through the vine drape and into the tunnel. The temperature dropped a full ten degrees. Monk kept a grip on Graff's elbow. The man trembled and shook, but he followed Monk's lead and hurried up the steps into the dark.

Behind them he heard the scrape of hull on sand and the victorious shouts of the pirates, confident their prey was trapped. Monk continued up, around and around, feeling in the dark.

It would not take long for the pirates to find the tunnel. But would they pursue or simply take off? The answer came soon enough.

Lights flared below . . . along with more furtive barked orders.

Monk hurried.

He heard the anger in the voices.

He had indeed pissed them off.

Slowly the darkness overhead turned to gray. Walls became discernible. Their pace increased. Graff was mumbling under his breath, but Monk could not understand the man's words. A prayer, a curse . . . he would take either if it would work.

At last the upper end of the stairs appeared. The pair burst out of the tunnel and into the fringe of rain forest that frosted the cliff. Monk pushed onward, grateful for the dense cover of the jungle. As he entered the forest, he saw the toxic kill zone was not limited to the beach below. Dead birds littered the forest floor. Near his toes lay the furred body of a flying fox, crumpled like a crashed jet fighter.

But not all the forest's denizens were dead.

Monk stared ahead. The forest floor churned and eddied in a red tide of its own. But this was no bacterial bloom. Millions of crabs covered the forest floor, every square inch. Some were latched onto trunks and vines.

Here were the missing Christmas Island red crabs.

Monk remembered his earlier study. Throughout the year, the crabs remained docile until aroused or stirred up. During their annual migration, the crabs were known to slash tires of passing cars with their razor-sharp claws.

Monk took a step back.

Stirred up described the crabs at the moment. They climbed all over one another, agitated, snapping. In a feeding frenzy.

Monk now understood why the creatures were missing from the beach below. Why go *down* when there was plenty to eat up here?

The crabs not only feasted on the dead birds and bats—but also on their own brothers and sisters, in a cannibalistic free-for-all. At the men's appearance, massive claws lifted in warning, snapping like broken sticks.

Welcome to the party!

Behind them, from the tunnel opening, excited voices echoed forth.

The pirates had spotted the tunnel's end.

Graff took a step forward, clutching his shoulder. A large crab, hidden under a fern leaf, swiped at his toe and cleaved clear through the plastic.

The doctor retreated back, mumbling under his breath again. It was the same mantra as on the stairs, only now Monk understood it . . . and couldn't agree more.

"We really should have rubbed that Buddha's belly."

3

Ambush

"WHAT THE HELL is going on?"

"I don't know, Dad." Gray hurried with his father to close the carriage doors to the garage. "But I intend to find out."

The two had hauled the assassin's motorcycle into the garage. Gray had not wanted the bike left in the open. In fact, he wanted *no* trace of Seichan left here. So far there had been no sign of whoever had shot her, but that didn't mean they weren't coming.

He rushed back to his mother. As a biology professor at George Washington University, his mother had taught plenty of pre-med students and knew enough to belly-wrap Seichan's wound in order to stanch any further hemorrhaging.

The assassin hovered at the edge of consciousness, drifting in and out.

"It looked like the bullet passed clean through," his mother said. "But she's lost a lot of blood. Is the ambulance on its way?"

Moments ago Gray had made an emergency call with his cell phone—but not to 911. Seichan could not be taken to any local hospital. A gunshot wound required answering too many questions. Still, he had to move her, get her medical attention as soon as possible.

Down the street, a door slammed. Gray listened, jumpy

at any noises, his senses stretched to a piano-wire tautness. Someone called out, laughing.

"Gray, is the ambulance on its way?" his mother persisted in a harder tone.

Gray just nodded, refusing to lie out loud. At least not to his mother. He turned to his father, who joined them, wiping his palms on his work jeans. His parents thought he was a laboratory technician for a D.C. research company, a lowly position after being court-martialed out of the Army Rangers for striking a superior officer.

But that had not been the truth either.

Only a cover.

His parents knew nothing about his true profession with Sigma, and Gray meant to keep it that way. Which meant he needed to bug out of here ASAP. He had to get moving.

"Dad, can I borrow the T-bird? All this Fourth of July commotion, emergency services are overloaded. I can get the woman to the hospital faster myself."

His father's eyes narrowed with suspicion, but he pointed toward the back door to the kitchen. "Keys are on the hook."

Gray ran and leaped up the rear porch steps. Cracking open the screen door, he reached inside and grabbed the jangling key fob from the hook. His father had restored a 1960 Thunderbird convertible, raven black with a red leather interior, tricked out with a new Holly carburetor, flamethrower coil, and electric choke. It had been moved out to the curb for the party.

He ran to where it was parked with its top down, hopped over the driver's door, and slid behind the wheel. A moment later, he was roaring in reverse and backed into the driveway, bouncing a bit in the seat as he hit the curb. His father was still troubleshooting the rebuilt suspension.

He choked it into park, engine running, and ran to where his mother and father knelt at Seichan's side. His father was already scooping her up.

"Let me," Gray said.

"Maybe we shouldn't move her," his mother opined. "She took quite the fall and roll."

Gray's father ignored them both. He heaved up, cradling Seichan in his arms. His father might be missing a part of a leg and mentally slipping a few gears, but he was still as strong as a draft horse.

"Get the door," his father ordered. "We'll get her spread out across the backseat."

Rather than arguing, Gray obeyed and helped get Seichan inside. He opened the door and folded the front seat down. His father climbed into the back and draped her with deliberate gentleness, then settled into the rear seat, supporting her head.

"Dad . . ."

His mother climbed into the passenger front side. "I've locked the house up. Let's go."

"I . . . I can take her on my own," Gray said, waving them both out.

He was not headed to any hospital. His earlier phone call had been to emergency dispatch, where he was immediately put in contact with Director Crowe. *Thank God he'd still been there.*

Gray had been ordered to a safe house, where an emergency medical evacuation team would rendezvous to evaluate and treat Seichan. Painter was taking no chances. In case this was all a trap, she was not to be taken to Sigma's headquarters. A known assassin and terrorist, Seichan was on the most-wanted lists of Interpol and a score of intelligence agencies around the world. Rumor had it that the Israeli Mossad maintained a shoot-on-sight order on her.

His parents had no place being here.

Gray stared at the steel in his father's eyes. His mother's arms were already crossed over her chest. They were not going to budge easily.

"You can't come," he said. "It's not . . . not safe."

"Like here's any safer," his father said, waving an arm back toward the garage. "Who's to say whatever gangbangers or drug dealers who shot her aren't already on their way here?"

Gray had no time to explain. The director had already dispatched a security detail to protect and watch over his parents. They would be arriving in the next couple minutes.

"My car . . . my rules," his father finished with a rumble of finality. "Now *go,* before she starts seeping through your mother's bandages and messes up my new leather seats."

Seichan groaned, stirring in pain and confused agitation. One arm lifted to her bandage, clawing. His father caught her fingers and lowered her hand. He kept hold of it, reassuring as much as restraining.

"Let's go," his father said.

The rare tenderness more than anything broke through his constraint.

Gray climbed into the driver's seat. "Buckle in," he said, knowing the sooner he got Seichan to the safe house, the better for all of them. He'd deal with the fallout later.

As he started the engine, he caught his mother staring at him. "We're not fools, you know, Gray," she said cryptically, and turned away.

His brows furrowed, more in irritation than understanding. He shifted the car into gear and shot down the driveway. He took the turn onto the street rather sharply.

"Careful!" his father barked. "Those are new Kelsey wire wheels! If you goddamn scratch them up . . ."

Gray sped down the street. He made several fast turns, minding the wheels. It felt good to be moving. The 390 V8 growled like a beast. An ember of grudging respect for his father's handiwork burned through his exasperation.

His mother glanced down the street as he turned in the opposite direction from the nearest hospital, but she remained silent and settled deeper in her seat. He would find some way of dealing with his folks at the safe house.

As Gray sped through the midnight city, he still heard occasional firecrackers popping. The holiday was ending, but Gray feared the true fireworks had yet to begin.

12:55 A.M.
Washington, D.C.

SO MUCH FOR holidays off . . .

Director Painter Crowe stalked down the hall toward his office. Central Command's skeletal night staff was rapidly swelling in numbers. A general alert had been dispatched. He'd already fielded two calls from Homeland Security. It wasn't every day you had an international terrorist fall into your lap. And not just any terrorist, but a member of the shadowy network known as the Guild.

Often competing with Sigma, the Guild hunted and stole emerging technologies: military, biological, chemical, nuclear. In the current world order, knowledge was the true power—more than oil, more than any weapon. Only in the Guild's case, they sold their discoveries to the highest bidder, including Al Qaeda and Hezbollah in the Middle East, Aum Shinrikyo in Japan, and the Shining Path in Peru. The Guild operated through a series of isolated cells around the world, with moles in world governments, intelligence agencies, major think tanks, even international research facilities.

And once, even at DARPA.

Painter still felt the sting of that betrayal.

But now they had a key Guild operative in custody.

As Painter entered the anteroom to his offices, his secretary and aide, Brant Millford, shifted back from his desk. The man used a wheelchair, his spine severed by a piece of shrapnel following a car bombing at a security post in Bosnia.

"Sir, I have a satellite call coming in from Dr. Cummings."

Painter stopped, surprised. Lisa was not scheduled to report in so soon. A thread of worry cut through the tangle of responsibilities this night.

"I'll take it in my office. Thank you, Brant."

Painter crossed through the door. Three plasma monitors hung on the walls around his desk. The screens were dark for now, but as the night wore on, they would soon be flowing with data, all pouring into Central Command. For now, that could all wait. He reached across his deck to the phone and tapped the blinking button.

Lisa had been scheduled to report in just around dawn, when it was nightfall among the Indonesian islands. Painter had requested the full day's debriefing at that time, just before she went to bed. Such scheduling also offered him the perfect chance to wish her a good night.

"Lisa?"

The connection proved spotty with occasional drops.

"God, Painter, it's great to hear—voice. I know you're busy. Brant mentioned a crisis—little else."

"Don't worry. Not so much a crisis, as an opportunity." He rested his hip to the edge of the desk. "Why are you calling in early?"

"Something's come up here. I've transmitted a large batch of technical data to research. I wanted someone over there to start double-checking the results from the toxicologist here, Dr. Barnhardt."

"I'll make sure it gets done. But what's the urgency?" He sensed the tension in her voice.

"The situation here may be more dire than originally projected."

"I know. I've heard about the aftermath of the toxic cloud that blew over the island."

"No—yes, that was horrible, certainly—but things may be growing even worse. We've isolated some strange genetic abnormalities showing up in secondary infections. Disturbing findings. I thought it best to coordinate with Sigma researchers and labs as soon as possible, to get the ball rolling while Dr. Barnhardt completes his preliminary tests."

"Is Monk helping the toxicologist?"

"He's still out in the field, collecting samples. We'll need everything he can bring us."

"I'll alert Jennings here in R and D. Get him to roust his team. I'll have him call and coordinate at our end."

"Perfect. Thanks."

Despite the resolution, Painter could not escape his own worry. Since assigning this mission, he was doing his best to balance his responsibilities as director, to maintain that necessary professional distance, but he could not achieve it, not with Lisa. He cleared his throat. "How are *you* holding up?"

A small amused snort escaped her, tired but familiar. "I'm doing okay. But after this, I may never take another cruise in my life."

"I tried to warn you. It never pays to volunteer. *I wanted to contribute. To make a difference,*" he said, mimicking her with a ghost of a smile. "See what it gets you. A passport to the Love Boat from Hell."

She offered him a halfhearted laugh, but her voice quickly lowered into a more serious tone, halting and unsure. "Painter, maybe it was a mistake . . . me coming here. I know I'm not an official member of Sigma. I may be in over my head."

"If I thought it was a mistake, I wouldn't have assigned you. In fact, I would have grabbed any excuse to keep you from going. But as director, I had a duty to send the best people suited to oversee a medical crisis on behalf of Sigma. With your medical degree, your doctorate in physiology, your field research experience . . . I sent the right person."

A long stretch of silence followed. For a moment, Painter thought the call had dropped.

"Thank you," she finally whispered.

"So don't let me down. I have a reputation to maintain."

She snorted again, her amusement ringing more true. "You really have to work on concluding your pep talks."

"Then how's this: Stay safe, watch your back, and get back here as soon as possible."

"Better."

"Then I'll simply have to go for the gold." He spoke firmly. "I miss you. I love you. I want you in my arms."

He truly did miss her, with a physical ache in his chest.

"See," she said. "With a little practice, you can actually be a pretty good motivational speaker."

"I know," he said. "The same line worked with Monk earlier."

A true laugh followed. It helped shatter his worry from a moment ago. She would do fine. He had faith in her. And in addition, in Painter's stead, Monk would keep her safe. That is, if Monk ever wanted to show his face again . . .

Before Painter could respond further, his aide appeared at his door, knocking softly. Painter waved for him to speak.

"I'm sorry to disturb you, Director. But I've another call holding. On your private line. From Rome. Monsignor Verona. He seemed quite urgent."

Painter's brow furrowed. He spoke into the phone. "Lisa—"

"I heard. You're busy. Once I coordinate with Monk, we'll conference with Jennings on the situation here. Get back to work."

"Stay safe."

"I will," she said. "And I love you, too."

The line blinked off.

Painter took a breath to collect himself, then twisted around to hit the button on his private line. *Why was Monsignor Verona calling?* Painter knew Commander Pierce had been romantically involved with the monsignor's niece, but that had ended almost a year ago.

"Monsignor Verona, this is Painter Crowe."

"Director Crowe, thank you for taking my call. I've been trying to reach Gray for the past two hours, but there's been no answer."

"I'm sorry to hear that. Is there a message you'd like me to forward?"

Painter didn't bother to explain about the current situation. Though Monsignor Verona had helped Sigma in the past, the matter here was on a need-to-know basis, already coded in black.

"There's been an incident here at the Vatican . . . in the

Secret Archives precisely. I'm not entirely sure of its import, but it strikes me as a message or warning. One left for both myself and perhaps Commander Pierce."

Painter stood up and circled around his desk to his chair. "What sort of message?"

"Someone broke into a vault here last week and painted the symbol for the Royal Dragon Court on the floor."

Painter sank into his seat, disturbed by the coincidence. Two years ago, Gray and Monsignor Verona had teamed up to root out and destroy a brutal sect of the Dragon Court. They had succeeded—but not without help, requiring an alliance with an enemy, an operative from the Guild.

Seichan.

And now the assassin was here.

Painter was not one to swallow coincidences easily. Not in the past, and certainly not now. If nothing else, his stint as director of Sigma had honed his edge of paranoia to a razor's sharpness.

"Did anyone get a look at this trespasser?" he asked.

"Briefly. Whoever it was, they came alone. Slipped past all of Vatican security. We captured only a shadowy image on one security camera. This was no casual thief. Only one person I know could have crossed into the inner sanctum and out again with no more than a shadow captured. The same someone connected to our joint involvement with the Dragon Court in the past."

So it seemed the monsignor was no less suspicious than Painter.

"And the dragon painting on the floor," Vigor continued. "It was plainly a message, perhaps even a reminder of a debt owed."

"You believe it was the Guild operative, Seichan," he said. "The one who helped you defeat the Dragon Court?"

"Exactly. If we could find her, ask her—"

Painter knew that any further secrets would only hamper discovering the true threat. It seemed the need-to-know status of the situation had just extended to Rome.

"Seichan is here," he said, cutting the monsignor off. "We have her in custody."

"What?"

He quickly related the night's return of the assassin, dropping out of nowhere, bloodied and on the run.

Vigor was stunned for a moment—then spoke in a rush. "She must be interrogated. If for no other reason than to ask her why she painted the message on the floor."

"We'll do that. Once she's treated, we'll conduct a thorough interview. Behind very stout bars."

"You don't understand. There's something larger going on. Possibly larger than the Guild itself."

"What do you mean?"

"The dragon symbol was painted around an ancient inscription carved into the floor of the archive vault. Carved possibly back when the Vatican was first being built, back to the time of Galileo. The symbols are the characters from what some conjecture might be the most ancient of all written languages. Older than proto-Hebrew. A writing that may even predate mankind."

Painter heard the anxiety in the other's voice. "What do you mean *predate* mankind? How could that be?"

Vigor answered him.

Painter kept the shock out of his reaction, along with his disbelief. He ended the call with a deep frown. The monsignor's assertion was plainly impossible, but true or not, he immediately understood the monsignor's distress. They needed to question Seichan as soon as possible—before anything else happened to her.

Painter hurriedly confirmed ETA on the medical team, then had his aide patch him through to the guard stationed at the safe house.

Who was on duty out there?

He called for Brant to contact security and have them forward video feed from the safe house to his office plasma screens.

As Painter waited, Vigor's final words echoed through him.

Those symbols . . . carved into the stone . . .

Painter shook his head.

Impossible.

. . . they are the language of the angels.

1:04 A.M.

GRAY SPED DOWN Greenwich Parkway into the exclusive Foxhall Village subdivision. He reached the end and made a left turn onto a tree-lined street. He slowed. He let the Thunderbird's idling engine carry him forward. The safe house appeared ahead, a two-story red-brick Tudor with forest-green shutters, a match to the woods of Glover-Archibold Park upon which the home backed.

With the top down, he could smell the damp forest.

Nearing the house, he noted the front porch light was on, as was a lamp in the upper corner window.

The all-clear sign.

He turned and bumped into the driveway, earning a groan from their injured passenger.

"Where are we?" his mother asked.

Gray braked under an overhanging porte cochere on the left side of the house. A side door to the house lay steps away. He had attempted repeatedly to get his parents to vacate the car, but with every hospital and medical center they passed, they only became more stubborn. Or at least his mother did. His father remained at the same level of muleheadedness.

"This is a safe house," he said, seeing little reason to dissemble now. "Medical help should be on its way. Stay put for now."

Gray cut the engine and climbed out.

On the far side of the car, the side door to the house opened. A large shadowy figure filled the doorway. A hand rested on a holstered weapon at his hip. "You Pierce?" the man asked, gruff and short, eyeing the additional passengers with suspicion.

"Yes."

The figure stepped out into the light. He was an ape of a man, thick-limbed, stubble-cut brown hair. He was dressed in military fatigues. Not exactly keeping a low profile.

"Name's Kowalski. I have Crowe on the horn for you." He raised his other hand and held out a cell phone.

Gray headed around the back of the car. He had not been looking forward to this conversation with the director, to explain his blown cover. It was not exactly *covert* to have your parents tagging along.

Even the guard stationed here seemed baffled by the elderly pair sharing the open convertible. He studied the new arrivals with his brows bunched into a knot over his forehead. He scratched his chin.

"Three fifty-two?" he asked as Gray came around.

Gray could not fathom what he meant.

His father answered from the backseat. "No, it's a *three-ninety* block. Rebuilt V8 from a Ford Galaxie."

"Sweet ride."

Plainly the guard hadn't been studying his parents, only the car.

Seichan stirred in the backseat, perhaps somehow noting the lack of wind and motion. She struggled weakly to sit up.

"Can you help get her inside?" Gray asked the guard. He noted the lower half of a U.S. Navy anchor on the man's right biceps as he accepted the phone. Ex-military. No surprise there. If there had been a picture under *jarhead* in the dictionary, it would've been this man's mug shot.

His mother opened the passenger door. "Where's that medical help?" She seemed to find little hope in the large form of the guard, even clutching her purse a bit tighter to her side.

Gray held up a palm, asking for patience.

"Ma'am," Kowalski said, and pointed to the kitchen.

"There's a medkit on the kitchen table. Morphine stabs and smelling salts. I've laid out a suture pack."

His mother eyed the man with a more studied appraisal. "Thank you, young man."

With a more withering glance in Gray's direction, his mother headed inside.

Stepping out of the way, Gray spoke into the phone. "Director Crowe, Commander Pierce here."

"Is that your mother who just got out of the car?"

How the hell . . . ?

Gray searched up and spotted the video camera hidden under the porte cochere. It must be sending a live feed to Central Command. He could feel heat rise at his collar.

"Sir—"

"Never mind. Explain later. Gray, we've intel out of Rome, related to our new arrival. How is the prisoner holding up?"

Gray eyed the back of the convertible. The guard and his father were discussing the best way to move Seichan's limp form. He noted the fresh bloom of blood in the center of her belly wrap.

"She's going to need immediate attention."

"Help should be there any minute."

The trundle of a heavy vehicle sounded. Gray swung around. A large black van turned and headed down the street.

"I think they're here," he said with a relieved sigh.

The van reached the house, shifted to the curb, and braked at the foot of the driveway. Gray felt a twinge of unease, hating to be blocked in, but he recognized the van. It was Sigma's medical response team. The camouflaged ambulance was based on the same design as the vehicle that accompanied the president, capable of handling emergency surgery if necessary.

"Give me an update as soon as their evaluation is over," Painter said. The director must have spotted the van also.

The side doors of the van shoved open. Three men and a woman, all in surgical scrubs and matching loose black bomber jackets, exited the van with coordinated skill. Two men yanked a stretcher, legs unfolding beneath it. They followed the third man and the woman, who strode forward to meet Gray. The man held his hand out.

"Dr. Amen Nasser," he said.

Gray shook his hand, appreciating the cool, dry grip. Calm and in control. The doctor could be no older than thirty, yet he carried himself with firm authority. His complexion was the hue of polished mahogany, unlike the woman, whose skin was more the color of warm honey.

Gray studied her.

Though of Asian heritage, the woman plainly sought to downplay it. She had shaved her head to a crew cut and bleached her remaining hair an ice blond. Entwining tattoos also circled her wrists in a Celtic pattern. While such severity had never appealed to Gray before, there remained something strangely seductive about her. Perhaps it was the emerald of her eyes, a feature that needed no other embellishment. Then again, it may have been the way she moved, leonine, muscular, balanced. Like much of Sigma, she must have had some military training.

The woman nodded to Gray. No introduction was offered.

"I've been informed of the situation," the team leader continued, his words precise, plainly foreign-born, with a trace of an accent. "I'll ask you all to stand back and let us work. We will transfer the patient to the surgical bay inside the van. I will send out Anni with a status report shortly." He finally acknowledged the woman.

The other two men rushed past with the stretcher. The doctor followed, while Anni remained where she was, leaning on a hip.

The cell phone in Gray's hand began to vibrate as he stepped aside. The team leader spoke rapidly. Gray finally recognized the accent of the team leader.

Dr. Amen Nasser.

He was Egyptian.

1:08 A.M.

PAINTER STOOD IN front of the wall monitor directly behind his desk. The plasma screens on the other two walls displayed live video of the first and second floor of the safe house. The one behind his desk pixilated with digital feed from the exterior camera.

"Pick up the phone, Gray!" he yelled at the screen.

The controls for the cameras were down a floor in main security. Painter had no way of swiveling the camera. He had seen the med van park at the edge of the screen, but it wasn't until a second ago that he had spotted the pair who had stepped into view in front of Gray.

Neither of them worked for Sigma.

Painter knew all the personnel.

The van might be Sigma's, but the team inside was not.

A trap.

On the screen, Gray flipped open the cell and raised it to his ear. "Director Crowe—?"

Before Painter could answer, a thin foot kicked out and smashed the phone against Gray's head. With a snap of cellular crackle, he went down, caught off guard.

"Gray . . ."

The image on the screen suddenly jumped—then went black.

1:09 A.M.

THE FIRST SHOT took out the camera.

Head ringing, Gray heard the muffled cough and splintering shatter. He twisted around.

"What the hell?" his father bellowed as the camera's debris rained down on him. He was still crouched in the backseat with Seichan.

The guard, Kowalski, was on the other side of the car. He froze like a deer in headlights, a grizzled two-hundred-pound deer. But the pistol at the back of his neck was a strong deterrent against moving.

The orderlies had shoved the stretcher into the side yard. One held a gun on Kowalski, the other waved for Gray's father to get out of the car.

"Stay where you are," a harsh voice warned behind him.

Gray glanced over his shoulder. The woman, Anni, held a black Sig Sauer at his face, standing out of reach of a leg sweep, but close enough that she would not miss a head shot.

Recognizing this, Gray faced the Thunderbird.

Dr. Nasser carried a matching pistol in his hand.

Gray somehow knew that it was the weapon that had shot Seichan.

Nasser came around to Gray's father's side. He searched down to where Seichan lay sprawled. He shook his head sadly, then pointed to the gunman on that side. "Get the old man out of the car. See if the bitch has the obelisk, then drag her to the van."

Obelisk?

Gray watched as his father was manhandled out of the backseat. He prayed his father would not aggravate the situation. But it proved unnecessary. Plainly stunned, his father offered no resistance.

"She doesn't have it," the man in the backseat finally said, straightening up.

Nasser stepped to the car and scanned the interior himself. He did not find what he was looking for. The only sign of consternation at this lack of discovery was a single crinkle between his eyes.

He stepped away from the car and faced Gray.

"Where is it?"

Gray fixed the man with a steady stare. "Where is what?"

He sighed. "Surely she told you, or you wouldn't be making such an effort for an enemy." Without turning, he signaled the man who had searched Seichan. The man pressed his pistol against his father's forehead.

"I don't ask questions a second time. You probably don't know that. So I'll give you this moment of leeway."

Gray swallowed, noting the raw fear in his father's eyes.

"The obelisk," Gray said. "The one you mentioned. She had it with her, but it broke when she crashed her bike at the house. She passed out before she could say anything about it. For all I know, it's still there."

And it might be.

He had forgotten about it in the rush to deal with Seichan. Where *had* it gone?

The man kept his eyes fixed on Gray. He studied him with a calculating and steady gaze.

"I think you're actually telling me the truth, Commander Pierce."

Still, the Egyptian signaled his gunman.

The shot was deafening.

1:10 A.M.

A MINUTE AGO Painter had noted movement on the plasma screen to the left. The interior video cameras of the safe house were still working. He spotted Mrs. Harriet Pierce crouched behind the kitchen table.

The attackers seemed unaware she was hiding inside.

No one except Gray had known he was coming to the safe house with an extra two passengers. The van had arrived *after* Gray's mother had gone inside. With the one guard stationed at the house immobilized, they had assumed the scene was locked down.

Painter knew it was his only advantage.

He called for a silent alarm to be raised at the house and a line opened. He watched the amber light beside the house phone blink and blink.

See the flashing light, he willed her.

Whether it was the alarm light or the simple instinct to call for help, Harriet crept over to the kitchen phone, reached up, and pulled the receiver to her ear.

"Don't talk," he said quickly. "It's Painter Crowe. Don't let them know you are inside. I can see you. Nod if you understand."

She nodded.

"Good. I have help coming. But I don't know if they'll reach you in time. The attackers must know this, too. They will be cruel and quick. I need you to be crueler. Can you do this?"

A nod.

"Very good. There should be a pistol in the drawer below the phone."

1:11 A.M.

THE GUNSHOT WAS deafening.

Deafening.

Not a silencer like before.

Gray knew the truth the fraction of a second before the gunman holding a weapon to his father's head fell to the side, half his skull splattering against the front quarter panel of the Thunderbird.

He knew the shooter.

His mother.

She was Texas bred, raised by an oilman who worked the same fields as Gray's father. Though his mother constantly petitioned for gun control, she was not shy around them.

Gray had both feared and hoped for some distraction from her. He'd kept ready for it, legs braced. Before the gunman's body even hit the ground, Gray leaped straight back. He had been watching the Asian woman's form in the polished chrome of the rear bumper.

The loud gunshot and the sudden backward leap caught her by surprise. Gray raised his right arm and hooked her arm, the one holding the Sig Sauer. As he struck her, he smashed his boot onto the inseam of her foot and cracked his head backward.

He heard something *crunch* below and behind.

Ahead, Kowalski had already elbowed his gunman, grabbed him by the scruff, and slammed his face into the edge of the convertible's door.

"Eat steel, jackass."

The gunman dropped like a sack of coal.

Without a pause Gray cradled Anni's captured fist and swung her arm toward Dr. Nasser. He squeezed the woman's finger against the trigger. She fought. Compromised, Gray's aim was off. His shot struck the brick wall with a ringing spark.

Still, it succeeded enough. Dr. Nasser ducked to the right, diving into the bushes that fronted the house, vanishing away.

Gray yanked the pistol from the woman's grip and back-kicked her away from him. She stumbled but kept her feet. Bloody-nosed, she twisted around and fled toward the van, sprinting like a gazelle, oblivious of her smashed foot.

Going for more weapons.

Gray did not want an encore of *Anni Get Your Gun*.

He raised the pistol toward her, but before he could fire, a round sizzled past the tip of his nose. From the bushes.

Nasser.

Startled, Gray stumbled backward, going for shelter under the porte cochere. He fired blindly into the bushes, not knowing where the bastard hid. He backpedaled until his calves struck the rear bumper of the T-bird. He fired another two rounds toward the med van.

But Asian Anni had vanished inside.

His shots ricocheted off the van. Like the president's med van, this one was armor-plated.

Gray yelled. "Everyone inside the car! Now!"

His mother appeared at the kitchen door, holding a smoking pistol. She had her purse over her other arm, as if she were going out for groceries.

"C'mon, Harriet," his father said. He reached up and hauled her toward the passenger door.

Kowalski leaped headlong into the backseat. Gray feared his bulk might finish Seichan off quicker than anything Nasser planned.

Gray vaulted over into the front seat and crashed hard. He twisted the key, still in the ignition, and the hot engine roared.

The passenger door slammed. Both his parents crowded the one seat.

Gray glanced into the rearview mirror.

Anni stood braced in the opening of the van. She balanced a rocket launcher on her shoulder.

The show is Anni Get Your Gun—*not* rocket launcher, *you bitch!*

Gray shifted into gear and slammed the accelerator. Three hundred horses burned the rear tires, rubber smoking and screaming.

His father groaned from the next seat—Gray suspected more about the wear on the glossy new tires than his own safety.

The wheels finally caught a grip, and the Thunderbird leaped forward, crashing through the wooden gate to the backyard. Once through, Gray yanked the wheel hard to avoid hitting a massive hundred-year-old oak. The tires dug a half-doughnut trench across the rear lawn, then sped them deeper into the yard.

Behind them, a sonorous *whoosh* was followed by a fiery explosion.

The rocket struck the large oak, blasting it to a ruin of flaming branches and bark. Blazing debris shot high. Smoke rolled.

Without glancing back, Gray punched the accelerator.

The Thunderbird smashed through the back fence and barreled into the woodlands of Glover-Archibold Park.

But Gray knew one certainty.

The hunt was just beginning.

4

High-Sea Piracy

BOXERS AND BOOTS.

That's all that stood between Monk and a sea of cannibal crabs. The feeding frenzy continued throughout the jungle, fighting, clacking, ripping. It sounded like the crackle of a forest fire.

Stripped, with his bio-suit in hand, Monk crossed back to Dr. Richard Graff. The marine researcher crouched at the edge of the jungle. He had also removed his bio-suit as instructed by Monk, wincing as he pulled the plastic fabric from his wounded shoulder. At least the marine researcher was better dressed, in shorts and a Hawaiian shirt.

Monk's nose crinkled as he stepped up to him. Out from beneath the thicker jungle canopy, the air burned, and the stench of the dead pool below was like being slapped in the face with a rotting salmon.

"Time to go," Monk said with a scowl.

A shout echoed up from the tunnel that led down to the toxic beach. The pirates were approaching more carefully, cautious. Graff, stationed there, had been lobbing chunks of limestone down the tunnel. Moreover their pursuers didn't know that Monk's pistol was down to one shot. But fear and rock throwing would only hold the pirates off for so long.

For the hundredth time Monk wondered at the strange persistence of their attackers. Hunger and desperation certainly made men do stupid things. But if the pirates wanted to raid and steal the Zodiac, to get ahold of their supplies and equipment for the Indonesian black market, then nothing was now stopping them. Most of these local pirates, brutal and ruthless as they might be, operated on a smash-and-grab modus operandi.

So why this persistence? To just silence them, to cover their tracks? Or was it something more personal? Monk pictured the one masked man toppling into the waters, clipped by one of his wild shots. Or was it revenge?

Whatever the reason, the raiding party was not settling for just the spoils—they wanted blood.

Graff choked at the burning air as he straightened. "Where are we going?"

"Back to visit our friends."

Monk led Graff into the jungle fringe. Steps away, the crimson sea of crabs chattered and clattered. If anything, their numbers had grown over the past few minutes, perhaps drawn by their voices or the fresh blood from Graff's seeping shoulder.

The marine researcher balked at the edge of the clearing. "There's no way through those crabs. Those giant claws can rip through leather. I've seen them take off fingers."

And they were fast.

Monk danced back as a pair of crabs, locked in mortal combat, rushed past them, sharp legs a blur, as fast as any jackrabbit.

"It's not like we have much choice," Monk said.

"And there's something wrong with these crabs," the researcher continued. "I've witnessed some of their aggression during migrations, but nothing of this caliber."

"You can psychoanalyze them later." Monk pointed to a large neighboring tree. A Tahitian chestnut. The evergreen was draped with many low branches. "Can you climb that?"

Graff clutched his wounded arm to his belly, trying to

keep from moving it too much. "I'll need help. But why? It won't hide us from the pirates. We'll be sitting ducks."

"Just climb." Monk walked him to the tree and helped him scale the first few terraces. The branches were thick and easy to grab. Graff managed well even on his own, climbing higher.

Monk dropped down, landing near a crab. It raised both pincers in threat. *No leaving the party early, buddy*. Monk kicked him back into the hordes of his brethren, then called back to Graff. "Can you see the tunnel opening?"

"I think . . . yes, I can." Graff shifted in the tree. "You're not leaving me up here, are you?"

"Just whistle when you see the pirates."

"What are you—?"

"Just do it, for Christ's sake!" Monk regretted the harshness of his tone. He had to remind himself that the man was not military. But Monk's mind was stacked with worries of his own. He pictured his wife and baby girl. He was not about to lose his life to a bunch of cutthroats or a forest full of Red Lobster entrées.

Monk crossed to the jungle clearing and stepped to the edge of the churning, snapping horde. He lifted his pistol in one hand and balanced his grip with his prosthetic one. He tilted his head and breathed through his nose.

C'mon, let's see what you got . . .

He heard a noise from the chestnut tree behind him. It sounded like air leaking out of a half-deflated balloon.

"They're coming!" he heard the man whisper, tension plainly sucking the wind out of his whistle.

Monk aimed across the clearing. He had one round, one shot.

Across the forest glade a pair of air tanks rested against the foot of a boulder. Earlier, as they were stripping out of their suits, Monk had Graff pass him his bio-suit's air tank. The portable air cartridges were lightweight, constructed of an aluminum alloy. Using the ankle holster from his pistol, Monk had quickly bound the doctor's tank together with his own and pitched the package in an underhanded throw across to the far side of the jungle clearing. The tanks had crashed amid the crabs, crushing a pair and sending their neighbors scurrying.

Monk took a bead upon the tanks now, steadying his aim with both flesh and prosthetics.

"They're here!" Graff moaned.

Monk squeezed the trigger.

The blast froze the image in his mind for a split second—then one of the pressurized tanks spat a brief flash of flame. The bound tanks spun and clattered, hissing and jumping. Then the second tank's nozzle cracked and the dance became more frenzied, smashing into crabs and sweeping and bouncing.

It was enough.

In the past Monk had strolled beaches covered with crabs that—once a seabird or stranger appeared—would clear in a heartbeat, crabs diving back into their sandy burrows. It was the same here. Those crabs nearest the commotion fled, climbing over their neighbors, jarring them into a panic. Soon a trickle became a stampede. The crabs, already riled up, fled on instinct.

The sea of crabs turned their tide—toward Monk—literally becoming a surging, churning wave of claws, climbing over one another to escape.

He fled back to the chestnut tree, pincers snapping at his heels.

He leaped and scurried up into the branches. One crab latched on to his boot. He cracked the shell against the trunk. It fell away. The pincer was still snagged tight to his boot. He felt the sharp edge cutting into his heel.

Damn.

Below, the tide of crabs swept past, obeying some instinct, possibly tied to their annual migration patterns. They fled toward the sea.

Monk climbed up to join Graff. The researcher had one arm hooked around the trunk. He eyed Monk, then turned back toward the slice of open rock that lay around the mouth of the sea tunnel.

The pirates, six of them, were out of the tunnel, spread a bit, but they had ducked low with the pistol shot. Only now were they rising to their feet, unsure.

Then from the jungle, the roiling sea of crabs burst forth.

It struck the man closest to the jungle fringe. Before he could react, comprehend what he was seeing, they scrambled up his legs to the level of his thighs. He suddenly screamed, stumbling back. Then one leg gave out under him.

During combat, a fellow Green Beret had had his Achilles tendon cut by a bullet. He had dropped in the same crooked manner as the pirate.

The man fell to one arm, screaming.

He was overrun, crabs scrabbling across his writhing body. But his wails continued, buried under the mass. For a moment, he surged back up. His mask had been stripped away, along with his nose, lips, and ears. His eyes were bloody ruins. He screamed one last time and fell back under the tide.

The other pirates fled in horrified panic, back to the tunnel, vanishing away. One man was cut off from the tunnel, pinned out on a spur of rock jutting off from the sea cliff. The crabs swelled toward him.

With a final cry he turned and leaped off the cliff.

More screams echoed up from the tunnel.

Like water down a drain, the sea of crabs swirled into the mouth of the tunnel, spiraling away in a red tide of razored claws.

Monk found Graff panting heavily beside him, eyes unblinking.

He reached and touched the man. He flinched.

"We have to go. Before the crabs decide to return to their forest."

Graff allowed himself to be led down to the forest floor. There were still hundreds of crabs down here; they moved cautiously through them.

Monk broke off a feathery branch of the chestnut tree and swept away any of the crabs that got too near.

Slowly Graff seemed to return to himself, to settle back into his own skin. "I . . . I want one of those crabs."

"We'll have a crabfeed when we get back to the ship."

"No. For study. Somehow they survived the toxic cloud. It could be important." The researcher's voice steadied, in his element.

"Okay," Monk said. "Considering we left all our samples behind, we shouldn't return to the ship empty-handed."

He reached down and snagged up one of the smaller crabs with his prosthetic hand, grabbing it by the back of its shell. The feisty fellow snapped its claws backward at him, straining to get him.

"Hey, no marring the merchandise, buddy. New fingers come out of my paycheck."

Monk went to smash it against a tree trunk, but Graff waved his good arm. "No! We need it alive. Like I said before, there's something odd about their behavior. That bears examination, too."

Monk's jaw tightened in irritation. "Fine, but if this bit of sushi takes a chunk out of me, you're paying for it."

They continued through the plateau forest, wending across the island.

After forty minutes of trekking, the forest thinned and a panoramic cliff-top view opened. The island's main township—named simply The Settlement—spread out along the beach and port. Out in the surrounding sea, beyond Flying Fish Cove, the white castle that was the *Mistress of the Seas* floated, a cloud in a midnight-blue sky.

Home, sweet home.

Movement drew Monk's eyes to a group of smaller boats, a dozen, rounding Rocky Point, each leaving a contrail of white wake. The group traveled in a wide V, like an attack wing of fighter jets.

A matching group appeared on the other side of the township's port.

Even from here Monk recognized the shape and color of the crafts.

Blue speedboats, long in keel and shallow draft.

"More pirates . . ." Graff moaned.

Monk stared between the two converging groups, two pincers, even more deadly than any red crab. He gaped at what was trapped between them.

The *Mistress of the Seas*.

1:05 P.M.

LISA STARED AT the radiograph X-ray.

The portable light box was set up on a desk in the cabin. Behind her, a figure lay sprawled on the bed, a sheet fully covering the patient.

Dead.

"It looks like tuberculosis," she said. The radiographs of the man's lungs were frothy with large white masses or tubercles. "Or maybe lung cancer."

Dr. Henrick Barnhardt, the Dutch toxicologist, stood at her side, leaning a fist on the table. He had called her down here.

"*Ja,* but the patient's wife said he'd shown no signs of respiratory distress prior to eighteen hours ago. No coughing, no expectorating, and he does not smoke. And he was only twenty-four years old."

Lisa straightened. They were in the cabin alone. "And you've cultured his lungs?"

"I used a needle to aspirate some of the fluid from one of the lung masses. The content was definitely purulent. Cheesy with bacteria. Definitely a lung abscess, not cancer."

She studied Barnhardt's bearded face. He stood with a bit of a hunch as if his bearish size somehow embarrassed him, but it also gave him a conspiratorial posture. He had not invited Dr. Lindholm into these discussions.

"Such findings are consistent with tuberculosis," she said.

TB was caused by a bacterium, *Mycobacterium tuberculosis,* a highly contagious germ. And while the clinical history here was definitely unusual, TB could be dormant for years, slow-growing. The man could have been exposed years ago, been a ticking time bomb—then his exposure to the toxic gas could have stressed his lungs enough to cause the disease to spread. The patient would have definitely been contagious at the end.

And neither she nor Dr. Barnhardt wore contamination suits.

Why hadn't he warned her?

"It wasn't tuberculosis," he answered. "Dr. Miller, our team's infectious disease expert, identified the organism as *Serratia marcescens,* a strain nonpathogenic bacteria."

Lisa remembered her discussion earlier, regarding the patient with normal skin bacteria that was churning out flesh-eating poisons.

The toxicologist confirmed the comparison. "Again we have a benign nonopportunist bacterium turning virulent."

"But, Dr. Barnhardt, what you're suggesting . . ."

"Call me Henri. And I'm not just suggesting this. I've spent the past hours searching for similar cases. I found two others. A woman with raging dysentery, literally sloughing out her intestinal lining. Caused by *Lactobacillus acidophilus,* a yogurt bacterium that is normally a healthy intestinal organism. Then there is a child demonstrating violent seizures, whose spinal tap is churning with *Acetobacter aceti,* a benign organism found in vinegar. It's literally pickling her brain."

As she listened, Lisa found her vision narrowing, focusing on the implication.

"And these can't be the only cases," Henri said.

She shook her head—not disagreeing, only in the growing, terrifying certainty of the truth of his words. "So something is definitely turning these benign bacteria against us."

"Turning friend into foe. And if this turns into an all-out war, we are vastly outnumbered."

She glanced up to him.

"The human body is composed of a hundred trillion cells, yet only *ten* trillion are ours. The other ninety percent are bacteria and a few other opportunistic organisms. We live cooperatively with this foreign environment. But if this balance should tip, should turn against us . . . ?"

"We need to stop it."

"It's why I called you down here. To convince you. If we're going to move forward, Dr. Miller and I need access to your partner's forensic suite. We must begin answering critical questions. Was this a toxic or chemical alteration to these bacteria? If so, how do we treat it? And what if it's contagious? How do we isolate or quarantine against it?" He grimaced through his beard. "We need answers. Now."

Lisa checked her watch. Monk was already an hour late. Either he's lost in his work or appreciating the island's beauty and beaches. But now was not the time for sightseeing.

She nodded to Henri. "I'll have someone radio Dr. Kokkalis. Get him back here ASAP. But in the meantime, you're right. Let's get started."

She led the way out of the cabin. Monk's forensic suite was near the top of the ship, five decks up. Sigma had commissioned one of the largest cabins to accommodate his equipment. Some of the crew had even unbolted beds and furniture to open space for the makeshift lab. The suite also had a wide balcony overlooking the starboard side. Lisa wished she was there now, needing sunlight, a fresh breeze on her face, something to chase away the mounting fear.

As she headed toward the ship's elevator, she knew she'd have to call Painter yet again. She could not bear this responsibility on her own. She needed the full support of Sigma's R&D team.

Plus she wanted to hear his voice again.

She pressed the button to call the elevator.

As if the button were attached to a detonator, a loud *boom* echoed from the other side of the ship, from the direction of the ship's docking bay, where the tender boats ferried folks between the shore and the ship.

Had there been an accident?

"What was that?" Henri asked.

A second louder explosion rattled on their side of the ship, somewhere near the bow. Screams distantly echoed. Then Lisa heard a familiar sound, the strafing ping of automatic fire.

"We're under attack," she said.

1:45 P.M.

MONK BOUNCED THE rusted Land Rover down the steep slope. He had hot-wired the old truck from a parking lot near the island's phosphate mine, abandoned during the evacuation. They sped along a dirt track that led down the back side of the mine toward the coastal township.

Dr. Richard Graff was belted into the seat next to him, one arm raised to the roof to help hold him in place. "Slow down."

Monk ignored him. He needed to reach the coast.

The two had broken into one of the mine's workshops and tried the phone. No service. The island was all but empty at this point. They were at least able to find a first-aid kit in the shack. Graff's shoulder was slathered in antibiotic salve and wrapped up in gauze.

The researcher had managed his own care while Monk had hot-wired the truck. Graff still had the first-aid kit clutched to his belly with his wounded arm. Once emptied, it served as a nice cage for their crab specimen.

A curve of jungle road forced Monk to downshift. He flew around the bend, carting the truck up on two wheels by a couple inches. They slammed back down, jostled in their restraints.

Graff gasped. "You're not going to do anyone any good if you bury our front end into the jungle."

Monk slowed—not because of Graff's words of caution, but because the road ended at a paved crossroads. They had reached a remote section of the island's coastal highway, a narrow two-lane blacktop. The dirt track dropped just to the south of Flying Fish Cove. To the north, the bulk of the township rose, a mix of seaside hotels, Chinese restaurants, dilapidated bars, and tourist traps.

But Monk's attention remained focused out into the waters, beyond Flying Fish Cove. The *Mistress of the Seas* was surrounded by burning ships, blasted yachts, and the ruins of the Australian Coast Guard cutter. Smoke choked high into the midday sky. Like circling sharks, a score of blue speedboats sped and roared through the water.

A single yellow-and-red helicopter, a Eurocopter Astar, circled the cove, an angry hornet stirring up the smoke. From the flashes of muzzle fire out its open hatch, it was no friend.

Monk had caught glimpses of the sea assault as he swept down the switchbacks from the highlands: explosions, flashes of gunfire, shattering eruptions of flaming debris. The blasts had echoed up to their truck like the sound of distant fireworks.

Boom . . . boom . . . boom . . .

Off to the north, a resounding blast cast up a gout of smoke and flame, coming from the township. Close enough to rattle the Land Rover's windows.

"Telstra substation," Graff said. "They're cutting off all means of communication."

Other sections of The Settlement were already burning.

These were no ordinary pirates. It was a full-on assault.

Who the hell were they?

Monk shifted back into gear and headed away from the township, along the coastal road.

"Where are you—?" Graff began to ask.

Monk rounded a bend. A small beachside hotel, isolated within a couple of tamed acres of rain forest, appeared ahead. Monk took a sharp turn at a sign that read

THE MANGO LODGE AND GRILLE. He sped down the entry road. The hotel rose into view, a two-story building that dissolved into a few freestanding jungle bungalows. A swimming pool glistened.

The place appeared deserted.

"You'll be safe here," Monk said as he braked to a stop at the side of the hotel under the shielding bower of the lodge's namesake, a mango tree.

Monk hopped out.

"Wait!" Graff struggled with his door, finally fighting it open. He all but fell out of the Land Rover. He chased Monk down.

Monk did not slow. He half trotted toward the beach. Like all seaside hotels, the Mango Lodge and Grille offered all the activities a beachcomber might want: snorkeling, kayaking, sailing. At the rear of the establishment, Monk spotted the hotel's activities center, a small cinder-block outbuilding with a thatched roof. It was boarded-up because of the evacuation.

On the fly, Monk snatched up a pole used to clean the pool. In no time, he was prying boards free and smashing through the glass door.

Graff caught up with him.

Monk reached out and hauled the researcher inside, out of the sun. The helicopter roared past overhead, low, its rotor wash whipping palm fronds. Then it swept away, continuing its patrol of the shoreline.

"Keep out of sight!" Monk warned.

Graff nodded vigorously.

Monk stalked through the front of the activities center, packed with beach towels, sunglasses, suntan oils, and a host of souvenirs. The place smelled of coconut and damp feet. Monk circled the counter and proceeded through a doorway draped in rattling beads.

He found what he was looking for.

Scuba gear hung along the back wall.

Monk kicked off his boots.

On the beach side of the room, lined up before a roll-up door, rested a variety of crafts for fun in the sun. Monk bypassed the paddleboats, a pair of kayaks, and stopped before the lone Jet Ski watercraft. It rested on a wheeled trailer, ready for easy hauling to and from the water.

At least the seas on this side of the island were clean of that toxic soup.

Monk turned to Graff. "I'm going to need your help."

Eighteen minutes later, Monk rubbed his elbow across the grease-stained window in the roll-up door. His wet suit squeaked against the glass. Craning his neck, Monk waited for the helicopter to circle by overhead and swing back north toward Flying Fish Cove. The cove lay out of direct sight, hidden by Smith Point. All that Monk could make out of the war zone was the smudged pall of smoke rising over the ridgeline.

At last, the helicopter turned tail and headed back toward the cruise ship.

"Okay, here we go!"

Monk bent down and hauled the door up, snapping it into place overhead. Behind him, Graff lifted the trailer hitch, and Monk swung around to the front. He grabbed the back of the Jet Ski, and together they ran the trailer down to the water. The large rubber sand tires made it quick work.

Graff loosened the craft from the trailer while Monk ran back and hauled on his BC vest and tanks. Once outfitted, he slipped a souvenir Mango Lodge windbreaker over all his equipment.

Heavily burdened, Monk plodded back to the water and helped float the Jet Ski off its trailer. "Stay hidden," he instructed Graff. "But if you can find some means of communication, a radio or anything, try to raise someone in authority."

Graff nodded. "Be careful."

In another minute Monk was gunning the engine to a high whine and racing off toward Smith Point. Behind him, Graff trotted the empty trailer back to its garage.

Monk bent lower in the seat and cranked the craft to full throttle. Flying faster, the windbreaker snapped in the breeze. Sea and salt sprayed. Smith Point grew in front of him. At last, he reached the rocky spur and, without slowing, sped around it.

On the far side of the cove, the *Mistress of the Seas* rose like a besieged white castle. Closer still, the waters burned with spills of flaming oil and smoking husks of ships. Even the jetty was a blasted ruin. And throughout the war zone, the roar of the pirates' speedboats growled.

On the hunt.

Here we go.

Like a skimming torpedo, Monk shot into the fray.

2:08 P.M.

"THERE MUST BE something we can do," Lisa said.

"For now, we sit tight," Henri Barnhardt warned.

They were holed up in one of the empty outside cabins. Lisa stood near one of the room's two portholes. Henri took a post by the door.

An hour ago they had fled through the ship, only to discover the place in full chaos. Uniformed crew and wild-eyed passengers, both the sick and the healthy, crowded the hallways. Explosions and gunfire were almost drowned out by the nerve-rattling klaxon of the ship's alarm bell. Whether automated or purposeful, someone had tripped the ship's fire doors, dropping them, isolating sections.

Meanwhile masked gunmen cleared the halls, one after the other, shooting anyone who resisted or moved too slowly. Lisa and Henri had heard the screams, the gunfire, the trampling feet from the deck above. They came close to being shot themselves. Only a swift race through the ship's gilded showroom and down another hallway had saved them.

They did not know how much longer they could hold out.

The rapidity of the takedown of the *Mistress of the Seas* suggested some of the crew must have been involved.

Lisa stared out the porthole window. The sea was on fire. From this same window, she had watched a handful of desperate passengers leap from upper balconies into the waters, hoping to make it to shore.

But the gunboats swept the cove, peppering and strafing the water.

Bodies floated amid the flaming debris.

There was no escape.

Why was this happening? What was going on?

Finally, the alarm klaxon went silent, cutting off with a final whining squelch. The silence that remained felt heavy, a physical weight. Even the air seemed thicker.

Somewhere above someone sobbed and wailed.

Henri met Lisa's eyes.

From the room's speaker a stiff voice began speaking in Malay. Lisa didn't speak the Malaysian language. Still staring at Henri, she watched the toxicologist shake his head. He was just as lost. But whatever was said was eventually repeated in Mandarin Chinese. They were the two most common languages spoken on the island.

Finally, the speaker switched to English, heavily accented.

"The ship is now ours. Each deck is patrolled by guards. Anyone caught out in the halls will be shot on sight. No one will come to harm as long as we are obeyed. That is all."

The speech ended with a snap of static.

Henri tested to make sure the cabin door was locked, then stepped toward Lisa. "The ship's been hijacked. Someone must have been planning this for some time."

Lisa flashed back to the *Achille Lauro,* an Italian cruise ship hijacked by Palestinian terrorists back in 1985. And more recently in 2005, Somalian pirates attacked another cruise ship off the east African coast.

She turned to the porthole, staring out, and studied the boats patrolling the waters below, operated by teams of masked gunmen. They appeared to be pirates, but she suspected otherwise.

Maybe some of Painter's paranoia had rubbed off on her.

This was all too coordinated for a random act of piracy.

"Surely," Henri said, "they'll ransack the ship and steal everything not locked down, then flee back among the islands. If we can keep alive, avoid any confrontation . . ."

The speaker screeched again, and a new voice spoke through the general shipboard communications. In English. It didn't repeat in Malay or Chinese.

"The following passengers will report to the ship's bridge. They will be expected here in the next five minutes. They will come with their hands on their heads, fingers clasped. Failure to appear will result in the death of two passengers for every minute you are late. We will shoot the children first."

The names were stated.

Dr. Gene Lindholm.

Dr. Benjamin Miller.

Dr. Henri Barnhardt.

And last: *Dr. Lisa Cummings.*

"You have five minutes."

The radio went silent again.

Lisa still faced the porthole. "This is no hijacking."

And these were no ordinary pirates.

Before she turned away from the window, she spotted a Jet Ski racing across the water toward the cruise ship. A rooster tail of water jetted high behind it, making it easy to spot. It weaved through the debris with skill. She could not make out who was aboard the craft. The rider was hunkered low.

And with good reason.

Two speedboats were in tight pursuit, crashing through flames and smoking planks. Muzzle flashes sparked from the boat.

She shook her head at the Jet Skier's foolishness.

From over the top of the cruise ship, a helicopter dove

into view, sweeping down toward the Jet Ski. She didn't want to watch, but she felt some obligation. Some acknowledgment of the rider's suicidal assault.

The helicopter tilted in a sharp arc, side door open.

A blast of smoke spat from its interior.

Grenade launcher.

Wincing, Lisa glanced down in time to see the Jet Ski explode in a fiery ball of smoke and charred metal.

She swung away, numb and trembling all over. She faced Henri. They had no other choice.

"Let's go."

2:12 P.M.

MONK SANK INTO the depths of the sea, dragged down by his weight belt and tanks. He did not fight it and held his breath. Overhead, the blue of the water blazed with fire. Shrapnel from the blasted Jet Ski sizzled through the water. Two meters away, the watercraft sank nose first into the depths.

As Monk followed, he struggled out of his Mango Lodge windbreaker. There was no reason to keep his tanks hidden any longer. He pulled up his scuba mask and swept his arm out to gather his air hose. He used the regulator to blow his mask clear, then secured it.

The depths turned crystalline clear.

He seated the regulator and drew his first breath.

More a sigh of relief.

Had his bit of subterfuge worked?

A moment ago, as the helicopter had dove toward him, drawn like a hawk to a mouse, Monk had eyed the gunman in the open hatchway. As the grenade launcher was pointed at him, Monk flipped the Jet Ski over at the last second, diving beneath it and into the depths. The explosion had still struck him like an anvil to the head, ears popping.

He sank toward the sea bottom. Flying Fish Cove had

deep-water moorings to a depth of thirty meters. But he didn't need to go that deep.

Monk adjusted his buoyancy compensators, swelling his vest with air from his tanks. His descent slowed to a hover. He craned up and watched the bottoms of the trolling speed-boats, propellers churning the water white. They circled and circled, looking for any signs of the Jet Ski's rider, ready to fire if he surfaced.

But Monk wasn't planning on surfacing, and if his ruse had worked, no one knew he had scuba gear. Monk twisted around, checked his glowing wrist compass, and headed along the bearings he had already calculated.

Toward the *Mistress of the Seas.*

He had always wanted to take a cruise.

5

Lost and Found

"THIS IS AS FAR as we dare go," Gray said.

He had spent the last seven minutes creeping and edging the Thunderbird through Glover-Archibold Park, following an old weedy service road, bushes scraping against the flanks of the convertible. The left front tire was a punctured ruin, slowing them, making steering damn near impossible.

Though most people considered Washington, D.C., to be a place of historic buildings, wide parade malls, and museums, it also featured one of the longest, interconnected series of parklands, threaded throughout the heart of the city, covering well over a thousand acres. Glover-Archibold Park marked one end, terminating at the Potomac River.

Gray had headed away from the river. It was too far and too open. Following a back alley that paralleled the park homes, he had wended north with his headlights off, discovering an old fire road that led deeper into the dense woods. He took it. He needed to stay lost, yet the Thunderbird was on its last legs.

Recognizing he could go no farther, he slowed.

They were at the bottom of a ravine. Steep wooded hills climbed on either side. Ahead, an old abandoned train trestle crossed the narrow valley. Gray edged the Thunderbird under the bridge of rusted red iron and wooden slats. He braked next to one of the cement walls holding the trestle up. The wall was scrawled with graffiti.

"Everybody out. We go on foot from here."

On the far side of the trestle, lit by stars and a sliver of moon, a wooden trail marker indicated a hiking trail. The path looked more like a tunnel, cutting into the heavily bowered forest.

All the better to hide them.

Off in the other direction, the sirens of emergency vehicles wailed. Gray spotted a flickering orange glow in the night sky. The fiery rocket blast must have started a house fire.

Closer still, the woods were dark, painted in shades of black.

Gray knew Nasser and his assassination team could be anywhere.

Behind them, ahead of them, closing in already.

Gray's heart pounded. His fears gathered tight around him—not for himself, but for his parents. He needed to get them somewhere safe, to put distance between them and the dangers circling around him. The only way to do that was to get Seichan patched up.

And he had to do that away from all eyes.

Even if he still had his scrambled cell phone, he dared not contact Sigma or Director Crowe. Lines of communication were compromised, as evidenced by the ambush at the safe house. Protocol dictated he go cold and dark. There was a leak somewhere, and until he had his parents holed up someplace safe, he wasn't going to lift his head above the weeds.

So that meant they'd have to seek an alternate means to care for Seichan. His mother had suggested one option and had already implemented her plan, making two calls on her personal cell phone. After that, Gray had her remove her cell phone's battery, lest someone use the device to track them.

"The morphine seems to have relaxed her," his mother reported from the backseat.

During a short stop, Gray's mother had shifted into the backseat with Kowalski. Seichan lay draped between them. His mother had injected Seichan with a premeasured morphine syrette, taken from some medical supplies at the safe house.

"If we're going to make it," Gray said, "we'll have to carry her from here."

"I've got her." Kowalski waved everyone out of his way.

Gray's father helped his mother exit the convertible. Once out, his father eyed the state of his car and shook his head, swearing under his breath.

Kowalski stood up, hauling Seichan in his arms. Even in the dark beneath the trestle, Gray noted the black stain on her belly wrap. The movement stirred Seichan awake. She struggled a moment in Kowalski's arms as he clambered out, startled, dazed. She cried out and struck the heel of her hand into his cheek.

"Hey . . . !" the large man exclaimed, avoiding another strike.

Seichan began to yell, an angry stream, an unintelligible mix of English and an Asian dialect.

"Quiet her down," his father said, glancing at the dark forest.

Kowalski tried to muffle her mouth, but almost got a finger bitten off. "Son of a bitch!"

Seichan's agitation grew more fierce.

His mother moved closer, searching in her large tote. "I have another dose of morphine."

Gray shook his head. "Wait." With Seichan's blood loss, he feared the respiratory depression that accompanied morphine. A second dose might kill her, and he still needed answers.

He held a palm out toward his mother. "Smelling salts." He remembered Kowalski had mentioned them as among the contents of the emergency medkit.

His mother nodded. She reached to her bag, fumbled a long second, then handed him a few capsules. Gray grabbed one and stepped to Kowalski's side.

The guard now bore a long bloody scratch down one cheek. "Christ, do something about her!"

Gray grabbed a fistful of her hair, arched her neck, and cracked the capsule under her nose. Her head wrenched, fighting, but he kept the capsule at her upper lip. The delirious cries cut off, replaced by gagging.

A hand rose to push him away.

He held tight.

"Enough . . ." Seichan coughed out, and grabbed Gray's wrist.

He was surprised at the strength in her fingers. He let his arm drop.

"Let me breathe. Set me down."

Gray nodded to Kowalski. He didn't have to be told twice. He settled Seichan to her feet but kept an arm under her shoulders. She'd overestimated her own strength. Her legs sagged. She hung in the large man's arms.

Wincing, she glanced around her. Gray read the confusion in her eyes, behind the war between pain and morphine. She quickly focused back to him.

"I . . . the obelisk . . ." she said with strained worry.

Gray was tired of hearing about the damned obelisk. "We'll have to get it later. It broke after you crashed. I left it back at the house."

His words seemed to cause her more pain than her bullet wound. But perhaps his earlier lapse was a bit of luck. Maybe Nasser had gone after the obelisk rather than pursuing them.

His mother, overhearing their conversation, stepped forward. "You're talking about that broken black pillar." She patted her large purse. "I picked it up when I went inside to get the bandages. It looked old and maybe valuable."

Eyes closing with relief, Seichan nodded to both those assessments. Her head hung in exhaustion. "Thank God."

"What's so important about it?" he asked.

"It could . . . it might save the world. If we're not too late already."

Gray glanced to his mother's tote, then back to Seichan. "What the hell do you mean?"

She waved an arm weakly, fading again. "Too complicated. I need your help . . . can't . . . not alone . . . we must, must get away."

Her chin dropped to her chest as she slipped into unconsciousness again. Kowalski caught her weight on his hip.

Gray was tempted to use another capsule of smelling salts, but he feared exerting her any further. Fresh blood trickled from her bandage.

His mother seemed to make the same assessment. She nodded to the trail. "We can't be far from the hospital now."

Gray turned to the dark path on the far side of the trestle. It was the other reason he had taken the Thunderbird north through the woods, following a suggestion from his mother. On the far side of Glover-Archibold Park spread the campus of Georgetown University. The school's hospital bordered the edge of the forest. His mother had former students who labored there.

If they could reach it in secret . . .

But was the destination too obvious?

There were a thousand exits out of the park system, but Nasser knew his quarry bore a seriously injured woman and that she needed immediate medical attention.

It was a huge risk, but Gray saw no way of avoiding it.

He remembered Nasser's eyes as the bastard asked about the obelisk. Hungry, ruthless. The Egyptian had believed Gray's assertion that the obelisk had been left behind— mostly because Gray had believed it. But which was more important to the man: obtaining the obelisk or seeking revenge?

He stared around at their small group.

All their lives balanced on that answer.

2:21 A.M.

A HALF HOUR later Painter stalked the length of his office, a hands-free headset fixed to his ear. "They're all dead?"

Behind him, the plasma screen displayed live feed of the fiery blaze of three homes, along with a section of the neighboring parkland. It had been a dry summer, turning forest into kindling. Fire engines and emergency personnel swarmed the cordoned-off area. Television vans were already raising satellite antennas. A police helicopter circled above, floodlight spearing down, searching.

But it was too little, too late.

Neither the convertible Gray had driven to the safe house nor the hijacked medical van was among the wreckage. The raging fires hampered further investigation.

The only solid news was bad. The original med-van team had been discovered in an abandoned field, each shot in the head. He had four folders on his desk. He sank to his seat. On top of everything else, he had four hard calls to make before dawn. To their families.

Painter's aide, Brant, wheeled into his doorway. "Sorry, sir."

Painter nodded to him.

"I have Dr. McKnight holding on your third line. He's available for phone or video conferencing."

Painter pointed a thumb at the fiery screen. "I've seen enough of this for the moment. Patch Sean through."

Painter peeled the headset out of his ear. He swore he might as well have one surgically implanted. He swung around to face the screen as the emergency scene dissolved away, replaced by the face of his boss.

Sean McKnight had founded Sigma but had since been promoted to the head of DARPA. Painter had placed a call to him as soon as Seichan had crashed into Gray's life. Both for his advice and expertise. But also for one more pressing reason.

"So the Guild is back on our doorstep," Sean said. He combed his fingers through his graying red hair. It was mussed, and it looked like he had been summoned directly from his bed. But his white shirt was creased and pressed. A navy pinstripe jacket lay over an arm of his chair. Ready for a long day.

"The Guild may be more than on our doorstep," Painter said. "Current intel suggests they may be through the door already." Painter tapped a folder behind him. "You've already read the sit-op."

A nod answered him. "Plainly the Guild knew about the safe house. Knew Gray was headed there with their AWOL operative. We have a leak somewhere."

"I'm afraid we have to assume that."

He shook his head. If true, it was disastrous. The Guild had infiltrated Sigma once before, but Painter would swear his organization was clean now. After the last mole had been exposed, Painter had burned Sigma to its roots and rebuilt it from the ground up, with hundreds of safeguards and countermeasures.

All for nothing.

If there was still a leak, the very foundation of Sigma might be suspect. It could mean the dissolution of the organization. An internal audit was already under way, a cost-benefit analysis of Sigma's basic command structure, under the guise of unifying U.S. intelligence-gathering services within Homeland Security.

But worst of all, there was a more intimate cost.

Painter had the four folders waiting on his desk to remind him.

Sean continued. "It is not just our division that is plagued by this terrorist-for-hire network. Two months ago, MI6 cleared a cell that had infiltrated a British Aerospace's black-ops project outside of Glasgow. They lost five agents in the process. The Guild is everywhere and nowhere. Here at home, the NSA and the CIA are still trying to figure out who the Guild's Osama is. We know next to nothing about their leader or their main players. We don't even know if they are called the Guild. The derivation of that name came out of a nickname by an SAS officer, now deceased. Still, apparently the various cells have taken on the name as their own, at first mockingly, then perhaps more genuinely. We know *that* little about the network."

He left this last hanging.

Painter understood. "And now we have a defector."

Sean sighed. "We've been trying to get a foothold in the organization for years. I've proposed several scenarios. But nothing as efficient as having an operative, one of the Guild elite, drop into our laps. We must secure her."

"And the Guild will try just as hard to stop that from happening. They've made that plain. To eliminate her, they've chosen to expose their own infiltration into Sigma. A costly choice. And to carry it out, they've sent their best and most elusive operative. Another of their elite."

"I saw the video of the man at the safe house. Read his dossier." Sean grimaced.

Painter had read the same. The Butcher of Calcutta. His true origin and allegience was unknown. Of mixed descent, he had posed in the past as Indian, Pakistani, Iraqi, Egyptian, and Libyan. If Seichan had a male counterpart, it would be this man.

"We have one lead," Painter said. "We were able to pick out his name off the video feed. *Nasser*. But that's the best we could manage."

Sean waved a dismissive hand. "His aliases are as numerous as his assassinations. He's left a bloody trail all around the world, mostly concentrating in North Africa and throughout the Middle and Near East. Though just recently he's extended deeper into the Mediterranean. The garroting of an archaeologist in Greece. The assassination of a museum curator in Italy."

Painter's attention hardened back to the screen. "In Italy? Where?"

"Venice. A curator found shot in the prisons below the

Duke's Palace. Nasser—or whatever his real name is—was seen in surveillance footage of the piazza outside."

Painter rubbed his chin, hard enough to burn the stubble. "I received a call earlier from Monsignor Verona at the Vatican. The details should be in the sit-op report. There is a good chance that Seichan was also attempting some action in Italy at around that time."

Sean's eyes slowly narrowed. "Interesting. It's a coincidence that bears further investigation. Both assassins in Italy. Now they're here. One hunting the other. Two master assassins, the best of the Guild. And if nothing else, Nasser has driven Seichan into our arms."

Or rather into Gray's arms, Painter added silently.

"We need that woman in custody. Immediately. To lose this chance is beyond acceptable."

Painter understood the severity of the situation, but he also knew Gray, how his mind worked. If anyone had a level of paranoia equal to his own, it was Gray. Custody could prove to be a problem.

"Sir, Commander Pierce is on the run. Ambushed at the safe house, he must suspect a leak like we do. He'll go into hiding with her. Lay low until he feels it's safe to come out of the cold."

"We may not have that long to wait. Not with the Butcher of Calcutta hunting them both now."

"What do you want me to do?"

"Commander Pierce must be found, brought back in with her. I have no choice but to expand the search, to contact local authorities and the FBI. I've already ordered a search of all hospitals and medical facilities. We can't let him go to ground."

"Sir, I would prefer to give Commander Pierce some leeway to address the situation. The more light shone in his direction, the more likely it will draw the attention of Nasser."

"If so, then we attempt to apprehend *two* Guild operatives."

Painter could not keep the shock from his voice. "By using Gray as bait."

Sean stared out of the monitor. Painter read the stiffness of his posture. He also noted again the pressed jacket and shirt. Painter suddenly realized he had not been the first one to have Sean's ear this night.

"This decision was made by Homeland. Signed by the president. There will be no countermanding it." Sean firmed his voice. "Gray and this Guild agent must be found and brought in by whatever force necessary."

Painter found no words to argue. There could be none. It was a new world. He slowly nodded. He would cooperate.

Still, in his heart, he knew Gray.

On the run, hunted by both sides, the man would prove formidable.

He would hide deep.

3:04 A.M.

"I spotted a Starbucks in the lobby downstairs," Kowalski mumbled. "Maybe it's open now. Anyone want a cup of Joe?"

"We stay put," Gray said.

Kowalski shook his head. "No fucking kidding. It was a joke."

Ignoring him, Gray continued to examine Seichan's broken obelisk. They were gathered in the small reception room of a dental office. At his elbow, a table lamp illuminated the cramped space, decorated in the typical cookie-cutter manner: months-old magazines, generic watercolors, an anemic potted ficus plant, and a dark wall-mounted television.

Forty minutes ago the group had followed the woodland trail to the edge of Glover-Archibold Park. It had ended at a street that separated the park from the Georgetown University campus. At that hour, there had been no cars, no traffic. They had hurried across the street, slipped between two darkened research buildings, and reached the university's Dental Annex. The hospital proper lay beyond, lit brightly. They had dared not go that far, risk that level of exposure.

So they made other arrangements.

Across the dental-room reception, Kowalski swore quietly and folded his arms, plainly bored but still on edge. They all awaited word.

"What's taking so goddamn long?" Kowalski grumbled.

Gray had learned the man was a former seaman with the U.S. Navy. He'd been recruited into Sigma following his assistance with a Sigma operation in Brazil, not as an agent, but as muscle. He had tried to show Gray his scars from that mission as they waited, but Gray declined. The man did not know how to shut up. No wonder he'd been assigned to guard duty. Alone.

But Kowalski's ongoing commentary had not fallen on deaf ears.

Across the room, Gray's father lay sprawled over three chairs, eyes closed but not sleeping. It took an effort to maintain that deep frown.

"So you're some sort of science spy," his father had said earlier. "Figures . . ."

Gray still didn't know what his father meant by that, but now was not the time to confront the issue. The sooner he could get Seichan patched up and away from his parents . . . the better for all of them.

Gray continued his examination. He turned the obelisk around, studying every surface. The black stone was ancient, pitted and scored, but was otherwise nondescript. It looked Egyptian, but it was not his area of expertise. Even his assessment of origin might have been clouded by the failed assassin's Egyptian accent.

But one feature of the obelisk was definitely not natural to the stone.

He turned the broken top section on end. Protruding from the bottom was a bar of silver, about the thickness of his smallest finger. He touched it. Gray knew it was the tip of the proverbial iceberg. Something had been hidden at the heart of the obelisk. Looking more carefully at the broken end, he was able to make out an old cemented seam in the stone, invisible from the outside. The obelisk was really two pieces of marble craftily glued together, hiding something within. Like carving out the pages of a book to hide a gun or valuables.

He remembered Seichan's words.

It might save the world . . . if we're not too late already.

Whatever she meant, it was important enough for her to come seek him out, to betray the Guild.

He needed answers.

The creak of the door drew his attention. Gray's mother pushed into the dental suite. She pulled a surgical mask from her face.

Gray stood up.

"She's damn lucky," his mother said. "We've cauterized the bleeding and hung a second unit of blood. Mickie thinks she'll do fine. He's finishing her dressing."

Mickie was Dr. Michael Corrin, a former teaching assistant of his mother's who had gone on to medical school, largely based on his mother's recommendation. The depth of their relationship and trust extended to this midnight house call, a secret rendezvous at the hospital's neighboring dental facility. A quick ultrasound revealed the night's first bit of good news. The bullet hadn't pierced Seichan's abdominal cavity. The shot had passed just lateral to her pelvic bone.

"When can she be moved?" Gray asked.

"Mickie would rather she spend a few hours here, at the very least."

"We don't have that much time."

"I explained that to him."

"Is she awake?"

A nod. "After the first unit of blood, she grew more responsive. Mickie's loaded her with antibiotics and analgesics. She's already sitting up."

"Then it's time to go." Gray went to push past his mother.

He had observed the ultrasound, but he'd been chased out when the doctor set to work on the wound. No amount of arguing would make the doctor budge.

Gray hadn't liked letting Seichan out of his sight, so he'd left with the broken obelisk. Seichan was not going anywhere without it.

With the two pieces of the obelisk in hand, Gray shoved through the door. His mother followed. Gray crossed to the first dental suite. He almost ran into Dr. Corrin as he was stepping out. The young doctor stood as tall as Gray, but he was sandy-haired and whip-thin. A manicured line of beard traced his jawline. Wearing a scowl, Dr. Corrin nodded back to the room.

"She yanked her catheter and asked that I fetch you. And an ultraviolet light." He waved a hand toward the rear of the dental office. "My brother uses one to cure dental composites. I'll be right back."

With the way open, Gray entered the suite.

With her back to him, Seichan was sitting in a dental chair, naked from the waist up, struggling to pull a borrowed Redskins T-shirt over her head. A steri-drape lay crumpled at her feet. Even with her bare back to him, Gray read the strain of the effort. She had to catch herself on the armrest.

His mother sidestepped him. "Let me help you. You shouldn't be doing that by yourself."

Seichan resisted. "I've got it." She lifted an arm to ward off any help, but flinched with a gasp.

"Enough, young lady."

Gray's mother went to her side and helped her tug the T-shirt over her bare breasts and bandaged midriff. Turning around, Seichan discovered Gray standing there. Her face darkened, abashed. But Gray suspected her embarrassment lay not in being almost caught naked, but in showing weakness.

She slowly stood, face hardening against the pain. Leaning her rear end against the reclined chair, she rebuttoned her pants, still tight to her hips.

"I need to speak to your son," she said to Gray's mother, voice hoarse, dismissive.

His mother glanced to Gray. He nodded to her.

"I'll go check on your father," his mother said coldly, and left.

Down the hall, the muted sound of a television started. Apparently Kowalski had found the remote.

Alone now, Gray and Seichan stared at each other. Neither spoke, both taking a moment to size the other up.

Dr. Corrin stepped to the door with a handheld lamp. "This is all we have."

"It will do." Seichan tried to raise a hand to ask for it, but her arm trembled.

Gray accepted it, cradling the pieces of obelisk in one arm. "We'll need a minute."

"Of course." Dr. Corrin followed after Gray's mother, sensing the tension in the room.

Seichan's eyes had never left Gray's face. "Commander Pierce, I'm sorry I put your family at risk. I underestimated Nasser." She gingerly touched her bandaged wound. Acid entered her voice. "I won't make that mistake again. I thought I had lost him in Europe."

"You didn't," Gray snapped back.

Her eyes narrowed. "I *didn't* because Sigma command is compromised. The Guild used your own resources to track and expose me. The blame does not fall squarely upon me."

Gray had no argument against that.

She touched her forehead as if she had forgotten something, but Gray suspected she was stalling, weighing what to say and what to leave out. "You must have a thousand questions," she mumbled.

"Only one. *What the hell is going on?*"

Her left eyebrow lifted. A strangely familiar gesture, a reminder of their shared past. "To answer that, we have to start there." She nodded to the obelisk. "If you'll set it on the instrument table . . ."

Needing answers, Gray obeyed, balancing the broken piece atop the base.

"The lamp . . ." she said.

A moment later, with the overhead lights off, Gray bent over and studied the rows of illuminated letters glowing upon the black stone, across all four surfaces.

He did not recognize the lettering as any hieroglyphs or runes he'd ever seen. He glanced across at her. The whites of Seichan's eyes glowed in the ultraviolet backwash.

"What you're looking at is *angelic* script," she said. "The language of the archangels."

Gray's brow crinkled with his disbelief.

"I know," she said. "Insane. The script's origin traces back to both early Christianity and ancient Hebrew mysticism. If you want to know more—"

"Skip it. I'd rather find out what you meant when you said that the obelisk could save the world."

She leaned back, glancing away—then her eyes flicked to

him. "Gray, I need your help. I have to stop them, but I can't do it alone."

"Do what alone?"

"Go against the Guild. What they are attempting . . ." Again there was that flash of fear from her.

Gray frowned. When he'd first run into Seichan, she had been attempting to explode weaponized anthrax over Fort Detrick. Considering such callousness, what would scare her now?

"I helped you in the past," she said, trying the guilt card.

"To defeat a mutual enemy," he countered. "And to save your own skin."

"And that's all I'm looking for here again. Cooperation to defeat a mutual enemy. And it's not just my life in jeopardy this time. Hundreds of millions are threatened. And it's already started. The seeds are planted."

She nodded to the obelisk's glowing writing. "All that is stopping the Guild is locked in this riddle. If we could solve it first, there would be some hope. But I've gone as far as I can alone. I need fresh eyes, someone with more knowledge."

"And you expect the two of us to be able to solve what thwarts the Guild with its vast resources. If we brought all of Sigma into the picture—"

"You'd be handing the Guild their victory. There is a mole in Sigma. Whatever Sigma learns, the Guild will know."

She was right. It was worrisome, to say the least.

"So you propose we go it alone. Just the two of us."

"And one other . . . if he'll cooperate."

"Who?"

"When it comes to dealing with angels and archaeology, there is only one other person I respect."

Gray knew immediately to whom she was referring. "Vigor."

She nodded. "I left Monsignor Verona a calling card, a mystery to begin solving on his own. If you cooperate, we'll continue on." She touched the obelisk, wobbling the broken half. "To the next step on the angelic path."

"And where is that?"

Another shake of her head. She certainly was not going to make this easy. "I will tell you when we are away. As it is, we must get moving. The longer we sit in one place, the greater risk of our exposure."

She reached for the obelisk.

Gray beat her to it. He snatched up the larger half of the broken obelisk and raised it over his head. He'd had enough.

"Destroy it if you want," Seichan warned. "I still won't tell you anything more. Not until we're safely away and you agree to help."

Gray ignored her. "I assume you already made copies of the script here, probably even photos."

"Several in fact," she said.

"Good."

He brought his arm down and smashed the obelisk against the floor. It shattered into several pieces, skittering across the linoleum. A small gasp of surprise escaped Seichan, indicating she had no clue anything was hidden inside the statue.

"What . . . what have you done?"

Gray bent down and picked through the pieces to retrieve the chunk of silver from the debris. He straightened. In his fingers, he held what was hidden inside the stone. He was momentarily stunned silent.

He lifted the large silver crucifix.

Seichan's eyes widened with recognition. She jerked closer, oblivious of any pain. "It cannot be. You found it."

"Found what?"

"Friar Agreer's cross." Her voice lowered, both angry and mortified. "I had it all along."

"Who is Friar Agreer?"

"Friar Antonio Agreer. The priestly confessor to Marco Polo."

Marco Polo?

Tired of the riddles and half statements, Gray snapped harshly. "Seichan, what the hell is going on?"

She waved to a side chair, where her ripped leather bomber jacket had been tossed. "We have to get out of here."

He refused to move, blocking her as she stepped toward the chair.

She lowered her chin, her eyes going hard. "Gray, make up your damned mind. I don't have the time." She made to push past him.

He grabbed her upper arm. "And what's to stop me from just turning your ass over to Sigma."

She twisted free. All the freshly transfused blood was now in her face, livid and furious.

"Because you know goddamn better, Gray! If the Guild catches me, I'm dead. If your government captures me, I'll be locked far away forever, beyond any ability to stop what's about to happen. That's why I came to you. But fine. I'll sweeten the deal. Make you a trade. How's that? Help me, convince Vigor of the same, and afterward I'll give you the name of the mole at Sigma. If saving lives isn't good enough . . . the wolves are already at Sigma's door. You may not know it, but the powers that be are seeking to castrate you all, to put you all out to pasture, and now that another mole—a *second* mole—is hidden in your midst, they'll burn you down and salt the ground. End of Sigma. Forever."

Gray found himself swaying. He had indeed heard of such rumors, engendered by the internal audit by NSA and DARPA. But he also remembered a different Seichan, bent over him, gun in his face. She had attempted to kill him when they'd first met. How much could he trust her?

Before the standoff could be resolved, a shout came from the reception area. "Commander Pierce! Come see this!"

Gray swore under his breath at the man's loud bark. What about *covert* didn't Kowalski understand?

Gray met Seichan's gaze. She was still burning with raw

anger, but it failed to lay waste to what he'd first heard in her voice, bleeding across his parents' driveway. Terror.

He stalked to the side chair, picked up her jacket, and handed it to her. "We'll do it your way for now. But that's all I'll promise."

She nodded.

"Commander!"

With a shake of his head, Gray headed out of the suite. He heard the television turned up louder. He hurried forward. Still clutching the silver crucifix in his palm, he pocketed it before stepping into the reception area.

He found everyone staring up at the television. Gray noted the familiar logo for *CNN Headline News*. On the screen, three homes burned at the edge of a forest fire.

". . . possibly arson," the report continued. "To repeat, the police are looking for this man. Grayson Pierce. A local Washingtonian."

A picture of Gray flashed in the corner of the screen, in uniform, his black hair shaved to a stubble, eyes angry, mouth grim. It was his mug shot from when he was incarcerated in Leavenworth. Not a flattering picture. He looked like a feral criminal.

His father grumbled at his side. "Looks like your past just bit you in the ass."

Gray concentrated on the news report.

"For the moment, the police are calling this former Army Ranger *a person of interest*. That is all. He is wanted only for questioning. The police request anyone with the knowledge of his whereabouts to contact authorities immediately."

Kowalski lifted the remote and muted the sound.

Dr. Corrin stepped back from them all. "In the light of all this, I can't keep silent any—"

Kowalski pointed the remote toward the doctor. "In for a penny, in for a buck, doc. Aiding and abetting. Keep quiet or you can kiss your medical degree good-bye."

Dr. Corrin blanched, backing another step.

Gray's mother reached and touched the doctor's arm reassuringly. "Nonsense." She scowled at Kowalski. "Quit scaring him."

Kowalski shrugged.

"Someone is just trying to flush us out," Gray said.

"But it makes no sense," his mother argued. "I spoke with Director Crowe on the phone back at the safe house. He knows we were ambushed. Why is he letting these lies spread?"

The answer came from behind them. "Because they really want me." Seichan stepped into the room. She had donned her jacket. "They don't want to risk having me slip between their fingers."

Gray faced the others. "She's right. They're tightening the noose. We have to leave now."

Kowalski confirmed this assertion. After being chastised by Gray's mother, he had crossed to the lone window, peeking through the blinds. "Folks, we've got company."

Gray joined him. The window faced the main hospital. The curve of the ambulance bay was visible. Four police cars careened into view, silent, lights twirling. Local authorities had begun canvassing hospitals.

Turning, he faced his mother's former teaching assistant. "Dr. Corrin, we've asked much of you, but I'm afraid I must ask more. Can you get my parents somewhere safe?"

"Gray," his mother said.

"Mom, no argument." He kept his eyes on the doctor.

Corrin slowly nodded. "I own a few rentals. One off Dupont Circle is currently furnished but vacant. No one would think to look for your parents there."

It was a good choice.

"And, Dad, Mom . . . no outside communication, use no credit cards." He turned to Kowalski. "Can you watch over them?"

Kowalski sagged, plainly disappointed. "Not goddamn guard duty again."

Gray started to order, but his mother cut him off. "We

can take care of ourselves, Gray. Seichan is still in poor shape. You may need an extra pair of hands more than we will."

"And the apartment building has around-the-clock security," Dr. Corrin added, a bit too briskly. "Guards, cameras, panic alarms."

Gray suspected the doctor's support was less for his parents' security than to keep Kowalski off his property. Even now, Dr. Corrin was careful to remain a few steps away from the man.

And his mother was right. With Seichan compromised, they might need the large man's strength. He was Sigma's muscle, after all. Might as well put him to work.

Kowalski must have read something in Gray's expression. "About time." He rubbed his hands together. "Let's get this party started then. First, we'll need guns."

"No, first we need a car." Gray turned again to Dr. Corrin.

The doctor did not hesitate. He pulled out a key chain. "Doctor's lot. Slot 104. A white Porsche Cayenne."

He was more than happy to part with their company.

Another was not.

His mother hugged him hard and whispered in his ear. "Keep safe, Gray." Her voice lowered to a breath. "And don't trust her . . . not fully."

"Don't worry . . ." he said, agreeing to both.

"A mother always worries."

Still in her arms, he whispered one final instruction, meant only for her ears. She nodded, and with a final squeeze, she let him go.

Gray turned to discover his father's hand out. He shook it. It was their way. No hugs. He was from Texas. His father turned to Kowalski.

"Don't let him do anything stupid," he said.

"I'll try my best." Kowalski nodded to the door. "We ready?"

As he turned away, his father placed a hand on Gray's

shoulder and gave it a firm squeeze, followed by a pat good-bye. It was as close to *I love you* as he'd get from the man. And it warmed Gray more than he'd care to admit.

Without another word, he led the others out.

3:49 A.M.

"STILL NO WORD on Commander Pierce's whereabouts," Brant reported over his intercom.

Painter sat at his desk. The lack of news both disheart-ened and relieved him. Before he could analyze his own in-ternal reaction, Brant continued.

"And Dr. Jennings has just arrived."

"Send him in."

Dr. Malcolm Jennings, head of R&D, had called half an hour ago, eager for a meeting, but Painter had to put him off because of the crisis at the safe house. Even now, Painter could only give him five minutes.

The door opened and Jennings strode into the office, a hand already up. "I know . . . I know you're busy . . . but this couldn't wait."

Painter motioned to the seat before his desk.

The former forensic pathologist lowered his lanky frame into the chair, but he remained perched at its edge, plainly anxious. A file folder was clutched in his hand. Jennings, close to sixty years old, had been with Sigma since before Painter took over as director. He adjusted his glasses, whose half-moon lenses were tinged a slight shade of blue, better to prevent eyestrain during computer use. They also comple-mented his dark olive skin and graying hair, giving him a hip professorial air. But right now, the pathologist merely looked worn from the long night, though there remained a manic vein of excitement in his eyes.

"I assume this meeting is about the files Lisa transmitted from Christmas Island," Painter began.

Jennings nodded and opened the folder. He slid over two

photographs, gruesome shots of some man's legs, riddled with what appeared to be gangrene. "I've gone through both the toxicologist's and the bacteriologist's notes. Here is a patient whose skin bacteria suddenly turned virulent, consuming the soft tissues of his own legs. I've never seen anything like it."

Painter studied the pictures, but before he could even ask a question, the doctor was back up on his feet, pacing.

"I know we initially classified the Indonesian disaster as a low-level priority, merely a fact-gathering operation. But after these findings, we need to upgrade. Immediately. I came here in person to petition for a promotion of the scenario to Status Critical Level Two."

Painter sat straighter. Such a classification would mean diverting massive resources.

"We need more than two people poking around," Jennings continued. "I want a full forensic team on the ground as soon as possible, even if we have to outsource with the general military."

"And you don't think this is jumping the gun? Monk and Lisa are due to touch base in"—Painter checked his watch—"in a little over three hours. We can strategize then, when we have more data."

Jennings took off his glasses and rubbed a knuckle into an eye. "I don't think you understand. If the preliminary conjectures by the toxicologist prove to be true, we may be facing an ecological disaster, one with the potential to alter the entire earth's biosphere."

"Malcolm, don't you think you're overstating your case? These results are preliminary. Most of it mere conjecture." Painter waved to the photographs. "All this could just be a onetime toxic event."

"Even if that were the case, I'd recommend firebombing that island and cordoning off the surrounding seas for several years." He faced Painter. "And if this threat proves in any way transmissible, we're talking about the potential for a global environmental meltdown."

Painter gaped at the pathologist. Jennings was not one to cry wolf.

The doctor continued. "I've compiled all the necessary data and written a brief abstract to summarize. Read it and get back to me. The sooner the better."

Jennings left his folder on Painter's desk.

Painter placed a palm atop it and pulled it toward him. "I'll do it now and get back to you in the next half hour."

Jennings nodded, grateful and relieved. He turned to leave, but not before adding one last warning. "Keep in mind . . . we still don't know for sure what killed the dinosaurs."

With that sobering thought, the pathologist left his office. Painter's eyes settled to the gruesome photographs still on his desk. He prayed Jennings was wrong. In all the commotion of the past hours, he had almost forgotten about the situation out in the Indonesian islands.

Almost.

All night long, Lisa had never been far from his mind.

But now new worries flared, ignited by the pathologist's urgency. He tried not to let it rule him. Over the course of the morning, Lisa had not reported in again. Apparently nothing had escalated over there enough to warrant another emergency call.

Still . . .

Painter tapped the intercom button. "Brant, can you ring up Lisa's satellite phone?"

"Right away."

Painter opened the file folder. As he began to read the report inside, a cold dread edged up his spine.

Brant came back on the intercom. "Director, it just keeps ringing through to voice mail. Do you want me to leave a message?"

Painter turned his wrist, checking his watch. His call was hours early. Lisa could be involved in any number of duties. Still, he had to force down a rising panic.

"Just ask Dr. Cummings to call in as soon as possible."

"Yes, sir."

"And, Brant, check in with the cruise ship's switchboard."

He knew he was being paranoid. He attempted to return to the folder, but he found it hard to concentrate.

"Sir . . ." Brant's voice returned a moment later. "I've reached the sea-band operator. They're reporting communication troubles shipwide, drops in satellite feed. They're still working out some of the bugs in the new ship."

Painter nodded. The *Mistress of the Seas* had been on its maiden voyage, also known as a shakedown cruise, when it had been commandeered for this medical emergency.

"They report no other major problems," Brant finished.

Painter sighed. So he was indeed being too paranoid. He was letting his feelings for Lisa cloud his judgment. If this had been any other operative, would he have even called?

He returned to his reading.

Lisa was fine.

And besides, Monk was with her. He would keep her safe.

6

Pestilence

WHAT THE HELL was going on?

Lisa stood with the other three scientists. They were all gathered in the ship's presidential suite. A uniformed butler poured single-malt whiskey into a row of tulip-shaped snifters, lined atop a silver tray. As a result of Painter's appreciation for malt whiskey, Lisa recognized the bottle's label: a rare sixty-year-old Macallan. The butler's hands trembled, jostling his aim, splashing the expensive whiskey.

The butler's poor stewardship could be blamed on the pair of masked gunmen, armed with assault rifles. They stood guard at the double doors that led into the suite. Across the room, French doors opened onto a balcony wide enough to park a municipal bus, where another gunman patrolled.

Inside, teak cabinetry and leather furniture appointed the grand suite. Vases of miniature island roses decorated the room, while a Mozart sonata whispered softly from hidden speakers. The scientists clustered in the room's center. It could have been the beginning of any university cocktail party.

Except for the raw fear in everyone's faces.

Earlier, Lisa and Henri Barnhardt had obeyed the summons to climb to the ship's bridge. What else could they do? Up in the bridge, they found the WHO leader, Dr. Lindholm, already there, wiping blood from his nose, plainly clubbed in the face. Benjamin Miller, the infectious-disease expert, arrived shortly thereafter.

They had been met by a towering figure, the leader of the pirates. He was the size of a linebacker, heavily muscled, with thick, cruel hands. He wore a khaki uniform, jungle-camouflaged pants tucked into black boots. He did not bother with a mask. His hair was the color of wet mud, clipped short, his skin polished bronze, except for a green-and-black tattoo across the left side of his face. It was of a Maori design known as Moko, all swirls and windblown lines.

He had ordered them to this suite, to wait in seclusion.

Lisa had been happy to abandon the bridge. A pitched battle must have been waged atop the ship, evidenced from the bullet-pocked windows and equipment. She had also noted the wide smear of blood across the bridge's floor, where a body had been dragged away.

Herded over to the presidential suite, Lisa had been surprised to discover one last captive caught in the net.

The owner of the cruise line, Ryder Blunt, stood beside his butler and gathered up a handful of the crystal snifters. Dressed in jeans and a rugby shirt, he looked like a young, sun-bleached Sean Connery.

He crossed over and passed around the snifters of whiskey. "I think we can all use a little of this Macallan heat," he said, puffing around the smoldering stump of a cigar. "If only to steady our nerves. And if not that, at least we'll drink through my best stores before the bloody bastards discover it."

Like most people, Lisa knew Ryder's story. Only forty-eight, the Aussie had earned his fortune during the silicon boom, developing encryption software for downloading copyrighted material. He then parlayed his profits into a series of wildly successful real estate and commercial ventures, including the cruise line. A lifetime bachelor, he was also renowned for his maverick ways: swimming with great whites, helo-skiing to remote parts of the world, base-jumping off buildings in Kuala Lumpur and Hong Kong. Yet he also had a reputation for generosity, joint-venturing a slew of philanthropic pursuits.

So it was no wonder he lent his ship to assist during this medical crisis. Though in hindsight, he might now regret his generosity.

He offered a snifter of whiskey to Lisa. She shook her head.

"Lass, no offense," he growled at her, still holding out the crystal snifter. "Who knows when we'll ever get another chance?"

She accepted the glass, more to get him to move away. His cigar smoke stung her eyes. She sipped the amber liquid. A fiery smoothness flowed into the belly, warming through her. She exhaled a bit of the warmth. It did help steady her.

Once the glasses were spread, the billionaire sank into a neighboring chair. He leaned his elbows on his knees, glaring toward the armed guards, puffing on his cigar.

At her side, Henri finally asked the question that had been plaguing all of them. "What do these pirates want with us?"

Lindholm sniffed, his eyes red, already bruising from the punch to the face. "Hostages." He glanced sidelong toward the seated billionaire.

"Perhaps in the case of Sir Ryder," Henri agreed, lowering his voice, using the man's knighted title. "But then why even bother with us? Our net worth combined wouldn't even equal the man's pocket change."

Lisa wafted cigar smoke from her face. "They clearly wanted all the main scientists here. But how did they know whom to summon?"

"They could have obtained a manifest from the ship's crew," Lindholm said sourly. He cast a second sidelong glance toward Ryder. "No doubt some of his crew were in league with the raiders."

Ryder heard and mumbled to himself, "And if I ever

find out who they are, I'll have them strung up from the yardarms."

"But wait . . . if they wanted all the main scientists here, why wasn't Dr. Graff summoned with us?" Benjamin Miller asked, naming the marine researcher who had left to collect samples with Monk. He turned to Lisa. "Or your partner, Dr. Kokkalis? Why summon us, but not the others?"

Miller sipped from his glass, his nose crinkling at the potency of the single malt. The Oxford-trained bacteriologist was not an unhandsome man, with thick auburn hair and green eyes. He stood barely over five feet, but he appeared even shorter due to the roll of his shoulders and hunched posture, possibly earned from decades of crouching over a microscope.

"Dr. Miller is right," Henri said. "Why weren't they called?"

"Maybe the bastards knew they weren't on board," Lindholm said.

"Or maybe they'd already been captured." Miller glanced apologetically in Lisa's direction. "Or were killed."

Lisa's chest hollowed out with worry. She had hoped Monk had escaped the trap, was even now summoning help, but she placed little faith in this dream. Before the assault, Monk had already been late getting back to the ship.

Henri shook his head and downed his drink in one swallow. He lowered his glass. "No use speculating on their fate. But if our captors knew our colleagues were out in the field, then that suggests whatever is going on here is more than a hostage situation."

"But what else could they want?" Miller asked.

The thumping of an approaching helicopter drew all their gazes toward the open balcony doors. It was too throaty for the smaller Eurocopter that had added air support to the sea battle. As a group, they moved to the doorway. Ryder stood up with a fierce exhalation of smoke and joined them.

A fresh breeze blew off the sea, smelling of salt and the barest hint of chemical bitterness, the aftermath of the toxic expulsion or perhaps it was just from the oil burning on the water. Nearby, the Australian Coast Guard cutter, gutted by a rocket blast, still smoked and foundered on its side, half sunk.

From over the top of the ship, a gray helicopter with double rotors, front and rear, military design, canted into view. It veered out over the water, stirring the smoke. It passed toward the seaside township, aflame in several spots now— then swung around, satisfied with whatever it had surveyed. It sped back to the ship and disappeared out of sight. From the path of its roar, it settled to the helipad atop the ship.

The thumping of the blades slowed and quieted.

In its absence, Lisa recognized a new rumble. A slight vibration tickled the soles of her feet.

"We're moving," Henri said.

Ryder swore around his clamped cigar.

Lisa saw it was true. Very slowly, like the hands of a clock, the view of the burning township was shifting.

"They're taking the ship out," Miller said.

Lindholm clenched a fist to his chest.

Lisa felt a similar fear. There remained a certain level of security in knowing land was so near. But even that was being taken from them. Her breathing grew heavier, yet drew less air. Surely someone would soon realize what had transpired and come to investigate. In fact, she was due to call Painter in only three hours. When she didn't call in—

The pace of their movement accelerated as the giant cruise ship fought its own inertia and began to roll away from the island.

She checked her watch, then turned to Ryder. "Mr. Blunt, how fast can your ship travel?"

He stubbed out his cigar in an ashtray. "The Hales Trophy benchmark for racing the transatlantic crossing in a cruise ship is forty knots. Bloody fast."

"And the *Mistress*?" she asked.

Ryder patted one of the bulkhead walls. "Pride of the fleet. German-designed engines, monohull construction. She is capable of forty-seven knots."

Lisa calculated in her head. If she didn't phone in three hours, when would Painter begin to worry? In four or five hours? She shook her head. Painter wouldn't wait a minute longer.

"Three hours," she mumbled to herself. *But was that still too late?* She turned to Ryder. "Is there a map in here?"

Ryder pointed and led the way. "A globe. In the library alcove."

He took her to a niche off the main room lined with teak bookshelves. A standing wooden globe rested in the center. She leaned over it and rotated the world to bring up the Indonesian islands. She calculated in her head and measured with her fingers.

"In three hours we'll be lost among the Indonesian chain of islands."

The region, dominated by the bigger islands of Java and Sumatra, was literally a maze of smaller atolls and islets. Over eighteen thousand of them, spread over an area equivalent to the size of the continental United States. Away from the main cities of Jakarta and Singapore, the region subsisted at a Stone Age level of technology. Cannibalism was still practiced on some of the outer islands. If you wanted to hide a cruise ship, here would be a good place to do it.

"They can't hope to steal an entire ship," Lindholm exclaimed, drawn to the library in the wake of the others. "What about surveillance satellites? You can't hide something as big as a cruise ship."

"Don't underestimate our captors," Henri said. "First someone has to know to look for us."

Lisa knew he was right. Given the swiftness of the assault, along with the collusion of key members of the ship's crew, the hijacking had to have been weeks in the planning. Someone knew what was happening on Christmas Island long before the rest of the world. Lisa remembered the patient in the isolation ward, the John Doe with the flesh-eating bacteria. He had been found wandering the island *five* weeks ago.

Did their captors' knowledge extend that far?

A commotion at the suite's double door drew them all around. A pair of men entered. In the lead, Lisa recognized the pirate leader with the tattooed face.

Stepping past the Maori warrior, a tall stranger pushed forward. He swept off a wide-brimmed panama hat and passed it to a woman who appeared from beyond the tattooed man's shoulder. Striding forward, the newcomer had apparently come dressed for a garden party, dapperly attired in a loose-fitting white linen suit with a matching cane, his salt-and-pepper hair cut rakishly long to the collar. His burnished features and close-set eyes cast him as Indian or perhaps Pakistani.

He crossed to the group, thumping his cane, but plainly not needing the support, all for show. His eyes glinted with a misplaced cheeriness.

"Namaste." He greeted them in Hindi with a slight bow of his head. "Thank you all for joining me here."

As the stranger settled to a stop, he nodded to the owner of the *Mistress of the Seas.* "Sir Ryder, I appreciate your hospitality and the use of your fine ship. We will do our best to return your ship to you unscathed."

Ryder merely glowered, sizing up the man.

Turning, the stranger acknowledged the scientists. "As we embark on this great endeavor, it is a privilege to have such leading experts from the World Health Organization gathered in one room."

Lisa noted Henri's brows pinch both in wariness and confusion.

The stranger's eyes settled last upon Lisa. "And of course, we must not forget our colleague from U.S. covert operations. Sigma Force, I believe, yes?"

Stunned silent, Lisa could only stare. How could he—?

The man offered the barest bow in her direction, genteel, not mocking. "I'm sorry your partner could not join us. It seems he met with a mishap while we attempted to fetch him. Something to do with indigenous crabs. The details remain sketchy. We lost several of our own men in the attempt. Only one fellow made it back alive."

Lisa's vision narrowed, closing down with dread.

Monk . . .

A hand touched her shoulder, consoling. It was Ryder Blunt. He faced the stranger. "Who the bloody hell are you?"

"Of course. My apologies." The man lifted a palm and formally introduced himself. "Dr. Devesh Patanjali, chief acquisition officer, specializing in biotechnology, for the Guild."

Despite her anguish, a cold stone settled into the pit of Lisa's stomach. She had heard all about the Guild from Painter . . . and the bloody swath that the terrorist organization left behind in its wake.

The man tapped his cane on the floor with a note of finality. "And I'm afraid we must not waste any more time on introductions. We have much work to do before we reach port in the morning."

"What work?" Lisa managed to force out, bitter with grief.

He cocked one eyebrow toward her. "My dear, together we must save the world."

3:45 P.M.

MONK CLAMPED HIS palm tight over the man's mouth. His other hand's prosthetic fingers tightened on the man's throat, just under his jaw, squeezing off his carotid, halting blood flow to the brain. The man struggled, but Monk's fingers were strong enough to crack walnuts between them. He waited for the man's kicking legs to go slack—then lowered him to the floor.

He hauled the man into a small equipment closet.

Monk noted the vibration underfoot, and a sonorous pitch to the engines. He straightened. The ship was moving. He had stowed away just in time.

After the explosion of his Jet Ski, Monk had boarded via one of the stabilizing anchor chains on the far side of the ship, shedding his scuba tanks and letting them sink to the bottom of the cove. His entry point was scantily guarded, most of the attention being directed toward shore. From the chain, he was able to leap to one of the hanging lifeboats, then clamber and roll to the Promenade Deck.

He had ducked quickly into hiding.

From the supply closet, he had waited a quarter hour for a lone guard to pass, one of the pirates, bearing a Heckler & Koch assault rifle. The guard was now sprawled in the same closet. Monk unzipped his wet suit and stripped the man of his loose pants and shirt. He changed quickly, but he was unable to cram his feet into the stolen boots.

Too small.

No choice, he left barefooted, but not barehanded.

The rifle's weight helped center him.

Stepping into the hall, he pulled the head scarf over his face, masking up like the other pirates. Monk knew the ship, having memorized the schematics while en route to the islands from the States. He hurried down a deck and along the starboard hallway. He met another two pirates at the stairwell, but he merely shouldered through them, appearing busy and hassled.

One of the guards yelled at him, jostled by his passage. Monk didn't understand the language, but he knew when he was being cursed. He lifted his rifle, acknowledging but not stopping.

He hurried down the hallway.

Lisa and Monk shared adjoining staterooms here. It was his first place to hunt for his missing partner. Monk had passed two sprawled bodies on his way down here, shot in the back, left where they had fallen. He had to find her.

He counted the staterooms. He heard someone crying behind one door, but he hurried until he reached their assigned cabins.

He tugged on his own door. Locked. He had left his

room's electronic key card back with his bags in the beached Zodiac. He moved to the next door, Lisa's cabin. The knob refused to budge—but he heard someone stir behind the door.

It had to be Lisa.

Thank God . . .

He tapped a plastic knuckle lightly on the door and leaned his lips close. "Lisa . . . it's me."

The peephole in the door darkened as someone shifted to peek through. Monk stepped back and lowered his head scarf, revealing himself. After a breath, the chain scraped on the other side, and the dead bolt released with a click.

Monk pulled up his mask and checked up and down the hall. "Hurry it up," he whistled out.

The door swung open, pulled inward.

Turning back to the door, he stepped forward. "Lisa, we have to—"

Monk immediately recognized his mistake and swung up his gun.

It was not Lisa.

Silhouetted against the brighter sunlight in the cabin, a young man crouched, half hidden by the door. "Don't . . . please don't shoot."

Monk held his rifle rock-steady while he scanned the cabin. Someone had ransacked the room: drawers opened and dumped, closets emptied. But his attention quickly fixed on the room's one other occupant: a dead body, facedown on the bed. It was one of the pirates. From the pool of blood soaked into the bedding, his throat had been slashed.

Eyes widening, Monk turned his attention back to the trespasser.

"Who are you?"

The young man waved an arm to encompass the room. "I came here to find Dr. Cummings. I didn't know where else to look."

Monk finally recognized the young nurse who had been helping Lisa. He could not recall the man's name.

"Jesspal, sir . . . Jessie," the young man mumbled, reading his confusion.

Lowering his gun, Monk nodded and pushed inside. "Where's Lisa?"

"I don't know. I was up in triage," he explained, trembling all over, close to shock. "Then the explosions . . . four of the crew opened fire in the hospital ward. I ran. Dr. Cummings had gone to speak with the toxicologist. I prayed to Vishnu that she had fled back to her cabin."

The young man glanced to the fouled bed, then just as quickly away. "Dr. Cummings had left her bag up in triage. I grabbed it. Found her key. But the man here had already been waiting inside. He got angry when I wasn't her. Made me kneel on the floor. He had a radio."

Jessie pointed to the portable radio on the floor.

"And what happened to his throat?" Monk asked.

"I couldn't let him report in. And Dr. Cummings had left more than her key card in her bag." From his waistband, Jessie pulled free a scalpel. "I . . . I had to . . ."

Monk squeezed his upper arm. "You did good, Jessie."

The young man sagged down atop the other bed. "I heard them over ship-wide radio. Calling for some of the doctors. Including Dr. Cummings."

"Where did they want them to go?"

"The ship's bridge."

"Did they repeat the order?"

Jessie stared for a moment, then slowly shook his head.

So Lisa must have obeyed . . .

Monk now had a destination.

He crossed to the door that linked their two rooms. It had been left ajar. A quick peek revealed his room was in no better shape. Someone had cleared his personal gear, including his satellite phone. He searched a bit more to be sure. No luck.

Monk also examined the dead body and discovered a surprise. The dark hue of the pirate's skin extended only to hands and face. The remainder of the man's skin was as pale as snow, sprinkled with a few freckles. This was no local islander—but some mercenary in disguise.

What was going on here?

Monk crossed back to his room to grab a pair of basketball shoes.

As he pulled them over his bare feet, he spoke to Jessie. "We can't stay here. Someone will come looking for your sleeping beauty over there. We'll find you somewhere else to hole up."

"What about you?"

"I'm going after Lisa."

"Then I'm coming with you." Jessie stood up a bit shakily.

The young man tugged his shirt over his head, plainly intending to go in a pirate disguise, too. The young man was all rib bones, but Monk supposed there were some wiry muscles under there, too. Jessie had jumped the man here, taken out someone twice his size.

Still . . .

"I'm better alone," Monk said firmly.

Jessie finally got his shirt over his head, mumbling something.

"What?"

The nurse turned to him, exasperated. "I've been trained in jujitsu and karate. Fifth-degree black belt in each."

"I don't care if you're India's answer to Jackie Chan. You're still not coming."

A knock at the door startled them both. Someone shouted at them in Malay, plainly a question. Monk didn't understand a word. He lifted his rifle. He had other means of communication.

Jessie slipped past him, shoving Monk's rifle barrel down as he passed. The nurse called through the door, sounding irritated, snapping back in Malay. An exchange followed, then whoever was at the door left, plainly satisfied.

Jessie turned back to him, cocking one eyebrow.

"Okay, maybe you could be useful," Monk admitted.

4:20 P.M.

LISA STOOD WITH the other scientists and Ryder Blunt. The group of captives had been led at gunpoint to the foredeck of the ship. The large helicopter rested on its pad, tethered down now. Its hatches were open and a beehive of activity buzzed around it. Men unloaded heavy crates from its cargo holds.

She noted some of the stamped names and corporate logos: SYNBIOTIC, WELCH SCIENTIFIC, GENECORP. One box bore a stenciled American flag and the letters USAMRIID. The U.S. Army Medical Research Institute of Infectious Diseases.

It was all medical equipment.

The crates vanished down the throat of an elevator.

She caught Henri Barnhardt's eye. The toxicologist had also noted the marked crates. One hand absently scratched his bearded chin. Deep frown lines bracketed his lips. Off to the side, Miller and Lindholm simply stood with their eyes glazed over, while Ryder Blunt attempted to light another cigar in the blustering breezes atop the cruise ship.

Standing under the helicopter's rotors, Dr. Devesh Patanjali continued to oversee the final unloading personally. He had never explained his cryptic statement about saving the world. Instead he had ordered them all up here.

The Maori leader of the gunmen stood to one side, hands free of any weapons, but his palm rested on a holstered horse pistol, a massive sidearm. He stood with squinted eyes, surveying the foredeck's activity, like a sniper sweeping a killing field. Lisa knew nothing escaped his notice, including the young woman who had accompanied Dr. Devesh Patanjali.

She remained a mystery, having spoken not a single word, her face an unwavering mask. She stood atop the foredeck with her sleek black boots together, her hands folded at her waist, a formal posture of waiting and servitude. And though her face might be unreadable, the shape and curve of her form had fully captured the attention of the Maori gunman.

Lisa had overheard her name when Dr. Patanjali had passed out of the presidential suite below. *Surina.* The doctor had given her a chaste kiss on the cheek as he left. It had been accepted without a flicker of emotion. The woman appeared to be of mixed Indian blood, dressed in a long sari wrap of muted oranges and rose silk, draped over which was a long ebony braid. If untied, her hair must sweep the floor behind her heels. Marking her heritage, she bore a crimson dot, the traditional *bindi,* on her forehead. But her complexion, a polished teak, was much lighter than Devesh Patanjali's, suggesting a European bloodline somewhere in her past.

Whether she was Devesh's sister, wife, or merely a companion, Lisa could not discern. But there was also something menacing in her silence, possibly heightened by the coldness in her eyes. Also her left arm was gloved in black, so skintight it was hard to tell if it was leather or rubber. But it looked like her limb had been dipped in black India Ink.

Crossing her arms, Lisa turned and searched the receding profile of Christmas Island. In the short time they'd been under way, the island had shrunk to a misty green silhouette, trailing a smudge of dark smoke into the sky. But who was there to see it as a signal? Painter would surely grow suspicious if neither she nor Monk called in to report. And for the moment, she placed all her hopes on his paranoia.

Luckily it was a safe bet.

A wind gusted as the tradewinds kicked up. Gulls coasted the breezes overhead, catching her eyes. If only she could fly away as easily . . .

A shout drew her attention back to the helicopter.

Two men in surgical scrubs hauled a stretcher from the rear hold of the helicopter. Wheels dropped and locked. Devesh hovered over them, checking the patient strapped to the gurney. Portable monitoring equipment lay nestled haphazardly around the patient for transport. The figure was sealed in an oxygen tent. The patient appeared to be a woman from the rise and fall of her chest. Facial features were obscured by a respirator and a tangled octopus of tubes and wires.

Devesh pointed his cane, and the two orderlies guided the gurney toward the elevators, following the train of medical equipment.

He finally crossed back to his captives.

"We'll have all the labs and medical suites set up in the next hour. Luckily, Dr. Cummings and her partner were very kind to have brought pieces of equipment that were beyond even my reach. Who would have known your Defense Department's research-and-development branch had perfected a portable scanning electron microscope? Along with electrophoresis equipment and protein sequencer? Quite a bit of serendipity to have such tools land in our laps."

He tapped his cane and set off. "Come. Let me show you the true face of what assails us."

Lisa followed with the others. In this instance, she didn't need the rifles at her back to make her obey. Mysteries were piled atop mysteries here, and she wanted answers, some clue to the reason for this assault and for Devesh's words.

My dear, together we must save the world.

They were led down three decks. Along the way, Lisa had noted crews of men in chemical suits, working along the lower passageways, moving within stinging clouds of sprayed disinfectant.

Devesh continued to the forward section of the ship. The hall ended at a wide circular space, off which the pricier cabins extended. Monk had commandeered one of the large suites here for his own laboratory. It seemed Devesh had commandeered all the rest.

Tucking under an isolation drape, he waved them into the busy central workspace. "Here we are," he said.

A score of men were cracking open crates, yanking out packing straw and Styrofoam, hauling free plastic-wrapped medical and laboratory equipment. One man emptied a boxful of petri dishes used to culture bacteria. The door to Monk's lab lay open. Lisa noted a man inside with a clipboard, inventorying Sigma's equipment.

Devesh marched them to a neighboring cabin. He swiped a personal key card and shoved open the door.

Turning, he spoke to the tattooed leader of the mercenary force. "Rakao, please have Dr. Miller taken to the bacteriology suite." He turned to the scientist. "Dr. Miller, we've taken the liberty of bringing up and expanding your bacteriology station. New incubation ovens, anaerobic growth media, blood culture plates. I'd like you to coordinate with Dr. Eloise Chénier, my team's virologist, down the hall, to complete the infectious-disease lab."

The Maori leader waved for one of his men to escort Miller down the hall. The bacteriologist glanced around at the others, plainly not wanting to leave their company, but the rifle at his back discouraged any argument.

As Miller left, Devesh nodded to their group. "And, Rakao, would you personally escort Sir Ryder and Dr. Lindholm up to the radio room? We'll join you momentarily."

"Sir." The tattooed man did not like this decision, his one word heavy with warning, eyeing Lisa and Henri with suspicion.

"We'll be fine." Devesh held open the cabin door and bowed his head for the young Indian woman to enter. "I believe Dr. Cummings and Dr. Barnhardt would like to hear what I have to say. And Surina will be with me."

Lisa and Henri were ushered into the cabin.

Devesh stepped after them, closing the door—then stopped and turned back to the Maori leader.

"Oh, yes, and Rakao, gather the children, if you'd be so kind. The ones I picked out. That's a good man."

Devesh closed the door, but not before Lisa noted the Maori leader's face darken into a glower. His tattoos stood out more starkly, an indecipherable map.

As the lock clicked, Devesh strode over to the cabin's desk. It was actually two desks joined together, one unbolted and moved from another cabin. The pair of desks supported three LCD monitors linked to two tower HP computers. They were the only additions to the suite. The remainder of the cabin consisted of a comfortable seating area of teak furniture facing patio doors and a shaded balcony.

Surina stepped to one of the sofas and lowered herself, bending only at the knees, to perch on one of its arms. And while the movement had a measure of demure modesty, Lisa sensed power and threat: the focused eyes, the smooth control of a geisha, but mostly it was the pair of sheathed daggers exposed on both ankles as she sat.

Lisa glanced away. A bedroom opened behind the desk. A pair of large steamer trunks rested at the foot of the bed. This must be Devesh Patanjali's personal room. But why had he brought them here?

Devesh awoke the sleeping computers with the tap of a few buttons, drawing her attention back. All three monitors bloomed to a brilliant glare in the dim room.

"Dr. Barnhardt . . . or *Henri,* if I may presume . . . ?" Devesh glanced back.

The toxicologist merely shrugged.

Devesh continued. "Henri, I must commend you on your assessment of the true threat hidden within the shroud of the toxic assault. It had taken our scientists weeks to ascertain what you managed to discern in less than twenty-four hours."

Lisa's skin went cold. *Weeks.* So their captors had been aware of the threat at the island long before the full crisis broke. But what did any of this have to do with the Guild?

"Of course, we did not so much appreciate the general alarm you raised, reaching all the way to Washington. It required accelerating our timetable . . . and some improvisation. Like utilizing the scientific talent here and merging it with my own. But so be it. We must move quickly if there is to be any hope."

"Hope for what?" Lisa finally asked.

"Let me show you, my dear." Devesh patted one of the two chairs, inviting her to sit.

She remained standing, but he seemed to take no offense, busy with the computer keyboard. On the center monitor, a video began playing. It depicted a dense microscopic field of twitching chains of rod-shaped bacteria.

"How much do you know about anthrax?" Devesh asked, glancing back.

Lisa's skin went cold at his question.

Henri answered, "*Bacillus anthracis.* It mostly infects ruminants. Cows, goats, sheep. But spores can also infect humans. Often proving fatal."

It was a clinical assessment, devoid of emotion. But Lisa noted the tense hold to the toxicologist's shoulders.

Devesh nodded. "*Bacillus* species are found worldwide in soil. Harmless for the most part. For example, here is one such benign organism, *Bacillus cereus.*"

The screen image changed to a microscopic close-up of a single bacterium. Rod-shaped with a thin membranous wall, the cell's DNA strands were stained to stand out in the center.

"Like other members of the species, this little bug can be found in gardens around the world. Happily feeding on microorganisms and nutrients in the soil. It causes no harm to anything larger than an amoeba. But its brother, *Bacillus anthracis*—" Devesh clicked to bring up another image—side by side with the first, a second bacterium that looked identical.

"Here is the organism that causes anthrax," he continued, "one of the most deadly bacterium on the planet. It shares the same genetic code with its peaceful, garden-dwelling brother." Devesh tapped the two cells' stained twists of DNA. "Gene by gene, nearly identical. So why does one kill and the other remain harmless?"

Over a shoulder, Devesh stared back at Lisa and Henri.

Lisa shook her head. Henri remained silent.

Devesh nodded as if satisfied by their reticence. Turning back, he toggled a key and the anthrax bacterium zoomed on the screen. The mass of DNA swelled on the monitor. Within the cytoplasm of the interior cell, separate from the main tangle of DNA, floated two perfect rings of genetic material, like a tiny pair of eyes staring back at them.

"Plasmids," Henri said, naming the rings.

Lisa's brow tightened as she was forced to draw upon her pre-med education. As well as she could recall, plasmids were circular strands of DNA separate from main chromosomal DNA. The free-floating bits of genetic code were unique to bacteria. Their role was still poorly understood.

Devesh continued. "These two plasmids—pXo1 and pXo2—are what turn ordinary *Bacillus* species into super-killers. Remove these two rings, and anthrax transforms back into an innocent organism, living happily in any garden. Put those same plasmids into any friendly *Bacillus* and the bug turns into a killer."

Devesh finally swung around to face them. "So I ask you, where did these extraneous and deadly bits come from?"

Lisa answered, intrigued despite herself. "Can't plasmids be shared directly from one bacterium to another?"

"Certainly. But what I meant was, how did these bacteria *first* acquire these foreign bits of genetic material? What's their *original* source?"

Henri stirred, moving closer to study the screens. "The evolutionary origin of plasmids remains a mystery, but the current theory is that they were acquired from viruses. Or more specifically *bacteriophages,* a category of viruses that only infect bacteria."

"Exactly!" Devesh turned back to the screen. "It's been theorized that, sometime in the ancient past, a viral bacteriophage injected a peaceful *Bacillus* with this deadly pair of plasmids, creating a new monster in the biosphere and transforming a sweet little garden bug into a killer."

Devesh tapped more rapidly, clearing the screen. "And anthrax isn't the only bacterium thus infected. The bacterium that causes the black plague, *Yersinia pestis* . . . its virulence is also enhanced by a plasmid."

Lisa felt a prickling chill as realization dawned. All this talk of transforming bacteria reminded her of the patients on the ship. The girl with seizures from vinegar bacteria, the woman with choleric dysentery from yogurt bacteria, the John Doe whose skin bacteria were eating his legs away . . .

"Are you suggesting it's happening here again?" she mumbled. "This same corruption of bacteria."

Devesh nodded. "Indeed. Something has risen again out of the depths of the sea, something with the ability to turn all bacteria deadly."

Lisa remembered Henri's example of how prevalent bacteria were in the world, how 90 percent of the cells in our own bodies were composed of bacteria. Nonhuman. If that tide should shift against us . . .

Devesh continued. "From studying the genetics of anthrax and other toxic bacteria, microbiologists have predicted the existence of an ancient strain of viruses. A strain that created the early ancestors of anthrax and other plague bacteria. Scientists have even coined a name for this ancient strain of viruses, one that turns friend into foe: the Judas Strain."

Henri must have read something in Devesh's face, a brightness to his eyes, an excitement. He straightened. "Something tells me you've isolated the causative agent in the outbreak here, haven't you? This Judas Strain. Or you wouldn't be here."

"We think so."

Devesh tapped another two keys. The bacterium vanished, replaced with a rotating figure on the screen, an image from an electron micrograph, all in shades of silver. It made the organism depicted seem more mechanical than biological. It looked like some lunar lander. The main shell was geometric, an icosahedron, made up of twenty flat triangular pieces. Out from every corner stretched thin tendrils, spiked at the tips, made to latch on and pierce.

Lisa had seen many such images back in medical school. A virus.

"We discovered it in a sample of the cyanobacteria from the toxic tide. It turned the innocent phosphorescent sea bacteria into a flesh-boiling, poison-spewing killer. And within such windblown steaming clouds of toxin, the virus spread onto land, beginning the slow alteration of the island's bacteria into monsters."

"And now we're seeing it happen among the patients," Henri said. "Turning our own bodies against us."

Devesh tapped the screen. "The ultimate betrayer of life. This organism has the capability to travel through the planet's biosphere, transforming all bacteria into lethal, life-destroying organisms. It's nature's neutron bomb, a viral explosion with the potential to wipe out all higher life-forms, leaving behind only a toxic soup of deadly bacterial ooze. If unchecked, we've already seen a peek of what the world may become on the windward side of Christmas Island."

"And if it should spread . . ." Henri's face had paled. "We'd have no way of stopping it."

Devesh finally stood and retrieved his cane. "Perhaps. But we've barely begun to analyze the organism. The good news is that so far the virus appears to be short-lived and does not infect human cells. Only bacteria. So the virus poses little *direct* risk to us. It hijacks a bacterial cell, uses the cell to churn copies of itself, then leaves behind the toxic plasmids. Outside the cell, the new virus is fragile. It can easily be killed with simple disinfectants and controlled with good hygiene."

Lisa pictured the work crews moving through the ship in a cloud of disinfectant. They were sterilizing the ship.

"But unfortunately, the virus leaves behind a killer in its wake. Deadly bacteria that divide and multiply, each a new monster added to the microbial world, contaminating the biosphere forever with never-before-seen life-forms."

Henri placed a worried palm on his forehead. "If the viral exposure breaks free into the general biosphere . . . we're talking about a thousand different new diseases hitting the world simultaneously. A plague with the capability of changing faces faster than we can react. The world has seen nothing like this before."

"That's not necessarily true," Devesh countered cryptically.

Henri focused back to their captor.

"My employers and I believe this is not the first outbreak of this Judas Strain. There are historical reports from the region of a similar outbreak. Back almost a millennium ago." His voice lowered to a contemplative whisper. "The stories were accompanied by some strange and disturbing claims."

"What historical reports are you talking about?" Lisa asked.

Devesh waved away her question. "It doesn't matter. We've got others looking into that question, following that historical trail. We must stay focused on our goal. Our mission aboard the ship lies not in the past, but the present. My employers orchestrated the evacuation of the island, arranged to have Mr. Blunt's cruise ship detoured here. We needed to isolate the currently infected in one place. Here we have the rare opportunity to study how this disease unfolds. Its epidemiology, its pathology, its physiologic effects. And we've a full shipload of test subjects."

Lisa backed away a step, unable to mask her horror.

Devesh leaned on his cane. "I sense your distaste, Dr. Cummings. Now you understand why the Guild had to act. When faced with an organism of such virulence, there could be no hand-wringing. No politically correct response to such an onslaught. Action must be swift, and hard choices made. In Tuskegee, did not your own government allow people infected with syphilis to die of the disease while scientists dispassionately recorded the suffering, the advancing symptoms, and the eventual deaths? To survive this, we must be as brutal and cold. Because, believe me, this is a war for the survival of the human species."

Lisa sought some counter to his words, too shocked.

Henri interceded, but not in the manner Lisa had expected. "He's right."

Lisa turned to the toxicologist.

Henri's eyes remained locked on the screen depicting the

microscopic image of the Judas Strain. "This is a planet killer. And it's already loose. Remember how fast the bird flu circled the world. We have a week, possibly only days. If we don't find a way to stop it, all life—at least all higher life—will be wiped off the earth."

"I'm glad we have a meeting of the minds," Devesh said with a bow of his head in Henri's direction. His eyes found Lisa's. "And possibly when I show Dr. Cummings here her role in our endeavor, she may also find the same such enlightenment."

Lisa frowned at his puzzling statement.

Devesh swung away toward the door. "But first we must join your friends up in the radio room. We have some fires to put out."

7:02 A.M.
Washington, D.C.

PAINTER STARED AT the news reports on his three plasma screens: Fox, CNN, NBC. All reporting on the blast near Georgetown.

"So everything is fine," Painter said, standing behind his desk. He held the earpiece more firmly in place. Lisa's voice was faint, traveling from halfway around the world. "You scared Jennings in R and D. He was just about ready to have the island firebombed."

"Sorry for the false alarm," Lisa said. "It was nothing more than laboratory contamination. Everything is fine here . . . or at least as fine as a shipload of burned patients might be. The initial conjecture is a bloom of something called fireweed. It's been plaguing these waters for years, spews off a corrosive pall, clearing beaches. This was just a perfect storm of the weed. The matter should be resolved in the next day or so, then Monk and I will head back."

"That's the first bit of good news I've heard all day," Painter replied.

His eyes kept flickering back to the plasma screens on his walls. They showed the fires being finally put out in the woods behind the safe house. Fire trucks arced water from engines parked along the forest's fire road.

Lisa whispered in his ear. "I know you're busy. I'll report in again in another twelve hours as scheduled."

"Great. You get some sleep. I imagine the sunsets out there must be beautiful."

"They are. I . . . I wish you were here to enjoy them with me."

"Me, too. But it won't be much longer until you're back. And right now I have a fire of my own to put out."

On the screen a news helicopter swung away to reveal the charred remains of the safe house for the morning news. He had already heard the report from the arson investigators. Tire tracks in the backyard had led to the discovery of an abandoned Thunderbird, the same convertible in which Gray had arrived on the scene a couple hours ago. It seemed he had not fled to the streets, but into the woods. But where did he go after that? There had still been no sign of Gray, his parents, or the wounded Guild operative.

Where had they gone into hiding?

"I have work here, too," Lisa said.

"Is there anything you need?"

"No . . ."

He heard a hesitation in her voice. "Lisa? What is it?"

"Nothing." She snapped a bit. "I guess I'm just tired. You know how I get this time of the month."

His aide Brant wheeled into the office with a sheaf of faxes in hand. He noted the letterhead on the top. Washington PD. It was another of the progress reports of their canvass of the local hospitals. He spoke as he accepted the papers from Brant.

"Then make sure you get some rest," he said, already reading the first line on the report. "You just stay safe and don't forget the sunblock. I can't have you making me look like some ghost next to your island tan."

"Will do." Lisa's voice had faded to the barest whisper. The ship's satellite connection was spotty. Still, he heard the disappointment in her voice. He missed her, too.

"I'll see you soon," he finished. "Talk to you in another half day. Now go get some sleep."

The line died without further word. He removed the earpiece and settled to his desk. Prioritizing, he shifted the pile of reports in front of him. He would scan them, then pass on the all clear to Jennings.

At least, one catastrophe had been put to bed.

6:13 P.M.
At sea

LISA LOWERED THE telephone handset. Her heart thudded heavily in her chest. The line had been cut off at a signal from Devesh Patanjali. He stood in the doorway to the ship's state-of-the-art communication shack, bracing both palms on his cane.

He shook his head, displaying his disappointment.

Lisa's stomach churned uneasily. Did he know what she had attempted? She rose from her seat beside the radioman. One of the guards grabbed her elbow.

"All you had to do was stick to the script, Dr. Cummings," Devesh said, his voice thick with exasperation. "It was a simple request, and the consequences were duly explained to you."

Panic iced Lisa's blood. "I . . . I followed your script. I didn't say anything out of turn. Painter thinks everything is fine. Just like you ordered."

"Yes. Lucky for that. But don't think your attempt at subtle communication, a hidden context, escaped me."

Oh God . . . She had taken a chance during the phone conversation. Surely he couldn't know. "I don't understand—"

" 'You know how I get this time of the month,' " Devesh quoted her, cutting her off. He turned and headed out the door to the hallway. "In fact, you finished your cycle ten days ago, Dr. Cummings."

An icy numbness spread through her.

"We have a full dossier on you, Dr. Cummings. Which I've read. And my memory is eidetic. Photographic. I encourage you not to underestimate my resources again."

The guard manhandled her out of the room. She stumbled along.

She had been a fool to try to secretly communicate with Painter, no matter how subtly.

What have I done?

Out in the passageway, other key captives stood lined up in the hall: Dr. Lindholm, Ryder Blunt, and an Aussie captain in a bloody khaki uniform. All of them had called their respective agencies, reporting all was well and under control at the remote island, whitewashing the scenario, buying the hijackers time to add distance between ship and island before anyone grew wiser.

But there were also others gathered in the hall. Four children cowered at the back of the passageway. Boys and girls. Ages six to ten. One for each of those sent into the radio room. Each child's life was balanced upon their cooperation. Lisa had been assigned a little girl, eight years old, with large almond eyes, terrified, huddled on the floor, hugging her knees to her chest. Her brother, a couple years older, kept an arm around her.

The Maori leader stepped over to the child, pistol in hand.

Devesh joined him and faced back to the group, a fist resting on his hip. "You were all warned if you strayed from the script in any significant regard, attempted any subterfuge, there would be consequences. But as this is Dr. Cummings's first mistake, I'll be lenient with her."

"Please," Lisa begged. She could not bear the child's blood on her hands. In the radio room, she had reacted instinctively. It had been a stupid ploy.

Devesh's gaze settled to her. "Instead of the little girl, Dr. Cummings, I'll let you choose another child to die in her place."

Lisa's breath caught in her chest.

"I'm not a cruel man, only practical. This is a lesson all of you must take to heart." He waved to Lisa. "Pick a child."

Lisa shook her head. "I can't . . ."

"Choose or I'll have them *all* shot. Let this be a lesson to everyone. We have too much to accomplish to tolerate insubordination, no matter how slight."

The guard dragged her forward at a signal from his tattooed leader.

"Choose a child, Dr. Cummings."

Lisa bit back a sob, staring at the four children's faces. None spoke English, but they must have read something in her face, understood her agony, and it scared them. Fresh tears flowed. They all hunched tighter.

Lisa caught Devesh's eyes, pleading with him. "Please, Dr. Patanjali. It was my mistake. Punish me."

"I believe that is exactly what I'm doing." He stared back at her, unmoved. "Now pick."

Lisa stared across the four faces. She could not pick the little girl, or her brother. She had no choice. She lifted a trembling arm and pointed a finger to another of the boys, the oldest of the group at ten years of age.

May God forgive me.

"Very good. Rakao, you know your duty."

The Maori gunman stepped over to the boy, whose frightened face lifted hopefully.

A moan escaped Lisa. She took a step forward, trying to retract her decision. The guard tightened his grip on her elbow. Restrained, her legs trembled—then she was on her knees, boneless with terror and grief.

The gunman lifted his pistol and pointed it at the boy's head.

"No . . ." Lisa gasped.

He pulled the trigger—but there was no blast of fire. The gun's hammer clicked sharply in the confined space, snapping on an empty cylinder.

Rakao lowered his weapon.

In the silence a gurgling cry erupted from the other side of the hall. Lisa turned in time to watch Dr. Lindholm sink to his knees, matching Lisa's posture. He met her gaze, eyes wide with shock and pain. His hands clutched his throat. Blood poured between his fingers.

Behind his shoulder, Devesh's companion, the woman Surina, stepped back, her head bowed down as if she had just served tea and was now exiting. Her hands were empty, but Lisa had no doubt the woman had slashed the doctor's throat, her dagger vanishing away as quickly as it had struck.

Lindholm slumped and fell to his chest on the carpeted floor. Blood soaked into the plush weave and overspilled into a growing pool. One hand twitched on the carpet, then stopped.

"Motherfucker . . ." Ryder growled, his face stony, turning away.

Devesh stepped back to Lisa.

"Wh-why?" she managed to force out, heartsick and cold.

"Like I said, nothing escapes our notice, Dr. Cummings. Including Dr. Lindholm's skill. Or rather *lack* thereof when it comes to research and fieldwork. He served his purpose in keeping the WHO off our backs with his call, but beyond that, he is more a liability than an asset. His death at least served one last function. A demonstration. Not only to show the cost of insubordination." Devesh fixed her with a hard stare. "Can I assume you've learned that cost, Dr. Cummings?"

She slowly nodded, staring at the pool of blood.

"Very good." He faced the others. "The death also demonstrates a lesson to everyone. Of the seriousness of our venture here. Your lives depend upon your usefulness. It is that simple. Perform or die. I encourage you to pass on this lesson to your other colleagues before further demonstrations prove necessary."

Devesh clapped his hands together. "Now, with that little bit of unpleasantness over, we can begin our work." He motioned to the Maori leader. "Rakao, please guide everyone to their respective posts. I'll escort Dr. Cummings personally to her patient."

Holstering his pistol, Rakao dispersed his men. Devesh led Lisa down the hall, away from everyone else. She passed the line of children. Shell-shocked, they were being gathered for a return to the ship's day care.

Surina, trailing Lisa and Devesh, paused by the little brother and sister. She bent to the girl, still cowering under her brother's arm. Surina held out an empty palm; then with a flicker of fingers, a small wrapped sweet appeared in her hand, as if out of the air. She offered it to the terrified girl, but the child only pulled tighter against her older sibling. Her brother, more practical, reached out and snatched the candy from Surina's palm, as if grabbing it out of a baited mousetrap.

Surina straightened in a smooth flow of embroidered silk, lightly brushing her fingers along the girl's cheek as she rose. Her fingertips came away damp with the child's tears. Lisa wondered if it was the same hand that had slashed Lindholm's throat. The woman's face remained perfectly still.

Lisa turned away, following Devesh.

He took her down to the very last cabin on this level and keyed his way inside. Another suite. A massive amount of equipment was being assembled in the outer room. Ignoring it all, Devesh crossed to the adjoining bedroom.

Lisa kept near him.

As Devesh passed inside, Lisa spotted a familiar figure sprawled atop the room's bed, draped in an isolation tent: a woman, tangled amid monitoring equipment, her blond hair a match to Lisa's own, but shaved to a close crop. Lisa had spotted the gurney used to transport the patient here out in the main room. It was the woman taken off the helicopter. Her features were still obscured behind an oxygen mask that covered her full face.

Two men, the same orderlies who had transported the patient down here, were busy hooking and securing the final leads and lines that ran from the woman to a neighboring bank of monitoring equipment. Lisa took it all in with a glance: electroencephalogram, EKG, Doppler blood pressure monitor. A central lead was already established in the patient's chest, tied to an intravenous drip. One of the men straightened the drape of a urinary catheter.

Devesh lifted a hand toward the figure in the bed. "May I introduce you to Dr. Susan Tunis, a marine biologist out of Queensland. One of the first people to encounter the toxic bloom of cyanobacteria. I believe you have met another of her party already. The John Doe down in the isolation ward."

Lisa remained near the door, unsure why she was brought here, still numb from the casual slaughter of Dr. Lindholm. Even if this was one of the first victims, what did it have to do with her? She was not a virologist or a bacteriologist.

"I don't understand," she said, voicing her confusion. "There are more qualified medical doctors aboard the ship."

Devesh waved away her statement. "We have technicians to meet her medical needs."

Lisa frowned. "Then why—?"

"Dr. Cummings, you're a proficient physiologist. With significant field research experience. But more importantly, you've proven yourself quite resourceful in your service to Sigma in the past. We'll need that innovation and experience here. To assist me personally. With this one case."

"Why her? Why this case?"

"Because this one patient holds the key to everything."

Devesh stared down at the woman. His eyes narrowed with worry for the first time. "She holds a riddle, one that extends deep into the historical past, back to Marco Polo and his trips through these waters . . . and into a larger mystery."

"Marco Polo? The explorer?"

Devesh waved a hand. "Like I said earlier, that's a trail we are leaving to another arm of the Guild." He nodded to the woman. "All our efforts here, all the research aboard the ship, all the sacrifices to come, center on this one woman."

"I still don't understand. What's so important about her?"

Devesh's voice lowered. "This woman . . . she's changing. Like the bacteria. The Judas Strain is growing inside her."

"But I thought you said the virus doesn't infect human cells."

"It doesn't. It's doing something else inside her."

"What?"

Devesh faced Lisa. "It's incubating."

INCUBATION

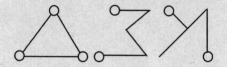

7

Of a Journey Untold

JULY 6, 6:41 A.M.
Istanbul

IN LESS THAN A DAY Gray had escaped halfway around the globe—and landed in another world. From the minarets of Istanbul's countless mosques, muezzin called the Islamic faithful to morning prayer. Sunrise cast long shadows and ignited the city's domes and spires.

Gray had a bird's-eye view from the rooftop restaurant where he waited with Seichan and Kowalski. No one looked happy. They were jet-lagged and on edge. But the dull ache behind Gray's eyes had more to do with his own concerns. Pursued by assassins, hunted by his own government, he had begun to doubt the wisdom of this current partnership.

And now this strange summons to Istanbul. Why? It made no sense. But at least for once, Seichan seemed equally baffled. She dripped honey into a tiny gold-rimmed cup of Turkish tea. The tea waiter, dressed in a traditional blue-and-gold embroidered vest, offered a refill to Gray.

He shook his head, already buzzing from the caffeine.

The waiter did not bother with Kowalski. The large man—dressed in a pair of jeans, black T-shirt, and long gray duster—had skipped the tea and gone straight for dessert. He nursed a chilled glass of grape brandy, called *raki*. "Tastes like licorice and asphalt," he had commented with a curl of his lip, but it did not keep him from consuming two glasses. He had also discovered the buffet table, buttering up a pile of bread, stacking on olives, cucumbers, cheese, and a half-dozen hard-boiled eggs.

Gray had no appetite. He was too full of worries, too full of questions.

He stood up and crossed to the half wall that encircled the rooftop terrace, careful to stay in the shadow of a table's umbrella. Istanbul, a terrorist hot spot, was under constant satellite surveillance. Gray wondered if his features were already being run through a facial-recognition program in some intelligence agency.

Was Sigma or the Guild closing in even now?

Seichan joined him, resting her teacup on the tiled ledge. She had slept the entire flight here, reclined in first class. With the rest, her color had much improved, though she still walked with a limp, favoring her wounded side. Aboard the jet, she had changed into a looser outfit, donning khaki pants and a billowing midnight-blue blouse, but she'd kept her black Versace motorcycle boots.

"Why do you think Monsignor Verona called us all the way here?" she asked. "To Istanbul."

Turning, Gray leaned a hip on the wall. "What? So we're talking now?"

Her eyes rolled ever so slightly, exasperated. Since they had left the doctor's office back in Georgetown, Seichan had refused any further explanations. Not that they'd had much time. On the run, Seichan had stopped only long enough to make one call. To the Vatican. Gray had listened in on the conversation. It seemed Vigor had been expecting her call and was not at all surprised to find Gray with her.

"Word has spread," the monsignor had explained. "Interpol, Europol, everyone is searching for you. I assume it was you, Seichan, who left me that little message in the Tower of Winds."

"You found the inscription."

"I did."

"You recognized the writing."

"Of course."

Seichan had sounded relieved. "Then we don't have much time. Many lives are in jeopardy. If you could gather your resources, figure out what—"

"I know what the inscription means, Seichan," Vigor had scolded, cutting her off. "And I know what it implies. If you want to know more, you'll both meet me at Hotel Ararat in Istanbul. I'll be there seven in the morning. At the rooftop restaurant."

After the call, Seichan had hurriedly arranged false papers and coordinated their transportation. She had assured him the Guild knew nothing of her contacts. "Just favors owed," she had explained.

Seichan twisted with a wince to face him, drawing him back to the present. Her elbow bumped her cup of tea. Gray caught it before it went tumbling to the street below. She stared at the jostled cup with the slightest pinch of concern at the corner of her eyes. Gray suspected such carelessness was rare for this woman, someone always in control.

Just as quickly, her expression hardened again.

"I know I've kept you in the dark," she said. "Once Monsignor Verona arrives, I will explain everything." She nodded toward him. "But what about you? Did you make any headway with the obelisk's writing?"

He merely shrugged, letting her think he knew something.

She stared—then sighed. "Fine."

She returned to their table.

Seichan had supplied Gray with photographs and a printed copy of the angelic script. En route here, he had attempted to break whatever code was locked within the script, but there were too many variables. He needed more information. And besides, Gray suspected he already knew the message of the code: *break open the obelisk and find the treasure inside.*

They'd already done that.

Gray wore the silver crucifix on a cord around his neck.

He had already examined it. It was definitely old, well worn. Even under a magnifying lens, he could discern no writing, no clues of any significance that would confirm Seichan's wild claim that the cross once belonged to the confessor of Marco Polo, the world traveler and explorer.

Alone at the railing, Gray studied the city, already bustling in the early morning. Below, buses competed with cars and pedestrians. The bleat of horns attempted to drown out the sharper cries of hawkers and the continual babble of early-morning tourists.

He searched the immediate vicinity, watching for any sign of threat or suspicious approach. Had they shaken Nasser? Having put half the world between them, Seichan seemed confident. But Gray refused to let his guard down. Below, in the hotel's courtyard, a pair of men rose from beaded blankets, finished with their morning prayers, and vanished back into the hotel. Alone now, a child splashed absently in the lobby fountain.

Satisfied, Gray allowed his gaze to shift momentarily higher. Hotel Ararat stood in the heart of Istanbul's oldest district, the Sultanahmet. All the way to the sea, ancient structures rose like islands from the muddle of the lower streets. Right across from the hotel, the lofty domes of the Blue Mosque climbed into the sky. Farther down the street, a massive Byzantine church stood half swallowed by black scaffolding, as if the ironwork sought to clutch the structure to the earth's bosom. And beyond the scaffolding, the Topkapi Palace sprawled amid courtyards and gardens.

Gray felt the weight of ages in these grand architectural masterpieces, stone monuments of history. His fingers absently fingered the cross around his neck. Here was another piece of antiquity, its provenance ripe with historical significance. But what did it have to do with Seichan's global threat? A cross that once belonged to Marco Polo's priest?

"Hey, Ali Baba," Kowalski called out behind him. "One more of these licorice drinks."

Gray bit back a groan.

"It is called *raki*," a new voice corrected, full of professorial authority.

Gray turned. A familiar and welcome figure stepped from the shadowed stairway onto the rooftop terrace. Monsignor Vigor Verona spoke in Turkish to the tea waiter, polite, apologetic. *"Bir sise raki lütfen."*

The waiter nodded with a smile and stepped away.

Vigor approached their table. Gray noted the lack of Roman collar around the man's neck. Plainly the monsignor was traveling incognito. Free of the collar, Vigor appeared a decade younger than his sixty years. Or maybe it was the casual manner of his dress: blue denim jeans, hiking boots, and a black shirt with the sleeves rolled up. He also carried a weathered backpack over one shoulder. He looked ready to scale the mountain for which Hotel Ararat was named, off on a search for Noah's Ark.

And perhaps once upon a time, the monsignor had made that very trek.

Before rising to prefect of the Vatican's archives, Vigor had served the Holy See as a biblical archaeologist. Such a position had also allowed him to serve the Vatican in one other manner. As spy. Vigor's cover as an archaeologist had permitted him to travel broadly and deeply, perfect for filtering intelligence and information back to the Holy See.

Vigor had also helped Sigma in the past.

And it seemed his expertise was needed once again.

Vigor settled to the seat with a long sigh. The tea waiter returned and settled a steaming cup of tea in front of their new arrival.

"Teşekkürler," Vigor said, thanking the man.

Kowalski shifted straighter as the waiter departed, staring between his empty glass and the back of the man's embroidered vest. He slumped, swearing softly under his breath about the poor service.

"Commander Pierce. Seichan," Vigor began. "Thank you for honoring my request. And Seaman Joe Kowalski. Wonderful to make your acquaintance."

A few other pleasantries were passed around. Vigor haltingly mentioned his niece Rachel. It was an awkward subject. Rachel and Gray's breakup had been a mutual understanding, but Vigor was still very protective of his niece. Not that she needed it. It seemed Rachel was faring well as a lieutenant with the Italian carabinieri, even gaining a pay grade.

Still, Gray was happy when Seichan interrupted. "Monsignor Verona, why did you summon us all the way to Istanbul?"

Vigor silenced her with a raised palm, sipped from his tea, then lowered his cup precisely to the tabletop. "Yes, we'll get to that. But before that, I want two things settled at the start. First, wherever this leads, I'm coming with you." He pinned Gray with a firm, unwavering stare—then swung his sights on Seichan. "Second, but no less important, I want to know what all this has to do with our illustrious Venetian explorer Marco Polo."

Seichan started. "How did you . . . I never mentioned anything about Marco Polo?"

Before Vigor could respond, the waiter returned. Kowalski glanced up, hope in his eyes. Those same eyes widened further when the waiter produced a full bottle of *raki* and propped it in front of the former seaman.

"I ordered you a half liter," Vigor explained.

Kowalski reached over and squeezed Vigor's arm. "Padre, you're all right in my book."

Gray turned his attention to Seichan. "So what does all this have to do with Marco Polo?"

MIDNIGHT
Washington, D.C.

THE BLACK BMW sedan turned off Dupont Circle and glided through the darker streets. Its xenon headlights carved a bluish path down the elm-lined avenue. Rows of apartment buildings framed the street, creating an urban canyon.

It was nothing like the canyons of Nasser's own land, where only goats roamed and caves and tunnels served as homesteads for the wandering Afghani tribes. Yet even that land was not truly his home. His father had left Cairo when Nasser was eight years old, off to Afghanistan after its liberation from Russian forces, to join those who sought a purer Islam. Nasser's younger brother and sister had been dragged there, too. They'd had no choice. On the eve of their departure, his father had strangled his mother, using Nasser's own school scarf. His mother had not wanted to leave Egypt, to vanish forever beneath a burka. She had talked, complained in the wrong ears.

The children had been forced to watch, kneeling in obeisance, as their mother's eyes bulged, tongue swollen, punished by their father's hand.

It was a lesson Nasser learned well.

To be cold. In all ways.

The xenon lamps swept around a corner. From the passenger seat, Nasser motioned to the middle of the block. "Stop there."

The driver, his broken nose bandaged after the failed kidnapping, slid the sedan to the curb. Nasser twisted around to face the rear seat. Two figures huddled close together.

Annishen, dressed all in shades of black, almost faded into the leather furniture. She even wore a hood over her shaved scalp, giving her a monkish appearance. Her eyes shone brightly out of the darkness. She had one arm around her companion, leaning close, intimate.

He still mewled around the gag. Blood blackened one side of his face and throat. In his bound hands, clutched between his knees, he still held his own right ear. Nasser had discovered the man's name in a Rolodex.

A doctor.

"Is this the place?" Nasser asked.

The man nodded vigorously, squeezing his eyes shut after verifying the address.

Nasser studied the building's lobby. A night watchman

was stationed behind a desk inside. A security camera protruded above the bulletproof glass doors. Full security. Nasser rubbed his thumb along the edge of the electronic key in his hand, a gift courtesy of their passenger.

After a full day, Nasser was finally back on the trail of the American and the Guild traitor. Last night, he had searched the small home in the Takoma Park neighborhood. He had discovered Seichan's damaged motorcycle in its garage, but little else. There had been no sign of the obelisk, except for a broken fragment of Egyptian marble in the driveway.

But inside the house, Allah had smiled upon him.

Nasser had discovered a Rolodex.

With several doctors' names.

It had taken the rest of the day to find the right one.

He turned around again.

"Thank you, Dr. Corrin. You've provided the leverage I'll need."

Nasser had no need to nod to Annishen. Her blade slipped between the man's ribs and opened his heart. It was a Mossad technique that Nasser had taught Annishen. He had employed it himself only once before.

As his father knelt in prayer.

Not a child's vengeance. Only justice.

Nasser shoved open the door to the sedan. He owed his father—if only for the lesson taught to an eight-year-old boy, kneeling before his strangled mother.

Such a lesson would serve him again this night.

To be cold. In all ways.

Exiting the car, Nasser crossed and opened the rear door. Annishen unfolded out of the backseat, rising with a rustle of black leather, resplendent in an Italian-designed calfskin jacket and a dark suede outfit, a match to his Armani suit. There was not a drop of blood on her, proving again the artistry of her craft. He slipped his arm around her and closed the door.

She leaned against him. "The night is just beginning," she whispered with a contented sigh.

He pulled her closer. Just two lovers returning from a late dinner.

The summer night was still muggy, but the apartment lobby was air-conditioned. The doors sighed open to greet them with a swipe of Dr. Corrin's key card. The guard glanced up from his desk.

Nasser nodded to him, striding toward the neighboring elevator bank. Annishen offered a tinkling giggle, purring up against Nasser's side, plainly anxious to get to their apartment. Her hand sidled to the holstered Glock at his waist.

Just in case . . .

But the guard merely nodded back, mumbled a "good evening," and returned his attention to the magazine he was reading.

Nasser shook his head as he reached the elevator bank. Typical. What passed for security here in America was more show than substance.

He called the elevator with a press of a button.

Shortly thereafter, Nasser and Annishen stood before apartment 512. He swiped the same key card across the door lock. The indicator light changed from red to green.

He glanced to Annishen. He read the dance in her eyes, stirred from the earlier bloodshed.

"We need at least one of them alive," he warned.

She feigned a pout and drew her weapon.

Using one finger, Nasser pushed the door handle down. He edged the way open on well-oiled hinges. Not even a creak. He entered first, slipping into the marble foyer. A light flowed from a bedroom in back.

Nasser paused just inside the door.

One eye narrowed.

There was something too still about the air. Too quiet. He needed to go no farther. He held his breath. He knew the apartment was empty.

Still, he waved Annishen to one side. He took the other. In moments, they swept the apartment's rooms, checking even closets.

No one was here.

Annishen stood in the master bedroom. The bed was made and looked untouched. "The doctor lied to us," she said with clear irritation and a moderate note of respect. "They're not here."

Nasser was in the master bathroom. Down on one knee. He had spotted something on the floor, rolled under the edge of the bathroom's cherry vanity.

He picked it up.

A red prescription bottle. Empty.

He read the label. The patient. Jackson Pierce.

"They were here," he muttered hard, and straightened up.

Dr. Corrin had not lied. He had told them the truth—or at least, what he thought was the truth.

"They've moved on," Nasser said, and strode back to the bedroom.

He clenched the empty pill bottle in his fist, swallowing his fury. Commander Pierce had tricked him yet again. First with the obelisk, now with this shuffle of his parents.

"What now?" Annishen asked.

He lifted the pill bottle.

One last chance.

7:30 A.M.
Istanbul

"To begin," Seichan said, "what do you know about Marco Polo?"

She had donned a set of blue-tinted sunglasses. The sun had risen enough that the rooftop restaurant was a mix of shadows and glaring brightness. They had moved to a secluded corner table, sheltered under an umbrella.

Gray heard the clear hesitation in her voice—and maybe a trace of relief. Her will teetered between a wary desire to control the flow of knowledge and a compulsion to release the burden of its weight.

"Polo was a thirteenth-century explorer," Gray answered. He had read up a bit on the man on the journey here. "Along with his father and uncle, Marco spent two decades in China as honored guests of the Mongol emperor Kublai Khan. And after returning to Italy in 1295, Marco narrated his travels to a French writer named Rustichello, who wrote it all down."

Marco's book, *The Description of the World,* became an instant hit in Europe, sweeping the continent with its fantastic tales: of vast and lonely deserts in Persia, of China's teeming cities, of far-off lands populated by naked idolaters and sorcerers, of islands fraught with cannibals and strange beasts. The book ignited the imagination of Europe. Even Christopher Columbus carried a copy on his voyage to the New World.

"But what does any of this have to do with what's going on today?" Gray finished.

"Everything," Seichan answered, glancing around the table.

Vigor sipped his tea. Kowalski leaned his ear on a fist propped up by an elbow. While the man looked bored, Gray noted how his eyes clocked around, studying them all, tracking the interplay. Gray suspected there were depths to the man as yet unplumbed. Kowalski absently fed crumbs of tea cakes to scrabbling sparrows.

Seichan continued, "Marco Polo's tales were not as clearcut as most people believe. No original text exists of Marco Polo's book, only copies of copies. And in any such translations and reeditions, marked differences have cropped up."

"Yes, I read about that," Gray said, trying to hurry her along. "So many disparities that some now wonder if Marco Polo ever really existed. Or if he was merely a fabrication of the French writer."

"He existed," Seichan insisted.

Vigor nodded his head in agreement. "I've heard the case against Marco Polo. Of the significant gaps in his descriptions of China." The monsignor lifted his cup. "Like the Far East's passion for drinking tea. A concoction unknown to

Europeans at the time. Or the practice of foot binding or the use of chopsticks. Marco fails to even mention the Great Wall. Plainly these are glaring and suspicious omissions. Yet Marco also got many things right: the peculiar manufacture of porcelain, the burning of coal, even the first use of paper money."

Gray heard the certainty in the monsignor's voice. Maybe it was just Vigor's Italian pride, but Gray sensed a deeper confidence.

"Either way," Gray finally conceded, "what does this have to do with us?"

"Because there was another serious omission in all the editions of Polo's book," Seichan said. "It concerns Marco's return trip to Italy. Kublai Khan conscripted the Polos to escort a Mongol princess named Kokejin to her betrothed in Persia. For such a grand undertaking, the Khan supplied the group with fourteen giant galleys and over six hundred men. Yet when they reached port in Persia, only *two* ships had survived the journey and only *eighteen* men."

"What happened to the rest?" Kowalski mumbled.

"Marco Polo never told. The French writer Rustichello hints at something in the preface to the famous book, a tragedy among the islands of Southeast Asia. But it was never written. Even on his deathbed, Marco Polo refused to tell of what happened."

"And this is true?" Gray asked.

"It is a mystery that was never solved," Vigor answered. "Most historians guessed disease or piracy beset the fleet. All that is known for certain is that Marco's ships drifted among the Indonesian islands for five months, only escaping with a fraction of the Khan's fleet intact."

"So," Seichan asked, pressing the significance, "why would such a dramatic part of his journey be left out of Marco's book? Why did he take it to his grave?"

Gray had no answer. But the mystery stirred a nagging worry. He sat a bit straighter. In his head, he began to get an inkling of where this might be leading.

Vigor's countenance had also grown more shadowed. "You know what happened among those islands, don't you?"

She dipped her head in acknowledgment. "The first edition of Marco Polo's book was written in French. But there was a movement during Marco's lifetime: to reproduce books in the Italian dialect. It was driven by a famous contemporary of Marco Polo."

"Dante Alighieri," Vigor said.

Gray glanced to the monsignor.

Vigor explained, "Dante's *Divine Comedy,* including the famous *Inferno,* were the first books written in Italian. Even the French came to nickname the Italian language *la langue de Dante.*"

Seichan nodded. "And such a revolution did not pass by Marco. According to historical records, he translated a French copy of his book into his native language. For his countrymen to appreciate. But in the process, he made one secret copy for himself. In that one book, he finally related what befell the Khan's fleet. Wrote that last story."

"Impossible," Vigor mumbled. "How would such a book have remained hidden for so long? Where has it been?"

"At first, at the Polos' family estate. Then eventually in a place more secure." Seichan stared at Vigor.

"You can't mean—"

"The Polos were sent abroad by order of Pope Gregory. There are some who claim that Marco's father and uncle were the first Vatican spies, sent as double agents into China to scout the strength of the Mongol forces. The veritable founders of the agency you once served, Monsignor Verona."

Vigor sank back into his seat, retreating into his own thoughts. "The secret diary was hidden in the archives," he mumbled.

"Buried away, unregistered. Just another edition of Marco's book to all outside eyes. It would take a thorough reading to realize that there was an extra chapter woven near the end of the book."

"And the Guild got ahold of this edition?" Gray asked. "Learned something important."

Seichan nodded.

Gray frowned. "But how did the Guild get their hands on this secret text in the first place?"

Taking off her sunglasses, Seichan stared him full in the face, accusing, angry.

"You gave it to them, Gray."

7:18 A.M.

VIGOR READ THE shock in the commander's face.

"What the hell are you talking about?" Gray asked.

Vigor also noted the steel flash of satisfaction in the emerald eyes of the Guild assassin. She seemed to gain a measure of enjoyment in taunting them. Still, he also noted the thinness of her face, the bit of pallor to her cheeks. She was scared.

"We're all to blame," Seichan said, nodding also to Vigor.

Vigor kept his reaction placid, not playing this game. He was too old for his blood to be so easily stirred. Besides, he already understood.

"The Dragon Court's symbol," Vigor said. "You painted it on the floor. I thought it was meant as a warning to me, a call to investigate the angelic inscription."

Seichan nodded, leaning back. She read the understanding in his eyes.

"But it was more," he continued. He remembered the man who formerly filled his seat at the Vatican Archives: Dr. Alberto Menardi, a traitor who secretly worked for the Royal Dragon Court. The man had pilfered many key texts from the archives during his tenure, stole them away to a private library in a castle in Switzerland. Gray, Seichan, and Vigor had been instrumental in exposing the man, destroying the sect of the Dragon Court. The castle ended up being bequeathed to the Verona household, a cursed estate with a long bloody history.

"Alberto's library," Vigor said. "At the castle. After all the bloodshed and horror, once the police allowed us on-site, we discovered the entire library gone. Vanished away."

"Why wasn't I told about this?" Gray asked, surprised.

Vigor sighed. "We supposed it was local thieves . . . or possibly some corruption among the Italian police. There had been many priceless antiquities in the traitor's library. And because of Alberto's interest, there were many books of arcane knowledge."

As much as Vigor despised the former prefect, he also recognized Alberto Menardi's brilliance, a genius in his own right. And as prefect of the archives for over thirty years, Alberto knew all its secrets. He would have treasured and been intrigued by such a discovery, an edition of Marco's *The Description of the World* with a hidden extra chapter.

But what had the old prefect read? What made him steal it away? What had piqued the interest and attention of the Guild?

Vigor stared at Seichan. "But it wasn't ordinary thieves who cleared out the library, was it? *You* told the Guild about the treasures to be found there."

Seichan did not even have the temerity to flinch at his accusation. "I had no choice. Two years ago, the library bought me my life after I helped the two of you. I had no idea what horror it hid."

Gray had remained silent during their exchange, watching, eyes narrowed. Vigor could almost see the gears turning, tumblers falling into new slots. Like Alberto, Gray had a unique mind, a way of juggling disparate fragments and discovering a new configuration. It was no wonder Seichan had sought him out.

Gray nodded to her. "You read this text, Seichan. The true account of the return voyage of Marco Polo."

As answer, she shoved her chair back, leaned down, and

unzippered her left boot. She removed a sheaf of three papers, folded and tucked into a hidden inner pocket. Straightening, she smoothed the papers open and slid them across the table.

"Once I began to suspect what the Guild intended," she said, "I made a copy of the translated chapter for myself."

Vigor and Gray shifted closer, shoulder to shoulder, to peruse the sheets together. The large seaman leaned over, too, his breath spiced with anise from the *raki*.

Vigor scanned the title and the first few lines.

CHAPTER LXII.

Of a Journey untold; and a Map forbidden

Now it came to pass, a full month beyond the last port, we sought to restore our waters from a fresh river and repair two ships. We ported in small boats, at which time the abundant bird and thickness of vine astounded. Salted meat and fruit were also depleted. We came with forty and two of the Great Kaan's men, armed with spear and arrow; and as nearby islands were populated by naked Idolaters who ate the flesh of other men, such protection of body was considered wise.

Vigor continued reading, recognizing the cadence and stiffly archaic prose from *The Description of the World*. Could these words truly be Marco Polo's? If so, here was a chapter only a few eyes had ever laid eyes upon. Vigor craved to read the original, not fully trusting the translation—but more importantly, he wanted to peruse the original dialect, to be that much closer to the famous medieval traveler.

He read on:

From a bend in the river, one of Kaan's men shouted and pointed to a steep rise of another peak from out of the valley floor. It lay a score of miles inland and deep within the thickness of the forest; but it was no mountain. It was the spire of a great building; and other towers were now spotted, half hid in mists. With ten days to idol in repairs and as the Kaan's men wished to hunt the many birds and beasts for fresh meat, we set off to seek these builders of mountains, a people unknown and unmapped.

After the first page Vigor sensed a palpable menace growing behind Marco's simple narrative. In plain words, he related how "the forest grew quiet of bird and beast." Marco and the hunters continued, following a trail far into the jungle, "trampled by these mountain builders."

At long last, as twilight neared, Marco's party came upon a stone city.

The forest opened upon a great city of many spires, each covered with the carved faces of Idols. What devilish sorcery were employed by such a people, I would never discover; but God in His merciful vengeance had smote this city and the forest proper with a great blight and pestilence. The first body was a naked child. Her flesh was boiled to bone and covered with large black ants. Everywhere one turned, the eye came upon another and another. A count of several hundred would not match the slaughter here; and the death was not constrained to the sin of man. Birds had fallen from the sky. Beasts of the forest lay in twisted piles. Great snakes hung dead from branches of trees.

It was a City of the Dead. Fearing pestilence, we sought to leave with much haste. But our passage was not unwatched. From the deeper forest, they came: their naked flesh was no more hale than those strewn across the stone steps and plazas, or floating in the green moats. Limbs were rotted to expose the flesh beneath. Others bore bubbling welts and boils that covered most their skin; and still more carried bellies

*heavy with bloat. All around, wounds wept and
steamed. Some came blind; and others scrabbled. It
was as if a thousand plagues had blighted this land; a
legion of pestilence.*

*From out the leafy bower, they swarmed with teeth
bared like wild animals. Others carried severed arms
and legs. God protect me even now, many of those
limbs were gnawed.*

A chill washed over Vigor, despite the growing heat of
the morning. He read with numbing horror as Marco described how his party fled deeper into the city to seek refuge
from the ravening army. The Venetian described in great detail the slaughter and cannibalism. As twilight fell, Marco's
party retreated to one of the tall buildings, carved with
twisting snakes and long-dead kings. The group set up a final stand, sure their small party would be overwhelmed as
more and more of the diseased cannibals entered the city.

Gray mumbled under his breath, no words audible, but
his disbelief was plain.

*Now as the sun sank, so did all our hopes. Each in his
own way cast prayers to the heavens. Kaan's men
burned bits of wood and smeared the ashes on their
faces. I had only my confessor. Friar Agreer knelt with
me and offered our souls to God through whispered
prayers. He clutched his crucifix and daubed my forehead with Christ's suffering cross. He used the same
ashes as the Kaan's men. I looked upon the other
men's marked faces and wondered: in such trial, were
we all the same? Pagan and Christian. And in the end,
whose prayer was it that was finally answered? Whose
prayer brought the Virtue against this pestilence into
our midst; a dark Virtue that saved us all.*

The story stopped there.
Gray flipped the paper over, looking for more.

Kowalski leaned back and made his only contribution to the historical discussion. "Not enough sex," he mumbled, and attempted to hold back a burp with a fist and failed.

Frowning, Gray tapped a name on the last page. "Here . . . this mention of Friar Agreer."

Vigor nodded, having spotted the same glaring error. Surely this text was false. "No clergymen accompanied the Polos to the Orient," he stated aloud. "According to Vatican texts, two Dominican friars left with the Polos, to represent the Holy See, but the pair turned back after the first few days."

Seichan collected the first page and refolded it. "Like this secret chapter, Marco edited the friar out of his chronicles. *Three* Dominicans actually left with the Polos. One for each traveler, as was custom for the time."

Vigor realized she was right. It was indeed the custom.

"Only *two* of the friars fled back," Seichan said. "The presence of the third was kept hidden . . . until now."

Gray shifted back and tugged at his neck. He pulled free a silver crucifix and placed it on the table. "And you claim this is actually Friar Agreer's cross? The one mentioned in the story."

Seichan's firm stare answered his question.

Shocked into silence at the sudden revelation, Vigor studied the crucifix. It was unadorned, with the barest representation of a crucified figure. Vigor could tell it was old. Could it be true? He gently collected it from the table and examined it. If true, its very weight gave substance to Marco's harrowing words.

Vigor finally found his voice. "But I don't understand. Why was Friar Agreer cut out of the story?"

Seichan reached over and collected the scattered papers. "We don't know," she said simply. "The remaining pages of the book were ripped out and replaced with a false page, stitched into the binding, but the quality and age of the new page dated it centuries later than the original binding."

Vigor frowned at such strangeness. "What was on the new page?"

"I was never able to see it myself, but I was told what it said. It contained a rambling rave, full of references to angels and biblical quotations. The writer clearly feared Marco's story. But more importantly, the page spoke at length of a map included in the book, one drawn by Marco himself. A map they deemed to be evil."

"So what happened to it?"

"Though they feared it, whoever edited the book also worried about destroying the map completely. So the writer, along with a handful of others, rewrote the map in a code that would protect and bless it."

Gray nodded his understanding. "So they buried it in angelic script."

"But who inserted the page?" Vigor asked.

Seichan shrugged. "It was unsigned, but there were enough references on the page to suggest that the Polos' descendants had handed Marco's secret book over to the papacy following the ravage of the Black Plague in the fourteenth century. Maybe the family feared the plague was the same pestilence that struck the City of the Dead, come at last to destroy the rest of the world. It was then the book was added to the archives."

"Interesting," Vigor said. "If you're right, it might explain why all trace of the Polo family vanished about then. Even Marco Polo's body vanished out of the Church of San Lorenzo, where he'd been buried. It was as if there was a systemic attempt to erase the Polo family. Did anyone ever date that rambling new page?"

Seichan nodded. "It was dated to the early sixteen-hundreds."

Vigor squinted his eyes. "Hmm . . . another great outbreak of bubonic plague swept Italy at about that time."

"Exactly," Seichan said. "And it was also at that time that a German named Johannes Trithemius first developed the angelic script. Despite his claim that it was a script from before man walked the earth."

Vigor nodded. He had performed his own historical study of angelic script. Its creator believed that by using his angelic alphabet—supposedly gained from deep meditative study—one could communicate with the heavenly choir of angels. Trithemius also dabbled in cryptography and secret codes. His famous treatise, *Stenographia,* was considered to be of occult nature, but it was actually a complex mix of angelology and code breaking.

"So if you wanted to hide a map during that time," Gray concluded, "one you deemed *evil,* then locking it up inside angelic script might seem a good way to ward against its dangers."

"That is exactly what the Guild came to believe. There were clues in that secret page as to the location of this coded map, a map now carved onto an Egyptian obelisk and hidden in the Gregorian Museum of the Vatican. But the obelisk had vanished, lost in time, shifted around. Nasser and I played a cat-and-mouse game searching for it. But I won. I stole it from under Nasser's nose."

Vigor heard the bitter pride in her voice, but he frowned and searched the others' faces. "What obelisk are you all talking about?"

7:42 A.M.

IN SKETCHY HIGHLIGHTS, Gray explained about the Egyptian obelisk that was used to hide the friar's cross and described the code painted in phosphorescent oils.

"Here is the actual text." Gray handed over his copy.

Vigor studied the complex jumble of angelic code and shook his head. "It makes no sense to me."

"Precisely," Seichan said. "The rambling letter in Marco's text also references a *key* to the map. A way to unlock its secret. A key hidden in three parts. The first key was tied to the inscription in the room where the secret text was originally hidden."

"In the Tower of Winds," Vigor said. "A good hiding place. The tower was under construction during that century. Built to house the Vatican Observatory."

"And according to the false page in Marco's book," Seichan continued, "each key would lead to the next. So to begin, we need to solve that first riddle. The angelic inscription in the Vatican." She turned fully to Vigor. "You claimed you'd succeeded. Is that true?"

Vigor opened his mouth to explain, but Gray placed a hand on his arm. He wasn't about to give Seichan all of their cards. He needed to hold at least one ace in the hole.

"Before that," Gray said, "you've still not said why the Guild is involved in all this. What gain is there in pursuing this historical trail from Marco Polo to the present?"

Seichan hesitated. She took a deep breath—whether to lie or steel herself for telling the truth, he wasn't sure. When she spoke, she confirmed Gray's own growing fears.

"Because we believe Marco's disease is loose again," she said. "Freed from some ancient timbers of Marco's original galleys found among the Indonesian islands. The Guild is already on-site, ready to follow the scientific trail. Nasser and I were assigned to follow the historical trail. As was custom for the Guild, the right arm was not supposed to know what the left one was doing."

Gray understood the cell-like compartmentalization of the Guild, a pattern taken to heart by many terrorist organizations.

"But I stole some information," she said. "I learned the nature of the disease, and its ability to alter the biosphere forever."

Seichan continued with the Guild's discovery of a virus— something called the Judas Strain—and its capability of turning all bacteria into killers.

She quoted from Marco's text. " 'A legion of pestilence.' That is what struck Indonesia. But I know the Guild. I know what they plan to do. By harvesting and harnessing this pathogen, they hope to create a slew of new bacterial bioweapons, an inexhaustible source born of this virus."

As Seichan related details about the disease, Gray had gripped the edge of the table. His knuckles ached. A greater terror had taken hold of him.

Before he could speak, Vigor cleared his throat. "But if the scientific arm of the Guild is pursuing this virus, what is so important about this historical hunt along Marco Polo's trail? What does it matter?"

Gray answered, quoting the last line of Marco's text. " 'A dark Virtue that saved us all.' That sounds like a cure to me."

Seichan nodded. "Marco survived to tell his story. Even the Guild wouldn't dare unleash such a virus without some means of controlling it."

"Or at least to discover its source," Gray added.

Vigor stared out toward the city, his face limned against the rising sun. "And there are other unanswered questions. What became of Father Agreer? What scared the papacy?"

But Gray had a more important question of his own. "Exactly where in Indonesia did this new outbreak happen?"

"At a remote island, luckily far from any large population."

"Christmas Island," Gray filled in.

Seichan's eyes widened in surprise.

Confirmation enough.

Gray shoved up. Everyone stared at him. Monk and Lisa had gone out to Christmas Island to investigate the same disease. They had no idea what they were about to confront— or of the Guild's interest. Gray's breathing grew heavier. He had to get word to Painter. But with Sigma compromised, would his alarm put his friends in more danger, paint a bull's-eye on them?

He needed more information. "How far along is this Guild operation in Indonesia?"

"I don't know. It was difficult learning what I did."

"Seichan," Gray growled at her.

Her eyes narrowed with concern. In his agitation, he almost believed it was genuine. "I . . . I truly don't know, Gray. Why? What's wrong?"

With a hard exhalation, Gray crossed to the railing, needing an extra second to think, to let everything he'd learned settle through him.

For the moment, he knew only one thing for certain.

He needed to get word to Washington.

1:04 A.M.
Washington, D.C.

HARRIET PIERCE STRUGGLED to calm her husband. It was especially difficult as he'd locked himself in the hotel bathroom. She pressed a cold damp rag to her split lip.

"Jack! Open the door!"

He had woken two hours ago, confused and disoriented. She had seen it before. Sundowner's syndrome. Common with Alzheimer's patients. A condition of heightened agitation after sunset, when the familiar surroundings become confusing in the dark.

And it was worse here. Away from home.

It didn't help that the Phoenix Park Hotel was their second accommodation in less than twenty-four hours. First, Dr. Corrin's apartment, and now here. But Gray had been firm when he whispered his good-byes and added a private instruction to her. Once Dr. Corrin left them at the apartment, she had been told to leave, cross the city, and check into another hotel, paying cash, using a false name.

An extra precaution.

But all the moving had only worsened Jack's status. He had been off his Tegetrol mood stabilizer for a full day. And he had finished the last of his Propranolol, a blood pressure medication that reduced anxiety.

So it was no surprise that Jack had woken earlier in a panic, disoriented. The worst she had seen in months.

His shouts and heavy-footed blundering had woken her. She had inadvertently fallen asleep, seated in a chair in front of the hotel room's small television. The channel had been tuned to Fox News. She had the volume on low, just loud enough to hear if Gray's name was mentioned again.

Startled awake by her husband's shout, she had hurried to the bedroom. A foolish mistake. One didn't surprise a patient in his state. Jack had slapped her away, striking her in the mouth. With his blood up, it took him a full half minute to recognize her.

When he finally did, he had retreated to the bathroom. She'd heard his sobbing. It was the reason he had locked the door.

Pierce men didn't cry.

"Jack, open the door. It's okay. I've called a prescription into the pharmacy down the street. It's all right."

Harriet knew it was a risk, calling in the prescription. But she couldn't take Jack to a hospital, and if untreated, his dementia would only grow worse. And his shouting threatened to draw the wrath of the hotel's management. What if they called the police?

With no choice, her teeth aching from the blow, she had made a decision. Using the phone book, she had called a twenty-four-hour pharmacy that delivered and ordered a refill. Once the medication arrived and her husband was treated, she would check out, move to a new hotel, and disappear again.

The doorbell chimed behind her.

Oh, thank God.

"Jack, that's the pharmacy. I'll be right back."

She rushed out of the bedroom and across to the front door. Reaching for the dead bolt, she paused. She leaned forward instead and peeked through the door's peephole. It offered a fish-eye view of the hallway. A lone woman, black hair cut into a bob, stood outside the door. She wore a white jacket with the pharmacy logo on the lapel and carried a white paper bag, stapled with a clutch of receipt.

The woman reached out of view. The bell chimed again. The woman checked her watch and began to step away.

Harriet called through the door. "Hold for a moment!"

"Swan Pharmacy," the woman called back.

To be extra cautious, Harriet crossed to the telephone on an entryway table. She caught a look at herself in the wall mirror above it. She looked haggard, a melted wax candle of a woman. She tapped the button on the phone and rang the front desk in the lobby.

It was answered immediately.

"Phoenix Park. Front desk."

"This is room 334. I wanted to confirm a pharmacy delivery."

"Yes, ma'am. I checked her credentials three minutes ago. Is there a problem?"

"No. Not at all. I just wanted—"

A crash sounded from the bedroom behind her, followed by a spat of cursing. Jack had finally opened the bathroom door.

The receptionist spoke in her ear. "Is there anything else I can do for you, ma'am."

"No. Thank you." She hung up the phone.

"Harriet!" her husband called, a note of distress behind the anger.

"I'm here, Jack."

The doorbell chimed again.

Frazzled, Harriet undid the door's dead bolt, hoping Jack would not fuss about taking his pills. She pulled open the door.

The delivery woman lifted her face, smiling—but there was no warmth, only a feral amusement. A shock of recognition froze Harriet. It was the woman who had attacked them at the safe house. Before Harriet could move, the woman kicked the door the rest of the way open.

Startled, the edge struck Harriet in the shoulder and knocked her into a stumbling fall onto the hard tile. She tried to absorb the impact with an outstretched arm—but her wrist exploded under her with a sharp snap. Fiery pain shot up her arm.

Gasping out, half on her hip, she rolled away.

Jack stalked out of the bedroom, only in his boxers. "Harriet . . . ?"

Still addled, Jack took too long to register the situation.

The woman stepped over the threshold and raised a thick-barreled pistol. She pointed the weapon at Jack. "Here's your medication."

"No," Harriet moaned.

The woman pulled the trigger. A snapping *pop* of electricity exploded from the barrel. Something spat past Harriet's ear, trailing wire. It struck Jack in the bare chest, sparking and crackling blue in the dim light.

Taser.

He gagged, arms flying out—and crashed backward.

He didn't move.

In the stunned silence a Fox News announcer whispered from the half-muted television: "Metro police are still continuing a manhunt for Grayson Pierce, wanted in connection to the arson and bombing of a local D.C. home."

8:32 A.M.
Istanbul

ALONE AT THE roof rail Gray struggled to think of some secure channel to communicate to Washington. About the dangers at Christmas Island. He would have to be circumspect, some private communication that would not spread beyond Painter. But how? Who was to say that the Guild was not monitoring all manner of communication?

Seichan spoke behind him, back at the table. Her words were not directed at Gray. "Monsignor, you still have not explained why you called us to Istanbul. You claimed to have understood the angelic inscription."

Curiosity drew Gray back to the table, but he could not sit. He stood between Seichan and Vigor.

The monsignor swung up his backpack and settled it in his lap. He fished through it and pulled out a notebook, flipping it open on the table. Across the page was a charcoal-etched line of angelic letters.

"Here is the inscription on the floor of the Tower of Wind," Vigor said. "Each letter of this alphabet corresponds to a specific tonal word. And according to the father of angelic script, Trithemius, when combined in the right sequence, such groupings could open a direct line to a specific angel."

"Like long-distance dialing," Kowalski muttered from the other side of the table.

With a nod, Vigor flipped the sheet to the next page. "I went ahead and marked the name for each letter."

ALEPH   IOD   GIMEL   AIN   HE

Gray shook his head, not seeing any pattern.

Vigor slipped out a pen and drew a line under the first letter of each name, reciting as he did so. "A. I. G. A. H."

"Is that some angel's name?" Kowalski asked.

"No, not an angel, but it is a name," Vigor said. "What you have to understand is that Trithemius based his alphabet on Hebrew, claiming power in the Jewish letters. Even today, practitioners of Kabbalah believe that there is some form of divine wisdom buried in the shapes and curves of the Hebrew alphabet. Trithemius just claimed his angelic script was the *purest* distillation of Hebrew."

Gray leaned closer, beginning to understand the direction of Vigor's track. "And Hebrew is read opposite from English. From right to left."

Seichan traced a finger across the paper and read backward. "H. A. G. I. A."

"Hagia," Vigor pronounced carefully. "The word means 'divine' in Greek."

Gray's eyes had narrowed—then widened with sudden understanding.

Of course.

"What?" Seichan asked.

Kowalski scratched the stubble on his head, equally clueless.

Vigor stood and drew them all up. He walked them to face the city. "On his journey home, Marco Polo crossed through Istanbul, named Constantinople at the time. Here is where he crossed from Asia and finally reentered Europe, a significant crossroads of sorts."

The monsignor pointed out to the city, toward one of the ancient monuments. Gray had noted it before. A massive flat-domed church, half covered in black scaffolding as restoration work was under way.

"Hagia Sophia," Gray said, naming the structure.

Vigor nodded. "It was once the largest Christian church in all the world. Marco himself commented on the wonders of its airy spaces. Some people mistake Hagia Sophia to mean 'Saint Sophia,' but in fact, the true name of the structure is the Church of Divine Wisdom, which can also be interpreted as the Church of *Angelic* Wisdom."

"Then that's where we must go!" Seichan said. "The first key must be hidden there." She swung away.

"Not so fast, young lady," Vigor scolded.

The monsignor returned to his backpack, reached inside,

and drew out a cloth-wrapped object. Gently resting it on the table, he peeled back the layers to reveal a flat bar of dull gold. It appeared very old. It bore a hole at one end, and its surface was covered in a cursive script.

"Not angelic," Vigor said, noting Gray's attention to the lettering. "It's Mongolian. It reads, 'By the strength of the eternal heaven, holy be the Khan's name. Let he who pays him not reverence be killed.' "

"I don't understand," Gray said, crinkling his brow. "Did this belong to Marco Polo? What is it?"

"In Chinese, it is called a *paitzu*. In Mongolian, a *gerege*."

Three blank faces stared back at Vigor.

Vigor nodded to the object. "In the modern vernacular, it's a VIP passport. A traveler bearing this superpassport could demand horses, supplies, men, boats, anything from the lands governed by Kublia Khan. To refuse such aid was punishable by death. The Khan granted such passes to those ambassadors who traveled in his service."

"Nice," Kowalski whistled—but from the glint in the man's eyes, Gray suspected it was the *gold* more than the story that had won the man's awe.

"And the Polos were given one of these passports?" Seichan asked.

"Three of them, in fact. One for each Polo. Marco, his father, and his uncle. In fact, there is an anecdote concerning these passports. A famous one. When the Polos arrived back in Venice, it was said no one recognized them. The trio came worn, tired, in a single ship. Looking little better than beggars. None would believe them to be the long-vanished Polos. Upon stepping to shore, the trio sliced open the seams of their clothes, and a vast wealth of emeralds, rubies, sapphires, and silver spilled out. Included in this treasure trove were the three golden *paitzus*, described in great detail. But after this story, the golden passports vanished away. All three of them."

"The same number as the map's keys," Gray commented.

"Where did you find this?" Seichan asked. "In one of the Vatican museums?"

"No." Vigor tapped the open notebook with the angelic script. "With the help of a friend, I discovered it under the marble tile upon which this inscription was written. In a secret hollow beneath the marble."

Like the friar's cross, Gray realized. *Buried in stone.*

Seichan swore slightly. Again the prize had been right under her nose all along.

Vigor continued, "I believe this is one of the very *paitzus* granted to the Polos." He faced them all. "And I believe this is the first key."

"So the clue leading to Hagia Sophia . . ." Gray began.

"It's pointing to the *second* key," Vigor finished. "Two more missing passports, two more missing keys."

"But how can you be so sure?" Seichan asked.

Vigor flipped the gold bar over. Inscribed in great detail, a single letter adorned the back side. An angelic letter.

Vigor tapped the letter. "Here is the first key."

Gray knew he was right. He glanced up, toward the massive church. Hagia Sophia. The second key had to be hidden there, but it was a huge structure. It would be like finding a golden needle in a haystack. It could take days.

Vigor must have read his worry. "I already have someone scouting ahead at the church. An art historian from the Vatican who helped me back at the Tower of Wind with the angelic riddle."

Gray nodded. As he studied the single letter, he could not shake a deeper worry. For his two friends. Monk and Lisa. Already in harm's way. If he could not contact Washington safely, perhaps there was another way he could help his friends: by beating the Guild to whatever lay at the end of this mystery.

To find the City of the Dead, to discover the cure.

Before the Guild did.

As he stared toward the sunrise, Gray remembered Vigor's words about Istanbul being the crossroad of Marco's journey. In fact, since its founding, the ancient city had been the crossroads of the geographic world. To the north lay the Black Sea, to the south the Mediterranean. The Bosporus Strait, a major trade route and seaway, flowed between them. But more important to history, Istanbul straddled two continents. It had one foot in Europe, the other in Asia.

The same could be said about the city's place in the gulf of time.

One foot in the present, one in the past.

Forever at a crossroads.

Not unlike himself.

As he pondered this, a cell phone chimed to the side. Vigor turned and fished his phone out of the backpack's front pocket. He studied the caller ID with a frown. "It's a D.C. area code," Vigor said.

"Must be Director Crowe," Gray warned. "Don't mention anything. Stay on as short as possible to avoid any trace. In fact, we should pull the cell's battery afterward so it's not passively tracked."

Vigor rolled his eyes at his paranoia and flipped his phone open. *"Pronto,"* he greeted.

Vigor listened for a few moments, his brow growing more and more furrowed. *"Chi Parla?"* he asked with a bit of heat. Whatever he heard seemed to shake him up. He turned and held the phone out for Gray.

"Is it Director Crowe?" he asked sotto voce.

Vigor shook his head. "You'd better take it."

Gray accepted the phone and lifted it to his ear. "Hello?"

The voice that came on the line was instantly recognizable, the Egyptian accent clear. Nasser's words drained all the heat from the air.

"I have your mother and father."

8

Patient Zero

SO MUCH FOR his rescue efforts . . .

Standing in the midship elevator, Monk balanced a lunch tray on an upraised palm. He carried his assault rifle over his other shoulder. From small speakers, an ABBA song played, an acoustic version. The ride from the ship's cramped kitchens to the top deck took long enough that he was humming along with the music by the time he reached his floor.

Oh, dear God . . .

The doors finally opened, allowing Monk to escape. He tromped down the hall toward the guards who flanked the double doors at the end. He mumbled under his breath, practicing his Malay. Jessie had stolen some dye to stain Monk's face and hands to match the other pirates, similar to the disguise of the dead man in Lisa's cabin, whose body Monk had discreetly dumped overboard.

Out of sight, out of mind.

To finish his own disguise Monk kept his head scarf over the lower half of his face, playing the role to the hilt.

When in Rome.

Over the past day and night Jessie had trained Monk in some of the more common Malay phrases, the official language of the pirates here. Unfortunately Monk hadn't learned enough to talk his way past the cordon of security established around Lisa. He and Jessie had scouted the ship and discovered that all the scientific heads and their immediate support staff had been herded to one floor, while the medical staff continued ministering to the sick throughout the ship.

Unfortunately, Lisa's background in physiology must have been discerned. She was isolated in the scientific wing, barricaded and under tight security. It seemed only the elite of the pirates, under the immediate supervision of their leader, a tattooed Maori named Rakao, manned these posts. The radio room was equally guarded. Jessie had learned that much by folding himself into the pirate's flock with his fluent use of their language.

In the interim Monk had become little more than Jessie's muscle. There was not much else he could do. Even if Monk tried a John Wayne assault on the scientific wing, how would he escape with Lisa? And go where? While still cruising at top speeds, they'd have to make a jump overboard. Not the wisest plan.

Earlier this morning Monk had studied the waters from an open deck. The *Mistress of the Seas* cruised deep among the Indonesian islands. They were lost in a maze of smaller atolls, a thousand jungle-frosted fingers pointing skyward. If they escaped, swam to one of those islands, they'd be easily hunted down.

That is, if they made it past the tiger sharks.

So Monk had to bide his time.

But that didn't mean he couldn't accomplish something.

Like now.

Serving lunch.

It was a good plan. He needed to open a means of communication with Lisa. To let her know she wasn't alone, but more importantly so they could coordinate whenever Monk was ready to take action. And as he could not reach Lisa directly, he needed an intermediary.

Monk reached the double door. He lifted his tray toward the pair of guards and mumbled his way through the Malay equivalent of "the lunch bell has rung."

One of them turned and pounded the butt of his rifle against the door. A moment later, a guard, who was stationed inside, opened the door. He spotted Monk and waved him into the presidential suite of the ship.

A butler in full tails and regalia met Monk at the entrance. He tried to take the tray from Monk, but playing up the pirate act, Monk tried a fierce Malay equivalent of *aaargh,* and shouldered the man roughly aside. The butler tumbled back, arms wheeling, which earned a chuckled grunt from the door guard.

Monk entered the main salon of the suite. A puff of smoke from a deck chair on the outside balcony alerted him to his target.

Ryder Blunt lounged in a ship's robe and flowered swim trunks, ankles crossed, his hair an unkempt blond mop. He was smoking a thick stogie, watching the steep islands slowly pass. Escape was so close, yet so far away. To match the ominous mood, a stack of dark clouds climbed the horizon.

As Monk joined him, the billionaire didn't even bother to glance his way. It was the habit of the rich, ever a blind eye to their wait staff. Or maybe it was merely disdain toward the pirate serving his lunch. Ryder's butler had already set up a side table.

Silver and crystal and ironed napkins.

It must be good to be king.

Monk lowered the tray to the table and whispered in the man's ear as he bent down. "Don't react," Monk said in English. "I'm Monk Kokkalis with the American envoy."

The only reaction from the billionaire was a more fierce exhalation of smoke. "Dr. Cummings's partner," he sighed back. "We thought you were dead. The pirates sent after you—"

Monk didn't have time to explain. "Yeah, about them . . . they caught a bad case of the crabs."

The butler came to the doorway of the balcony.

Ryder waved him off, speaking loudly. "That'll be all, Peter. Thank you."

Monk unloaded the tray. He lifted one of the silver covers over the hot plate and revealed two small radios beneath it. "An extra serving for you and Lisa." He covered it back up and revealed what was under the second plate. "And of course, a bit of dessert."

Two small-caliber handguns.

One for Ryder and one for Lisa.

The billionaire's eyes widened. Monk read the understanding.

"When . . . ?" Ryder asked.

"We'll coordinate with the radios. Channel eight. The pirates aren't using it." Monk and Jessie had been using that bandwidth all day, with no one the wiser. "Can you get a radio and gun to Lisa?"

"I'll do my best," he said, but followed it with a determined nod.

Monk straightened. He dared not tarry any longer or the guards would get suspicious. "Oh, and there's rice pudding under the last tray."

Monk headed back to the main salon. He heard Ryder's mumbled comment: "Bloody disgusting stuff . . . whoever thought to put rice in pudding?"

Monk sighed. The rich were never happier than when they had something to complain about. He reached the double doors and headed out. One of the guards asked him something in Malay.

As answer, Monk dug a finger in his nose, looking very busy and determined, grumbled nonsensically, and continued down to the elevator.

Luckily, the cage was still there and the doors opened immediately. He ducked inside just in time to hear the next ABBA melody begin.

He groaned.

The radio at his side chirped. Monk freed it and brought it to his lips. "What is it?" he said.

"Meet me in the room," Jessie said. "I'm heading down there now."

The two of them had found an empty cabin to share and made it their base of operations.

"What's up?"

"I just heard. The ship's captain expects to reach some port today. They're spiking the engines to reach it before nightfall. Word from the weather band is that a storm cell, moving through the Indonesian islands, is escalating toward typhoon status. So they have to go to port."

"Meet you down at the room," Monk said, signing off.

Hooking the radio to his belt, Monk closed his eyes. Maybe this was their first bit of luck. He calculated in his head, while reflexively mouthing the words to "Take a Chance on Me" by ABBA.

It was a pretty good song.

1:02 P.M.

LISA STARED DOWN at her patient. The woman was dressed in a blue hospital gown, wired and tubed to all manner of monitoring equipment. A pair of orderlies waited in the other room.

Lisa had asked for a moment of privacy.

She stood beside the bed, fighting a thread of guilt.

Lisa knew the patient's statistics by heart: Caucasian female, five-foot-four, 110 pounds, blond hair, blue eyes, an appendectomy scar on her right side. Radiographs had revealed an old healed break to her left forearm. The Guild's biographical background check even revealed the cause of the break: from a youthful accident between a skateboard and a broken curb.

Lisa had memorized the woman's blood-test results: liver enzymes, BUN, creatinine, bile acids, cell blood counts. She knew her latest urinalysis and fecal culture results.

To one side stood an instrument tray neatly arranged with examination tools: otoscope, ophthalmoscope, stethoscope, endoscope. She had used them all this morning. On a neighboring nightstand, the previous night's EKG and EEG printouts lay accordion-folded. She had examined every inch of strip. Over the past day, she had read through all the medical history of the patient and much of the findings by the Guild's virologists and bacteriologists.

The patient was not in a coma. The more accurate status of the patient was catatonic stupor. She displayed marked *cerea flexibilitis,* or waxy flexibility. Move a limb and it would stay in that position, like a mannequin. Even painful positions . . . as Lisa had tested these herself.

By this time Lisa knew everything about the woman's body.

Exhausted, she took a moment to better examine the patient.

Not with tools, not with tests, but with empathy.

To see the woman behind the test results.

Dr. Susan Tunis had been a well-regarded researcher, on her way to a successful career. She had even found the man of her dreams. And except for being married for five years, the woman's life paralleled Lisa's. Her fate now was a reminder of the fragility of our lives, our expectations, our hopes and dreams.

Lisa reached out with gloved fingers and squeezed the woman's hand as it lay atop the thin bedsheet.

No reaction.

Out in the other room, the orderlies stirred as the suite's cabin door opened. Lisa heard Dr. Devesh Patanjali's voice. The head of the Guild's science team pushed into the room.

Lisa released Susan's hand.

She turned as Devesh entered the room. His ever-present shadow, Surina, slipped to a chair in the outer room and sat, hands neatly folded on her lap. The perfect companion . . . - perfectly deadly.

Devesh leaned his cane beside the door and joined her. "I see you've been getting well acquainted with our Patient Zero this morning."

Lisa simply folded her arms. This was the first time Devesh had spoken to her in any significant regard, leaving her to her study. He had been spending more time with Henri in the toxicology lab and Miller in the infectious-disease lab. Lisa had even been taking her meals alone in her room or here in the suite.

"Now that you've gained a complete picture of my prize patient, what can you tell me about her?"

Though the man smiled, Lisa sensed the threat behind his words.

She remembered Lindholm's cold murder. All to teach a lesson: be useful. Devesh expected results from her, insights that had escaped all the other researchers. She also sensed that the time left alone with the patient was intended to isolate her from any preconceived bias.

Devesh wanted her unique take on the situation.

Still, she remembered his early words about the virus, what it was doing inside the woman. *It's incubating.*

Lisa crossed to the patient and exposed the length of her forearm. From the medical reports, boils and bloody rashes had once coated her limbs. But presently, her skin was clear of any blemish. It seemed the virus was *more* than incubating inside her.

"The Judas Strain is healing her," Lisa said, knowing it was a test. "Or more precisely, the virus suddenly decided to reverse what it had started doing to her bacteria. For some unknown reason, it has begun reverting the deadly bacteria in her body back to their original benign state."

He nodded. "It's flushing out the very plasmids it had once put into the bacteria. But why?"

Lisa shook her head. She didn't know. Not for sure.

Devesh smiled, a strangely warm and companionable expression. "It's stumped us, too."

"But I have a hypothesis," Lisa said.

"Truly?" His voice rang with a note of surprise.

Lisa faced him. "She's healing bodily, but it made me wonder why she remains in a catatonic state. Such stupor only arises from head trauma, cerebrovascular disease, metabolic disease, drug reactions, or encephalitis."

She stressed the last cause.

Encephalitis.

Inflammation of the brain.

"I noted one test conspicuously absent from all the reports," she said. "A spinal tap along with a test of cerebrospinal fluid. It was missing. I'm assuming it was performed, to examine the fluids around her brain."

Davesh nodded. "*Bahut sahi.* Very good. It was tested."

"And you found the Judas Strain in the fluid."

Another nod.

"You said the virus only infects bacteria, turning each into a new nasty bug, and that the virus cannot invade human cells directly. But that doesn't mean the virus can't float around in the brain's fluid. That's what you meant by *incubation*. The virus is inside her head."

He sighed his agreement. "That does seem to be where it wants to get."

"So it's not just this one patient."

"No, eventually it's all of the victims . . . at least those that survive the initial bacterial attack."

He waved her to a corner of the room, where a computer station had been set up. He began clicking through various computer screens.

Lisa continued while he worked, pacing at the foot of the bed. "No organism is evil for the sake of being evil. Not even a virus. There has to be a purpose to its toxification of bacteria. Considering the broad spectrum of bacteria it converts, it can't be random chance. So I wondered: What does it gain by doing so?"

Devesh nodded, urging her to continue. But plainly her conclusions were not anything new. He was continuing to test her.

Lisa stared at the patient. "What does it gain? It gains access to forbidden territory: the human brain. Dr. Barnhardt mentioned how ninety percent of the cells that make up our body are nonhuman. Mostly bacterial cells. One of the few places that remain off-limits to viral or bacterial infections is our skulls. Our brains are protected against infection, kept sterile. Our bodies have developed an almost impenetrable blood-brain barrier. A filter that lets blood's oxygen and nutrients reach the brain, but little else."

"So if something wanted to get inside our skulls . . . ?" Devesh prompted.

"It would take a major assault to bridge the blood-brain barrier. Like turning our own bacteria against us, to weaken the body enough that the virus could slip through the barrier and into the brain's fluid. That's the biologic advantage gained by the virus when it turns bacteria toxic."

"You do amaze," Devesh said. "I knew there was a reason to keep you alive."

Despite the compliment buried in there, Lisa drew little comfort at the implied threat.

"So the ultimate question is *why*," Devesh continued. "Why does the virus want to get inside our heads?"

"Liver fluke," Lisa said.

The non sequitur was strange enough to finally regain Devesh's full attention. "Come again?"

"Liver flukes are an example of nature's determination. Most flukes have a life cycle that involve three hosts. The human liver fluke produces eggs that pass out of the body in feces, which are then washed into sewers or waterways and consumed by snails. The eggs then hatch into little worms that drill out of the snail and seek out their next host: some passing fish. The fish is then caught, consumed by humans, where the worm travels to the liver, and grows into an adult fluke, where it lives happily ever after."

"Your point being?"

"The Judas Strain may be doing something along this line. Especially if you consider the *Lancet* liver fluke. *Dicrocoelium dendriticum*. It also uses three hosts: cattle, snail, and ant. But what it does in the *ant* stage is what I find most intriguing."

"And that is?"

"Inside the ant, the fluke controls the insect's nerve centers, changes its behavior. Specifically, whenever the sun sets, the fluke compels the ant to climb a blade of grass, lock its mandible, and wait to be eaten by a grazing cow. If not eaten, the ant returns to its nest at sunrise—only to repeat the same thing again the next night. The fluke literally drives the ant like its own little car."

"And you think the virus is doing that?" Devesh said.

"Possibly in some manner. But I mostly bring this up to remind you how insidious nature can be in finding territory to exploit. And the brain, sterile and off-limits, is certainly virgin territory. Nature will try to exploit it, like the fluke with the ant."

"Brilliant. Definitely an angle to pursue. But there may be a fly in that particular ointment." Devesh returned to the computer. He had been uploading a Quicktime video. "I mentioned that the virus has been penetrating into the cerebrospinal fluid of all the patients that survived the initial bacterial assault. Here is what happens when it does."

He clicked the play button.

A silent video began to run. Two white-smocked men struggled to strap down a writhing naked man, his head shaved, wires running from electrodes attached to skull and chest. He fought, snarling and frothing. Though he was plainly debilitated, with sores and blackened boils, one arm ripped free of the tied cuffs. A clawed hand raked one of the restrainers. The patient then reared up and bit deep into the same man's forearm.

The video ended.

Devesh switched off the monitor. "We're already getting reports of similar manic responses from some of the patients, those earliest exposed."

"It could be another form of catatonia. Catatonic *stupor* is just one form." Lisa nodded to the patient in the bed. "But there is also an opposite reaction, its mirror image:

catatonic *excitement*. Characterized by extreme hyperactivity, severe facial grimaces, animal-like shrieks, and psychotic violence."

Devesh stood and turned back to the hospital bed. "Two sides of the same coin," he mumbled, and studied the prone woman.

"The man in the video," Lisa asked. She had noted the background in the video. The film had not been taken aboard the cruise ship. "Who was he?"

Devesh nodded sadly toward the bed. "Her husband."

Lisa tensed at the revelation. She stared at the woman sprawled on the bed. *Her husband* . . .

"The pair were exposed at the same time," Devesh said. "Found on a yacht that had become grounded on a reef near Christmas Island. Your John Doe below, with the flesh-eating disease, must have swum to shore. We recovered these two, still aboard the yacht. Too weak, near to death."

So that was how the Guild first learned about all this.

Devesh nodded to the woman. "Which of course begs the question, Why did her husband have a complete schizoid breakdown, while our patient here is on the way to healing her external wounds and remains happily complacent and catatonic? We believe a possible cure for everyone lies in that answer."

Lisa did not argue. She was no fool. Despite what Devesh claimed, Lisa knew the Guild's operation was not motivated by altruistic reasons. Their search for a cure was not to save the world. They had plans for this virus, but before they could utilize it, they needed to fully understand it. To develop an antidote or cure. And in this regard, Lisa was not at cross-purposes with the Guild. A cure *needed* to be discovered. The only question: How to find it without the Guild's knowledge?

Devesh turned on a heel and headed toward the door. "You've made excellent progress, Dr. Cummings. I commend you. But tomorrow is another day. And we'll need more progress." He glanced back at her, one eyebrow raised. "Is that understood?"

She nodded.

"Most excellent." He paused again. "Oh, and our cruise ship's esteemed owner, Sir Ryder Blunt, has invited everyone for afternoon cocktails in his suite. A small celebration."

"Celebration for what?"

"A welcome as we come into port," Devesh explained, gathering up his cane. "We're almost home."

Lisa was in no mood to toast such an event. "I have much work here."

"Nonsense. You'll come. It won't take long, and it will help recharge your batteries. Yes, the matter is settled. I'll have Rakao escort you. Please wear something appropriate."

He left, Surina trailing in his wake.

Lisa shook her head as they departed.

She glanced back to the bed.

To Dr. Susan Tunis.

"I'm sorry," she mumbled.

For the woman's husband and for what was to come.

Lisa remembered her earlier comparisons to the patient, how their two lives had followed similar paths. She pictured Susan's husband, wild-eyed and feral. Reminded of her own love, she hugged her arms around herself and wished for the thousandth time that she was back home with Painter.

She had spoken to him again this morning. At another of their assigned debriefings. She knew better than to attempt any subterfuge this time, reporting all was well. Still, she had been in tears by the time she was yanked from the radio room.

She wanted his arms around her.

But there was only one way to make that happen.

To be useful.

She crossed to the tray of examination tools and picked up the ophthalmoscope. Before she proceeded to the cocktail party, she wanted to follow up with an aberration, something she had kept from Devesh.

Something that was surely impossible.

2:02 A.M.
Washington, D.C.

ONE STEP BEHIND.

Painter descended the stairs two at a time toward the lobby of the Phoenix Park Hotel, too impatient even to wait for the elevator. A Sigma forensic team was still a floor above, sweeping room 334. He had left a pair of FBI field agents arguing with the local authorities.

A pissing contest for jurisdiction.

This was insanity.

Either way, Painter doubted any solid evidence would be found.

An hour ago he had been woken from a catnap in the dormitory of Sigma Command. One of their tracers had finally hit. An order for a prescription refill for Jackson Pierce. The Social Security number had matched. It was the first hit since Gray and company had fled the firebombed safe house. Painter had tagged all of Gray's aliases, along with his parents' names, coordinated through NSA's tracking network.

Painter had sent out an emergency response team to the pharmacy while joining another team headed to the delivery address on the prescription. The Phoenix Park Hotel. The pharmacy had confirmed the order, but the delivery person had not yet returned. An attempt to reach him by cell phone had so far failed. The pharmacy had even tried calling the hotel, but no one picked up at the extension for the room.

Upon arriving here, Painter learned why. The room was deserted. Whoever was here had already bolted. The register was signed under Fred and Ginger Rogers, an elderly couple according to the desk clerk. They had checked in alone. And paid cash. Gray was apparently not with them. Besides which, Gray would not have made such a blatant mistake, ordering a refill, triggering an alert.

And if so, what made his parents make such a risky move? Harriet was a bright woman. The need must have been dire. So why didn't they wait? What made them cut and run? Was it meant merely to misdirect? To send them all along a false trail?

Painter knew better. Gray would not use his parents like that. He would get them to hole up anonymously and lay low. Nothing more. Something was wrong here. No one had seen the elderly couple leave.

And then there was the question of the missing deliveryman.

Painter shoved through the stairwell door and into the lobby.

The night manager nodded to him, wringing his hands. "I have the security footage from the lobby pulled and waiting."

Painter was led into the manager's back office. A television with a built-in VCR stood atop a filing cabinet.

"Key it to an hour ago," Painter said, checking his watch.

The manager started the tape and fast-forwarded to the time-stamped hour. The lobby was deserted, except for a lone woman behind the desk, seated doing paperwork.

"Louise," the manager introduced, tapping the screen. "She's quite shook up by all this."

Painter ignored his commentary, leaning closer to the screen.

The lobby door swung open, and a figure in a white smock strode to the front desk, presented an ID, and stepped toward the elevator bank.

Louise returned to her work.

"Did your night clerk ever see the delivery person leave?"

"I can ask . . ."

Painter paused the tape as the figure adjusted the smock.

A woman.

Not the pharmacy's *man*.

The security footage was grainy, but the woman's Asian features were evident. Painter recognized her. He had seen her on the video surveillance back at the safe house.

One of Nasser's team.

Painter punched the eject button and grabbed the tape. He swung around so fast that the startled manager backed away a step. Painter held up the security tape.

"No one knows about this," he said firmly, fixing the manager with a steady stare, doing his best to look threatening, and considering his mood, it wasn't hard. "Not the police. Not the FBI."

The man nodded vigorously.

Painter headed out the door, clenching a fist, wanting to pound something.

Hard.

Painter understood what had happened here.

Nasser had snatched Gray's parents.

Out from under their noses.

The bastard had beat Sigma by only minutes. And Painter could not blame any mole for losing this particular race. He knew the reason. Bureaucracy. Seichan's background as a terrorist had everyone on full alert, which meant everyone was stepping on everyone else's toes. Too many goddamn cooks in the kitchen . . . and all of them blindfolded.

Unlike Nasser.

All day long Painter had been running into roadblocks, mostly due to bureaucratic territoriality. With Sigma under a government oversight review, other agencies tasted the blood in the water. Whoever could nab the Guild turncoat, the big fish amid all the chum, could almost guarantee some security. As such, there was little true cooperation, more a nod in its general direction.

If Painter had any hope of thwarting Nasser, he needed to cut the red tape binding his wrists. There was only one way to do that. He pulled out his cell phone. To hell with diplomacy.

He pressed a button and speed-dialed to Central Command.

The line was picked up by Painter's aide.

"Brant, I need you to patch me through to Director McKnight at DARPA. On a secure line."

"Certainly, sir. But I was just about to call you in the field. Communications just patched up some strange news. About Christmas Island."

It took a moment for Painter to switch gears. "What's happened?" he asked after a steadying breath. He paused before the hotel's revolving door.

"Details are sketchy. But it appears the cruise ship used to evacuate the island was hijacked."

"What?" he gasped out.

"One of the WHO scientists was able to escape. He used a shortwave radio to reach a passing tanker."

"Lisa and Monk . . . ?"

"No news, but details are flooding in now."

"I'll be right there."

His heart pounding, he signed off, pocketed the phone, and pushed through the revolving door. The cool air did little to take the heat out of his blood.

Lisa . . .

He ran over his last conversation with her in his head. She had sounded tired, maybe a tad on edge, wired from lack of sleep. Had she been forced to make those calls?

It made no sense.

Who would have the audacity to hijack an entire cruise ship? Surely they must know word would get out. Especially in the age of satellite surveillance.

There was nowhere to hide a ship this size.

3:48 P.M.
Aboard the Mistress of the Seas

MONK GAPED AT the sight.

Sweet Jesus . . .

Monk stood on the starboard deck, alone, waiting for Jessie. A mist-shrouded island rose directly ahead. Cliffs climbed steeply out of the ocean, offering no beach or safe harbor, topped by jagged peaks. The whole place looked like an ancient stone crown, draped in vine and jungle.

It appeared especially ominous backlit by the black skies behind it. The cruise ship had been outrunning a storm. Off in the distance, patches of dark rain brushed from the low clouds and swept the whitecapped ocean. The winds had picked up, snapping flags and gusting with shoves to the body.

Monk kept one hand clamped to the rail as the large boat rolled in the rising storm surges, taxing the ship's stabilizers.

What the hell was the captain thinking?

Their speeds had slowed, but their course remained dead-on. Straight toward the inhospitable island. It looked no more welcoming than the hundreds they'd already passed. What made this one so special?

Ever resourceful and fluent, Jessie had ascertained some details about the island from one of the ship's cooks, a native of the region who recognized the place. The island was called Pusat, or Navel. According to the cook, boats avoided the place. Supposedly the Balinese witch queen Rangda was born out of this navel, and her demons still protect her birthplace, beasts who rose out of the deep to drag the unsuspecting down to her watery underworld.

Jessie had also offered an alternative explanation: *But more likely it was just bad reefs and tricky currents.*

Or was it something else entirely?

From seemingly out of the sheer rock of the island, a trio of speedboats jetted into view. Blue, long-keeled, and low.

More pirates.

No wonder no one dares come here, Monk thought. *Dead men tell no tales.*

Monk glanced around him as some men hurried past, shouting in Malay. He strained to make out the words. He checked his watch. Where was Jessie? A little translation right about now would be handy.

Monk studied the island ahead.

From international reports, the Indonesian islands were riddled with hundreds of secret coves. Over eighteen thousand islands made up the Indonesian chain; only six thousand were known to be populated. That still left twelve thousand places to hide.

Monk watched the trio of boats buzz toward them, then split away, spinning sharply with a spray of seawater. They positioned themselves to either side of the cruise ship's bow and one directly in front. They headed back toward the island, puttering slowly in the chop.

Escorts.

The smaller ships were guiding their big brother to port.

As the island drew nearer, Monk was able to spot a narrow chasm in the cliff face, angled in such a manner as to be easy to miss. The gap appeared too small for the cruise ship, like passing a camel through a needle's eye. But someone had done proper soundings, compared them to the ship's dimensions and draft.

The cruise ship pushed its bow between two sheer walls of black rock. The rest of the ship had no choice but to follow. The port side scraped with a screech and tremble. Monk danced back as a spar of cliff on his side ground away a pair of lifeboats, smashing and raining down pieces.

The entire ship squealed.

Monk held his breath. But they did not have far to go. The way opened again. The *Mistress of the Seas* slid out of the chasm and into a wide, open-air lagoon, the size of a small lake.

Monk crossed back to the rail and gaped around. *I'll be damned. No wonder they call this place a navel.*

The island was really an old volcanic cone with a large lagoon at the center. Jagged walls circled all around and made up the crown of the island. Inside, the cliffs were less steep, lush with jungles, threaded with silver waterfalls, and lined by sandy beaches. The far side of the wide lagoon was littered with palm-thatched buildings and clapboard homes.

Scores of wooden docks and stone jetties prickled from the small town. Several boats were pulled up on shore for repair; others were rusted down to ribbings.

Home sweet home for the pirates.

More boats sped out to meet the arriving cruise ship.

Monk expected they weren't coming to sell trinkets.

He searched upward, noting how the character of the light had grown shadowy when they had pushed into the lagoon. As if the storm clouds had blown over suddenly.

But it wasn't clouds that shaded the lagoon.

Someone's been busy, Monk thought as he craned upward.

Crisscrossed over the open cone of the volcano, a vast net had been strung. It looked fairly patchwork, built piecemeal, surely decades in its construction, possibly centuries. While the main sections were supported with steel cable and latticework, strung from one peak to the next, other areas were formed of rope and reef nets, and even older sections appeared to be merely twined grass and thatch. The entire construct spanned the lagoon like a meshed roof, an engineering marvel, artfully camouflaged with leaf, vine, and branch. From above, the lagoon would be invisible. From the air, the island would appear to be just a continuous jungle.

And now the vast net had captured the *Mistress of the Seas* and hid it forever from prying eyes.

Not good.

The engines cut and the ship slowed to a drift. Monk heard the chug and gentle vibration as the ship's anchors were dropped.

A commotion toward the bow drew his attention forward.

Monk headed over to investigate. Other pirates were less stealthy and ran past him, assault rifles held in the air, cheering.

"That can't be good," Monk muttered.

Keeping back, Monk discovered a large crowd of the

pirates gathered on the forward deck, massed around the pool and hot tub. Bahamian music blasted, courtesy of Bob Marley and his Rastafarian riffs. Many had bottles of beer, whiskey, and vodka, reflective of the mix of mercenary and local pirate. It seemed a welcome-home party was under way.

Along with games.

The pirates' attention focused toward the starboard side of the ship. Assault rifles were shaken in upraised fists; encouraging shouts rang out. Someone had unscrewed the diving board and had it protruding out from the rail, over the water. A man was dragged forward, his arms tied behind his back. He had been beaten, bloody-nosed, split lip.

Shoved around, Monk caught a glimpse of his face over the crowd.

Oh, no . . .

Jessie babbled desperately in Malay—but his words fell on deaf ears. He was forced at gunpoint over the rail and onto the diving board. It seemed these were fundamentalist pirates, sticking with tradition.

Jessie teetered on the plank, poked and prodded to the end.

Monk made a step in his direction.

But a mass of pirates stood between him and the young nurse. And what could he do? Plainly Monk could not shoot his way through the throng of pirates here. It would just get them both killed.

Still, Monk's hand drifted to his rifle.

He should never have involved the kid. He'd come to lean too heavily on him, pushed him too far. Jessie had left an hour ago, searching for any local maps of the region. Someone must have a map or could sketch one. The pirates had to be getting their supplies from somewhere nearby. Monk had urged caution, but Jessie had scampered away, eyes bright.

And look what it bought him.

With a final wail, Jessie fell from the plank's end and tumbled into the water, striking it hard. Monk rushed to the rail, along with most of the pirates, standing shoulder to shoulder as they catcalled, cheered, and cursed. Bets were placed.

Monk let out a held breath when Jessie resurfaced, kicking hard, on his back, gasping. A pair of pirates near the bow leveled rifles at the struggling victim.

Oh God . . .

Shots cracked crisp, especially loud under the muffle of the netting.

Spats of splashes marked the impact.

At Jessie's heels.

More laughter.

The kid kicked harder and writhed, swimming away from the boat.

He would never make it to shore.

One of the blue speedboats aimed straight toward his floundering shape, meaning to run him over. But at the last moment, it dodged away, swamping Jessie with its wake.

He sputtered up, looking more angry than frightened.

On his back, he scissor-kicked and used his bound arms as some sort of rudder. The guy was strong and wiry.

But the speedboat was faster.

It swung around again, sweeping back for another pass.

A laughing gunman in the back of the boat braced himself and aimed his assault rifle. He strafed the water as the boat passed between the cruise ship and the boy.

Monk cringed, knowing Jessie could not have survived this time.

The speedboat buzzed past.

And there Jessie was, coughing and sputtering. He paddled and kicked. A small cheer arose from the pirates.

Monk's hands clenched on the rail, hard enough to rip it away. Goddamn assholes were toying with Jessie, stretching out the torture.

Although he was unable to act, refusing to turn away, Monk's fingers tightened into a knot. His face, heated to a red-hot fire, must be glowing through the nut-brown makeup.

All my fault . . .

Jessie fought toward shore, on his side now, searching for how far he had to swim to reach the beach. The speedboat circled back. Laughter echoed over the water.

Jessie kicked faster. Suddenly he popped up, finding sand under his toes. He ran, fell, shoved, and dove toward shore. Then his legs were high-stepping through the lapping water. He pounded across the beach toward the dense jungle.

Go, Jessie . . .

The speedboat raced by. Shots were fired. Sand exploded, leaves shredded. Then Jessie dashed the last steps and vanished headlong into the forest, arms still tied behind his back.

More cheers, some disappointed groans.

Money changed hands.

But most were still chuckling, as if at some private joke.

Monk nudged his neighbor. *"Apa?"* he asked.

As the band of pirates here was a mix of locals and foreign mercenaries, Monk had learned that pigeon Malay passed okay. Not everyone was as fluent as the native pirates.

The gentleman at his side was missing several teeth, but was happy to show how many he had left by grinning broadly. He pointed toward shore, but he aimed higher up. A few wisps of smoke could be seen near the ridgeline. Some camp was up there.

"Pemakan daging manusia," the pirate explained.

Same to you, bud.

The pirate must have noted his confusion and only smiled wider, showing his decaying wisdom teeth. He tried again. *"Kanibals."*

Monk's eyes widened. That was one Malay word Monk could translate himself. He stared back toward the empty beach, then up toward the trails of smoke. It seemed the pirates shared the island with a local tribe of cannibals. And like any good guests returning home, the pirates had thrown their caretakers a bone.

Literally.

The pirate at his side continued to babble and pointed toward the water. Monk only caught a few phrases, a word here and there.

". . . lucky . . . at night . . . bad . . ." The man pantomimed with his hand, a claw rising up and grabbing something and dragging it down. *"Iblis."*

The last was a Malay curse word.

Monk had heard it enough times, but he was fairly certain the man was using its direct translation.

Demon.

"Raksasa iblis," he repeated, and babbled a bit more, ending in a whispered name, drying his grin into more of an ache. "Rangda."

Monk frowned and straightened, leaning over a bit to stare at the water. He remembered Jessie's old wives' tale. Rangda was the name of the Balinese witch queen, whose demons were supposed to haunt these waters.

"At night . . ." the man mumbled in Malay, and pointed to the water. *"Amat, amat buruk."* Very, very bad.

Monk sighed. Just great. He stared with concern toward the forest, toward where Jessie had vanished.

Demons and cannibals.

What's next? Club Med?

9
Hagia Sophia

WITH THE SUN blazing across the rooftop restaurant, Gray listened to the threat. It sapped all warmth out of the morning.

"If you don't follow my directions precisely, I'll kill your parents."

Gray strangled Vigor's cell phone within his grip. "If anything happens to them . . ."

"Something will. I promise that. I'll send you pieces. In the mail. Over months."

Gray heard the simple certainty in the man's words. He turned his back on the others, needing to concentrate, to think.

"If you attempt to contact Sigma," Nasser continued in a dispassionate voice, "I will know. You will be punished. With the blood of your mother."

Gray's throat had tightened to a strangled knot. "You bastard . . . I want to know they're alive . . . unharmed."

Nasser didn't even respond. Gray heard a shuffle of the phone, muffled voices, then his mother came on the line. "Gray?" she gasped out. "I'm sorry. Your father. I needed his pills." Her words ended in a sob.

Gray's whole body trembled, teetering between fury and grief. "Doesn't matter. Are you okay? Is Dad?"

"We're . . . yes . . . Gray—"

The phone was snatched from her, and Nasser came back on the line. "I will be leaving them in the care of my colleague Annishen. I believe you met her at the safe house in D.C."

Gray pictured the Eurasian woman with the dyed crew cut and tattoos.

Asian Anni.

Nasser continued, "I will be joining you in Turkey. At nineteen hundred hours. You will not move from where you are."

Gray checked his watch. A little over nine hours.

"I have men closing on your position in the Sultanahmet as we speak. Do not try to be clever. We've been tracking Monsignor Verona's phone since he left Italy."

Vigor's sudden departure from the Vatican must have triggered a red flag. Gray wanted to be angry at the monsignor for being so careless, but he knew Vigor did not operate at the same level of paranoia as he did. Few people did. And at the moment, Gray had no room for recriminations, too consumed by his own guilt.

He had left his parents alone.

"I would like to speak with Seichan now," Nasser said.

Gray waved Seichan over. She went to take the phone, but Gray kept hold of it. He motioned for her to come close so he could listen in on their conversation.

With heads together, ear to ear, Seichan spoke into the phone. "Amen," she said, using Nasser's first name, "what do you want?"

"You bitch . . . for this betrayal, I'll make you suffer in ways—"

"Yes, and you'll beat my dog and kick my cat. I get it, sweetheart." Seichan sighed, her breath tickling Gray's neck. "But I'm afraid we'll have to say our good-byes here. I'll be long gone by the time you arrive."

Gray tensed and turned slightly to glance at her. She held up a silencing palm and shook her head. She wasn't going anywhere.

"My men already have you surrounded," Nasser warned. "You try to leave, and they'll put a bullet between your cold eyes."

"Whatever. As soon as this little conversation is over, I'm heading out of this damn *church*." Seichan glanced significantly at Gray and pointed over the rooftop wall toward Hagia Sophia.

She continued on the phone, "We weren't making any progress here at Hagia Sophia anyway. Too many damned murals. It's all yours, baby. You'll never see me again."

Gray frowned. She was plainly lying. But why?

Nasser paused, then spoke, fury thawing his icy manner. "You'll not make it ten steps! I've got all the exits to Hagia Sophia covered."

Seichan rolled her eyes at Gray, indicating her ploy.

"I'm sure you do, Amen," Seichan finished. "Ciao, baby. Kiss, kiss."

Seichan stepped back from the phone and held a finger toward Gray, warning him to be careful.

Gray played along. "What did you just tell her?" he snapped into the phone. "Seichan just grabbed her gun and took off out of the church. What the hell are you and that bitch up to?"

Seichan nodded with a tight smile.

Listening to Nasser swear sharply, Gray calculated in his head, struggling to catch up with Seichan's subterfuge, pushing back his guilt and anger. It would not serve him, or his parents.

He met Seichan's eyes. The Guild might have traced Vigor's call, but their triangulation was not perfect. That's what Seichan had tested with her claim of being at Hagia Sophia. The Guild knew they were somewhere in the old district in Istanbul, but not exactly where.

At least not yet.

Gray stared across a neighboring park toward the massive hulk of Hagia Sophia, with its giant flat dome, surrounded by four spiked minarets.

"What are you doing at Hagia Sophia?" Nasser asked.

Gray judged how much to say. He had to be convincing, and the best way to do that was with a bit of the truth. "We're looking for Marco Polo's key. Monsignor Verona decoded the script at the Vatican. It led here."

"So Seichan told you what we're seeking." Another curse. "For letting her escape, I'll have to teach you how serious we are."

Gray read the intent to harm his parents.

"Seichan is no longer important," Gray cut in sharply, protecting his parents the only way he could. "I have what you're seeking. The angelic code off the Egyptian obelisk. I still have a copy."

Nasser remained silent. Gray pictured him closing his eyes with relief. Nasser needed the angelic script, more than he needed to punish Seichan.

"Very good, Commander Pierce." The strain from a moment ago died out of his voice. "Continue cooperating in such a manner and your mother and father will live out the rest of their lives in peace and grace."

Gray knew that such a promise was as thin as the air he breathed.

"I'll meet you inside Hagia Sophia at nineteen hundred hours," Nasser said. "Search the church for Polo's key if you like. But I have snipers at all the exits."

Gray forced down a sneer.

"And, Commander Pierce, if you think to set up any trap, I'll be checking back with Annishen every hour. If I'm late by a minute, she'll start with your mother's toes."

The line clicked off.

Gray snapped Vigor's phone closed. "We have to get to Hagia Sophia. Before the Guild's men triangulate our true location."

They began quickly gathering up their material.

He turned to Seichan. "That was risky."

Seichan shrugged. "Gray, if you ever hope to survive this, certainly don't underestimate the Guild. They are powerful, with many allies. Yet, at the same time, don't *over*estimate them. The Guild will prey upon your fears of their omnipotence. To use that fear to weaken your morale. Just stay focused. Be cautious, but use your head."

"And if you'd been wrong?" Gray asked with a bite of anger.

Seichan tilted her head. "I wasn't."

Gray breathed heavily through his nose, trying to shed his anger. His mother and father would have suffered if she'd been wrong.

"Besides," Seichan said, "I needed a solid excuse not to be here when Nasser arrives. He'll keep you and Monsignor Verona alive. You're both useful. And with your mother and father as collateral, Nasser will believe he can ride you like a well-broken horse. But Nasser would shoot me on sight. That is, if I was lucky. So I needed an exit strategy that saved my life, yet still allowed me the freedom to maneuver on my own. If I'm going to have any chance of helping you."

Gray finally got hold of his anger. Seichan's parents weren't the ones in danger. It was easier for her to be cavalier and take risks. She had made a cold decision, acted swiftly, and the results would serve them all.

Still . . .

Seichan turned away and pointed. "And I'm going to need that guy."

"Who? Me?" Kowalski asked.

"Like I said, Nasser will shoot me on sight. Probably Kowalski, too."

"Why me?" The large man's face wilted. "What the hell did I ever do to him?"

"You're useless."

"Hey!"

Seichan ignored his outburst. "Nasser needs no other hostages, not with Mr. and Mrs. Pierce in hand. He'll see no value in keeping you around."

Gray held up a hand. "But what if Nasser already knows Kowalski is here with us?"

Seichan just stared at him, exasperated.

He slowly understood.

Don't overestimate the Guild.

Frowning, Gray struggled to rid himself of his view that the Guild was omnipotent. It threatened to cripple him from acting. Steadying himself, considering all the angles, he realized she was right.

He turned to Kowalski. "You'll go with Seichan."

"And I'll put him to good use," Seichan said, swatting the former seaman on the rear.

"At least someone thinks I'm useful," Kowalski grumbled, rubbing his backside.

With all their gear gathered up, they headed down. Seichan and Gray went last. Gray grabbed her arm as she tried to pass.

"What are you going to do?" he asked once they were alone on the rooftop. "To help us?"

"I don't know. Not yet."

She held his gaze a moment too long, then tried to turn away. She plainly wanted to tell him something more, but she hadn't quite gotten the nerve yet. It was evident in the tightness of her breathing, the slight waver to her eyes.

"What is it?" he asked softly, concerned.

His tenderness only seemed to make her want to pull away more. But she sighed. "Gray . . . I'm sorry . . ." she started, looking away again. "Your parents . . ."

There was more than worry in her eyes and manner. There was also a measure of guilt. Why? Guilt implied responsibility. But Seichan's involvement of Gray's parents had been accidental. Gray had come to accept that. So where was this sudden guilt coming from?

His mind ran through various possibilities, reviewing the recent conversations. With Nasser, with Seichan. What was bothering her—

—then suddenly he knew.

Seichan had practically told him a moment before.

Don't overestimate the Guild.

His grip tightened on her arm. He thrust Seichan against the wall beside the doorway. He leaned close, their lips almost touching.

"Oh my God . . . there is *no* goddamn mole at Sigma. There never was."

Seichan stammered to explain.

Gray would not let her. "Nasser warned me against calling Sigma, even threatening me. Why? He knew I was aware of a Guild mole in Sigma. So why even bother threatening?" He shook her. *"Unless there was no mole."*

She flinched, struggled for a moment to knock his arm away, but he clenched tighter, bruising to the bone.

"When were you going to tell me?" he asked sharply.

She finally found her voice—and it was angry, unapologetic, defensive. "I was going to tell you. After this was all over." She sighed in irritation. "But with your parents captured, I couldn't keep it a secret any longer . . . not if there is to be any hope of freeing them. I'm not that callous, Gray."

Seichan tried to turn away, but Gray shifted to keep his eyes locked on her.

"Then if there was no mole," he asked, "how did Nasser know about the safe house? The ambush he set up?"

"A miscalculation on my part." Her eyes grew flinty. "And that's all I'll say. You'll have to trust me that I acted in good faith."

"Trust you," he scoffed.

His reaction seemed to wound her, the barest lowering of her chin.

Gray did not let up. "If I had Sigma's support from the start—"

Her face hardened. "You'd have been bogged down, Gray. And I'd be locked in some prison. Useless. I needed both of us out and away as cleanly and as quickly as possible. So I let you believe what you thought."

Gray searched for some micro-expression, a fleeting glimpse of a contrary emotion indicative of a lie. There was none. She maintained her fixed gaze, clear-eyed, challenging. She did not even bother to hide that there was more left unsaid.

Gray scowled at her, cursing himself for not being more careful with her. "I should just let Nasser shoot you."

"Then who is going to watch your back, Gray? Who do you have out here? Kowalski? You're better off alone. You've got me. That's goddamn it. So let's get past this. We can continue arguing, waste what little time you have left to call Sigma, or we can sort this all out later."

She nodded to the door. "There's a phone in the hotel lobby. It's another of the reasons I wanted Nasser to think we were somewhere else. By now, he probably has a trace on all public phones in Hagia Sophia. The one in the lobby should be safe. Or at least safe enough. And you'll have to be short. We're already running out of time."

Gray let her go, thrusting her away.

Again a wounded expression flashed across her face.

Let her be wounded.

If he had known there was no mole, he could've contacted Painter from the start. At least arranged for his mother and father to be secure.

She must have read the source of his anger. She wiped her face, her voice softening, sounding bone-tired. "I thought they would be safe, too, Gray. I truly did."

Gray wanted to snap back at her, but no words came out. Both because he was angry, but more importantly because he could not unload all his guilt on Seichan.

There was no denying the simple truth.

He had left his parents alone.

Not anyone else.

3:04 A.M.
Washington, D.C.

"DIRECTOR CROWE, I have a secure call coming in from Istanbul."

Painter glanced up from the bank of satellite feeds and over to the communications chief. Who was calling from Istanbul?

For the past hour Painter had been arguing with the powers that be at the National Reconnaissance Office and the National Security Agency, attempting to gain full access to ECHELON, their satellite surveillance system, to prioritize a search around Christmas Island. But such remote territory, sparsely populated, was designated low risk and not under constant surveillance. Going outside the box, Painter had finally convinced the Australian Joint Defence Facility at Pine Gap to task one of their satellites to the area. But it would still take another fourteen minutes.

"It's from Commander Pierce, sir," the communications chief said and held out the telephone receiver.

Painter swiveled in his seat. *What the hell?* He took the phone. "Gray? This is Director Crowe. Where are you?"

The voice came faint. "Sir, I don't have much time, and I have a lot of intel to pass on."

"I'm listening."

"First, my parents have been kidnapped by a Guild agent."

"Amen Nasser. We know. We have a wide sweep already under way."

Surprised silence followed, then Gray continued. "You also have to reach Monk and Lisa. They're in danger over in Indonesia."

"We're aware. I'm attempting a satellite pass as we speak. If you're done telling me what I already know, why don't you start at the beginning?"

Gray took a deep breath and quickly related what had happened since Seichan had crashed back into his life. Painter asked a few questions and pieces began to fit together like a scattered jigsaw. He had already made several realizations while he waited for the NSA to respond. He had already suspected the Guild might be involved with the incident at Christmas Island. Who else had the resources to steal an entire island's population and vanish away? Gray just confirmed this conjecture and answered why this was all happening, even giving it a name.

The Judas Strain.

An hour ago Painter had summoned Dr. Malcolm Jennings back into Sigma's R&D offices, hauling him from his bed. On the car ride back to Sigma from the site of the kidnapping, Painter had gone over Lisa's last conversations. Clearly coerced, it made all her statements suspect. Like claiming the disease that so disconcerted her earlier was now just a false alarm. He had remembered Jennings's earlier panic about the threat of an environmental meltdown. And the man's last chilling statement. *We still don't know for sure what killed the dinosaurs.*

Plainly here was something that might interest the Guild.

Painter had even guessed that Seichan's sudden appearance and Gray's disappearance might be related to Indonesia. Two major Guild actions, striking at the same time. Painter was not a fan of coincidences. There had to be a connection. But he never would have guessed who connected it all together.

"Marco Polo?" Painter asked.

Gray finished his story. "The Guild is operating on two fronts. A scientific arm is pursuing the current outbreak, seeking a cure and the source. At the same time—"

Painter cut him off. "A historical arm is following Marco's path back to the same: a cure and the source."

It now made a certain awful sense.

"And now Nasser is heading out to Istanbul," Painter said.

"He's probably already in the air."

"I can mobilize resources out there, have assets on the ground in the next couple hours."

"No. The Guild will know. According to Seichan, Istanbul is one of their major hubs of activity. They're in all agencies out here. If they realize you've activated forces, they'll know we've talked. My parents . . . you can't. I'll have to handle Nasser on my own."

"But you've taken a huge risk as it is, Gray. Sigma's compromised. I'll do my best to keep this from leaking any further, but the mole here could—"

"Director, there is no mole in Sigma."

Painter started. It took him a moment to regroup, to consider this possibility. "Are you certain?" he finally asked.

"Certain enough to stake my parents' lives on it."

Painter sat for a moment. He believed Gray. The prickling frustration of dealing with all the interagency squabbling washed away. If there was no mole . . .

Gray's voice grew fainter. "I can't risk staying on the line any longer. I have to go. I'll do my best to follow this trail, to see where it leads."

The line went silent for a moment. Painter thought Gray might have cut the connection, but then he returned. "Please, Director, find my folks."

"I will, Gray. You can be certain of that. And when I do, tell Vigor to expect a call from his niece. It will ring a few times, then hang up. That will be the signal that your parents are safe."

"Thank you, sir."

The phone clicked off.

Painter leaned back.

"Sir," the communications officer interrupted, "we should have feed in another two minutes."

10:15 A.M.
Istanbul

DESPITE THE NEED to hurry, Gray could not stop his feet from slowing as he approached the western facade of Hagia Sophia, awestruck by its size.

Vigor noted his craned neck. "Impressive, isn't it."

There was no denying it.

The monumental Byzantine structure was considered by many to be the Eighth Wonder of the World. Seated atop a hill where once a temple to Apollo had stood, it overlooked the magnificent blue expanse of the Sea of Marmara and much of Istanbul. Its most striking feature, the massive Byzantine dome, glowed like polished copper in the morning sun, climbing twenty stories into the air. Other lower half domes buttressed it to the east and west, while additional cupolas spread out to either side like attendants to a queen, expanding the breadth of the massive structure.

Vigor continued an ongoing history lesson about the place and pointed to the giant archways ahead that led into Hagia Sophia. "The Imperial Doors. It was through those doors that in 537, Emperor Justinian dedicated the church and declared, 'Oh, Solomon I have surpassed thee.' And it was through those same doors, during the fourteen-hundreds, that Sultan Mehmed, the conquering Ottoman Turk who had sacked Constantinople, poured soil over his head in a humble act before entering the church. He was so impressed that rather than destroying Hagia Sophia, he converted it into a mosque."

The monsignor waved an arm to encompass the four towering minarets that now rose at each corner of the grounds.

"And now it's a museum," Gray said.

"As of 1935," Vigor confirmed, and pointed to the scaffolding on the south side of the structure. "Restoration work has been almost continuous since that date. And not just on the outside. When Sultan Mehmed converted the church to a mosque, he plastered over all the Christian mosaics, as it is against Islamic law to depict human figures. But over the past decades, there's been a slow and meticulous attempt to restore those priceless Byzantine mosaic murals. At the same time, there's been an equal desire to preserve the ancient Islamic art from the fifteenth and sixteenth centuries, impressive sweeps of calligraphy and decorated pulpits. To balance such a project, the restoration work at Hagia Sophia required bringing in experts from all fields of architecture and art. Including consulting the Vatican."

Vigor led the way across the open plaza toward the arched entrance, following the flow of tourists. "As such, I thought that I might bring someone familiar with restoration, someone who has been consulted by Hagia Sophia's curators in the past."

Gray remembered Vigor mentioning that he had sent someone ahead to begin the hunt for the golden needle in a massive Byzantine haystack.

As they reached the doors, Gray noted a bearded giant of a man inside the doorway, blocking the flow of tourists. He stood with his fists on his hips, glowering at everyone. But when he spotted Vigor, he raised an arm in greeting.

Vigor motioned him back into the depths of the church.

Gray followed, anxious to get off the streets, unsure if any of the Guild trackers had reached their location. Until his parents were safe, he didn't want to rankle Nasser in any way, to make the man question Seichan's earlier subterfuge.

Passing through the door, Gray glanced back toward the open plaza. He saw no sign of Seichan or Kowalski. Their two parties had separated as soon as they left the hotel. Seichan had purchased a prepaid throwaway cell phone. Gray had memorized her number. It was the only way of contacting her.

"Commander Gray Pierce," Vigor introduced, "this is my dear friend Balthazar Pinosso, dean of the art history department at the Gregorian University."

Gray's hand was swallowed up by Balthazar's grip. He stood just shy of seven feet.

Vigor continued, "Balthazar was the one who first discovered Seichan's message in the Tower of Winds and helped me with the angelic translations. He's also good friends with the museum's curator here."

"Lot of good that'll do," Balthazar groused in a deep

baritone, and led the way into the main church. He waved an arm ahead. "We've got a lot of ground to cover."

The man stepped aside and the view opened.

Gray gaped at the sight. Vigor noted his reaction and patted him on the shoulder.

A long barreled vault stretched a vast distance ahead, not unlike entering a train station. Overhead, a series of arches and cupolas climbed to the central main dome. A second-floor colonnade framed both sides. But the most impressive sight was not anything constructed of stone—it was simply the play of light in the space. Windows pierced walls and lined the bottoms of domes, allowing sunlight to reflect off emerald-and-white marble, off gold-encrusted mosaics. The sheer volume of empty space, unsupported by interior pillars, seemed impossible.

In awed silence Gray followed the two men down the long nave.

Reaching the heart of the church, Gray stared up at the scalloped vault of the main dome, twenty stories over his head. Its ribbed surface was decorated with rippling gold-and-purple calligraphy. Around its bottom circumference, forty arched windows allowed in morning sunlight, creating an appearance that the dome was hovering over one's head.

"It's like it's floating up there," Gray mumbled.

Balthazar joined him. "An architectural optical illusion," the art historian explained, and pointed up. "See those ribs along the underside of the roof, like the braces on an umbrella? They distribute the weight around the windows down to the flared pendentives seated atop massive foundation piers. Also the roof itself is lighter than it appears, constructed of hollow bricks kilned in Rhodes from the city's porous clay. It's a masterpiece of illusion. Stone, light, and air."

Vigor nodded. "Even Marco Polo was awed, to quote the great man, by 'the apparent weightlessness of the dome, and the bewildering abundance of direct and indirect lighting effects.' "

Gray understood. It was also strange to know that where he now stood, Marco Polo had also stood, the two men joined across the ages by their mutual wonder at and respect for the ancient builders.

The only blemish to the effect was the wall of black scaffolding along one side that climbed from the marble floor to the top of the dome.

It helped ground Gray in his situation. He checked his watch. Nasser would be arriving before nightfall. They had less than a day to solve this riddle.

If his plan was going to work . . .

But where to start?

Vigor was asking the same of his friend. "Balthazar, were you able to question the museum staff? Has anyone seen anything like angelic script in here?"

The man rubbed his beard and sighed. "I interviewed the curator, talked to his staff. The curator knows Hagia Sophia from its underground crypts to the tip of its highest dome. He insists nothing like angelic script can be found anywhere. He expressed one thought, though . . . something you're not going to like to hear."

"What?" Vigor asked.

"Remember how much of Hagia Sophia was plastered over from when the church was converted into a mosque. What we may be looking for could be hidden under inches of old plaster. Or it could have been inscribed on plaster that has since been cleaned away." Balthazar shrugged. "So there's a very real possibility that what we seek may be gone."

Gray refused to believe it. While Vigor and Balthazar discussed such matters in more detail, he walked away. He needed to think. He checked his watch again, a reflexive gesture. Nervous and worried. He didn't even really see the time. He dropped his arm and crossed to the scaffolding. He should never have left his parents alone. His mother's few words over the phone haunted him.

I'm sorry. Your father. I needed his pills.

Something must have happened. Gray had refused to take into account his father's illness, his need for medication. Was his neglect a purposeful blindness, a refusal to accept his father's true condition? Either way, his recklessness now threatened his parents' lives.

Gray sank down, cross-legged, and stared up toward the dome. He fought to clear his mind. His worries, fears, and doubts would not serve him. Or them. Taking a deep steadying breath, he exhaled slowly and let the drone of the tourists fade into the background.

He pictured the church as it must have looked back in the sixteen-hundreds. In his mind, he repainted the walls again, whitewashing over the golden mosaics with plaster. He did so with concentrated deliberation. A meditative exercise. If only in his head, the old mosque came alive again. He heard the muezzin calling from the minarets over the ancient city. He pictured the supplicants knelt atop rugs, rising and falling, in faithful prayer.

In such a place, where would the next key be hidden? Where in all this vast space, with its countless anterooms, galleries, and side chapels?

As he sat, Gray spun his view of the church behind his eyes, like a three-dimensional computer model, studying it from all angles. As he did so, his finger absently traced in the plaster dust on the floor. He finally became aware of what he was drawing: the glyph of angelic script, the one inscribed on the back of Marco's golden passport.

He stared down at the single letter while still spinning the architectural structure of Hagia Sophia around in his head.

"It was already a mosque," he mumbled.

He tapped the four circles, what Vigor called *diacritical marks*.

Four circles, four minarets.

What if the symbol was more than the first key to solving the riddle of the coded map? What if it was meant also to be a clue leading to the second key? Didn't Seichan say something about that? How the one key would lead to the next?

In his mind's eye, he superimposed a schematic of Hagia Sophia over the symbol, positioning the minarets so it overlaid the diacritical marks. Four circles, four minarets. What if the symbol was supposed to also represent Hagia Sophia? A crude map with the minarets as anchors.

If so, then where to begin looking?

In the dust, Gray added an additional dotted line.

"*X* marks the spot," he mumbled.

11:02 A.M.

VIGOR NOTED GRAY crawling on his hands and knees near the center of the nave, sweeping the marble floor with his hands.

Balthazar noted the man's actions with a raised eyebrow.

The two men crossed over to Gray's side.

"What are you doing?" Balthazar said. "If you're planning on checking the entire floor by hand, you'll be here for weeks."

Gray sat back, stared up at the dome as if gauging his position, then continued his sweep of the floor, working along the edge of the scaffolding. "It has to be here somewhere."

"What?" Vigor asked.

Gray pointed back to where he had originally been seated. Vigor strode over and stared down at the smudged drawing in the dust. His brow crinkled.

Gray spoke. "It's a rudimentary map of Hagia, indicating where we should be searching for the next clue."

Vigor sensed the truth of Gray's assessment, surprised yet again at the man's unique ability to cogitate and analyze. It slightly frightened him.

Gray continued to crawl, slowly working a specific section of the floor, gaining a few strange glances from some passing tourists.

Balthazar tracked at his heels. "You think someone carved a bit of angelic script into the marble."

Gray stopped suddenly, his shoulder brushing the black scaffolding. His fingers returned to a spot he had just swept over. He leaned down and blew on the tile.

"Not angelic script," Gray said, and reached to his shirt collar.

Vigor joined him. Both he and Balthazar knelt around the tile that intrigued Gray. Reaching out, Vigor felt the marble with his fingertips.

Faintly inscribed in the tile, worn by ages and the erosion of treading feet, was the barest outline of a cross.

Gray pulled out the silver crucifix from around his neck. Friar Agreer's cross. He tested its dimensions and shape against the inscription on the tile. A perfect fit.

"You found it," Vigor said.

Balthazar already had a small rubber mallet in hand, removed from his belt. He tapped at the tile. Gray's brow pinched at the man's deliberate work.

Vigor explained, "It was how we found the hollow spot beneath the inscribed tile in the Tower of Winds. Percussion. Listening for any hidden cavity."

Balthazar worked across the tile, meticulous, but the furrows across his forehead deepened. "Nothing," he finally mumbled.

"Are you sure?" Vigor said. "It has to be here."

"No," Gray said. He sprawled out on his back, staring up. "What's Jesus staring at?"

Vigor glanced to the vague figure of Christ in silver on the crucifix, then back up.

"He's staring at the dome," Gray answered. "The same dome that transfixed Marco Polo. A dome lightened in weight through the use of *hollow* bricks. If you wanted to hide something that would last the ages . . ."

Vigor craned, mouth wide. "Of course. But which brick?"

Balthazar leaped to his feet. "I have an idea." He ran off toward the rear of the building, shoving through a German tour group.

Vigor offered a hand and helped Gray back to his feet. Gray collected the cross and hung it back around his neck.

"Brilliant, Gray."

"We haven't found the second golden *paitzu* yet."

Vigor knew Gray had pulled Seichan aside for a private few words before they separated. "What's the urgency, Gray? With Nasser coming in a few hours, why even bother finding the second key?"

"Because I want Nasser happy," Gray said. Vigor read the worry in the young man's eyes for his parents. "And to prove our use to him. We need him to keep us alive."

Vigor sensed the man was leaving some bit of the plot unspoken. Before he could question Gray further, Balthazar reappeared and hurried back to them. Breathless, he held out a small tool. "With all the construction going on, I figured someone had to have a laser pointer or level. Handy when working across such vast spaces."

Vigor's colleague knelt down and positioned the laser device atop the inscribed cross and switched it on. Nothing seemed to happen.

Balthazar picked up a pinch of plaster dust and cast it above the device. A scintillation of ruby brilliance lit up the dust. "It's working." He craned up. "Someone will have to climb up the scaffolding to find which brick is lit up by the pointer."

Gray nodded. "I'll do it."

Balthazar glanced around guiltily—then handed him a chisel and hammer. "I got these, too." He waved for Gray to hide the tools away. "You'll have to be discreet. No one's allowed up there without a special artisan's pass issued by the Turkish government. I got permission from the curator to allow one of us up there. To take some photographs. Briefly. But the guard"—he nodded to the armed sentinel by the scaffolding's ladder—"in this day of terrorist attacks, they've been trained to shoot and ask questions later. If they see you take a chisel to the roof . . ." His voice trailed off.

"Beyond getting shot," Vigor warned, "we can't be discovered in any regard. If we're kicked out . . . if the police are summoned . . ."

Vigor read the understanding in Gray's eyes.

Nasser would know.

"And it's not just our lives in jeopardy," Vigor acknowledged.

Gray's parents would suffer, too.

Sighing deeply, Gray lowered his voice, "Then we'll need a distraction."

11:48 A.M.

HALFWAY UP THE scaffolding, Gray kept his head ducked from the low bracings as he climbed. Reaching a landing of planks, he glanced below and spotted Balthazar. The tall man's features were barely discernible as he stood with the museum curator. Gray leaned out to spot the scaffolding's guard. The uniformed man had stepped away from his station to get a clear view of Gray's progress.

Under everyone's watchful gaze, Gray continued onward. He reached the ring of windows along the bottom edge of the dome. Sunlight blazed through the arched glass. Gray caught a glimpse of the Sea of Marmara through one of them. Then he was above the windows. The way grew more shadowy. After another two minutes of scaling, he finally reached the top of the scaffolding and could touch the domed roof. In fact, he had to crouch to keep from hitting his head.

All around, vast scripts of Islamic calligraphy cascaded down the scalloped walls. Immediately overhead, the dome's central vertex cupped an ornate spiral of gold Arabic lettering, painted against a rich purple backdrop.

Gray searched around the edge of the vertex. Small dust motes flickered with fire to the left, lit from below by the laser pointer. He spotted his target—a glowing ruby dot sighted on a deep purple section of plaster. Good. The color was dark enough that any hole in it should be hard to spot.

At least he hoped so.

Reaching the targeted brick required continuing on hands and knees as the domed roof arched downward.

Once there, Gray crouched up and felt across the plaster. There was no carving. No angelic script. No other marking.

He frowned. What if he was wrong?

Unfortunately, there was only one way to find out. Gray waved his hand across the path of the laser, lighting up his hand.

It was the signal.

Below, Balthazar bent down, casually collected up the pointer, and aimed it down the length of the cavernous nave.

As if the light had struck some gong, a loud police whistle blew from that end of the church, piercing the solemn quiet, echoing all around the interior. Confused shouts followed.

Gray stared in the direction and spotted a burst of flame. An improvised Molotov cocktail, derived from rubbing alcohol used to clean the mosaics. Vigor had set it off in a trash receptacle.

More shouts.

Gray swung around to keep the bulk of his form between the guard below and his desecration above. He lifted his tools from his belt, positioned the chisel tip where the pointer had been. He waited a tense breath, then a second whistle blew.

As it blasted, Gray struck one strong blow.

Plaster broke—along with the hollow crack of dry clay.

A chunk of brick shattered free, struck Gray's chest, and bounced off. He snapped out a hand and caught the lump in the hand with the chisel before it could tumble to the marble floor below. Cringing internally, Gray shoved the broken shard into his shirt.

Using the chisel, he quickly levered into the heart of the hollow brick, careful of the loosened pieces. Reaching up, he examined the cavity with his fingers. Rather than course clay, it felt glassy inside, watery smooth. He searched around.

Something was up there.

He fingered it out. Gray had been expecting the golden *paitzu,* but instead he pulled out an eight-inch-long tube of copper or bronze, capped at both ends, not unlike a cigar holder. The object ended up down his shirt.

Casting a sidelong glance, Gray noted the small trash fire had already been smothered with an extinguisher.

Hurrying, he searched again and felt something heavy, nudged with his index finger. It took another few seconds to work the second prize out of the secret vault: another gold *paitzu.*

The heavy passport fell free, bobbled out of his frantic fingers, and clattered to the rungs of the scaffolding at his feet. The metal rang like a struck bell, amplified by the cup of the dome. Unfortunately, it hit at the exact moment when there was a lull in the commotion below.

Crap . . .

As the noise echoed away, Gray grabbed up the golden passport and tucked it into his shirt. With shouts calling up from below, he did the only thing he could. He kicked the hammer off the scaffolding and tumbled after it, arms wheeling in midair, a shout on his lips.

11:58 A.M.

FROM THE SECOND-FLOOR colonnade Vigor watched Gray plummet off the top of the scaffolding.

Oh, no . . .

Moments before, Vigor had blown the whistle at the opposite end of the church and dropped the lit Molotov he had been holding, hidden inside an unattended trash receptacle. He barely got his arm out in time, hurrying away. He had blown the whistle again—then tossed it into a potted plant. Having already donned the Roman collar of his profession, he merely had to look confused and a little scared. The guards ignored him as he rushed the length of the upper floor back toward the central nave.

He reached the center of the church in time to hear Gray shout and fall headlong off the immense scaffolding. People came running, others scattered out of the way below. A hammer struck the marble floor with a resounding crack.

Overhead, Gray cartwheeled and snagged a strut of the scaffolding with an outstretched hand. He slammed back into the bracings. His feet kicked and struggled for a purchase. He found it and scrambled back into the heart of the scaffolding. He lay on his back, plainly collecting his wits from the fall.

The scaffolding guard yelled up at him and waved another security guard to pound up the stairs to check on him.

Gray rolled back and forth, clutching his left arm, moaning.

Vigor circled back to the stairs to reach the floor of the nave. He joined Balthazar and the museum curator. The security guard helped Gray up, and half supported by the guard, the pair descended with care.

As Gray limped along, his face purpled with anger. He pointed to the hammer, the very hammer Balthazar had given him. "Don't your workmen clean up after themselves," he sputtered in frightened outrage. "All that commotion down here, I accidentally stepped on the blasted tool. I could have been killed!"

The curator, a slender man with a bit of a paunch, collected the hammer. "Oh, my dear sir, my apologies. Such recklessness. I assure you. It will be attended. Your arm . . ."

Gray was holding it to his chest. "Sprained, maybe dislocated." He glowered at the curator.

"The police are already on their way here . . . for the fire," the curator said.

Gray and Vigor shared a worried look.

If Nasser heard the police had come here . . .

Vigor cleared his throat. "The fire. Surely it was just a cigarette tossed by a careless tourist. Or maybe a harmless prank."

The curator didn't seem to hear. He had already turned to one of the guards and spoke rapidly in Turkish.

Vigor understood.

This was even worse.

"No, no," Vigor insisted, glancing hard to Gray. "I'm sure our student doesn't need to be taken to the hospital. No ambulance is needed."

Gray's eyes widened. They could not leave the church. Their distraction had only succeeded in getting them deeper and deeper into hot water.

"The monsignor is right." Gray flexed and rotated his arm. Vigor noted a flinch. Gray really had hurt his arm. "Just sprained a bit. I'll be fine."

"No. I insist. It is museum policy. If anyone is injured on the premises, a hospital visit is mandatory."

Vigor saw that there was no way to dissuade the curator.

Balthazar stepped forward, clearing his throat. "That sounds prudent. But in the meantime, perhaps there's a place we could rest. Your office is in the basement, no?"

"Of course. No one will disturb you. I will deal with the police and summon you when the ambulance arrives. And Dr. Pinosso, please accept my sincere apologies. You've been so generous with your time and knowledge in the past and look how I repay you."

Balthazar patted his arm. "Hasan, do not worry. All is well. Nerves are just shaken up. It serves my student right for not watching where he steps when on a precarious perch."

Sirens sounded in the distance.

"This way," the curator said.

A short time later the three of them were alone in Hasan's basement office. It was sparsely furnished. The schematics for the church were tacked to the back wall, behind a cluttered desk. A single framed photograph of the curator, Hasan Ahmet, shaking hands with the Turkish president adorned the wall above a bank of steel filing cabinets. On the opposite wall was an ancient illuminated map of the Middle East.

Balthazar flipped the office door's dead bolt and paced the length of the room. "There is a maze of rooms down here in the basement. You two could hide out until that Nasser fellow comes. I can go up and tell Hasan that you both left."

"It will have to do." Vigor sank into a couch next to Gray, who was massaging his shoulder. "We won't have much time. Did you find anything up there?"

As answer, Gray unbuttoned the lower half of his shirt and pulled out a slab of gold and a tube of beaten bronze. He shook his shirt a bit more and a bit of ruddy clay pottery tumbled out. Gray bent down, picked it up, and placed it on the table.

Vigor began to turn away, but a bit of color from the pottery caught his eye. He retrieved the chunk of reddish clay from the tabletop.

"It's a piece of the hollow brick," Gray explained sourly. "I didn't want to leave it up there. Heaven knows, things went badly enough."

Vigor briefly examined it. On one side, a bit of purple plaster still clung to it, but on the other side, a thick skein of sky-blue glaze coated the clay. Why would someone glaze the inside of a hollow brick?

"Did you see any angelic script up there," Vigor asked, and returned the chunk to the table.

"No. No writing, nothing unusual."

Balthazar bent down and flipped the golden *paitzu* over. "But there is angelic writing here."

Vigor leaned closer. As expected, a single letter of angelic script decorated the back side. A crude circle enclosed it.

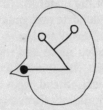

"The second key," Vigor said.

"But what's this?" Balthazar asked. He nudged the tube.

Vigor picked it up. It was as thick around as his thumb, unadorned, except for the old hammer marks of its forger. "It may be a scroll tube." He examined one end. A thin coin of bronze had been stamped over the end, sealing it.

"We'll have to open it," Gray said.

Vigor felt some discomfort at his suggestion. As an archaeologist, he feared mishandling such an ancient artifact. It needed to be photographed, its measurements taken, cataloged.

Gray reached to a pocket and slipped out a penknife. He opened the small blade and held it toward Vigor. "We're running out of time."

Taking a deep breath, Vigor accepted the knife. With a twinge of professional discomfort, he used the tip to pry the cap off the end. It popped cleanly, as if only crafted yesterday.

Vigor cleared a space on the coffee table, tilted the tube, and slid out its contents. A roll of white material dropped to the mahogany table.

"A scroll," Gray said.

Without touching it, Vigor made an assessment from his years of study and lifetime of experience. "It's not parchment, vellum, or even papyrus."

"What is it?" Balthazar asked.

Vigor wished he had examination gloves for handling the old scroll. Fearful of the oils in his hands, Vigor collected a pencil from the curator's desk and used the eraser to unroll the free edge of the material.

It fell away easily, delicate and gauzy.

"It looks like cloth," Gray said.

"Silk." Vigor unrolled more and more, teasing it across the length of the table. "It's embroidered," he said, noting the fine stitching of black thread across the white silk.

But the needlework did not form a picture or an intricate pattern. Instead, lines of cursive text, stitched into the material, spread down the length of the unrolled bolt of silk.

Gray twisted his head to read, but his frown deepened, not comprehending.

"It's *lingua lombarda,*" Balthazar declared with awe.

Vigor could not take his eyes from the writing. "The Italian dialect of Marco Polo's region." He reached a trembling hand and followed with the pencil eraser, translating the first line aloud. " 'Our prayer was answered in a most strange manner.' "

He glanced to Gray. He read the understanding in the American's eyes.

"It's the rest of Marco's story," Gray said, "continuing where the Guild's copy of his book ended."

"The missing pages," Vigor agreed, "embroidered onto silk."

Gray glanced to the door, plainly edgy, and waved to the silk diary. "Read the rest of it."

Vigor started from the beginning, continuing the story of Marco's party. The first section left them trapped in the City of the Dead and surrounded by a cannibal horde. Vigor carefully translated the next part of the tale, his voice tremulous with the power of Marco's original words.

Our prayer was answered in a most strange manner. And was thus brought about:

Night fell over the City of the Dead. From the vantage of our sanctuary, the moats and pools of the city below shone with light of a sepulchral nature; the hue and sheen was that of molds and mushrooms. It cast the scene below into some dread feast expelled from the Devil's bowels, as the dead fed on the dead. We saw no hope for salvation. What angel would dare tread these blasphemed lands?

But then it came to pass that three figures emerged from the dark forest. They appeared as such: their skin cast a sheen to match pond and moat, and the dread cannibals parted before their feet insomuch as the wind sweeps through a field of grain. The three crossed through the city with little haste but with clear direction. Once at the foot of the tower, these strange apparitions were seen to be of the same people as those that feasted on flesh. Yet their skin glowed with some Blessed light.

In great terror, the kaan's men dropped all weapons and hid their faces against the stone. The three entered our shelter and came upon us with no molestation. Their faces were gaunt and fever-worn; but they seemed sound of flesh, unlike their brothers below. But it was no flesh like unto man. The light of their skins seemed to penetrate their deeper bodies; and thus revealed the churn of bowel and shadowy beat of their hearts. It came also to pass that one of the three brushed against one of the kaan's men. He screamed and fell away; and where he was touched his skin did blister and blacken.

Friar Agreer lifted his cross against them; but the first of the three came forward with little fear and touched the Dominican's cross. He spoke in words that no one understood; but with much gesturing, their desire was communicated: to have us drink from the halved shell of an Indie nut.

One of the kaan's men must have understood enough of the strange tongue to communicate. A great healing virtue was offered us; and with its consumption, we would be protected from the pestilence that struck here. But Heaven forgive us all for what it would cost, what it would make of us in the end.

The story stopped there.

Vigor sat back in frustration. "There must be more."

"Hidden with the third and final key," Gray suggested.

Vigor nodded and tapped the stretch of silk diary. "But even from this much of the story, it is plain why this tale was never told."

"Why?" Gray asked.

"The descriptions of the strange apparitions," Vigor stressed. "Glowing with a 'Blessed light.' Offering salvation."

"Sounds like angels," Balthazar said.

"But *pagan* angels," Vigor stressed. "Such a concept would not have gone down well with the Vatican during the Middle Ages. And remember, whoever split up Marco's story did so during the sixteen-hundreds, during another Italian plague outbreak. Despite the disturbing content, the Vatican dared not destroy the message. Some mystics within the Church must have divided the text to both preserve and hide it. But the bigger question remains: What is still left untold?"

"If we're going to discover that," Gray said, "we'll need to find that third key. But where do we begin to look? There's no angelic script anywhere."

"Maybe no angelic script that we could *see* with the naked eye," Vigor added pointedly.

Gray nodded his understanding. He twisted around to his pack and began fishing through it. "I brought a UV light. In case we ran into any more glowing obelisks."

Balthazar dimmed the lights. Gray ran the UV over every artifact. Even the shard of broken clay brick.

"Nothing," he finally admitted.

Dead end.

12:43 P.M.

GRAY'S FRUSTRATION HAD stretched to the tautness of a piano wire. He gave up any hope on his original plan, though it had been a long shot.

"We can't wait any longer," he finally admitted, checking his watch. "We have to get into hiding. Let's gather this all together. Find a place to hole up."

They had spent the last five minutes racking their brains, searching for some clue as to where to seek the third key. Vigor attempted to decipher a hidden meaning in the text, going over it again. Balthazar had studied all surfaces of the golden *paitzu*. Everyone agreed that the crude line circling the single angelic letter had to be significant, but no one could guess what it might be.

Vigor sighed and began rolling up the scroll. "The answer must be here. Seichan said the Guild's copy mentioned how each key would lead to the next one. We just have to figure out what we're missing later."

Gray gathered up the last remaining artifact: the chunk of the brick itself. He tapped the plaster on the outside of the chunk. "Could there be some significance to the brick being plastered in purple? I'm assuming the false brick could have been any number of colors. They had the entire dome's palette to choose from."

Vigor barely seemed to hear him as he tucked the scroll back into its bronze tube. Still, he mumbled aloud. "Purple is the color of royalty or divinity."

Gray nodded. Grabbing his backpack, he shoved the chunk inside. His thumb ran over the thick blue glaze on the opposite side. Gray remembered the inside of the brick had felt glassy.

"Blue," he whispered aloud. "Blue and royalty."

Then it came to him.

Of course.

Vigor realized it at the same time and sprang straighter. "The Blue Princess!"

Balthazar slid the gold *paitzu* over to Gray to pack away.

"You're talking about Kokejin. The young Mongol woman who traveled with Marco."

Vigor nodded. "She gained her nickname because her name translates as *sky blue*."

"But what's the significance of her reference here?" Gray asked.

"Let's backtrack," Vigor said, ticking off on his fingers. "The first key was at the Vatican, in Italy, where Marco ended his journey. A major milestone. Following Polo's route backward, we come to the next milestone here, in Istanbul, where Marco crossed from Asia and stepped for the first time back into Europe."

"And if we trace Marco's route further back . . ." Gray said.

"The next major milestone would be at the site where Marco completed the task set to him by Kublai Khan, the whole reason for the journey: to bring Kokejin to Persia."

"But where exactly in Persia?" Gray asked.

"Hormuz," Balthazar answered. "In southern Iran. The island of Hormuz lies at the mouth of the Persian Gulf."

Gray glanced to the table. *An island.* He picked up the golden *paitzu* and traced the line encircling around the angelic symbol. "Could this be a crude map of that island?"

"Let's check," Vigor said, and stood up. He crossed over to the curator's old illuminated map on the wall.

Gray joined him.

Vigor pointed to a small island near the bottom of the Persian Gulf, close to the mainland of Iran. It bore the same rounded shape with a distinct teardrop tip. It was almost an exact match to the drawing around the gold glyph.

"We found it," Gray said, his breath quickening in anticipation. "We know where we have to go next."

And that meant his plan could still work.

"But what about Nasser?" Vigor asked.

"I haven't forgotten about him." Gray faced the monsignor and gripped his shoulder. "The first key. I want you to give it to Balthazar."

Vigor frowned. "Why?"

"In case anything goes wrong here, we can't let Nasser get ahold of it. We'll present the second key we found here as the *first* one. Nasser can't know that you found a key in the Vatican." Gray stared between them. "I assume you two kept it between yourselves."

Both men nodded.

Good.

Still, Vigor's frown had not dimmed. "Surely when Nasser gets here, he'll search Balthazar and find the other golden key."

"Not if Balthazar is already gone," Gray said. "Like with Kowalski, I doubt Nasser knows your colleague traveled with you. Why would he suspect you came here with the dean of the art history department? By tracking your cell phone, all Nasser knows is that *you* left to meet us. We'll use that to our advantage. We'll send Balthazar with everything he needs to know. Out to Seichan. Along with Kowalski, the three of them can get a jump start and head over to the island of Hormuz. It will be up to them to find the last key. Once Nasser arrives here, we'll have to stall the bastard for as long as possible. But for the sake of my parents, we may have to eventually send him on the right path."

"Where hopefully Seichan will have already found the last key," Vigor said.

"Then we'll have something to bargain with," Gray said.

Still, Gray knew all of these plans hinged on one last hope.

That Painter found a way to free his parents.

And of course, that Gray had not made any gross miscalculations himself.

1:06 P.M.

SEICHAN WAITED INSIDE the hotel room across from Hagia Sophia's west entrance. She sat by the fifth-floor

window. Her cheek rested against the stock of her Heckler &
Koch PSG1 sniper rifle. She stared down its telescopic sight,
focused on the plaza in front of the church.

She had watched the police come and go, stopping only
briefly.

What had happened?

Behind her, Kowalski lay stretched on the bed, chewing
on olives and cleaning five hand pistols and a 5.56 mm
NATO A-91 assault rifle.

They had gone shopping, stocking up on the essentials.

Kowalski whistled around an olive pit as he worked. It
was getting on her nerves as she kept her post. But at least he
knew his armaments.

From her vantage, Seichan had a clear view of the street,
park, and plaza. She watched for anyone taking an inordi-
nate interest in the church, more than the typical flash-and-
go tourist. She also watched for any telltale sign of someone
carting heavy weaponry.

So far so good. Either that or she was losing her edge.

Through her telescopic sight, she watched everyone
leaving or entering through the western Imperial Doors of
Hagia Sophia. She adjusted the focal length to get a clear
view of the faces. She kept inventory. To see if any of the
same faces came and went, indicating someone who was
canvassing the place.

She wanted to know where as many of the hostiles were
positioned as possible.

In case an assault proved necessary.

So far nothing. It made no sense.

Where were Nasser's men? They should have been here
by now, taking up positions. The Guild had many resources
and assets in Istanbul. The supply of arms behind her was
proof enough of that. Or was Nasser operating lean? Keeping his manpower to a minimum? It was easier to blend one
or two men into the scenery than a half dozen.

Still, Seichan wasn't buying it.

"Something's wrong," she muttered, bobbling her view.

What was his game?

She concentrated back on her duty. A large man exited the church, crossing in large strides, not attempting to hide. Seichan focused on him, bringing up his bearded face.

That's more like it.

She didn't know his name, but she had seen the man before, meeting with Nasser, two years ago. A fat envelope had passed between them. Nasser hadn't known Seichan had tailed him, spied on his rendezvous. Seichan had a series of photographs of the unknown operative somewhere in her Swiss bank vault. Something tucked away for a rainy day.

Or a sunny one like today.

"No wonder Nasser is operating lean," she mumbled.

The bastard had someone positioned *inside* Hagia Sophia. That did not bode well. If this man was leaving, that meant someone else had already relieved him. She watched him stop in the plaza and take out a cell phone.

Probably calling Nasser, letting him know his quarry was safe and sound inside the church.

Her cell phone rang.

Odd.

She reached blindly to the phone, pressed talk, and lifted it to her ear. "Ciao," she said.

"Hello," the caller responded, his voice bright. "I am looking to speak to a woman named Seichan. I was told to call at this number, to arrange for us to get together. A certain monsignor and an American would like us to meet."

Seichan's skin chilled as she listened, focused on the figure, watching his lips move in synchronization with the voice in her ear.

"This is Balthazar Pinosso, with the Vatican's art history division."

At least Seichan finally had a name for the man in the photograph with Nasser. Balthazar Pinosso. A Guild operative. She breathed through her nose. Nasser didn't just have someone positioned inside the church—he had someone inside their own goddamn inner circle.

Seichan mentally kicked herself. It wasn't Sigma that had a Guild mole. The Vatican did.

"Hello," the man repeated, with a trace of worry.

Seichan leaned her cheek tighter against the stock, taking dead aim.

Time to plug the leak.

"Kowalski . . ." she whispered.

"Yeah."

"The shit's about to hit the fan."

"Hell of about time!"

Seichan pulled the trigger.

10

Out of the Frying Pan

THANK GOD, the cocktail party had finally ended.

Lisa hurriedly unbuttoned the hand-beaded silk coat that overlay her black cocktail dress, a pleated silk charmeuse. The Vera Wang–designed ensemble was well over her budget, but she had found the dress spread out on her bed earlier when she returned to get ready for Ryder Blunt's soiree, welcoming the cruise ship to the pirates' home port.

Dr. Devesh Patanjali must have handpicked the dress himself from the ship's luxury shops down on the Lido Deck. That was reason alone to get it off her body. Lisa had not wanted to go to the party, but Devesh had left no choice. So she had joined the other senior staff up in Ryder's suite.

Champagne and chilled wine had flowed. Hors d'oeuvres were passed atop silver platters, borne aloft by liveried wait staff, while iced trays of caviar surrounded by toast points decorated the buffet table. Apparently there remained enough members of the ship's orchestra still alive to form a string quartet. The group played quietly out on the balcony as the sun set, but they were forced to disband when the winds kicked up and rain began to pelt down in heavy, stinging drops.

Thunder rumbled overhead even now as the storm grew in intensity. At least the ship remained steady, sheltered in the caldera of a sunken volcano. Still, word of a typhoon and countless responsibilities had soon ended Ryder's impromptu party.

It had lasted only a couple of hours.

Lisa stripped to her bra and panties, glad to be done with the matter. She climbed back into her jeans and slipped a loose blouse over her head, shimmying it in place. Barefoot, she crossed to the evening purse on the bed, another gift of Dr. Patanjali, a Gucci frame bag with silver tassles. The bag had a price tag still on it.

Over six thousand dollars.

Still, what it held was of far greater value. During the festivities, Ryder had discreetly passed to her a pair of party favors, which she had quickly tucked into her purse.

A small radio and a pistol.

And the news that accompanied the gifts was even more welcome.

Monk was alive!

And on board the ship!

Lisa quickly hid the gun in the waistband of her jeans and covered it with the edge of her loose blouse. Radio in hand, she crossed to the door and listened with her ear pressed against it.

There was no regular guard posted at her door. The entire wing had been cordoned off at the stairwell and at the elevator banks. Devesh had assigned an inside cabin for her, only two doors down from where her patient still slumbered in a catatonic stupor.

Satisfied she was alone, Lisa dialed the radio to channel eight and slipped on the radio's earpiece and microphone. She pressed the transmitter. "Monk, are you there? Over."

She waited.

A bit of static rasped, then a familiar voice spoke. "Lisa? Thank God! So Ryder got you a radio. Did you get the gun? Over."

"Yes." She desperately wanted to hear his entire story,

how he survived, but now wasn't the time. She had more important concerns. "Ryder said that you had some plan."

"A plan might be too generous a term. More like a seat-of-your-pants run for your life."

"Sounds great to me. When?"

"I'm going to coordinate with Ryder in another few minutes. We'll be ready at twenty-one hundred. You be ready, too. Keep the pistol with you." He gave her a brief overview of his plan to free her.

She filled in some necessary details to help him, then checked her watch. *Less than two hours.*

"Should I tell anyone else?" Lisa asked.

A long pause.

"No. I'm sorry. If we're going to have any hope of escaping, we're going to have to bolt with as few people as possible, using the cover of the storm. Ryder has a private boat in a slide launch on the starboard side. I've got a map from your friend Jessie. There's a small township about thirty nautical miles away. The best hope is to reach it and raise the alarm."

"Is Jessie coming with us?"

An even longer pause followed.

Lisa clicked the transmitter again. "Monk?"

A sigh filled her ear. "They caught Jessie. Threw him overboard."

"What?" Lisa pictured his smiling face and propensity for stupid puns. "He's . . . he's dead?"

"Don't know. I'll explain more when we meet."

She felt a well of grief for a young man whom she had only known for a few hours. Lost in that well, she could not find her voice.

"Twenty-one hundred hours," Monk repeated. "Keep your radio with you, but out of sight. I'll contact you again then. Out."

Lisa removed the headpiece and grasped the radio in both hands. The physicality of the hard plastic helped center her. They would talk again in a couple of hours.

Thunder rumbled.

She clipped the radio inside her pocket, folding and tucking in the headpiece. She kept its bulge hidden by the drape of her blouse.

She stared at the cabin door. If they were going to make an escape, Lisa did not want to leave empty-handed. She knew there were reams of data and files in the room with her patient.

Plus there was a computer . . . with a DVD burner.

She had talked with Henri and Dr. Miller up at the cocktail party. In hushed whispers, they had related how Devesh and his team were collecting samples of various toxic bacteria produced by the Judas Strain, the worst of the bunch, storing them in incubation chambers in an off-limits lab, run by Devesh's virologist.

"I think they're also doing experiments with the virus on known pathogens," Dr. Miller had reported. "I saw stacks of sealed plates marked *Bacillus anthracis* and *Yersinia pestis* disappear into the restricted lab."

Anthrax and the Black Plague bacterium.

Henri postulated that Devesh must be experimenting to produce a superstrain of these deadly pathogens. During their discussions, one word remained unspoken—the reason for all of this.

Bioterrorism.

Lisa checked her watch and crossed to her door. If the world was going to have any chance of stopping the myriad plagues that the Guild was collecting and producing, they needed as much data as possible from her patient. The woman's body was healing itself, ridding its tissues of the toxic bacteria, flushing it clean.

How and why?

Lisa knew Devesh was right about Susan Tunis.

This one patient holds the key to everything.

Lisa couldn't leave without gathering as much data as possible.

She had to take the chance.

Squeezing the door handle tightly, Lisa tugged it open. She crossed the five steps to Susan Tunis's room. Ahead, the circular bay of scientific suites was still busy with technicians coming and going. A radio was playing honky-tonk, but the singer crooned in Chinese. The air smelled of disinfectant and an underlying earthy smell.

Lisa briefly made eye contact with the armed guard who patrolled the central space, circling the pile of discarded crates and idle equipment. Down the hall behind her, she heard more guards talking.

She ducked over to Susan Tunis's room, swiped the card Devesh had given her, and pushed inside. As always, two orderlies manned the room. Devesh never left his prize patient unattended.

One man lounged in a chair in the main salon, feet up on the bed, watching television with the volume on low. It was some Hollywood movie shown on a shipwide broadcast. The other orderly was in the well-lit bedroom with the patient, clipboard in hand, recording the quarter-hour vitals.

"I'd like a moment alone with the patient," Lisa said.

The large man, shaved bald and dressed in scrubs, could be the identical twin of the other. She never learned their names, internally referring to them as Tweedledee and Tweedledum.

But at least they spoke English.

The orderly shrugged, handed her the clipboard, and crossed out with his partner.

Lightning flashed brightly through the balcony doors, and thunder grumbled. The world beyond—lagoon and surrounding forested island—appeared in stark relief, then vanished back into darkness with a fierce clap.

Rain pounded more heavily.

Lisa slipped on a mask and a pair of surgical gloves and crossed over to her patient. She again collected the ophthalmoscope from the tray of examination instruments. She had been monitoring a strange anomaly in the patient's eyes, something she had kept secret from Devesh. Before she left she wanted to check one more time.

She slipped back the flap of the isolation tent, leaned down, and used a fingertip to gently peel up the lid of the woman's left eye. Lisa clicked on the ophthalmoscope's light and adjusted the focus. Leaning down, nose to nose, she began a funduscopic exam of the patient's inner eye.

All the retinal surfaces appeared normal and healthy: macula, optic disk, blood vessels. The anomaly was easy to miss, as it wasn't structural. Holding her position, Lisa clicked off the ophthalmoscope's light source. She continued to stare through the instrument's lens.

The back of the patient's eye, the entire retinal surface, shone back at her, softly aglow with its own milky light. Some strange phosphorescence had infused the retinal tissues. It had started around the optic disk, where the main nerve bundle from the brain attached to the eye. But over the past few hours, the glow had spread outward and now encompassed the entire retinal surface.

She had read the historical reports of the first manifestation of the disease, an algal bloom, back at the island, how the seas had glowed with phosphorescent cyanobacteria.

And now the patient's eyes glowed.

There must be some clue here. But what?

Based on these earlier findings, Lisa had discreetly performed a second tap of the patient's cerebral spinal fluid. She wanted to know if anything had changed in the fluid around the brain. The results should be back by now, fed into the computer in the corner of the room.

Lisa finished her exam, shed her gloves and mask, and crossed to the computer station. It was out of direct view of the other room.

She brought up the menu for laboratory tests. Her CSF tap's results had indeed returned. She glanced through the chemical analysis. Protein levels were rising, but little else had changed. She switched over to the microscopic exam. Bacteria had been detected and identified.

Cyanobacteria.

As she had suspected.

When the blood-brain barrier had been weakened to allow the Judas Strain virus into the brain, it brought some company.

Company that was growing and multiplying.

Anticipating these very results, Lisa had done some earlier research. Cyanobacteria were one of the most ancient strains of bacteria. In fact, they had the distinction of being among the world's oldest known fossils. Almost four billion years old, one of the earth's first life-forms. They were also unique in that they were photosynthetic, like plants, able to produce their own food from sunlight. If fact, most scientists considered cyanobacteria to be the ancestor of modern plants. But these ancient bacteria also proved to be very adaptable, spreading into every environmental niche: salt water, freshwater, soil, even bare rock.

And with the help of the Judas Strain, apparently the human brain.

The glow of the patient's eyes suggested that the cyanobacteria in the brain must have traveled along the optic-nerve sheath to the eye, where they were now setting up house.

Why?

From the sample Lisa saw that a technician had performed a new microscopic scan of the Judas Strain virus. Curious, she brought the fresh image to the screen. Once again, she was faced with the true monster here: the icosahedron shell with the branchlike tendrils sprouting from each corner.

She remembered her earlier words. *No organism is evil for evil's sake.* It just sought to survive, to spread, to thrive.

The file was also cross-indexed to the original viral photos. She brought those up, too.

Old and new. Side by side. All the same.

She reached to close the file, but her finger hovered over the button.

No . . .

Her hand began to tremble.

Of course . . .

Lightning cracked, blindingly bright through the balcony doors, followed by an immediate clap of thunder that made her jump. The entire ship shuddered. The balcony doors rattled.

The lightning had struck right over the ship, maybe hitting it.

The cabin lights flickered. Lisa glanced up just as they went out. Darkness fell over the cabin.

The orderlies yelled out a complaint.

Lisa stood up.

Oh. My. God.

Then the lights zapped back on with a surge of current. The computer squelched a complaint and made a loud smoky *pop*. The television in the other room garbled, then settled into regular movie dialogue.

Lisa stayed where she was, frozen in shock.

She continued staring down at the figure in the bed. In the moment of brief darkness, Lisa had made another discovery about the patient. Had no one ever turned out the lights in here? Or was this phenomenon new?

It wasn't only the woman's *eyes* that glowed.

In the darkness, dressed only in a thin gown, the woman's limbs and face had glowed with a soft blush, a sheen of phosphorescence that was not evident in the bright light.

The cyanobacteria had not just spread to her eyes—but everywhere.

Lisa was so stunned that she failed to note one other detail for a full breath: the patient's eyes were open, staring back at Lisa.

Parched lips moved.

Lisa read those lips more than heard the words.

"Wh-who are you?"

8:12 P.M.

MONK LISTENED TO the radio's earpiece as he climbed the stairs from the lower decks. He had gone down to check the access to Ryder Blunt's private dock, where he kept his boat. It was unguarded. Few knew about the private slide launch.

"I have the electronic key to the dock's hatch," Ryder said. "Once I'm free, I'll head down there, get the boat gassed up, and be ready to launch. But can you free Dr. Cummings by yourself?"

"Yes," Monk said into the mouthpiece. "The less commotion the better."

"And you've got everything prepared."

"Yes, Mother." Monk sighed. "I'll be ready in a half hour. On my word, you know what to do."

"Roger that. Out."

Monk climbed to the next landing of the stair, crossed to a janitorial closet, and collected up the blanket, pillow, and clothes he had hidden inside earlier.

His earpiece buzzed again. "Monk?"

"Lisa?" He checked his watch. It was early. His heart thudded harder. "What's wrong?"

"Nothing. At least not exactly. We need a change of plans. We need room for one more."

"Who?"

"My patient. She's awake."

"Lisa . . ."

"We can't leave her here," she insisted in his ear. "Whatever is happening to her is critical to everything that's going on. We can't risk the Guild escaping with her before we can return."

Monk breathed hard out his nose, recalculating. "How mobile is she?"

"Weak but mobile enough. I think. I can't judge more with the orderlies in the next room. I'm in my room where I can talk. I left her back there, feigning still being catatonic."

"And you're sure she's that important."

"Positive."

Monk asked a few more questions, settled a few more details, revising on the fly. Lisa signed off to get ready at her end.

"Ryder?" Monk said.

"I heard," the Aussie billionaire said. "My radio was still on."

"We'll have to move up the timetable."

"No bloody kidding. When will you be here?"

Monk flipped the safety off his weapon. "I'm heading up there right now."

8:16 P.M.

LISA RETURNED TO the infirmary suite. She had donned a sweater. She had complained earlier to the orderlies that she was cold, a simple excuse to return briefly to her room and make the radio call to Monk.

As she entered, Tweedledee and Tweedledum were still engrossed in their movie. Some shoot-out was under way on the television. Life was about to imitate art.

If all went well.

Lisa turned and crossed to the bedroom—then stumbled back a step, startled.

Dr. Devesh Patanjali stood at the foot of the bed, hands behind his back. Ahead, Susan lay sprawled on the bed, under the isolation tent, eyes closed, breathing evenly.

Devesh was not supposed to be here.

"Ah," he said without turning, "Dr. Cummings, how is our patient doing?"

8:17 P.M.

THE ELEVATOR DOORS chimed open onto the level of the presidential suite. Monk, tired and irritable, strode out into the hall. He had a bundle of blankets and a pillow.

He crossed toward the pair of guards posted by the double doors.

One sat on a chair, the other straightened from where he was leaning against the wall.

"Go," Monk said crisply into his radio's microphone.

It was his signal.

A muffled gunshot rang out from behind the suite's door as Ryder took out the man posted inside.

Startled, the guard who'd been standing by the wall swung to the door.

Monk was on him immediately. He swung up both arms, a pistol in each hand, one tucked into a pillow, the other bundled in the blanket. He shoved the pillow against the man's back and pulled the trigger, taking out his spine. As the guard dropped, he fired a second round into the man's head.

Before the body even hit the ground, Monk turned to the seated man, lifting the blanket-wrapped pistol.

He pulled the trigger . . . twice.

8:19 P.M.

LISA ENTERED THE bedroom.

"Dr. Patanjali, I'm glad you're here," she said, swallowing the gall that came with the lie. She needed Devesh out of here. She had told Monk only two orderlies would be here.

Devesh turned to her.

Lisa swiped some loose hair over her ear, feigning exhaustion as her heart pounded. "I had come to get some test results on a CSF tap I performed earlier. But . . ." She waved to the computer. "The power surge knocked out the CPU. I was hoping to review the results before I went to bed."

"Why didn't you order one of the men to fetch them from Dr. Pollum's lab?"

"No one's there. I was hoping you might expedite matters."

Devesh sighed. "Certainly. I was just heading over to my room for the night. I'll call down and have Pollum send you a hard copy."

"Thank you."

Devesh headed away, but he stopped at the threshold and turned back to her.

Lisa tensed.

"You looked quite handsome at the cocktail party. Truly radiant."

Lisa kept her face impassive by sheer force of will. "Th-thank you."

Then he was gone.

Shaken a bit, Lisa hurried over to Susan. Leaning down, Lisa whispered in her ear. "I'm going to begin unhooking you from everything. We're getting out of here."

Susan nodded. Her lips moved, exhaling a soft "thank you."

As Lisa set to work on the IV catheter, she noted the tear tracks leaking from the outer corner of Susan's eyes to her pillow. Earlier, Lisa had quietly explained about the fate of the woman's husband. Lisa had read his autopsy reports, courtesy of Devesh.

Lisa squeezed the woman's shoulder.

Luckily, Devesh had not noted her glowing tears.

8:25 P.M.

MONK HURRIED ACROSS the outside starboard deck, hunched against the wind-lashed rain. Only a few pools of light spilled to the darkened deck. Black clouds whipped and roiled above the giant net woven across the top of the island. Flashes of lightning glowed like a distant war zone. The rumble of thunder was almost constant.

After his first talk with Lisa, Monk had scouted the proper section of deck and prepared everything he needed.

But he hadn't had time to ready a second sling. He'd simply have to haul the women up one at a time.

To accomplish that quickly, Monk needed more muscle.

Ryder pounded behind him, dressed in local rags like Monk.

Gassing up the billionaire's boat would have to wait.

"This way!" Monk yelled above the drench of rain and gusts of wind.

A deck chair skittered past him. The winds were picking up. They needed to be out of here in the next hour to escape the worst brunt of the coming typhoon.

Overhead, the island's woven roof shook and rattled.

Monk reached the section of deck where he had rigged a rope and fireman's sling, stolen from out of the ship's emergency rescue gear.

Monk pointed. "Haul it to the rail!" he hollered as he leaned over the edge.

He searched below. The curve of the ship's hull made it hard to be certain, but two levels below him should be the balcony to the cabin where Lisa had been tending her patient. It was the point of egress for this op.

Farther below, the dark lagoon reflected the ship's few lights, rippling gently, sheltered from the worst of the wind by the high volcanic walls. As Monk turned to Ryder, he noted some flashes of light in the water. Not reflections, something deeper. Bright blues and crimson fire.

What the hell?

A crackle of lightning shattered overhead, striking the roof net, lighting up the lagoon. Monk ducked from the thunder. Where the lightning struck, sparkling blue energies shattered outward along the steel bracings of the net, leaving momentary dances of St. Elmo's fire. The entire structure must be grounded, acting like a massive lightning rod.

Ryder joined him at the rail. He had the coil of rope over his shoulder and tossed the sling over the rail. He lowered it with the experience of a dock lineman. The sling reached the level of the balcony, swinging in the blustering wind.

"I'll go down," Monk yelled in his ear. "Secure the cabin. Then haul ass back up here. The two of us will have to pull the women up."

Ryder nodded. He had already heard the plan. Monk had repeated it, just to give the man one last chance to volunteer to go down instead.

Ryder didn't.

Smart man. No wonder he's a billionaire.

Monk grabbed the line, hauled himself over the rail, hooked his leg, and swung out on the wet rope. Controlling his descent with his prosthetic hand, he zipped down the rope until his feet hit the sling.

He faced the open balcony, swinging in the wind. The drapes were half closed, but the bright light inside revealed Lisa. A bear of a man had her pressed against the balcony doors, hand around her neck, lifted up on her toes.

Oh, this was already going well.

8:32 P.M.

LISA HUNG FROM Tweedledee's arm, his hand clenched around her neck. His nose was in her face, and spittle flew as he yelled.

"What the fuck were you doing with the IV lines, bitch?" The last word was spat at her in heavily accented English.

What Lisa had been doing was removing all of Susan's catheters—urinary, intravenous, her central line—readying her to leave as quickly as possible. Unfortunately, the orderlies' movie had ended, and Dee had gone to relieve himself, passing close enough to sense something was amiss.

Behind his brother, Dum checked on the patient. He turned and spoke rapidly in Russian. Lisa didn't understand, but plainly something was massively awry.

Not good.

Still pressed against the balcony door, Lisa felt someone tap the glass at her backside.

Please, God, let that be Monk.

She reached behind her and just managed to stretch her index finger to the locking latch. She flipped it up.

The door slid open behind her, taking her with it.

Surprised and caught off balance by the move, Dee stumbled forward and dropped her. She tried to keep her feet, but ended up falling hard on her backside.

An arm burst through the open balcony door, grabbed Dee by the collar of his scrubs, and yanked him outside. A muffled shot followed, followed by a fading scream.

Dee was going for a swim.

Dum, on the other hand, was backing toward the foot of the bed, snatching at his shoulder holster, startled and too stunned to yell out yet. Lisa went for her weapon, but she was sitting on it.

Monk appeared in the doorway, lit from behind by a flash of lightning, soaked to the skin. He had his pistol raised. The shot would be heard, but there was no avoiding it.

Then a figure rose behind Dum, kneeling up on the bed, wobbly.

Susan.

The woman stabbed out with a scalpel, piercing the man's neck clean through from behind. Forgetting his gun, the guard clutched both hands to his throat.

Monk lunged forward, grabbed the man's belt, and hauled him straight out the door.

"Time to go check on your brother."

This time there wasn't even a scream.

Monk returned, wiping his hands clean. "So, who's ready to go?"

The next few moments were a rush.

Lisa ran to the cabin's door and threw the security bolt while Monk helped free the last of Susan's leads and wires—EKG, EEG, Doppler pulse—unchaining her from the medical equipment.

Lisa slipped off her sweater and helped Susan don it, along with climbing into an extra pair of scrub pants. Though unsteady on her feet, Susan proved stronger of limb than Lisa had expected from her after five weeks of catatonia.

Maybe it was adrenaline, maybe something else.

Either way they were soon out on the balcony and into the storm. A sling bounced at the end of a rope. Monk caught it and glanced over to Susan, surprise making him pause. "Mind telling me why your friend's glowing in the dark?"

Shying away, Susan tried to pull the sweater farther over her arm. Lisa had already demonstrated the effect earlier to Susan, by turning off the bedroom lights briefly.

Lisa waved Monk to the rope. "We'll talk about it later."

Monk frowned, but he clambered up, proving the strength of his upper body and the grip of his prosthetic hand.

Lisa helped Susan into the sling. "Can you hold on okay?" she asked the woman.

"I'll have to." Susan shivered violently.

After a bit of maneuvering, Monk and Ryder began hauling her skyward, using a ship's post as a brace.

Lisa waited, pacing a bit.

A loud knock reached her, freezing her in place.

It came from the cabin.

She stepped to the threshold. An angry shout greeted her.

Dr. Devesh Patanjali.

He must have tried to use his key card and discovered it was privacy locked. More pounding.

Lisa backed up, leaned out over the rail, and stared up.

Susan's feet kicked. She was being helped over the rail.

Lisa pulled out her pistol from her belt and yelled up. "Hurry! Someone's coming!"

The wind and thunder ate her words.

A splintering crack erupted from the cabin. They were breaking inside. A rifle shot followed. Loud as a cannon blast. Startling her.

A shout echoed down to her from above.

Monk at least had heard the gunfire.

The sling dropped at her shoulder, tossed, not lowered. It banged into her. She ignored it, rushed forward to the open balcony door, grabbed the inside drape, and swept it fully closed. She slid the door shut, too.

Let them discover the empty room.

The ruse might not last long, but it could buy her an extra few seconds. She dove back around, snatched the sling, and squirmed into it. A sudden gust of wind caused it to strike her hand, knocking her pistol from her grip.

The weapon flew off into the darkness.

Damn it . . .

Frantic, she cinched the sling, climbed up onto the balcony rail, and kicked out.

She felt the sling jerk under her arms as the men hauled her up.

She swung back toward the balcony, just as the drape was ripped open. Lightning flashed overhead. She saw Devesh's face widen in surprise, uncomprehending at the view of her swinging toward him.

He fell back.

In his place, Surina appeared in a dressing gown, her long black hair loose. She shoved the door open while her other arm snaked back and grabbed the cane from Devesh.

Lisa reached the end of the arc of her swing. She kicked at the woman, but Monk and Ryder had hauled her up, shortening her rope enough that the tip of her boot whished through open air.

The sling swung away again.

Surina followed, out onto the balcony, her hair whipped into a furious swirl by the wind. She grabbed Devesh's cane in both hands, twisted it, and whipped it wide. A sheath of polished white wood flew back into the cabin, revealing the length of steel blade hidden in the cane.

Surina flew to the balcony rail.

Lightning lit the sky, turning the sword into blue fire.

Weaponless, Lisa swung back toward the woman waiting with the blade.

8:46 P.M.

MONK HAD NOT waited. With the first rifle blast, he knew Lisa needed more direct help, so he left the big Aussie to haul her on his own.

Monk rappelled out on a rope. The other end was tied to a life preserver, jammed between two posts of the ship's rail. His prosthetic hand clenched the rope with the strength of a steel clamp. His other hand pointed his pistol.

He leaped out far enough to see Lisa swinging back toward a woman with a sword. He aimed his pistol and fired.

A gust of wind threw off his aim.

The round tore a chunk out of the balcony's wooden railing.

But it was enough to ward off the swordswoman. She fell back with a smooth twist of her body.

Ryder bellowed as he hauled hard on Lisa's line.

At the same time, with strength born of adrenaline and terror, Lisa pulled herself up by her arms. She now stood in the sling, rather than hanging. She was above the balcony opening now. She hit the hull hard and bounced away.

Ryder yanked her another three feet up.

Monk emptied the remainder of his clip, another three rounds, discouraging anyone's approach. That should keep everyone back.

He was wrong.

The swordswoman appeared again and leaped to the top of the rail, like a gymnast mounting a balance beam—then she leaped straight up, sword pointed high.

Lisa screamed.

8:47 P.M.

THE BLADE SLID past her boot heel, sliced through her jeans, and bit deep into her left calf.

Then the sword fell away, succumbing to gravity.

Lisa stared between her toes. Surina landed on the balcony deck and stepped deftly away. She didn't even glance back up.

Ryder drew Lisa higher yet again.

Out of reach.

Lisa lost sight of the balcony, pulled beyond the curve of the hull. Hugging the rope, she trembled and shook. Blood poured down her leg and into her boot.

She spotted Monk to one side climbing back up to the railing.

Moments later, someone grabbed her shoulders and dragged her bodily over the rail. She fell to the deck, still shaking. Ryder appeared, unwrapping a head scarf that had fallen around his neck.

"This is going to hurt," he said, but it sounded far away.

He took the scarf, wrapped it around her burning calf, then swiftly tugged it tight. Pain bloomed through her, earning a strangled gasp from her. But the agony broke through the threatening shock.

Sound returned from out of the hollow well down which it had fallen.

Ryder helped her stand. "We have to go. They'll be up here any bloody moment."

She nodded. "Fine . . . go . . . yes."

It wasn't Shakespeare, but Ryder understood. He shouldered her up while Monk helped Susan. They were all drenched.

They set off toward the stern of the boat.

"Where . . . ?" she asked, hobbling as fast as she could.

"We'll never make my boat," Ryder answered. "They'll have the stairs and elevators covered."

Confirming this, an alarm began to wail, sounding deep in the ship, then exploding out to the decks.

Monk pointed over the rail and down. "The public tender dock," he said. "An hour ago, when I checked for any
guards at your private launch, I spotted one of the pirates'
blue speedboats tethered down there, unmanned and
abandoned."

"The tender dock lies just as many decks down."

Monk drew them in a limping group to the midship rail.
He leaned out. "Not if we take a more direct route."

He pointed down.

Lisa craned over. She could just make out the protruding
end of the tender dock. A speedboat with an outboard motor
was moored there. It must have been used to shuttle pirates
between their small village and the ship.

It seemed unguarded.

"We jump?" Susan asked, dismayed.

Monk nodded. "Can you swim?"

Susan nodded. "I'm a marine biologist."

Lisa balked. They were a good fifty feet above the water.
Shouts echoed in the direction of the bow. Monk glanced at
Lisa's leg, then up to her face.

She nodded. No other choice.

"We'll have to go as a group," Monk said. "One big
splash will draw less attention than four."

They climbed over and held themselves steady on the
rail.

Monk leaned farthest out. "Ready."

Nods all around.

Lisa's stomach churned, her leg throbbed. Pain made her
see stars in the dark water, brief flashes of electric streaks.

Monk counted down, and they all leaped.

Arms flailing for balance, Lisa plunged feet first. She
had done some cliff-diving in the past. Still, when she
struck the water it was like landing on hard-packed dirt.
The blow impacted her entire frame. Her knees buckled—
then the sea gave way. She shot deep into the warm water.
After the chill of the rain and wind, the lake felt like a welcoming bath.

Her momentum slowed, braking further with her arms out.

Then she was rising. She kicked and stroked back to the surface, breaking through with a gasp. All around, rain pebbled the water. Winds spat in contrary gusts.

Treading water, Lisa spotted the three others. Monk was already headed to the boat.

Ryder helped Susan. He glanced over to Lisa.

She waved him to the boat.

Her boots and sodden clothes made it harder, but she kept pace.

Monk reached the speedboat first and hauled himself up and into it like a beaching seal. He stayed low and surveyed the tender dock.

No shouts arose.

The ship still rang with alarms. Everyone was probably still heading to the upper deck, where the fugitives had last been spotted.

Ryder reached the boat next with Susan.

As Monk helped them aboard, Lisa closed the distance.

She was almost to the boat when—

—something struck her leg, bumping it hard.

Startled, she floundered a bit. She searched the dark waters. Something brushed against her hip. It left a tracery of green fire in the water, flashing, then gone.

Hands grabbed her shoulders.

She almost cried out. She had not known she had reached the boat. Ryder hauled her up and over the edge.

Lisa sprawled across the floor. Abandoned tools pinched her backside. She smelled oil in her hair. But she didn't move. She breathed deeply, slowing her heart.

The engine behind her suddenly gave a watery growl. Ryder yanked off the mooring lines. Monk edged the boat away from the dock. He went slow at first, keeping their noise to a minimum.

Lisa sat up and glanced back to the dock.

A shape stepped out of the ship and onto the planks of the tender dock. Even with his face shadowed, Lisa pictured his tattoos. Rakao. The Maori leader had not been fooled. He knew there were only so many ways off this ship.

"Go!" Lisa shouted. "Full throttle, Monk!"

The engine shook, coughed a bit of water, then roared.

As Lisa stared, Rakao lifted his arm. She remembered his giant horse pistol.

"Down!" she yelled. "Everyone down!"

Muzzle fire flashed. The metal side of the boat rang from a glancing shot. The boat's speed kicked up, churning a thick wake.

Rakao fired again, but even he must have realized it was wasted. He already had a radio to his lips.

Monk sped away from the cruise ship.

Lisa noted another speedboat appear from around the stern of the cruise ship, still some distance off. It must be returning from the beachside village. It suddenly sped faster, aiming for the tender dock.

Rakao must have summoned it, preparing to give chase.

But they had a good lead.

That is, until the engine choked with a loud clank and an oily gout of smoke. The speedboat shuddered and slowed. Lisa sat higher, twisting around. She stared down at the tools she had sprawled atop. The oily towel crumpled in the back.

The boat had *not* been waiting to ferry passengers between boat and village—it was being repaired.

The engine's smoking grew worse. Its roar became a putter.

Ryder swore, climbed past her, and opened the hatch on the engine.

More smoke poured out.

Ryder scowled. "This little tinny's gone tits up."

Back at the cruise ship, Rakao leaped from the dock to the speedboat. It took off after them.

"We have no choice," Monk said, turning the wheel as they weakly limped along. The engine sputtered a bit more speed. "We'll have to make for shore. Hope for the best."

Lisa stared at the beach, then back toward Rakao's boat. It would still be a close call.

Monk cajoled as much horsepower as he could. The dark forest rose before them. At least it looked dense enough to hide them.

A half minute later, the engine finally died completely.

"Swim for it!" Ryder said.

The beach was not far. Less than fifty yards.

"Abandon ship," Monk agreed. "And haul ass."

Once again, they all leaped into the lake. Lisa kicked off her boots and followed. Rakao's boat roared toward them.

Only after she hit the water did she remember something bumping her earlier, her momentary panic. But right now Rakao scared her more. Having been diving all her life, Lisa had been bumped by her fair share of inquisitive sharks.

Rakao was definitely scarier.

She kicked for shore.

Glancing behind her, she noted strange flashes in the water.

Emerald, ruby, sapphire.

Scintillations, like fire underwater.

They streaked through the water, aiming for their group.

Lisa suddenly knew what had bumped her, what sped toward them, a pack of hunters, communicating with flashes of light, a predatory Morse code.

"Swim!" she screamed.

She paddled faster.

They wouldn't make it.

IT FOLLOWS THE scent trail of blood in the water. Lateral fins undulate and glide. Muscles pump water through its mantle and out its rigid rear funnel, jetting its six-foot bulk through the water. It clenches its eight arms into a tight point, a sleek muscular arrow. Its two longest tentacles flash with brilliance at their tips. Streaks of luminescence shiver in stripes along its flanks.

Guiding the pack.

Large globular eyes read the messages of its brethren.
Some sweep wide, others go deep.
The blood scent grows richer.

LISA KICKED AND paddled in clean strokes.

Panic would only slow her.

The beach spread ahead, a silvery strand between the black water and dark jungle. It was a finish line she intended to cross.

Rakao's boat growled behind her.

But the Maori pirate was not who she was racing.

Streaks of watery fire jetted toward her.

Drawn by her sliced calf.

Blood.

Four yards ahead, Monk and Ryder slogged out of the water, dragging Susan between them. Lisa kicked harder.

"Monk!"

WITH ONE FINAL muscular squeeze, it sweeps toward the churn of water. It unfurls its arms, billowing them wide. Two longer tentacles shoot out, snaking through the water, blistering with yellow lights, lined by suckers barbed with chitinous hooks.

9:05 P.M.

MONK HEARD HIS name called out.

Lisa paddled toward shore, looking frantic.

Only three yards away.

Behind her the pirate boat skimmed at full throttle right toward their group. Rain poured from the open sky, dimpling the lake. Beneath the surface, winking flashes of fire, like tracer rounds in the night, shot toward Lisa.

Monk remembered the stories of this lagoon.

Told by a toothless local.

Demons of the deep.

He leaped back into the water. The shore fell away steeply. In two steps he was waist-deep. "Lisa!"

She glanced to him, eyes meeting.

Then suddenly she jerked to a stop, snagged.

Her eyes widened. "Go—"

Monk lunged for her, arms out. "Your hand!"

Too late.

A flurry of tentacles exploded from the water, enveloping her. With neck-breaking speed, Lisa was twisted and slammed below, swamped away. The monster rolled briefly into view, sleek and fringed with small lateral wings, rippling with thin bands of electric flashes. A large black eye stared back, then vanished away.

One sleeved arm broke the surface, already two yards farther out. Then with impossible speed, it ripped through the water, a fish on a zipping line. The limb snapped back into the deep.

Lisa . . .

Monk took another step, preparing to dive.

But blasts of gunfire shattered through his shock. Rounds peppered the water, driving him back, out of the water, to the sand.

"Here!" Ryder yelled.

More shots coughed up divots of sand. Rifle fire cracked.

He had no choice.

Monk stumbled back, into Ryder's grip, into the dark forest.

Lisa . . .

LISA STRUGGLED TO hold her breath, tangled within constricting arms.

Giant hooks bit into flesh, made painless by panic.

She kicked and writhed.

Eyes open.

Trailing flashes of light shot through the darkness.

This was how she would die.

9:06 P.M.

MONK ALLOWED HIMSELF to be pulled farther into the jungle. He had no choice. There was nothing he could do.

Through a break in the foliage, he stared back toward the black water.

The pirates' boat had slowed near the beach. Rifles bristled toward shore, searching. But Rakao stood braced in the bow, a dark silhouette with long spear in hand.

With a heave, the Maori hunter drove the length of steel into the lake.

Arcs of blue lightning sizzled outward from where it struck, brilliant in the darkness, lighting up the night and the depths of the lagoon. Waters hissed with a bubble of steam around the spear's shaft.

What was he doing?

BARELY CONSCIOUS, LISA gasped the last of her trapped air. A painful shock clenched through her. The squid's embrace locked harder, experiencing the same agony, possibly even more sensitive.

Then its arms released her with a final savage twist.

Seawater burned into her nose.

Her eyes open, she saw the creature streak down into the dark depths, an arrow of emerald fire. Others followed.

Buoyancy floated her up.

Then hands grabbed her, pulled by her hair.

They were too slow.

Lisa choked in water, mouth opening and closing like a fish, as darkness swallowed her away.

9:07 P.M.

FROM THE SHELTER of a boulder and heavy jungle, Monk watched as Lisa was hauled from the water by her hair. Limp and boneless. Her head lolled back at an impossible angle.

Rakao tossed aside his spear.

"Some sort of cattle prod," Ryder said. "Shocked the ink right out of the wankers."

Rakao bent Lisa over the rail and pushed on her back. A wash of seawater splashed from nose and mouth.

One arm lifted and swatted at him.

Alive.

The pirate hauled her around and dumped her to the floor. He stared toward the jungle, then higher up the cliffs. Lightning crackled in a shattering display across the roof of the island. Winds gusted up with a whip of rain, sheeting over the lagoon.

Rakao lifted an arm and made a circling motion.

The speedboat swung around with a surge of wake, then sped back out, trailing a rooster tail of water. They were returning to the ship.

Taking Lisa with them.

But at least she was alive.

"Why are they leaving?" Susan mumbled.

Monk glanced over. In the darkness of the forest, the woman's face and hands shone with a whispery glow, barely noticeable, but there. Like moonlight through thick clouds.

"Not like there's exactly anywhere we can go," Ryder said bitterly. "By morning, they'll be hunting us."

Monk pointed deeper into the forest. "Then we'd better get going."

With Susan at his side, Monk headed into the higher jungle. He glanced one last time back to the lagoon. "What were those things?"

"Predatory squid," Susan mumbled with some authority. "Some bioluminescent squids hunt in packs. Humboldt squids in the Pacific have attacked and killed people, swarming out of the deep. But larger specimens also exist. Like *Taningia danae*. The isolated lagoon here must be home to such a subspecies. Rising to feed. At night, when their luminescent communication and coordination work best."

Monk remembered a story from one of the pirates, about the island, of witches and demons in the water. Here must be the source of the story. He also remembered another story of the island.

He craned up toward the jagged cliffs, framed against the dark sky. Heard past the rumble of thunder, drums pounded.

Cannibals.

"What now?" Ryder asked.

Monk led the way. "Time to meet the neighbors . . . see what's cookin'."

9:12 P.M.

SUPPORTED ON THE tender dock, Lisa hung from the arms of one of the pirates. She was too weak to fight, too tired to care. Sodden to bone, bleeding from a score of lacerations, she awaited her fate.

Rakao was in midargument with Devesh.

In Malay.

Beyond her comprehension.

But Lisa suspected the fight was about the tattooed pirate not pursuing Susan Tunis into the jungle. Lisa understood only one word.

Kanibals.

Behind the men a robed Surina stood at the entrance to the boat, out of the rain, arms folded, back straight, patient. Her eyes were fixed on Lisa. Not cold—that implied some emotion. Surina's eyes were a total void.

Finally, Devesh turned and pointed an arm at Lisa. He spoke in English as a courtesy to their captive. "Shoot her. Now."

Lisa straightened in the pirate's arms. She coughed her voice to a hoarse mumble.

She offered the Guild scientist the only thing she could. To save her life.

"Devesh," she said firmly. "The Judas Strain. I know what the virus is doing."

II

Broken Glass

SHOCK SLOWED THE SCENE down to a breathless, silent stretch.

From a second-story window of Hagia Sophia, Gray watched the back of Balthazar Pinosso's head explode in a spray of blood and bone. His body crumpled at the waist from the impact. His arms went wide to the side. His cell phone, at his ear a moment before, went flying from his fingertips, struck the pavement, and skittered away.

The large man's body struck next.

Vigor gasped at Gray's side, breaking the tableau. "Oh, my Lord . . . no . . ."

Sound crashed back: the echo of the gunshot, screams from the plaza.

Gray drew back, taking an extra breath to realize the implication. *If Balthazar was shot . . .*

"Nasser knew about him," Vigor said, finishing his own slow thought. Stunned, the monsignor caught himself on the ledge of the window. "Nasser knew Balthazar was here. The monster's snipers killed him."

Gray fared no better, dazed with incomprehension and guilt. He had sent the man out to a firing squad.

The screams and shouts grew worse outside, spreading

inside. People ran—most fleeing to the nearest shelter, the sanctuary of Hagia Sophia.

Minutes ago, Gray and Vigor had climbed to the church's second floor, where there was less traffic, keeping hidden. Before heading out, Balthazar had informed the museum curator that Gray and Vigor had already left, denying the need for an ambulance. They had come up here to make sure all went well.

"The police will swarm here," Gray said. "We've got to hide."

Vigor grabbed Gray's sleeve. "Your mother and father . . ."

He shook his head. He had no time to consider that. Nasser had warned against any ruse. But once voiced aloud, Gray could not escape the terror. His breathing grew heavier; he became light-headed. Gray's parents would also suffer for this mistake.

How had Nasser known about Balthazar?

Vigor continued to stare out the window. The monsignor's fingers tightened on Gray's arms. "Dear Lord . . . what's she doing now?"

Gray turned his full attention back to the open plaza below the western facade. As people fled the square or crouched in fear, only one figure ran straight through all the confusion. She limped slightly, favoring her left side.

Seichan.

Why was she coming here?

Almost to the church, a chatter of sparks struck at her heels. Someone was shooting at her. Nasser's men. But her sudden appearance had caught the snipers off guard. With orders to keep Gray and his companions from leaving the church, they hadn't been expecting someone running *toward* the church.

Seichan sped faster, racing death.

1:58 P.M.

BLINDSIDED, SEICHAN CURSED. So Nasser did have a sniper or two positioned out here. She had missed picking them out earlier. Then again, the snipers had plenty of time to hide well. Seichan had not anticipated a traitor among their group. Balthazar had already been at Hagia Sophia all morning, setting up a snug snare.

She dashed through the Imperial Doors and ducked against the inside wall. Were gunmen in here, too?

She searched the cavernous length of the nave. People, frightened by the gunplay, cowered in corners or shifted in maddened tides of confusion and panic. She had to find Gray and Vigor.

Sirens sounded in the distance.

A hand snagged her shirt. Reflexively, she jabbed a pistol into ribs.

Her target didn't flinch. "Seichan, what happened?"

It was Gray, his face drawn and pale.

"Gray . . . we have to get out of here. Now. Where's the monsignor?"

He pointed toward a neighboring stairwell. Vigor kept half hidden at its entrance and watched the crowd.

Seichan herded Gray over to him.

The monsignor stared back at the arched doorway, his eyes wounded with grief. "Nasser shot him. Shot Balthazar."

"No," Seichan said, killing any misconception. "I did."

Vigor backed up a step. Gray swung around.

"He was working with Nasser," Seichan explained.

Vigor's voice turned angry. "How can . . . ?"

"I have photos from two years ago. Nasser and Balthazar together. Money changed hands." She fixed Vigor with a hard stare. "He's been working with him all along."

Seichan read the continuing disbelief. She hardened her voice. "Monsignor, who called your attention to the inscription in the Tower of Wind?"

Vigor glanced toward the doors, toward the dead man out of sight.

"Before involving you both," Seichan pressed, "Nasser and I were playing cat and mouse throughout Italy, searching for the first bits of the angelic puzzle. No one was supposed to discover my invisible mark in the Vatican until I called you, alerted you to search the tower's closet with an ultraviolet light. Do you think your friend just *accidentally* stumbled upon it?"

"He said . . . one of his students . . ."

"He was lying. Nasser told him. The bastard followed the same trail I did. Used Balthazar to recruit you into solving the riddle."

Vigor sank to the stairs, covering his face.

Seichan turned to Gray. He stood a step away, eyes glazed, reconfiguring all the morning's events in light of the revelation. He must have sensed Seichan's attention.

"Then Nasser knew we were trying to betray him," Gray said. "He knew we had the first key. He knows everything."

"Not necessarily." Seichan pulled Vigor up by the shoulder and shoved Gray toward the church. "It was why I had to take him out. I don't think he had the time to call Nasser after he left you. I took him out before he got the chance and made things worse."

"Worse?" Gray stopped, refusing to move, his eyes furious. "You could have captured him. We could have used him against Nasser. There were a thousand options!"

"All of them too risky!" Seichan stepped closer, walking into the fire. "Get this through your thick skull, Gray. Nasser's plan, our plans . . . they're all screwed. It's clean slate time here. And we have to act now."

His face darkened as anger boiled up. Even his eyes turned stormy. "When the bastard finds out what you did . . . what we did . . . you just got my parents killed!"

She cut him off with a resounding slap to the face, knocking him back a step. Stunned, he lunged at her. She didn't resist. He collared her. His other hand a fist.

She kept her voice calm against his storm. "With that

bastard dead, we have a small window of confusion here. We must take advantage of it."

"But my folks—"

She kept her voice even. "Gray, they're already dead."

The fist tangled in her shirt trembled. His face constricted tight, red and agonized. His eyes searched her, needing someone to blame.

"And if they're not dead," she continued, "if he's keeping them alive as extra insurance, then we have only one hope here."

Gray's hand dropped from her throat but remained clenched.

"We'll need a big bargaining chip," she continued. "Equal to the weight of your parents' lives."

In his eyes, she could see the rage beginning to subside, the tide going out, the words finally sinking in. "And the second key alone won't do it."

She shook her head. "We need to go silent. Have Vigor pull his cell phone battery so that it's not tracked."

"But how will Nasser reach us?"

"It's time we took that control from him."

"But when he tries to call us . . . ?"

"Nasser will be furious. He may hurt one or both of your folks, maybe even kill one. But until he finds us, he'll keep one alive. He's not a fool. And that is our only hope."

Vigor's phone began to ring. Everyone froze a breath. Then Vigor slipped it out of his pocket. He glanced to the caller ID, swallowed, and passed it to Gray.

He took it. "Nasser," he confirmed.

"Speak of the devil," Seichan hissed. "One of the snipers must have called him. Needing to get further instructions. It's probably the only reason they haven't stormed the place already. Killing Balthazar caught them off guard. This is the only window we have."

Gray stared down at the phone.

Seichan waited.

How strong was this man?

2:04 P.M.

GRAY'S FINGERS REFUSED to move, clamped around the phone.

It vibrated and rang again.

He could almost feel the fury emanating out of it, an anger ready to be unleashed against his mother and father. He wanted desperately to answer it: to scream, to beg, to curse, to bargain.

But he had no leverage.

Not yet.

"Nasser must still be in midflight," Gray finally mumbled to the phone.

"Due to touch down in five hours," Seichan agreed.

Gray let a coldness wash through him, but his fingers tightened harder. "Up in the air, he'll hesitate to make any major decisions. He'll wait until his feet are on the ground before making a final assessment."

"And if he hasn't heard from you by then . . ."

Gray couldn't say the words. He only nodded his confirmation. Nasser would kill his parents. He won't wait any longer than that. He'll punish Gray and move on to a new strategy.

Five hours.

"We'll need more than the second key we found here," he said. "More than even the third key."

Seichan nodded.

Gray stared up at Seichan. "We'll need to have solved the obelisk's riddle. We'll need Marco's map."

Seichan simply stared, waiting.

Gray knew what he had to do. He flipped the phone over. With fingers numb and uncooperative, he fumbled with the battery in back.

Vigor stepped up and covered his palm over Gray's fingers. "Are you sure, Gray?"

He lifted his eyes. "No . . . I'm not. I'm not sure of a damn thing." He slipped his hands free of the monsignor's and peeled the battery off the phone, cutting the last ring in half. "But that doesn't mean I won't act."

Gray turned to Seichan. "What now?"

"You've just thrown down the gauntlet. Nasser will be calling his henchmen. We've got maybe a minute or two." She pointed into the depths of the church. "This way. Kowalski's got a car. He'll meet us out at the east exit."

She led them down the nave. People milled, unsure, voices echoed. Sirens closed down upon their location. Seichan fished something out of her pocket.

"Nasser must have snipers at that exit, too," Gray said, striding up to her.

Seichan held out her palm. "Concussive grenade. A flash-bang. We'll detonate it in the center. As everyone goes rushing out the exits . . . out we'll go, too."

Gray frowned.

Vigor voiced his concern as they circled past a crowd of schoolchildren, all wide-eyed and fearful, clutched in a group. "If the snipers see any of us, they'll open fire. On the crowd."

"No other way." Seichan sped faster. "We'll have to take the chance. Nasser's men may already be coming—"

A gunshot cracked loudly in the church.

Gray felt something whine past his ear. A bit of wall mosaic blasted in a shower of gold.

The crowd panicked, fleeing in all directions.

Vigor was knocked to a knee. Gray dragged him up as a second shot sparked against a marble column. The blast echoed.

Staying low, the trio fled to the side and down the length of the nave. As they reached the center, Seichan prepared to pull the pin on the grenade.

Gray grabbed her hand, restraining her. "No."

"It's the only way. There could be more shooters ahead of us. We'll need to trample with them to reach the exit."

And if we're spotted amid the crowd, he thought, *how many innocent people will be killed?*

He pointed. "There's another way."

Still holding his hand clamped to hers, he led them all to

the south side, toward the wall of scaffolding he had scaled earlier.

"Up!" he said.

However, there remained one obstacle.

The scaffolding guard had not fled his post. He remained crouched behind a wooden barrier, his rifle up, ready to shoot.

Gray snatched the grenade out of Seichan's fingers, pulled the pin, and tossed the bomb behind the barrier. "Close your eyes!" he yelled at Vigor, pulling the monsignor down. "Cover your ears."

Seichan crouched, her head wrapped in her arms.

The explosion felt like a kick to the gut. A sonic boom trapped in stone. A flash seared through Gray's lids, even with his head turned away.

Then it was over.

Gray yanked Vigor up. Screams echoed, sounding muffled through the residual ring in his ears. He rushed toward the massive scaffolding. The crowds parted, fleeing toward the east and west exits.

But they weren't going with them.

At the scaffolding, the guard was down, dazed on his back, moaning.

He'd have a bad headache, but he'd live.

Gray took his rifle and waved Seichan and Vigor up the scaffolding staircase. They'd have to move fast. The stampede would slow the shooters, but only for so long.

He clambered up after Seichan and Vigor.

"Where are we going?" Seichan called down. "We'll be sitting ducks up here!"

"Go!" Gray said. "Get your asses up there!"

They fled around and around, leaping steps.

They reached the halfway point when a spray of automatic fire rang off the bracings, wildly shot, but effective enough to chase them off the outer stairs and into the heart of the scaffolding. They pounded along the planked flooring of this level.

Gray pushed ahead of the others. "This way!"

Running in a half crouch, Gray raced toward the nearest wall.

They were at the level where the dome rested atop the church. A row of arched windows, the same windows that both Gray and Marco had marveled over, ringed the dome's bottom.

Gray lifted his rifle and strafed the window that lay at the end of the level. Glass shattered out. He did not slow. He reached the window, used the butt of his rifle to clear more glass.

"Out!" he yelled to Seichan and Vigor.

They flew past him as more gunshots pursued them, ringing off the steel bars and chewing through wood.

Gray followed them out, perched on an encircling ledge.

The afternoon sun blazed.

Istanbul spread below them in all its jumbled beauty, its chaotic mix of ancient and modern. The Sea of Marmara glowed a sapphire blue. Farther out, the suspended length of the Bosporus Bridge was visible, spanning the strait that led up to the Black Sea.

But it wasn't that bit of engineering that held Gray's attention.

He pointed to the church's southern facade, to where the exterior scaffolding clutched that side of Hagia Sophia, under repairs.

"Down there!"

Obeying, Vigor led the way around the dome, sidling along the narrow ledge. Once even with the scaffolding, Gray leaped off the ledge and onto the sloped lower roof. He slid on his backside down to the scaffolding, holding his rifle high.

He banged into the bracings and turned around. Seichan was already coming, keeping on her feet, half running, half skiing, heedless of the risk. Vigor was more cautious, on his backside, scooting in spurts and starts.

Seichan came to a steady stop, arms out to grab a strut.

She had her cell phone out, yelling into it.

Gray caught Vigor and helped the monsignor under the

railing and over to the scaffolding stairs. They fled down. Luckily there was no guard on this side. The commotion must have drawn him off.

Reaching the ground, Seichan led the way across a small greenbelt to a side street. A yellow taxicab skidded in a wishbone around the far corner, spun its tires, and sped straight at them. Seichan backed away, with a wide-eyed look of confusion.

The beat-up taxi sideswiped at the last moment and braked to a squealing stop.

The driver leaned toward the open passenger windows. "What the hell are you all waiting for? Get your asses in here!"

Kowalski.

Gray climbed in front. Seichan and Vigor in back. Doors slammed.

Kowalski took off, smoking the tires and tearing away.

Seichan fought the acceleration enough to lean forward. "This isn't the car I left you with!"

"That piece of Japanese crap! This is a Peugeot 405 Mi16. Early nineties. Sweet for speed."

Proving it, Kowalski revved the engine's rpms, down-shifted for the next corner, twisted the wheel, throwing them all to the left, then planted back on the power and shot out of the turn like a rocket.

Seichan hauled back up, red-faced. "Where—?"

Sirens erupted behind them, streaking around the same corner.

"You stole it," Gray said.

Leaning forward, nose by the wheel, Kowalski shrugged. "You say carjacking, I say *borrowing*."

Gray twisted around. The blazing police car was fading back, outgunned by their engine.

Kowalski sped around the next corner, throwing them all in the other direction, dictating the features of the car. "It's got a perfect weight-to-horsepower ratio, power steering stiffens at higher speeds . . . oh! And it's got a sunroof."

He lifted his hand off the gearshift to point up. "Nice, huh?"

Gray leaned back.

Kowalski lost the police in another two turns. They found themselves a minute later, puttering with the busy traffic headed out of Istanbul's old district, lost in a sea of taxis.

Gray finally calmed enough to turn back to Seichan. "Five hours," he said. "We need to get over to Hormuz."

"The island of Hormuz," Vigor elaborated. "At the mouth of the Persian Gulf."

Seichan held a hand against her side. The exertion must be taking its toll on her. She looked pale, but she nodded. "I know the place. Lots of smugglers and gunrunners use the island, crossing from Oman to Iran. Shouldn't be a problem."

"How long?"

"Three hours. By private jet and seaplane. I know a man."

Gray checked his watch. That would leave them only two hours to find the last key and use it and the others to unlock the obelisk's riddle. His heart began beating harder again. The excitement had stemmed his fear for his parents. But now . . .

He held out his hand to Seichan. "I need your cell phone."

"To call Sigma command?"

"I have to update them on what's happened."

Gray read her expression. She knew he was sidestepping the real reason. Still, she gave him her phone.

He sat back. In another few moments, he had Director Crowe on the line. He did update Painter on all the recent events, from the discovery of the second key through their escape.

"So it was the Vatican that had been infiltrated by a Guild mole," Painter said, his words dropping in and out a bit. "But, Gray, I don't think there's much I can do for you at the island. It's Iranian territory. Especially in such a short span. Not without alerting intelligence agencies throughout the Middle East."

"I don't want you to intervene," Gray said. "Just . . . please . . . my parents . . ."

"I know, Gray . . . I get it. We'll find them."

Despite the promise, Gray heard the hesitation in the director's voice, the unspoken words.

If your parents are still alive.

8:02 A.M.
Arlington, Virginia

THEY WERE BEING moved again.

Harriet balanced a glass of water against her husband's lips. Dressed in sweatpants and a sweatshirt, he was tied to a chair. "Jack, you need to drink. Swallow."

He fought.

"Get that pill down," the woman barked, "or I'll shove it up his ass."

Harriet's hands shook. "Please, Jack. Drink."

Annishen was losing patience. The woman, dressed in black leather, had taken a call a few minutes ago and had called in the other guards, even those on the street. Harriet had been dragged out of the old walk-in freezer where she had been locked up all night. It was a frightening place. A single bare bulb shone upon a double row of meat hooks, hung along tracks in the ceiling. Fresh bloodstains had streaked the floor, only haphazardly washed toward the freezer's center drain.

Then the call.

Harriet had been hauled out to attend her husband. Jack had been kept apart from her. They wouldn't let her stay with him. She had spent the entire night fearing for his life. He had been barely conscious after being struck by the Taser in the hotel room. She was horrified to find him bound and gagged in the chair, but he seemed otherwise unharmed.

He had thrashed against his ropes when he first saw her

again. But he didn't really recognize her, not fully. He remained in a disassociative state, brought on by all the stress, the near electrocution, waking bound and gagged.

"Forget it," Annishen finally said, grabbing Harriet's shoulder. "The pills you gave him earlier didn't do anything."

"He was already agitated," she said, begging. "It takes time . . . and consistency of dosage. He needs this pill."

Annishen waved to her. "One more try."

Harriet leaned against her husband's cheek, holding his head with one hand, the glass in the other. He jerked back, but she held tight. "Jack, I love you. Please drink. For me."

She dribbled water over his mouth. His lips finally parted, an animal reflex. He must be thirsty. He finally drank, gulping the offered water. It even seemed to calm him. He sagged in his bonds.

Harriet sighed in relief.

"Did he take it?" Annishen asked.

"It should calm him in about an hour."

"We don't have an hour."

"I understand . . . but . . ."

Harriet knew someone must be looking for them. The longer they stayed in one place, the greater the chance they might be tracked. The more moves, the trail would grow colder.

"Get him up!" Annishen said.

The woman grabbed Harriet by the scruff of her shirt collar and hauled her to her feet. She was strong. She shoved Harriet toward the back exit. Her goons untied Jack. Her husband was slung between the two gorilla-size men, Armenian, heavy eyebrows. One held a pistol in a jacket pocket, against her husband's back.

Annishen gripped Harriet's elbow.

Jack howled as they began to move him, struggling. "Noooo."

"Maybe we zap him again," the guard said in a thick accent.

"Please don't," Harriet pleaded. "I can keep him calm."

The guard ignored her.

Annishen seemed to be weighing this choice.

"It's daylight," Harriet said. "If you carried him out unconscious . . ."

"There are taverns," one guard said. "On the street. I pour vodka on his shirt. No one think twice."

Annishen soured at the idea. Harriet imagined it was mostly because it wasn't her own. She pushed Harriet toward Jack.

"Keep him quiet or I'll Tase him into a drooling baby."

Harriet rushed to her husband's side. She took the place of one of the guards, an arm around Jack's waist. She rubbed his chest with her other hand.

"It's okay, Jack. It's okay. We have to go."

He looked suspiciously at her, but the angry set to his eyes and lips softened. "I want . . . to go home."

"That's where we're going . . . c'mon now, no fussing."

He allowed them to lead him to the back exit and out to a narrow alley, barely large enough for the overflowing trash bin. The sunlight stung her eyes.

They were marched out to the street.

They had been in a boarded-up butcher's shop, one of a row of closed businesses on the block. Harriet searched around for landmarks. They were somewhere in Arlington. Harriet knew they had crossed the Potomac after being kidnapped.

But where?

A black Dodge van was parked half a block away.

Morning traffic was already picking up. A few homeless men and women were gathered in an alcove of a Laundromat. A shopping cart stood by them, piled high with stuffed plastic bags.

Annishen ignored the homeless and led her group to the van. She unlocked it with her remote and the rear side door slid open on its own.

Jack walked in a leaden daze, barely noting his surroundings.

Harriet waited until they were even with the men gathered

around the shopping cart. Her right hand still rested on Jack's belly.

I'm sorry.

She pinched his skin through his shirt and twisted.

Jack jerked straight, snapping out of his passivity.

"Noooo!"

He fought the guard.

"I don't know you people!" he hollered. "Get away from me!"

Harriet tugged at him. "Jack . . . Jack . . . Jack. Calm down."

He swatted at her, striking her hard on the shoulder.

"Hey!" one of the homeless men called out. He was skeletally thin with a ragged beard. He clutched a bottle, snugged in a paper sack. "What are you doing to that guy?"

Some faces inside the Laundromat lifted to stare out the steamy, streaked windows.

Annishen stepped back toward Harriet. She wore a thin smile, staring straight at Harriet. One hand rested in the pocket of her light hooded sweater, the threat plain.

Harriet rubbed Jack's belly and faced the bearded stranger. "He's my husband. He has Alzheimer's. We're . . . we're taking him to the hospital."

Her words soothed the wary cast to the man's face. He nodded. "Sorry to hear that, ma'am."

"Thank you."

Harriet led Jack into the van. They were soon settled in, and the doors closed. Annishen sat in the front passenger seat. As they pulled away, she turned to Harriet.

"Those pills had better kick in," she said. "Or next time, we'll leave him hanging from one of those butcher's hooks."

Harriet nodded.

Annishen turned back around.

One of the men reached from the backseat and pulled a black hood over her head. She heard a moan of protest from Jack as the same was done to him. She reached a hand over and gripped her husband's hand. His fingers gripped hers back, if only in a reflex of love.

I'm sorry, Jack . . .

Harriet's other hand slipped into the pocket of her sweater. Her fingertips nudged the pile of pills—the pills she had only *pretended* to give her husband. Before and now. She needed to keep Jack agitated, confused enough to act out.

To be seen . . . to be remembered.

She closed her eyes, despairing.

Forgive me, Lord.

12

Of a Map Forbidden

JULY 6, 4:44 P.M.
Strait of Hormuz

THE RUSSIAN SEAPLANE, a Beriev 103, coasted up from Qeshm Island International Airport and sailed out over the aquamarine waters of the Strait of Hormuz.

Gray was impressed with the short turnaround at the airport. Their jet from Istanbul had touched down only ten minutes ago. The amphibious plane had been waiting: fueled, engine warmed, its twin propellers slowly turning. The seaplane sat only six people, including the pilot, three sets of paired seats, lined one behind the other.

But it was swift.

The sea crossing to the island of Hormuz would take no more than twenty minutes. They had made good time. Still, it would leave them only two hours to find the last key and use it and the others to decipher the angelic script on the obelisk.

Gray had used the time aboard the private jet, provided via Seichan's black-market connections, to study the obelisk's complicated code. Even on such a short flight as this, every minute counted. Seated in the back row by himself, he pulled out his notebook again, scribbled with notes and possibilities. He had already tried converting all the obelisk's scripts into letters, like Vigor had done with the Vatican's angelic script, which spelled out *HAGIA*. But he had made no real headway.

Even with Vigor's help.

Back on the jet, the two of them had poured over the cryptogram. Vigor was better with ancient languages. But it proved no use. Decoding was made especially difficult because they didn't know which of the four surfaces of the obelisk was the starting point, and in which direction it should be read, clockwise or counterclockwise.

That created eight possibilities.

Vigor had finally rubbed his eyes, admitting defeat. "Without the third key, we'll never figure this out."

Gray refused to believe that. The two had even gotten into a brief argument. They mutually decided to take some time apart, to quit banging their heads together over the riddle. Gray knew much of the shortness of his temper was tied to the knot in his stomach.

Even now he felt like vomiting. Every time he closed his eyes, he pictured his mother's face. He saw the blame in his father's eyes.

So Gray stopped closing his eyes and continued to work. It was all he could do.

Gray stared again at one of the letter-substitution pages.

C N	B A	C G	M A
A S P	Z Z P	B V P	S P Z
A Z H	A L M	A Z H	Z L H
M V B	H V C	M L Z	A V C
T L C	S T C	S T H	S T G
S N Z	S N G	G N B	V A C
A L H	A L B	B L A	A L H
M V B	M V H	M V A	M S B

Seven more possibilities covered the next pages.

Which was right? Where to even begin?

Ahead, a loud snort drew his attention forward. Kowalski had already fallen asleep. Probably before the wheels even left the tarmac.

Vigor shared the neighboring seat, poring over the silk diary yet again. It was surely a dead end. The monsignor scowled at Kowalski's racket and undid his belt. He slid back to join Gray and collapsed in the next seat. He held the scroll in his hands.

A moment of awkward silence stretched.

Gray closed his notebook. "Back there . . . earlier . . ."

"I know." Vigor reached out and gently patted his hand. "We're all worried. But I wanted to run something by you. Get your thoughts."

Gray straightened. "Sure."

"I know you want to solve the obelisk's code. But since we're about to land, maybe now's a good time to figure out where on Hormuz Island the third key might be."

"I thought we already knew where to search," Gray said.

Unable to resist he reopened the notebook and tapped the angelic symbol found on the back of the third gold *paitzu*.

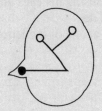

They had compared it to a map of the island and discovered that the blackened circle marked the location of the ruins of an old Portuguese castle, built about a century before the keys were hidden. In its prime, it had been a prominent stronghold. Built on an isthmus and separated by a moat, it had overlooked the town of Hormuz and the best anchorage ports. To those Vatican mystics looking to hide a key for the ages, the castle would have appeared to be a good place.

They were headed to its ruins now.

Vigor nodded. "Yes, the Portuguese castle. But what I meant was *why* are we searching there. If we knew that, we might figure out *what* to look for inside the castle ruins."

"Okay, so where do we begin?"

Vigor pointed out Gray's porthole window. The island could be seen ahead. "*Hormuz* was a major trading port, trafficking in jewels, spices, and slaves. Important enough that the Portuguese invaded during the sixteenth century and built their castle. But during Marco's time, it was also important enough for Kublai Khan to send a young woman of his household here to be married off."

"Kokejin, the Blue Princess."

"It was purely a commercial arrangement. In fact, the Persian king to whom she was betrothed died while Marco and Kokejin were en route. She ended up marrying the man's son. But again it was a marriage of convenience. She ended up dying only three years later. Some say at her own hand, some say because she was pining for another love."

Gray turned. "You don't mean—"

"Even Marco did not marry until after Kokejin was dead. And when Marco did die, he had two treasures in his room. The gold *paitzu* that Kublai Khan had given to him. But also a golden headpiece, encrusted with jewels." Vigor stared pointedly at him. "A *princess's* headpiece."

Gray straightened, imagining Marco's long two-year voyage, traveling and exploring exotic lands. Marco was still relatively young when he left Kublai Khan's palace, in his midthirties. Kokejin was seventeen when she left China, nineteen when she reached Persia. It was not impossible to imagine them falling in love, a love that could never last beyond Hormuz.

Gray rubbed at the headache he'd been fighting. He remembered the brick back at Hagia Sophia, the interior glazed in royal blue, a secret hidden in stone. But could the brick also represent Marco's heart, symbolic of his secret love for Kokejin?

"Then we've forgotten another clue left to us," Vigor continued. He lifted the scroll. "The story was embroidered on silk. Why silk?"

Gray shrugged. "It's a material from the Far East, where Marco had traveled."

"Yes, but could it signify something more?"

Gray remembered Vigor bent over the scripture, even examining it with a loupe. "What did you discover?" he asked.

The monsignor lifted the scroll. "This silk was not new when it was embroidered with the text. The silk was worn thin and uneven. I found oils and old stains."

"So it was a used piece of silk."

"But what was it *used* for?" Vigor asked. "One of the most common uses for silk—due to its expense and rarity—was as shrouds, burial shrouds of royalty."

Vigor waited, staring at Gray. He slowly understood, picturing a hollow blue brick. Amazement crept into his voice. "You think it might be *Kokejin's* burial shroud."

"Possibly. But if I'm right, then I know what we must search for within that old castle."

Gray knew, too.

"Kokejin's tomb."

4:56 P.M.

SEATED IN THE copilot's seat, Seichan had an expansive view of the island as the seaplane dove toward a sheltered bay. It was not a large island, no more than four miles across. Its center was rocky and hilly, with sparse veins of green. Most of its coastlines were cliffs and isolated jagged bays, home to many smugglers' coves. But to the north, the higher slopes fell more gently toward the sea. Here, the land turned greener with date palms and tilled fields, nestling a small township of thatched huts.

From the air, evidence of an older, more extensive city could be spotted: massive foundations, the stones quarried from the island's rock-salt hills; a few crumbled homes, looking more like rubble piles; and a single tall minaret, once used as a lighthouse by the Portuguese.

But none of this was their destination.

The seaplane tipped on a wing and banked over the isthmus that extended north from the old city. Upon the spit of land rested the remains of the old castle. It had once been separated from the ancient city by a wide moat, but it was now silted up, marked only by a sunken line drawn from east to west.

As the plane crossed over the ruins, Seichan studied their target. The massive fort was surrounded by tall seawalls, but the western side had long ago lost its battle with those seas, undermined and toppled by battering waves. The eastern side, sheltered by a gentle bay, had fared better.

The plane angled for a landing in this bay, diving low, then skimming the water. Seichan caught a glimpse of rusty iron cannons on the roof of the fort, and six more on the beach of the bay, now used as mooring ties for boats. In fact, a small tin boat was tied up to one. A small brown figure, naked except for a long pair of shorts, waved an arm at their approach.

Seichan expected that the young man was the guide she had ordered up from the village. With only two hours to spare, they needed someone who knew the castle grounds.

The seaplane coasted down to the water, spraying a fierce wash behind as the flying boat settled to the sheltered waters. Seichan was shoved forward in her seat belt, earning a twinge of complaint from her wounded side. She had checked the injury earlier, in the airport's bathroom. The bandages were damp with some leakage, but more pink than red.

She'd survive.

The pilot guided his ship around as the tin boat sped at them, bouncing through the plane's wake. Their guide sat in the rear, a hand on the rudder.

A few moments later, the hatches were opened, and the party climbed from plane to skiff. Their guide ended up being a boy of twelve or thirteen, all rib bones and smiles. And plainly he wanted to practice his English, as fractured as it might be.

"Good chaps, fine lady, welcoming to Hormuz! I am named Fee'az!"

Gray helped Seichan into the boat, cocking one eyebrow. "This is your experienced guide?"

"Unless you're willing to melt down one of those gold passports, that's the best money can buy here."

And she had already spent top dollar to get them here so quickly.

She watched Gray settle to a seat. His eyes were already studying the castle. She noted the worry in the hunch of his shoulders. In profile, his features were hard, all angles, from chin to cheekbones. But he was mortally torn, broken and weakened.

Over his mother and father.

With a slight dismissive shake of her head, Seichan turned away. She could not even remember her parents. Only one memory existed: of a woman being dragged through a door, weeping, reaching for her, then gone. She wasn't even sure it was her mother.

Fee'az whined up the small outboard and sputtered toward the palm-lined beach and the towering ruins of the castle. Kowalski trailed a hand in the water, yawning. Vigor stared over toward the village. Some celebration was under way, with music wafting over.

Gray glanced back at her. He wore a familiar expression, both eyebrows high, that asked, *Are you ready?*

She nodded.

As Gray turned back, he shook out of his light jacket. The sunlight blazed down. He wore only a khaki T-shirt. She noted a flash of sunlight at his collar. His right hand absently tucked back the bright bit of silver under his shirt.

A dragon charm.

She had given it to him mostly as a teasing joke from a past cooperation. But Gray had kept it and still wore it. Why? It made her feel inexplicably warm—not so much from affection as a mix of confusion and embarrassment. Did Gray think she had given the charm as some token, some sign of attraction? She should have been amused, but for some reason it just irritated her.

The boat's bow scraped against the sand, jarring her back.

They'd reached the shore and began unloading.

Seichan tossed Kowalski a satchel that contained additional gear, including a laptop computer, several more flash-bang grenades, and six boxes of ammunition for the four pistols.

Gray held out a hand to help her out of the boat.

She brushed him aside and hopped out.

Fee'az tied up the boat to one of the rusty cannons and waved them toward a square opening in the fort's walls. Higher up, narrow casements pierced the ramparts, where once Portuguese gunmen had defended the bastion.

The group passed under the wall and into the abandoned stone courtyard. Thorny weeds grew from cracks, a few steps away a large open cistern threatened a nasty fall, and a couple of scraggly date palms sprouted from an old garden patch. Everywhere else, loose sand whispered across the rock with the hissing voices of ghosts.

Fee'az lifted an arm toward the main bulk of the castle. It climbed in six stories to toothed ramparts, where the rusted tips of cannons still protruded.

"I will show you all!" Fee'az declared. "Much to watch!"

He began to set off, but Vigor touched the boy's shoulder. "Does the castle have a chapel?" he asked.

The boy frowned for a moment, then brightened again with his perpetual smile. "Chapple! You are thirsty."

Vigor smiled. "No. A church."

The boy's brow pinched, but his smile refused to fade. "Ah, you are Christian. That's okay. All good. Muslims like the Bible. It's a holy book, too. We have saints, too. Muslim saints. But the Prophet Mohammed is best." He shrugged sheepishly.

Vigor squeezed his shoulder, recognizing the boy was struggling between being a good tourist guide and being a good Muslim.

"The church?" he asked again.

The boy nodded vigorously. "The room of the crosses." He led them toward the dark opening, still babbling in a furious stream.

Kowalski shook his head at the boy's antics and set off after them. "He needs to cut caffeine out of his life."

Gray smiled, a rarity, sunshine through thunderclouds. "Let's go," he whispered to Seichan as he passed. He brushed close. His hand grazed hers.

She almost reflexively grabbed it. Instead, angry at herself, she clenched her fingers. But her reaction wasn't all fury or frustration.

There was guilt, too.

She hated lying to this man.

5:18 P.M.

"OH, THIS IS going to be a pain in the ass," Kowalski said.

Gray did not argue.

The chapel rested on the first floor of the castle, all the way to the rear. After passing through the entrance hall, they had needed flashlights to traverse the low, back passages. It grew quieter the deeper they traveled. The air went still. The only movement was from a few nesting rats, scurrying from the beams of their lights.

The hall had ended at a low door, requiring not just ducking one's head, but also bowing at the waist. Vigor had been the first to enter the room with their guide. A small gasp escaped him as he straightened inside. Gray had followed next.

He stood now, splashing his beam around the dark chapel.

Cut high into the far wall, a cross-shaped window allowed in some sunlight, but not much. The window was no more than a pair of crossed slits, certainly too narrow to squeeze through, but maybe another place from which to defend the castle.

The window cast a cross of sunlight across a waist-high slab of stone.

The chapel's altar.

The room was otherwise empty.

But not unadorned.

Across every surface—walls, floor, roof, even the altar—crosses had been carved into the stone. Hundreds, if not thousands of them. They varied from ones no larger than a thumbprint to ornate, life-size giants.

"No wonder they call it the room of crosses," Vigor said.

"Yeah, real serial-killer chic," Kowalski commented sourly. "Must be all that island inbreeding."

Gray studied the expanse of crosses, remembering the faint cross inscribed into the marble tile in Hagia Sophia. He pulled out the silver cross, Friar Agreer's crucifix. "Now all we have to do is find the one that matches this."

Vigor stepped over and asked Fee'az to leave them alone here.

He seemed confused until the monsignor pointed to the cross in Gray's fingers.

"We must pray," the monsignor explained. "We will come out when we are done."

The boy quickly stepped away, nodding. He could not dart out quick enough, plainly fearful of being caught while a Christian ceremony was performed. From his speed, he must suspect they'd be sacrificing babies.

Once they were alone, Gray scratched his head, momentarily daunted, too conscious of the press of time. "One of these crosses must be an exact match to Friar Agreer's crucifix. We must find which one."

He split the party up.

Four of them, four walls.

And that still left floor and ceiling.

Gray placed the cross on the altar, readily available for each person to grab and compare. He also ripped four pages out of his notebook and traced the cross's shape, crib sheets for each.

As they all searched, Gray noted the shift of the sunlight across the altar, creeping steadily as the sun set, as
time escaped him. He finished his wall. Nothing. Sweat
poured; his clothes clung to his skin. He started on the
floor. The others, one at a time, joined him. Seichan worked
on the altar.

The most important cross—the one formed of sunshine—
continued to inch inexorably across the room.

"Not on the floor either," Vigor said, red-faced, straightening from his knees. He stood, one hand supporting his
lower back.

Behind the altar, Seichan shook her head.

No luck either.

Gray stared up.

The roof was low, but not low enough to touch. It would
require much lifting to test every cross up there that might
be the right size.

"Maybe I was wrong," Vigor said. "Maybe Kokejin's
tomb is somewhere else in the castle. All these crosses may
be a false lead."

Gray shook his head. *No*. They had lost a full hour already. They didn't have time to search every nook and
cranny of the castle by hand. They had committed to the
chapel. There was no turning back, no second-guessing.

"Kokejin's tomb must be here," Gray insisted.

Vigor sighed. "Then that leaves us the ceiling."

Gray assigned Kowalski to help boost the monsignor up.
He stepped over to Seichan's side.

"Man, I got the raw end of this deal," Kowalski griped.

Ignoring him, Vigor pointed to the walls. "We'll start
along the outer edges. You two do the middle."

Seichan climbed onto the altar. "I can reach the ones above
here by myself."

As she stood, a cross of sunlight lit her back. She had
stripped out of her vest and only wore a black T-shirt. Gray
noted her curves as she reached up, the stretch of cotton over
breast. Despite all his worries, a part of him was still male

enough to appreciate it . . . yet he was still man enough to feel guilty about it.

Now wasn't the time . . .

"I think I see a possibility . . ." Seichan mumbled, extending to her toes, stretching higher.

Then she winced and came down on her heels. Her hand cupped her left side. She had strained her wound.

Gray climbed up next to her. "Let me help you."

He offered her a leg up, lacing his hands together into a stirrup.

She picked up the silver crucifix, then stepped into his hands.

As he straightened and lifted her, she balanced one hand atop his head and reached the crucifix toward the ceiling. Her left buttock was pressed against his cheek.

Oh, yeah, he was going to hell.

"I think . . . I think . . ." Seichan whispered. "It fits! This mark's carved deep, and the crucifix snugs right into it. A perfect match!"

Gray craned up, but all he could see were the underside of her breasts.

"Can you tell what Christ is staring at?" he asked, remembering Hagia Sophia.

"Down at the altar," she answered, but she seemed distracted. "The crucifix is seated in a circular block of stone. When I pushed the crucifix in there, I thought I felt something click. And the stone almost seems loose. With the crucifix in place, I think I can turn it. Maybe loosen it free."

"I don't think you should—"

He heard a scrape of stone. A loud clank sounded, but it came not from above. Gray stared down between his toes.

The altar dropped from under his feet, falling straight through the floor, taking Gray with it.

Seichan tumbled into his arms, hugging tight to his neck.

The stone slab hit the ground with a jarring impact, dropping Gray to one knee. Dust flumed up. One of the floor bricks broke away, smashed into the altar, and bounced away into the darkness that lay ahead.

Gray stared up. Though it had scared the breath out of him, they had fallen only four feet. Vigor and Kowalski stared down at them.

"I think you found something, Indiana," Kowalski said with a smirk. He passed over a flashlight.

Gray rolled his eyes, but he accepted the flashlight. Seichan climbed off him, dusting herself off. Crouching, Gray pointed his light into the chamber revealed under the chapel. A dark archway beckoned.

He slid off the altar stone to the floor, Seichan at his shoulder.

Vigor and Kowalski climbed down to follow.

Two crossed arches formed the roof of a small chamber, half the size of the upper chapel. Lit by his flashlight, a low niche was cut into the back wall, framed in another archway.

"A *loculi*," Vigor said. "A tomb."

Within the niche, a body lay stretched across the bare stone, covered in folds of white cloth.

"Kokejin's tomb," Vigor said. "We found it."

Despite the excitement, they approached solemnly. Gray and Vigor stepped up. They needed to be sure. Vigor blessed their trespass with the sign of the cross and a mumbled prayer.

The monsignor reached a hand to the burial shroud.

"If something moves," Kowalski whispered, dead serious, "I'm out of here. Just so you know."

Vigor ignored him and reverently lifted away a fold of cloth from one end. "Silk," he whispered.

Dust wafted as he pulled it back.

The dome of a skull was revealed. Resting atop it shone a gold headpiece, rubies and sapphires reflected the light. Diamonds glistened.

"The princess's headpiece," Vigor said in a hushed voice.

Gray remembered Vigor's story, how Marco had the headpiece with him at his deathbed.

Vigor's hand trembled. "Marco must have willed that it be returned. Possibly even arranged to have her body removed and secured in secret, before she finally came to her final rest here."

Gray reached out and covered Vigor's hand with his own. "The third *paitzu* . . . the third key."

They were short on time.

Gray drew the silk shroud away from the rest of the bones.

Vigor gasped and fell back a step.

Even Gray froze, stunned.

It was not just *one* body beneath all the silk trapping.

Two skeletons lay within the tomb, entwined in each other's arms.

Gray recalled Vigor's story of the Church of San Lorenzo, how Marco Polo was interred there in 1324, but a later renovation revealed the body to be gone.

"We haven't just found Kokejin's tomb," Vigor said.

Gray nodded. "We found Marco Polo's tomb, too."

He stared down at the entwined pair.

What the two couldn't have in life, they had finally achieved in death.

To be together.

Forever.

Gray wondered if he'd ever find a love that great. It reminded him of his parents, together through so much hardship, struggling through trials of debilitation and now dementia . . . yet they never gave up on each other.

Someone had to save them.

11:01 A.M.
Washington, D.C.

PAINTER WISHED HE could be on-site, but it would only delay the response team. From Sigma's com-center, he watched the live video feed. It was broadcast from a helmet camera of one of the strike team.

Ten minutes ago they'd had their first real break.

All morning Painter had busted balls to trace the international phone lugs from Monsignor Verona's cell phone back to U.S. shores. Gray had mentioned that Amen Nasser had called Vigor's phone. To trace that call, Painter had to rattle powers from the Vatican's Curia to Homeland Security's director of operations. At least with Seichan in tow, he had been able to play the terrorist card. It had opened doors normally closed.

Still, it took longer than he'd liked, but Painter finally knew from where the call had originated. A strike team waited on his word to begin the assault.

He leaned to the microphone. "Go."

Van doors slid open. The camera feed jittered and jumped. The team closed in from multiple directions, front and rear, running low, assault rifles in hand.

The strike team hit the building like a storm.

A battering ram smashed the front door open in one swing.

The feed went dark as his cameraman followed the others into the building. The team fanned out.

Painter waited.

Unable to sit any longer, he stood up, leaning his fists on the communication array. Technicians crowded either side, viewing other monitors as satellite feed streamed in from Indonesia. A major storm with hurricane-strength winds blanketed most of their region, hampering the search for the hijacked *Mistress of the Seas*. The storm also grounded a good number of the search planes out of Australia and Indonesia.

The lack of progress had boiled up Painter's frustration. His fear for Lisa, for Monk, had grown close to crippling.

Then the hit on the phone trace.

He needed a win.

At least here.

Within his earpiece, he heard the chatter of the strike team, crisscrossing reports and call-outs. Finally, one clear voice rang through, coming from the cameraman. He had stopped inside what looked like a meat locker. Hooks hung from the roof.

"Director Crowe, we've completed the sweep of the butcher shop. We're negative on the targets. The place is deserted."

The video jittered as the cameraman bent down—then straightened, lifting his fingers into view.

They were damp.

"Sir, we've got blood."

Oh, no . . .

One of the technicians glanced in his direction, saw something he didn't like in Painter's expression, and quickly turned back around.

A voice cut through his despair, coming from the door.

"Director Crowe . . ."

A woman stood in the doorway, dressed in navy blues. Her auburn hair was tied away from her face, shining with fear and worry. He understood the haunted look in her eyes.

"Kat . . ." he said, straightening. It was Monk's wife.

"My aunt is watching Penelope. I couldn't just sit at home any longer."

He understood and lifted an arm. "We could use your help."

She sighed and nodded.

It was all they could do.

Keep moving, keep fighting.

In any way they could.

6:04 P.M.

VIGOR STARED DOWN at the entwined bodies.

Marco and Kokejin.

The discovery still kept him frozen in front of the slab.

Others were not as moved. Seichan pushed between Gray and Vigor.

She pointed an arm. "The third gold passport."

Gray pulled the burial shroud fully aside. Nestled between the bodies, covered by the two skeletal hands, a glint of gold shone past the bones.

It was the third *paitzu*.

And resting beside it was a familiar length of bronze tube.

The third and final scroll.

With a reverential gentleness, Gray removed the items. He slipped the headpiece off the skull, too. "It might bear a clue," he justified.

Vigor didn't argue. With the burial chamber opened, it would be quickly stolen if left unattended.

They all climbed back up into the chapel.

Once there, they gathered in a corner of the room.

Gray turned over the golden passport to reveal a third angelic glyph.

"We have them all," Seichan said.

"But not the entire story," Gray said. He pulled out his notebook and nodded to Vigor. "Let's hear it."

Vigor needed no further prompting. He nicked open the bronze tube and extracted the scroll. "Silk again," he commented, and began unwrapping it with care.

The last piece of the story was longer, stretching a quarter of the way across the chapel floor. Vigor translated Marco's Italian dialect. The harrowing tale continued with the appearance of the glowing angelic figures, coming upon Marco's party trapped inside a tower room.

Vigor read the story aloud:

These strange apparitions held forth the crude chalice; and in plain and vigorous method insisted we drink. In such a manner, we would be preserved against the dread pestilence that had turned the City of Death into a vision of Hell, as man consumed the flesh of his brother.

With such a promise, we each partook of the drink, which upon closer sight and taste was found to be blood. We also were urged to eat a bit of raw meat upon a palm leaf, which upon closer sight and taste was some form of sweetbread. Only after such consumption did I think to inquire as to the source of such offerings. The kaan's man answered; and thus proved ourselves to be cannibals already; for it was blood and sweetbread drained and cut from a man.

Thus were we treated in such ill manner, which would later prove virtuous as it did indeed protect us from a great pestilence. But there was a cost for such a cure. Friar Agreer was not allowed to partake of the blood and sweetbread. There was much murmuring and pointing toward his cross and to the man who bore it. In the end, we were allowed only to depart if we left Friar Agreer behind.

In his great Grace and Blessed countenance, Friar Agreer insisted we escape. I wept hard, but obeyed the confessor. With his last word, he left me with his crucifix, so as to return it to the Holy See. The final sight of the noble man had him being led in the opposite direction; and I guessed their destination. Lit by the fullness of the moon, a great mountain towered above the forest, carved with a thousand faces of demons.

"Dear God," Vigor muttered.

He slowly read the rest.

Upon escaping the city, Marco Polo related how a plague struck his fleet, stranding the ships and crew at a remote island. Only those who consumed the medicine offered by these glowing men remained untouched. Marco left the City of the Dead with enough additional medicine to treat his father and uncle, along with Kokejin and two of her maids. They ended up burning the ships and bodies of the diseased, many of them still alive.

Vigor read the final section.

May the Lord forgive my soul for disobeying a promise to my father, now dead. I must make one final confession. In that dread place, I discovered a map of the city, a chart which I destroyed upon the will of my father; but set to mind not to forget. I've recorded it here anew, so as to keep such knowledge from being lost forever. May whoever reads this take good warning: the gateway to Hell was opened in that city; but I know not if it was ever closed.

6:22 P.M.

AS GRAY LISTENED to the story and its cryptic ending, he worked on the puzzle in the notebook. It helped him concentrate to listen to Vigor while contemplating the mystery in hand. It distracted him from the terror clutching his own heart.

And as the story unfolded, he began to understand.

He'd been a fool.

He studied his notebook, blurring his eyes, seeing the answer hidden in the code. And with the three keys, perhaps a way to read it.

He flipped through the pages, looking for the right one. When he found it, he leaned closer, tracing with a finger. Could this be right? He needed to investigate it more.

He checked his watch.

With less than a half hour left, do I have enough time?

Before he could find out, a rattle of automatic fire echoed to them, sounding like firecrackers. *Pop, pop, pop, pop . . .*

Gray leaped up.

God, no . . . had Nasser found them?

He crossed to the chapel opening and stared out into the dark halls.

"Get everything together," he urged without turning. "Now!"

Backlit by the filtering sunlight, Gray made out the slim shape of a figure running toward him. Bare feet slapped stone—then a voice called out, balanced between urgency and stealth.

"Hurry!"

It was Fee'az.

The boy did not slow and ran straight at them.

Farther out, coming from the direction of the castle courtyard, angry shouts in Farsi echoed.

Gray caught the thin boy's shoulder as he flew up to them, breathless.

"Hurry. Smugglers."

Fee'az did not wait and rebounded back into the outer hall and headed in the opposite direction, paralleling the rear of the castle.

Gray turned to the others. "Grab what you have . . . leave the rest!"

They set off after Fee'az.

The boy waited halfway down the hall, then fled onward.

Fee'az continued a running commentary. Apparently even the threat of smugglers did not stifle his tongue. "You take so long. With your prayers. I sleep. Under palms." He waved back in the general direction of the courtyard. "They not see me. Almost step on me. I wake and run. They shoot. Bang, bang. But I am fast on the legs."

Proving it, he flew through the back rooms and halls.

Behind them, shouts changed in timbre, indicating the raiding party had entered the castle.

Fee'az led them to crude stairs leading down. "This way."

They reached a narrow, low tunnel, barely taller than a crawlway. It shot off to the south. Fee'az scurried ahead.

After fifty steps, it ended at an old rusted iron grate. The bars had long been sawed away, leaving only stumps. They pushed through and out into the castle's silted-up moat. Crumbled stone walls marked the boundary.

Gray glanced behind him. The crawlway must have been the castle's old sewer line.

Waving them to stay low, Fee'az led them along the moat, toward the eastern bay. Shouts still echoed from the castle. The smugglers had not yet realized the mice had fled.

Reaching the water, Gray saw the plane still waited, unmolested.

Fee'az explained, "Dirty smugglers. Never steal plane. They pinch little." He demonstrated by holding his fingers apart, almost touching, then shrugged. "Sometime kill. Throw bodies to sharks. But never take something so big. Government will send bigger planes, bigger guns."

So not worth the risk.

Still, erring on the side of caution, they used oars to silently paddle the boy's boat out to the waiting seaplane. Fee'az waved them on board.

"Come again! Come again!" he said, formally shaking each hand.

Gray felt obligated to give him some bonus for pulling their asses out of the fire. He reached to his pack, fished inside, and handed him the princess's golden headpiece.

The boy's eyes widened, holding the treasure with both hands—then pushed it back toward Gray. "I can no take."

Gray folded his fingers over it. "It will cost you only a promise."

Fee'az glanced up to him.

"There are two bodies, two skeletons, in the castle. Under the room of crosses." He pointed to the castle, then out to the distant hills. "Take them away, dig a deep hole, and bury them. Together."

He smiled, unsure if Gray was joking.

"Will you promise?"

He nodded his head. "I will get my brothers and uncles to help."

Gray pushed the golden headpiece toward him. "It is yours."

"Thank you, sir." He shook Gray's hand and said with all the solemnity of a blessing, "Come again."

Gray climbed into the plane.

Minutes later they were airborne, shooting up out of the bay and headed back toward the international airport.

Gray returned to the rear seat, joining Vigor.

"You gave the boy the princess's headpiece?" the monsignor said, staring down at the boy's retreating skiff.

"To bury Marco and Kokejin."

Vigor turned to face him. "But such a discovery. History—"

"Marco has done enough for history. It was his last wish to be buried in peace with the woman he loved. I think we owe him that much. And besides, we don't need the headpiece."

Vigor stared at Gray, one eye narrowed, plainly sizing him up, judging his generosity. "But you thought the headpiece might hold a clue. That's why you took it." The monsignor's eyes widened and his voice raised. "Dear Lord, Gray, you actually solved the angelic code."

Gray pulled his notebook out. "Not quite. Almost."

"How?"

Seichan overheard their discussion and came back to join them, standing between the seats. Kowalski twisted around, peering over the seat back.

Gray answered the monsignor. "I solved it by throwing out all our old suppositions. We kept looking for a letter-substitution code."

"Like the inscription in the Vatican spelling out HAGIA."

"I think that was done to purposefully mislead. The big mystery on the obelisk is *not* a letter-substitution puzzle."

"Show us," Seichan said.

"In a moment." Gray checked his watch. Eight minutes left. "I still have part of the puzzle to figure out. The three keys. Keys organized in a certain order."

He opened his notebook and tapped the three angelic symbols.

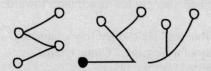

Gray continued, "With the obelisk's code always in plain sight, the keys only served one purpose. To reveal the correct way to read the code. The obelisk has four sides. But on which side do you start? In which direction do you read it?"

Gray flipped his notebook open and found the original page of script supplied by Seichan. "For the gold-inscribed symbols to be so important, they must be written somewhere on the obelisk. And so they are."

Gray circled them.

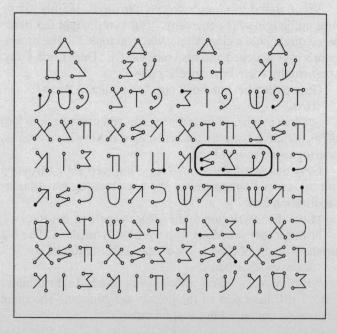

"This sequence only appears once. It's unique. Notice how it wraps from one of the obelisk's surfaces to the next. It's delineating where to begin reading and in which direction."

He added an arrow.

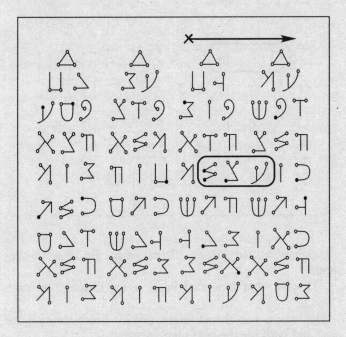

"So you must reorder the sequence to match the keys." He flipped the notebook pages, searching through the eight variations that he and Vigor had mapped out earlier. He found the right one and circled the key symbols. "This is the proper way the map must be laid out to be read correctly."

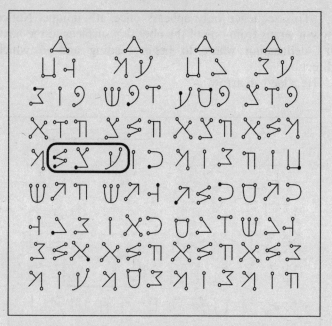

Seichan leaned closer. "What map are you talking about?"

"This is what I noticed back at the chapel," he said. "Watch."

He took a pencil and began poking holes through the page and marking the next blank page.

"What are you doing?" Vigor asked.

Gray explained, "Notice how some of the diacritical marks—those small circles in the angelic script—are darkened and others are not. We know from the second key how that symbol's black diacritical mark ended up being a marker for the Portuguese castle. So the blackened circles on the obelisk's code must be markers, too. But markers to what? If you poke out each dark circle onto a fresh page, stripping all else away, you get this."

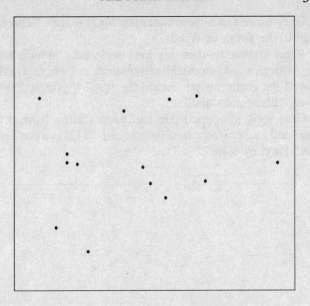

"Well, that sure helped," Kowalski said sarcastically.

Gray rubbed a hand over the stubble on his chin, concentrating. "Something's here. I can sense it."

"Maybe you're supposed to connect the dots," Kowalski said with no less sarcasm. "Maybe it'll form a big flashing arrow spelling out *go the fuck here.*"

Seichan frowned. "And maybe it's time for you to shut the hell up."

Gray did not need their bickering. Not now. Kowalski was fine as a getaway driver, good in a firefight, but Gray needed sage advice, not kindergarten suggestions, like connect the dots.

Then he saw it.

"Oh my God!" Gray sat up, fumbled his pencil, and grasped it more firmly. "Kowalski is right!"

"I am?"

"He is . . . ?" Seichan responded.

Gray turned to Vigor, clutching his forearm. "The first clue! In the Tower of Winds."

Vigor frowned—then his eyes widened. "Which holds the Vatican's astronomical observatory . . . where Galileo proved the earth moved around the sun!" Vigor tapped the sheet. "These are stars!"

Gray took his pencil. He had been staring hard at the sheet and recognized a familiar pattern. "This is a constellation." He drew it in.

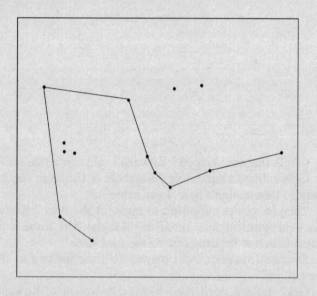

Vigor recognized it, too. "That's the constellation for Draco, the dragon."

Seichan cocked her head as she stared down. "Are you saying it's a navigational star map?"

"It looks that way." Gray scratched his head with his pencil's eraser. "But how does one constellation tell us where to go?"

No one answered.

"It can't," he finally conceded.

Gray's heart pounded in his throat. They were running out of time. Had he just taken them down the wrong path?

Vigor sat back. "Wait," he mumbled. "Remember Marco's story. The last stanza. Marco said he drew a map *of* the city, not a map *to* the city."

"And?" Gray asked.

Vigor took the paper, spun it around. "This can't be stars. It has to be the *layout* of the City of the Dead. That's what Marco's text stated. Possibly the Vatican made the same mistake we just did. They misinterpreted Marco's map in the same manner. They also thought it was a navigational star map."

Gray shook his head. "That's a rather strange coincidence that a city should be laid out in the exact pattern of the Draco constellation. If I'm not mistaken, even the stars outside the dragon line mark the placement of real stars."

Vigor nodded. "But remember, from my study of ancient civilizations . . . from the Egyptians through Mesoamerica, many civilizations built their monuments and cities patterned after the stars, made to mimic them."

Gray remembered a similar lesson. "Like the three Egyptian pyramids are supposed to represent the stars of Orion's belt."

"Exactly! Somewhere in Southeast Asia is a city patterned after the Draco constellation."

Seichan suddenly swung around. *"Choi mai!"* she swore under her breath. "I remember something . . . something I heard about . . . some ruins in Cambodia. My family has roots in the region. Vietnam and Cambodia."

Seichan rushed to her pack, pawed through it, and pulled out her laptop. "There's an encyclopedia program on here."

Seichan squatted down between the knees of Vigor and Gray. She called up the program and typed rapidly. She double-clicked on an icon and a digital map filled the screen.

"This is the temple complex of Angkor, built by the Khmer people of Cambodia in the ninth century."

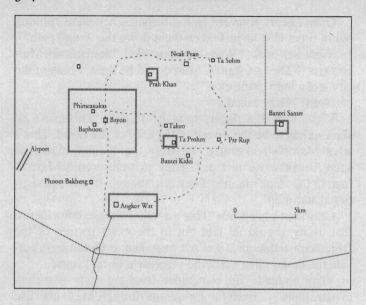

"Notice the layout of the temples," Seichan said, "where each one lies. I had heard stories of how these ruins were supposedly laid out in a starlike grid."

With his finger Gray drew a line connecting the temples in a pattern and tapped the remaining temples. He held up the first star map and placed it next to the open laptop.

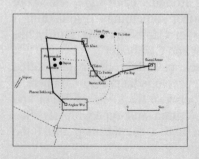 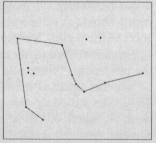

"They're an exact match," Vigor said, awed. "Marco's City of the Dead. It's the ancient city of Angkor Wat."

Gray leaned down and hugged Seichan's shoulders. She tensed, but didn't pull away. Gray owed everyone a debt of gratitude, even Kowalski, whose simplistic overview had broken the way to the solution.

Gray checked his watch.

Not a minute to spare.

He held out his hand toward Vigor. "Your phone. It's time to make a deal."

Vigor passed him the cell phone and battery.

Gray snapped the battery in place, praying for some measure of good fortune. He dialed Nasser's number, supplied by Seichan. Vigor reached over and gripped Gray's hand, offering support.

The phone rang once and was picked up.

"Commander Pierce," a cold and furious voice answered.

Gray took a steadying breath, struggling not to lash out. He needed to be deliberate and firm.

"My plane is about to land," Nasser continued, not even waiting for acknowledgment. "For your treachery, I will allow you to decide which of your parents will die first, your mother or your father. I will make you listen to their screams. And that parent, I promise, will be the luckier of the two."

Despite the threat Gray took some solace. If Nasser wasn't lying, both of his parents were still alive.

Taking comfort in that, Gray kept his voice even, his jaw muscles aching with the restraint. "I will offer you a trade for their lives."

"There is nothing you can offer," Nasser barked back.

"Even if I told you that I'd solved the obelisk's angelic code?"

Dead air answered him.

Gray continued. "Nasser, I know where Marco's City of the Dead lies." Fearing even this might not be enough to sway the bastard, Gray spoke the next words slowly, so there was no misunderstanding. "And I know how to cure the Judas Strain."

Vigor turned to him, startled.

Silence continued on the phone.

Gray waited. He stared at the digital map of Angkor Wat on the laptop. He sensed that the two arms of the Guild operation—the one following the scientific trail, the other following the historical—were about to slam together.

But who would be crushed between them?

Nasser finally answered, his voice a trembling rage.

"What do you want?"

OUTBREAK

13
Witch Queen

THE DRUMS POUNDED louder than the rumbles of thunder overhead. Lightning spattered, flashing the jungle into stark greens and blacks, limned in silver by the reflection off the wet leaves.

Bare-chested, Monk pulled Susan by the hand up a steep turn in the jungle path. They'd been following the trail for the past two hours in the dark, sometimes waiting for lightning to show them where to step next. Rain continued to pour through the canopy. The switchbacked trail had become a running stream. But the remainder of the jungle was a dense tangle of grappling vines, heavy leaves, thorny bushes, root-choked trunks, and sopping mud.

So they kept to the trail, heading up, always up.

Ryder climbed behind them. He had their group's one pistol. A 9mm Sig Sauer P228 with a Teflon finish. Unfortunately he had no spare magazines. Only the thirteen rounds already in the gun.

Not good.

Monk knew that once the storm broke, the jungle would be scoured by Rakao's men. This island was their base of operation, giving them the home-field advantage. Monk did not delude himself into thinking he could escape being tracked and captured.

He glanced back through a break in the jungle. They were about three hundred feet up. The giant cruise ship sat in the center of the lake, a quarter mile out. Somewhere on board was his partner, pulled alive from the black waters, out of the grip of some nasty calamari.

But was she still alive?

Until he knew for sure, Monk would not give up hope.

Not for Lisa, not for himself.

To that end, Monk needed allies.

Drums continued their perpetual beating, louder and more urgent, as if striving to drive the typhoon away. They had climbed high enough that each pound of leather drum now reverberated against his rib cage, down to the bone.

Monk pushed through a drape of branches, waterlogged and drooping low. He spotted a glow ahead, flickering.

Firelight.

He took another two steps and stopped.

Only now did he realize they weren't alone. To either side of the path, sentinels stood, half hidden by the dense foliage, but plainly in the open, wanting to be noted. Men stood, bare-chested, wearing wide grass hats tied to their heads. Their faces had been painted with oil and ash, turning their countenances pitch-black. Polished white boar tusks and yellowed rib bones pierced noses. Brilliant feathers and snail shells were threaded around upper arms.

With a shout, Ryder lunged forward, his pistol raised.

The sentinels were unimpressed.

Monk shoved down Ryder's arm and stepped forward, holding up his hands, palms forward. "Don't spook the natives," he whispered to Ryder.

One tribesman shifted onto the trail. He wore a breastplate of bone braided together by leather. His waist was circled by a kilt of long feathers. His legs and feet were bare, painted with grease and ash, too. He carried a sharpened shoulder blade of some animal.

At least Monk hoped it was an animal.

Monk heard a rustle behind him, knowing their back

trail was already being closed off. Drums pounded ahead. The firelight spat momentarily brighter.

The man on the path turned and led the way toward the glow.

"Looks like we're invited to the party," Monk said, putting his arm around Susan.

Ryder followed, pistol in hand.

If things went awry, they might need the billionaire's remaining thirteen rounds to blast their way to freedom. But for now, Monk knew their best bet was to cooperate.

The path ended at a cliff face in the volcanic rock. A natural coved amphitheater had been carved out of the reddish-black rock, roofed over with thick palm thatching. The downpour drained in a sheet of rain off the roof's front edge, creating a watery curtain.

Beyond the flow, lit by a massive bonfire within, Monk spotted lines of drummers along both walls, working hard, pounding away. Two massive drums, as wide as his outstretched arms, hung from the rock walls and were struck with bone hammers. Each stroke shook the thin waterfall that cascaded from the thatched roof to the rock floor.

They were led forward.

A single boar rooted through the open space in front and squealed back from the strangers' approach. More pigs huddled under an overhang, squeezed tight together, rump to rump.

Monk led Susan through the sheet of water and under the large overhang. He shivered as the rain cascaded over his bare chest. The heat of the fire inside was welcome, but the smoke choked and stung, doing its best to exit a narrow flue in the thatching.

Around the fire ahead, a crowd had gathered, some standing, some squatted. Monk estimated over a hundred. Men, bare-breasted women. But cave openings lined the walls. More faces peered out. A few naked children stood staring, wide-eyed. One cradled a piebald piglet.

At some signal, the drums suddenly stopped with one resounding note. The quiet intimidated.

In that sudden silence, a voice called out.

"Monk!"

Startled, he turned. A thin figure stood pressed up against the bamboo bars of a cage built into a back corner. He wore a torn shirt and a pair of muddy white briefs.

"Jessie?"

The young nurse was still alive!

But before they could continue their tearful and heartfelt reunion, a towering figure stepped forward, though for the tribe, *towering* was about five-foot-nothing. The old gray-beard looked like someone had sold him a skin suit two sizes too large. He was greased and daubed in ash, too. He wore some sort of twisted gourd over his privates and a shock of purpled feathers in his hair, sticking straight up, as if startled. And nothing else.

Monk recognized that this was the tribe's leader.

It was time to perform, to dance for his supper—or rather, to dance not to *become* supper.

Monk lifted his arm toward the elder. *"Boogla-boogla rah!"* he intoned solemnly, then tensed his forearm and reached his other hand to pull the toggle at his wrist.

Freed from its electromagnetic contacts, his prosthetic hand dropped to the muddy volcanic stone.

A gasp arose from the crowd.

The leader fell back a step, almost into the fire.

Monk lowered his arm, staring down at his disembodied hand.

Besides looking authentically fleshy, the prosthetic was a marvel of DARPA engineering, incorporating direct peripheral nerve control through its titanium wrist contact points. It also was bioengineered with advanced mechanics and actuators, allowing sensory feedback and surgically precise movements.

But that was only half the story.

Monk's stumped end of his wrist was encased in a polysynthetic cuff, surgically attached to the end of his wrist and wired into nerve bundles and muscle tendons. In actuality, it was the other half of his prosthesis. The hand might be the brawn, but the wrist cuff was definitely the brain.

With his remaining hand, he manipulated the titanium contacts on the cuff. It was the best feature of his artificial hand. Monk performed this stunt at parties all the time. So why should this be any different?

The cuff and hand were linked wirelessly, a digital radio interface.

As Monk tapped a practiced sequence on his wrist, his severed hand lifted up onto its fingers and began to dance across the rock like a five-legged spider.

This time the cannibal leader did step into the fire, searing his backside enough to yelp and leap away.

Monk sent his hand chasing after him.

By now a wide ring cleared around the party.

Ryder had drawn Susan back into the shadows of the cliff face, giving Monk the stage.

"Now that I have your attention," Monk bellowed.

He strode toward the fire.

Guessing no one spoke English here, he had to sell it with a bravado of expression and a great pounding of his bare chest. Still, it wasn't good enough just to scare the superstitious folk. He needed to win them over. It was time for an American-led coup of Cannibal Island.

Turning on a heel, Monk pointed back to Susan.

On his signal, she unwrapped Monk's borrowed shirt from around her head. Ryder reached and stripped the hospital gown from her shoulders and let it fall away. Susan lifted her arms, bare-breasted like the women here.

Only she glowed in the shadows.

A hushed amazement spread through the tribespeople.

Monk gaped at Susan himself. She glowed even brighter than when he had first seen her. Significantly brighter. Her skin shone with an inner moonlight, turning her skin almost translucent.

Ryder motioned to Monk, urging him from the sideline to continue.

Rattled, Monk collected himself. He stepped to Susan, dropped to his knees, and shouted the only word he knew in the cannibals' language, taught to him by a toothless pirate.

A name.

"RANGDA!" Monk called out, naming the cannibals' queen of the island, mistress of the lagoon's *glowing* demons.

Glowing like Susan.

He bowed down.

"All hail the witch queen of the islands!"

1:04 A.M.

DEVESH ENTERED LISA'S room, tapping his cane.

Sprawled in bed, hooked to an IV, Lisa knew she could not stall any longer. Earlier, as she was hauled back onto the ship from the tender dock, she had swooned in her guard's arms, catching him by surprise and collapsing with a bone-jarring thud to the deck.

Lisa had split her lip doing so, but she'd had to make it look convincing. It hadn't been hard. With her calf sliced open by a sword, her body torn and lacerated in hundreds of places by the clawed grip of the predatory squids, and her lungs still coarse from the near drowning, only adrenaline had kept her on her feet.

So she had collapsed, even passing out for a few breaths.

The act had her rushed up to the scientific suite, where she was treated by the ship's doctor and one of the WHO medical staff. Her leg had been cleaned and stitched, along with the worst of her lacerations. An IV catheter was established, streaming in fluids, antibiotics, and pain relievers. She now lay in her old room, an inside cabin with no balcony or window, under guard. Beneath the thin sheet, her body was a patchwork of bandages and taped gauze.

Such care was not administered out of mercy or compassion. It was done to serve one end: to make sure she completed her promise to Devesh atop the deck.

The Judas Strain. I know what the virus is doing.

For such a revelation, Devesh was not about to lose her, especially with Susan Tunis vanished somewhere on the storm-swept island. Devesh needed Lisa. So she stretched her advantage, stalling. She had tasked Devesh with some busywork, various assignments for the head of his clinical labs.

Her justification: to test and confirm her hypothesis.

But that could stretch for only so long.

"So," Devesh said. "Results are being compiled right now. It's time to have our little delayed chat. If I don't like what I hear, we'll begin slowly reversing all your medical care. I imagine reopening your wound with pliers will persuade you to cooperate."

Devesh turned on a heel and waved to a waiting nurse.

Lisa's IV catheter was quickly pulled and taped over.

Lisa sat up. The room swam a bit, then steadied.

Ever the gentleman, Devesh held out a thick cotton robe with the ship's logo. Lisa stood up, draped in a thin hospital gown, but naked underneath. She tolerated his politeness to pull on the robe and cover herself. She cinched the belt snugly.

"This way, Dr. Cummings." Devesh crossed back to the door.

Barefoot, Lisa was led out of her cabin. Devesh headed across to the infectious-disease suite.

The door stood open. Voices could be heard.

Following Devesh inside, Lisa immediately recognized two familiar faces: the bacteriologist, Benjamin Miller, and her confidant since arriving, the Dutch toxicologist Henri Barnhardt. The two clinicians were seated on one side of a narrow table.

Lisa glanced around. The back half of the suite had been emptied of all furniture and refilled with laboratory equipment, much of it stolen from Monk's gear: fluorescence microscopes, scintillation and auto-gamma spectrometers, carbon dioxide incubators, refrigerated centrifuges, microtiter and ELISA readers, and along one wall, a small fraction collector.

Some universities weren't so well equipped.

Dr. Eloise Chénier, the Guild's virologist and chief administrator of the infectious-disease lab, stood on the other side of the table, dressed in an ankle-length lab coat. In her late fifties, with salt-and-pepper hair and a pair of reading glasses hung on a chain around her neck, she looked like some quaint schoolmarm.

The virologist had an arm raised to a pair of computer stations behind her. Data flowed across one monitor, the other displayed a jumble of overlapping files. She was just finishing some explanation with Henri and Miller, accented heavily in French.

"We gained an excellent viral load by washing a sample of the cerebral spinal fluid through a series of phosphate buffers, then fixed it with glutaraldehyde, and pelleted it by centrifugation."

Chénier noted their arrival and waved them to the table.

Devesh joined his colleague while Lisa found an empty stool next to Henri. Her friend placed a reassuring hand on her knee. Henri glanced at her, his expression asking, *Are you okay?*

She nodded, glad to be seated.

Devesh turned to Lisa. "We've completed all the ancillary tests you requested, Dr. Cummings. Perhaps now you can explain why?"

His accusing gaze weighed heavily on her.

Lisa took a deep breath. She had delayed for as long as possible. Her only hope for further survival was to offer the truth and pray her ingenuity proved of great enough value to overcome her earlier betrayal.

She remembered Devesh's first lesson: *Be useful.*

Lisa started slowly, relating her discovery of the strange retinal glow in Susan's eyes. But as she spoke, she read the disbelief shining already in Devesh's expression.

Lisa turned to Henri, seeking substantiation. "Were you able to perform the fluorescent assay on the spinal fluid sample?"

"*Ja*. The fluid sample did demonstrate a low fluorescence." Chénier agreed. "I spun the sample down. The bacterial pellet did glow. And was confirmed to be cyanobacteria."

Miller, the bacteriologist, nodded his agreement.

Devesh's skepticism shifted to interest. His eyes focused back to Lisa. "And from this, you determined the bacteria migrated from the brain, down the optic nerve, and colonized the fluids of the eye. So you ordered the second spinal tap."

She nodded. "I see Dr. Pollum is not here. Was he able to finish the protein assay on the viral shell?"

Lisa had ordered this test, too. It wasn't truly necessary, but it had promised a good couple hours of extra labor.

"One moment," Chénier said. "I have the results here." She turned to one of the monitors and began collapsing screens while narrating. "It might interest you to know that we were able to classify the virus from genetic assays into the *Bunyavirus* family."

Henri noted the pinch to Lisa's eyes and explained. "It was what we were discussing before you arrived. Bunyaviruses typically infect avian and mammalian species, causing hemorrhagic fevers, but the vector for transmission is usually arthropods. Biting flies, ticks, mosquitoes."

He slid over a notepad.

Lisa glanced to the open pages. Henri had diagrammed the pathway of infection.

Human → Insect (arthropod) → Human
(infected) (carrier, not sick) (infected)

Henri tapped the center. "*Insects* are necessary to spread the disease. Bunyaviruses themselves are seldom transmissible directly from human to human."

Lisa rubbed her temples. "Unlike the Judas Strain." She

picked up a pencil and altered the diagram. "Instead of an *insect* to spread the disease, it takes a *bacterial* cell to pass the virus from one person to another."

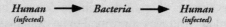

Henri frowned. "Yes, but why did—?"

Gunfire blasts cut off his words. All of them jumped.

Even Devesh dropped his cane. With a muttered curse, he recovered it and headed to the door. "You all stay here."

More blasts followed, along with guttural cries.

Lisa stood up. What was happening?

1:24 A.M.

DEVESH COLLECTED TWO guards stationed in the science wing and hurried over to the middeck security post by the elevators. Automatic gunfire erupted in sporadic bursts, as loud as detonations in the confined space.

Shouts rang out between the blasts.

Keeping his guards ahead of him, Devesh followed more cautiously as the post came into view. Six men manned the security detail. The leader, a tall African soldier from Somalia, noted Devesh and fell back to his position.

He spoke tersely in Malay. "Sir, a dozen of the afflicted broke out of one of the back wards. They rushed our line. Attacked."

The leader nodded to one of the guards, seated to the side, cradling a bloody arm. He had his sleeve rolled back, revealing a deep bite wound.

Devesh took a step forward and pointed absently to the wounded man. "Isolate him."

Beyond the security post, a hallway extended toward the stern. Some doors stood open, others closed. Down the passageway, a few bodies sprawled, riddled with bullets, blood soaking into the carpet. The closest two—a naked obese woman and a shirtless teenage boy—were tangled together. Devesh noted the bubbled rashes and the blackened boils on the corpses.

He fought to control his temper, breathing heavily through his nostrils. The stern section of this level housed the most debilitated patients, making them readily available to the research team. Devesh had outlined a firm protocol when dealing with patients on this level. Such lapses would not be tolerated. Not when he was this close to success.

"I've called in reinforcements," the sentry leader said. "When we started firing, some of the afflicted fled into open rooms. We'll have to flush them out."

A moan arose from farther down the hall.

A man rose up to an elbow. His other shoulder was a bloody ruin. He wore a medical smock. One of the doctors. Caught in the firefight.

"Help me," he croaked out.

From an open doorway at his shoulder, a hand lashed out and grabbed his jacket. Another tangled in his hair. He screamed as he was yanked halfway through the door. His legs still protruded into the passageway, his heels kicking and pounding.

The sentry leader glanced to Devesh, asking permission to proceed forward.

Devesh shook his head.

The doctor's screaming suddenly cut off—but his heels continued to beat a rhythm of agony.

Devesh felt no sympathy. Someone had been careless with a restraint or door lock. He heard the booted tread of reinforcements echoing up the stairwell.

Devesh turned away but waved an arm back to the hallway. "Exterminate them."

"Sir?"

"The entire deck. Clear it all out. Cabin by cabin."

1:54 A.M.

STILL IN THE virology lab, Lisa listened to the spats of rifle fire.

Screams also reached her.

No one spoke.

Devesh finally returned. He seemed unfazed, only a little red in the face. He pointed his cane at Lisa. "Come with me. There is something I would like you to see." He turned on a heel and stepped briskly away.

Lisa stood and followed, hurrying to keep up.

Devesh led her past the security station and down the next hallway.

It was a slaughterhouse. Blood splashed walls. Bodies lay rolled up against the walls, macerated by automatic gunfire.

Lisa swallowed hard, choking on the stench in the confined passageway.

As they passed along the hallway, the cabin doors to either side all lay open. She glanced inside and spotted more bodies, lifeless, twisted, bloody. Some had been shot while still handcuffed to their beds.

More gunfire blasted—not scattered, purposeful.

Farther down, a pair of guards exited a cabin, rifles smoking—then moved to the next room.

"You . . . you're slaughtering the patients," Lisa said.

"We're winnowing the patient load, that's all." Devesh lifted an arm and vaguely motioned ahead. "This is the second breakout. An hour ago, a pair of patients escaped their restraints, biting off their own fingers in order to free themselves. They attacked their doctor, killing him before they could be stopped. In such a deranged state, these patients are strong, hyped on adrenaline, oblivious of pain."

Lisa remembered the video footage of Susan Tunis's husband, raving and attacking. It was starting here now, too.

Devesh glanced back to her. "From EEG studies, it seems you were right. The pathology appears to be some form of catatonic excitement, accompanied by deep psychotic breaks."

More gunfire chattered, causing her to jump.

Responding to her reaction, he sighed. "This is for everyone's safety. We're seeing a rapid decline in condition among patients. Shipwide. With medical supplies already running low, we must be efficient. Once a patient devolves to this level of debilitation, they pose a grave physical threat to all around them and serve no real purpose."

Lisa understood the sentiment behind his words. Devesh and the Guild were using the ship's patients as the equivalent of living culture media for the Judas Strain, harvesting the deadly pathogens and storing them as potential bioweapons. And like any field after it had been thoroughly reaped, Devesh was plowing it over.

"Why did you bring me out here?" she asked, aghast.

"To show you this."

Devesh stepped to the only cabin door that was still closed. He keyed it and held the door open for her.

A stronger stench struck her.

Lisa crossed the dark threshold, unsure what to expect. The hall lights revealed an inside cabin, similar to her own: a small bath, a couch, a television, and a small bed in back.

Behind her Devesh reached inside and flicked on the lights. The bulbs flickered, then steadied into a low thrum of fluorescents.

Lisa stumbled back, a hand at her throat.

A body lay draped across the bed, soaked into the bedding and cushions. His two bare legs were tied to the bedposts, arms to the headboard. But it appeared as if a bomb had gone off in his belly, hollowing out his abdomen. Gore splattered ceiling and walls.

A hand over her mouth, Lisa went cold, falling reflexively back to the clinical, her only safe haven.

Where were his internal organs?

"They were found feeding on him," Devesh explained. "Patients whose minds had rotted beyond restraint."

Lisa shivered once violently. She was suddenly too

aware of her bare feet, her near-naked body under the robe.

"We've seen this before," Devesh continued. "In this state of catatonic excitement, the virus appears to stimulate a ravenous appetite. Insatiable, in fact. We've watched one of these victims gorge himself to the point his stomach exploded. And still he continued to eat."

Oh God . . .

Past the shock, Lisa needed another moment for the significance of his words to strike her. "You *watched . . .* where . . . ?"

"Dr. Cummings, you don't think we were just studying Susan Tunis. To be thorough, we must also understand every facet of the disease. Even this cannibalism. This insatiable hunger bears a striking similarity to Prader-Willi syndrome. Are you familiar with it?"

Numb, Lisa shook her head.

"It's a hypothalamic dysfunction, triggering an insatiable appetite that can never be quelled. An endless sense of starvation. A rare genetic defect. Many of the afflicted die at a young age of stomach ruptures from gorging."

Devesh's cold clinical assessment helped anchor her back inside her body, but her breathing remained heavy.

"Autopsy of one of the psychotic's brains showed toxic damage to the hypothalamus, similar to the pathology in Prader-Willi patients. And coupled with the catatonic excitement and adrenal stimulation. Well . . ." Devesh waved to the bed.

Lisa's stomach churned. As she turned away, she finally noted the victim's face: the agonized lips, the blank staring eyes, the corona of gray hair.

Her hand covered her mouth as she recognized the man. It was the John Doe patient, the one suffering from flesh-eating disease. From Susan's medical history, Lisa even knew the patient's name now.

Applegate.

To put a name to the cannibalism here, to personalize it . . .

Lisa hurried out of the room.

Devesh's eyes glinted with dark amusement. Lisa realized the bastard had brought her purposefully down here, half naked, unnerved, knowing she'd identify him. It was all some awful bit of sadism.

"So now you know what we truly face here," he said. "Imagine events magnified worldwide. That is the threat I'm trying to prevent."

Lisa held back a sharp retort. *Trying to prevent, my ass.*

"We are facing a pandemic," Devesh continued as he headed back down the hallway toward the scientific wing. "Before the World Health Organization had responded to Christmas Island, early patients had already been airlifted to Perth in Australia. Prior to that, tourists traveling through Christmas Island had spread to the four corners of the world. London, San Francisco, Berlin, Kuala Lumpur. We don't know how many, if any, were infected from early exposure, like Dr. Susan Tunis, but it would not take many. Without proper disinfection like we employ here, the virus may already be spreading."

Devesh led her back down the hall to the virology lab. "So perhaps now you'll be a bit more forthcoming and open."

As they reentered the lab, questioning glances were cast their way.

Lisa simply shook her head and sank to her stool.

Once they were settled, Dr. Eloise Chénier shifted from her seat in front of the computer. "While you were gone," she said, "I pulled up Dr. Pollum's files. Here is the protein schematic you ordered. From the virus in the toxic soup."

The doctor backed from the screen so all could see the rotating image, spinning like a toy top on the monitor.

It depicted the icosahedron shell of the virus: twenty triangular sections, forming a sphere, like a soccer ball. Except some of the triangles bulged out with alpha proteins, while others were sunken in by beta proteins. Lisa had wanted it all mapped out to better test her hypothesis.

Lisa pointed. "Can you stop the rotation?"

Chénier tapped a button on her mouse and the spinning halted, freezing the image on the screen.

Lisa stood back up. "Now, on the other monitor, can you bring up the protein map of the virus recovered from Susan Tunis's cerebral spinal fluid?"

A moment later, a second soccer ball appeared, spinning. Lisa moved closer, studying it. She manipulated the mouse button herself this time, freezing the image where she wanted it.

She faced the others.

Devesh shrugged, using his whole upper body. "So? It looks the same."

She stepped back. "Picture the two side by side."

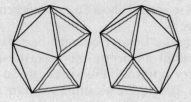

Henri stood up, eyes widening. "They're *not* the same!"

She nodded. "They're mirror images of each other. They may superficially look the same, but they are really exact opposites. Geometric isomerism. Two forms of the same geometric shape, just mirrored one upon the other."

"*Cis* and *trans*," Chénier said, using the technical term for the two sides of the same coin.

Lisa tapped the first screen. "Here is the *trans* form, or the bad form of the virus. It infects bacteria and turns them into monsters." She waved to the other screen, depicting the virus found inside Susan's skull. "Here is the *cis* form, or the good virus that heals."

"*Cis* and *trans*," Miller mumbled. "Good and bad."

Lisa elaborated her theory. "As we already know, the *trans* virus toxified bacteria in order to weaken the blood-brain barrier, thus allowing it to penetrate that virgin territory of the inner skull. It even brought along some company."

"The cyanobacteria," Miller said. "The glowing bacteria."

"And normally the toxins produced by the bacteria corrupted the brain in such a manner that it triggered catatonic excitement with psychosis. But in Susan's case, something else happened. The virus, when it hit her brain fluid, somehow altered. Changed from its evil *trans* form over to its beneficial *cis* form. And once altered, the new virus swept out and began reversing all the damage done by its evil twin, healing the patient and sending her into a deep recuperative stupor, contrary to the manic excitement phase of the other patients."

"Even if you're correct," Henri said, "which I believe you

are, what was so special about Susan's biochemistry to trigger this change?"

Lisa shrugged. "I wager over the next days or weeks, we'll see a handful of other patients make the same transformation. Susan was infected five weeks ago. So it may be too soon to judge. But I think it's still a very rare event. A random quirk in her genetics. For example, are you familiar with the Eyam phenomenon during the Black Plague?"

Chénier raised her hand as if in a schoolroom. "I am."

Lisa nodded. Of course, an infectious disease expert would know the story.

Chénier explained, "Eyam was a small village in England. Back in the sixteen hundreds, the Black Plague struck the village. But after a year, most of Eyam still lived. Modern genetic studies revealed why. A rare mutation was present in the villagers. In a gene called Delta 32. It was a benign defect that was passed from one family member to another, and in such an isolated township, inbred as they were, a good portion of the town had acquired the mutation. Then the plague struck. And this strange little mutation, just hanging about, saved them. Made them immune."

Devesh spoke up. "Are you suggesting our patient carries the Delta 32 equivalent against the Judas Strain? Some random protein that enzymatically switched the virus in her from *trans* to *cis*."

"Or maybe it's not that random," Lisa mumbled. She'd been struggling with this question ever since her discovery of the altered virus. "Only a very small percentage of our DNA is actually functional. Only three percent, in fact. The other ninety-seven percent is considered genetic junk. It doesn't code for anything. But some of that junk DNA bears a remarkable resemblance to *viral* code. The current belief is that such coding might serve a protective role, to help us survive future disease."

As Lisa continued, she pictured the body of Susan's friend, attacked and eaten. "Like cannibalism, for example."

Her strange statement drew everyone's eyes from the monitors.

Lisa elaborated. "Genetic markers found worldwide show that most humans carry a specific set of genes against diseases that can only be acquired by eating human flesh. These findings suggest that our ancient ancestors might have all been cannibals. Maybe Susan has a similar genetic marker to protect her brain against the attack by the Judas Strain virus. Something left over from our long-lost genetic history. Something buried in our collective past."

"Intriguing as usual, Dr. Cummings." Devesh rocked back and forth on his toes, plainly excited. "But whether the transformation was random chance or was triggered by some viral genetic marker from our past . . . it doesn't truly matter. Now that we know about this new virus, we can use this knowledge to produce a cure!"

Chénier looked less sure. "Possibly," she stressed. "It will take more study. Luckily we have a boatload of sick patients upon which to test potential treatment regimens. But first, we'll need more of that *cis* virus." She glanced significantly over to Devesh.

"No worries," he said. "With Rakao and his men already hunting the island, we'll soon have Susan Tunis and the others back. But with that matter settled—"

Devesh turned to Lisa. "It's now time to discuss your punishment."

As if on cue, a figure stepped forward, carrying a doctor's satchel in her hands.

Her long black hair had been retied into a braid.

Surina.

3:14 A.M.

MONK CLIMBED THE steep switchback, following the naked rear end of one of the cannibals. Another dozen tribesmen scaled the crooked trail in the rock ahead of him. Behind Monk, more followed, another forty strong.

His cannibal army.

Rain poured out of the dark skies. But at least the winds had mostly died down, snapping with only occasional gusts across the jagged peaks. Monk had purposefully timed this ascent, waiting for the eye of the storm to crest over the island. It had been an agonizing delay, but his patience had opened a small window of opportunity.

He continued on. Though the path they climbed was sheltered, cut deep into the rock, the downpour made the rocks slippery, treacherous, requiring crawling at times on hands and knees.

Monk glanced behind him.

Ryder and Jessie had his back. Strung out behind them, a line of tribesmen followed, dressed in feathers, shells, bark, bird claws, and bones.

Lots of bones.

The improvised strike team bore short spears, sapling bows, and sharpened clubs. But half of them also carried rifles and a smattering of old assault weapons—Russian AK-47s, United States M16s—along with bandoliers strapped with extra magazines and cartridges. It seemed the cannibals had been trading for more than just two-legged meat with the pirates that shared their cove.

From this height, Monk had a wide view of the dark lake. The cruise ship glowed like a sodden wedding cake in the middle. It was the goal of the cannibal strike team.

It seemed whatever Rangda, the witch queen, wanted, the mesmerized cannibals would make sure she got.

And Rangda wanted that cruise ship.

Her wishes and orders were translated by the young Jessie. He spoke Malay, and as it was the official trading language of the pirates, most of the cannibals understood it, too. They were much in awe of the young nurse, that he should understand the language of their queen and was able to pass on Rangda's desires. She even bestowed a kiss on her interpreter's cheek, blessing the young nurse.

No one dared disobey him.

But while Jessie had been integral in organizing the assault, the plan here was all Monk's.

He turned his back on the cruise ship. With the waters surely watched, they'd never manage an assault by boat. And swimming was certainly not an option. Even from this height, Monk noted the occasional flashes streaking through the lagoon far below. The storm had the denizens stirred up and hunting the shallows.

So it had left only one choice.

Monk climbed higher, all the way to the roof of the world. They had finally reached the giant steel support posts and massive cabling that anchored this section of the island's net.

Monk stared out across the net's underside.

Rain poured from it, soaking through all the camouflaging vegetation woven into the web's upper side. Someone had to be maintaining that illusion. And Monk guessed it wasn't just the pirates.

Proving this, one of the cannibals scurried up the nearest cable, his bare feet frogging his lithe form up the span. He vanished through the netting. A rope ladder cascaded back down.

Others began scaling up.

Monk turned to Jessie. "You can still go back down, join Susan at the beach. We can pick you both up there."

Jessie swept rain-soaked hair out of his eyes. "I'm going. Otherwise, who's going to translate for you?" Before Monk could argue, the nurse grabbed the ladder and scurried up.

Ryder followed next, clapping Monk on the shoulder as he passed. Once the billionaire had shoved through the net overhead, Monk grabbed the lower rung, staring back at the spread of his dark army. Feathered, armed to the teeth, ready to do the bidding of their queen.

Monk felt a momentary misgiving at abusing their superstitions in this regard. Many of them would die. But if Lisa was right, the whole world was threatened. He had no choice but to use the resources at hand.

They had to reach Ryder's boat. Get Susan out of here—and hopefully rescue Lisa. Monk refused to believe his partner was not still alive.

Monk pulled himself up the ladder.

He climbed through the whipping tangle of camouflage. Even in the eye of the storm, the gusting winds sought to kite him from his perch. He beached himself out onto a narrow ribbon of planking, bolted atop the net. It was a crude utility bridge. The span offered a means to crisscross the net, to maintain it, to refresh its camouflage as needed.

Already the forefront of his army headed across the bridge, on its belly, clinging to the bridge's slats.

With rain sweeping down in stinging sheets, Monk scooted after them. Occasional winds thrummed through the net, jumping and rolling it under him. Like riding Aladdin's flying carpet.

Monk craned around. Overhead the cloud cover had thinned enough to reveal a few stars, but all around dark clouds churned in a continual whirl. The eye of the storm was smaller than Monk had hoped. To all sides, lightning flashed and thunder rumbled.

Monk hurried onward. He and his army had to be off the net when the storm's eye swept away from the island. He recalled earlier lightning strikes, the cascades of electricity ripping across the metal skeleton.

It would be death to be up here then.

Slowly, they inched toward their goal.

As he followed, Monk stared below, between the slats. At least, Susan was out of harm's way.

4:02 A.M.

HER FACE GREASED with ash to hide her glow, Susan sat on a boulder, buried in the jungle, not far from the lagoon. She had spent the past hour trekking back down to the beach, to await Monk there.

But she was not alone.

A dozen tribesmen, her royal escort, stood guard in the jungle, buried in the forest. Only a woman, whose name was Tikal, kept her immediate company, knelt beside the rock, her forehead pressed to mud. She had not moved since they had stopped.

Susan had attempted to engage her, but the woman only shivered.

So Susan waited, seated on her rock. She wore a cloak of dried pigskin, draped with feathers, shells, and polished stone beads. Her head was crowned by a circlet of rib bones, tied to her forehead by bark fiber. All the bones splayed outward, like some macabre flower. She was given a polished staff, topped by an impaled human skull.

All fitting apparel for the witch queen of Pusat.

And despite the ghoulish ornamentation, the cloak was warm and her staff proved useful in climbing down from the highlands and back to the beach. Her escort had also woven a temporary shelter of thatched palm leaves overhead, keeping their mistress dry.

Susan stared up toward the vast netting. She had known she was too weak to attempt to cross with the others. So she had not argued when Monk ordered her down to the beach, to keep hidden, to await the outcome of the cannibal assault upon the cruise ship.

But she knew it would be a long vigil.

Too long.

Abandoned, she began to absorb the full impact of all that had happened after waking aboard the cruise ship. Though alive herself, those closest to her heart had not survived.

Gregg . . .

Her husband flooded back to her: his crooked grin, his galloping laugh, his dark eyes, the musky scent of his skin, the taste of his lips . . . on and on.

He filled her up.

How could all that be gone?

Susan knew she was still far from fully comprehending her loss. But she knew enough. Her body felt physically bruised, all the way down to her core. Her throat closed up, and she began to tremble. Glowing tears swelled and ran over her ash-blackened face.

Gregg . . .

She rocked in place for a long stretch, merely letting her grief rack through her. It was impossible to stop it. The surge of sorrow was a tidal force, as inescapable as the pull of the moon.

But after a stretch of time, even a tide must ebb. In its aching wake, another primal sensation remained, washed up from even deeper shoals, something she had again avoided acknowledging until now. But it was there, as inescapable as her grief.

Susan extended an arm from her cloak, staring at the breadth of her skin, glowing because of the cyanobacteria in her perspiration, in her pores. She turned her hand, palm up. The glow did not heat the skin, but there was a strange warmth—it harkened more to fever than sunlight.

What was happening to her?

As a marine biologist, Susan knew all about the organism. Cyanobacteria, commonly referred to as *blue-green algae,* were as ubiquitous as the sea itself. They grouped into myriad formations: thin filaments, flat sheets, hollow balls. They were instrumental to evolution, being the predecessors of modern plants. Early in the earth's history, cyanobacteria also generated the planet's first oxygen atmosphere, making the world livable. And since then, they had adapted to millions of ecological niches.

So what did the colonization of her body mean? How did it relate to her exposure to the Judas Strain virus? It made no sense.

Despite all her questions, Susan knew one truth.

Something was still coming.

She sensed it deep inside, a welling sensation that defied any description.

As unstoppable as any rising tide.

She stared across the forest, across the lagoon, beyond the island. As surely as she could sense the sun rising beyond the curve of the planet, Susan knew she was not done changing.

4:18 A.M.

FROM A HUNDRED yards away Rakao spied upon his quarry. Hidden in a rain poncho, he held the infrared goggles to his brow. He counted the red glows, body-heat signatures, spread along the edge of the beach. His hunters outnumbered the tribesmen two to one.

With a raised fist, Rakao signaled his team to spread out to either side, to keep their distance. His men knew to move only with each rumble of thunder. The tribesmen had keen senses. He did not want to spook his prey.

Rakao studied Susan Tunis, seated on a rock. He had followed the cannibal party down from the highlands to the lagoon. Where were her companions? They could not be far.

So while he could snatch her up at any time, he was a patient hunter. As his men spread out in a snare, securing the trap, Rakao knew the best use to put the woman.

As bait.

14
Ruins of Angkor

SIX HOURS OF TRAVEL deposited Gray in another century and a mishmash of cultures. He climbed out of the taxi into the heart of the old French district of Siem Reap, a small riverside hamlet in the middle of Cambodia, nestled between rice paddies and the great expanse of an inland lake. With dawn still an hour away, the place slumbered, air heavy and humid, buzzing with mosquitoes and hissing with the flicker of gas lamps. From the neighboring river, the lazy chirping of frogs added to the soft somnolence of the early morning.

A couple of low skiffs poled through the river's shallows, oil lamps hanging on extended poles as fishermen in wide bamboo hats checked crab and crayfish traps or stabbed at the unwary frog, fetching fresh catch for the town's many restaurants and cafés.

The rest of Gray's party climbed out of the taxi in various poses of exhaustion. Vigor, hunched and bleary-eyed, looked like someone had washed him and put him away wet in the humid air, whereas Seichan stretched like a waking cat, one hand protecting her wounded side. Her eyes smoldered past him to inspect their accommodations. Kowalski scratched at his armpit and did the same, whistling between his teeth, which set a dog to barking a block deeper into the village.

Nasser had arranged their spectacular accommodations.

It was where they were to await his arrival.

In another two hours.

Across a curved entry road the three-story colonial hotel spread from the river in yellow wings of plaster and timber, roofed in red stone, anchored in manicured French gardens. Its history typified the entire region. The seventy-five-year-old lodge used to be named the Grand Hôtel des Ruines, servicing French and British tourists wishing to visit the nearby complex of Angkor ruins, which lay only five miles away. Both hotel and village had eventually fallen into near ruin during the bloody and brutal years of the Khmer Rouge, where millions were murdered in one of the most heinous acts of genocide, annihilating one-fourth of Cambodia's population. Such atrocities put a damper on tourism. But with the fall of the Khmer Rouge, people had returned. The hotel rose from its ashes, meticulously renovated in all its colonial charm and renamed the Grand Hôtel d'Angkor.

Siem Reap had similarly been revitalized—if with a bit less care. Hotels and hostels had multiplied in a continual creep out from the river's east and west banks, along with restaurants, bars, Internet cafés, travel agents, fruit and spice stands, and myriad markets selling Cambodian carved curios, filigreed silver, postcards, T-shirts, and trinkets.

But here in the early hours—with neither tourist nor sun yet risen—some of the charm and mystery still remained in its architectural mix of Asian and French culture. An ox-driven cart laden with spiky-skinned durian fruit ambled down the road toward the Old Market, while a manservant in a pressed white jacket slowly swept the hotel's porch.

As Gray climbed the stairs, leading his group, the sweeper smiled shyly, set aside his task, and opened the door for them.

The lobby was bright with marble and polished woods, perfumed by large flowering displays of roses, orchids, jasmine, and lotus. An antique elevator cage, wrapped in intricately twined wrought iron stood beside an inviting curve of stairs.

"The Elephant Bar is around the corner," Seichan explained, pointing an arm. It was where they were to meet with Nasser.

Gray glanced to his watch for the hundredth time.

"I'll get us checked in," Vigor said.

As the monsignor headed over to the reception desk, Gray searched the lobby. Were there Guild agents already here? It was the question that Gray had been asking himself since they landed in Bangkok and switched planes for the short hop here. Seichan had confirmed that the Guild had operatives throughout the region, with deep ties in China and North Korea. It was practically Guild home turf.

Gray did not doubt that Nasser had spies planted along their entire route from the island of Hormuz to Cambodia. To spare his parents' lives, Gray had been forced to reveal where Marco's historical trail ended: the ruins of Angkor. It convinced Nasser to delay any immediate plans to murder his parents. But as Gray feared, it had not bought his parents their freedom.

With the sword still poised over his parents' heads, Gray had refused to elaborate on his second bombshell—the cure for the Judas Strain. Not until Nasser was face-to-face with him and supplied concrete evidence that his parents were released and safe.

So they had agreed to rendezvous here.

An exchange.

Information for his parents' freedom.

But Gray was no fool. He knew Nasser would never release his parents. This was all a trap by Nasser—and a pure delaying tactic by Gray. Both men knew this. Still, they had no choice but to continue this dance of deceptions. All Gray could do was keep Nasser strung along, to keep hanging that carrot in front of him, in order to buy

Director Crowe as much time as possible to find his mother and father.

Gray had risked a short call Stateside after hanging up with Nasser, using Seichan's disposable phone. Fearing that Nasser might quickly tap the cell towers in the remote region, Gray had to keep their talk short as he updated Painter. The director had only grim news in return. Sigma had no new leads on his parents, and there continued to be no word on Monk and Lisa's whereabouts. Gray had heard the frustration and fury in the man's voice.

Add raw terror to the mix, and it matched Gray's mood.

Painter had again offered to send assets to support Gray out here, but until his parents were safe and secure, he dared not accept them. As Seichan had warned, this was Guild home turf. Any mobilization would only reveal that Gray was still secretly in communication with Washington. It was a small advantage, but one Gray did not want to risk losing. But more importantly, if Nasser got a whiff that a line of communication was open between Gray and Sigma command, he would immediately kill his parents. Gray needed Nasser to feel fully confident that his team was cut off.

Still, Gray had taken one small risk and had asked for a tiny concession from Painter. Afterward, with the matter settled, all Gray had to do was keep extending that time frame.

He still had another two hours.

The elevator door chimed open behind him. He heard the old wrought-iron door ratchet back. "I see you all arrived safely," a voice spoke calmly behind him.

Gray turned.

Nasser stepped out of the cage and into the lobby, dressed in a dark suit, no tie. "It looks like we can get this meeting started early."

Men in khaki uniforms and black berets appeared from the halls to either side. Behind him, Gray heard the pound of boots on the porch outside. A score more soldiers clambered down the curved stairs ahead. Though no weapons were in sight, Gray did not doubt they were all armed.

Kowalski must have sensed this, too. He already had his hands in the air.

Seichan merely shook her head. "There goes my hot bath."

Vigor stepped back to Gray's side.

Nasser joined them. "So it is time to discuss this cure."

6:18 P.M.
Washington, D.C.

"FROM WHAT YOU just told me," Dr. Malcolm Jennings said, "Gray has nothing to offer the Guild. Nothing of real value."

Painter listened quietly, letting the man run through his thought processes. He had summoned Jennings, the head of Sigma's research-and-development department, up to his office to get his input. Luckily, Jennings had already been on his way up here.

"From the details in Marco's story," Jennings said, pacing in front of Gray's desk, "Polo and a handful of others were protected against the Judas Strain by consuming blood and sweetmeat, a delicacy derived from the thymus gland. And according to the story, the blood and gland were harvested out of another man."

"Basically cannibalism."

"Or as Gray had read into the text—and I believe he's correct—it could represent a crude form of *vaccination*. The thymus gland is a *major* source of white blood cells, the body's cellular defense against disease. And the blood is a *major* way antibodies against infections are distributed. By consuming such tissue, you could theoretically confer the equivalent of an immunization."

Painter agreed. "That's what Gray believes protected Polo's companions."

"But such a revelation is meaningless," Jennings argued. "It offers no real cure. Where did the blood and gland come from? Not from one of the sick. You'd just get infected. There is a missing piece of this puzzle. For such a cure to work, you'd need to harvest cells and antibodies from someone cured, someone who survived the Judas Strain. It's just circuitous logic. It takes a cure to find a cure."

Painter sighed. "And you can't think of anything in the story that might offer some elaboration."

The doctor slowly shook his head.

As Painter feared, Gray was running a dangerous bluff. Amen Nasser was not a fool. The bastard would also recognize the lack of any real answer. All Gray's bluff could hope to achieve was to buy time. And with the trail gone cold after the raid on the butcher shop, it seemed a wasted effort, a needless risk. Painter had hoped Jennings might have some new insight.

But no such luck.

Painter resigned himself. "So it seems Marco's story leads to a dead end."

"Not necessarily." Jennings waited a breath. "Director, there is something else I wanted to discuss. It was why I was headed up here. It may even relate to this topic. In fact, if you have an extra minute, perhaps you'd better see this for yourself."

Painter truly didn't have that extra minute. He stared at the pile of papers in front of him, a plethora of reports. Down the hall, Monk's wife, Kat, had taken over minding the satellite recon of the Indonesian islands. With her background in the intelligence services, Kat had proved skilled at enlisting foreign aid and orchestrating cross-satellite platform surveys. But still, hampered by the local storm, they'd had no success locating the cruise ship.

Anxious and short-wired, Painter wanted to get back down there himself. But he trusted Jennings not to waste his time with trivialities. "What do you want me to see?"

Jennings waved to one of the office's plasma wall monitors. "I'd like to conference with Richard Graff in Australia. He's expecting my call, if you're willing."

"Graff?" Painter asked. "The researcher who had been working with Monk at Christmas Island?"

"Exactly."

It was Dr. Graff who had radioed a tanker passing Christmas Island and had alerted the world about the hijacking of the cruise ship. The oceanographer was currently sequestered and quarantined in Perth.

"You've read his debriefing with Australian authorities?" Jennings asked.

Painter nodded.

"But there is something odd that the researcher has discovered since then."

Painter waved to the monitor. "Okay. Show me."

Jennings came around his desk and quickly established a live conference feed. "Here we go."

The monitor went dark, flickered, then a jittery image of the scientist appeared. Dr. Graff wore blue hospital scrubs and his arm was in a sling. He blinked behind his glasses at Painter and Jennings.

Introductions were made—though Jennings passed themselves off as researchers associated with the Smithsonian Institution.

"Can you demonstrate what you found?" Jennings asked. "What you showed me earlier? I think my colleague should see it."

"I have the specimen waiting right here." Graff slipped offscreen. The camera angle widened and shifted to reveal a white conference table.

Graff reappeared, carrying a large red object in one hand.

"Is that a crab?" Painter asked, sitting straighter.

"*Geocarcoidea natalis,*" Jennings explained. "The Christmas Island red land crab."

On the screen, Graff nodded and settled the crab to the tabletop. Its large pincer claws were rubber-banded closed. "The little bugger—or rather a horde of them—helped save my life back on the island."

Curious, Painter stood up and approached the screen.

Graff put the crab on the table and released it. It immediately scrabbled across the surface, aiming in a determined straight line. Graff hurried around to the table's far side to catch it.

Painter shook his head. "I don't understand. What are you trying to show me here?"

Graff explained. "Dr. Kokkalis and I found it strange that these crabs were not killed off by the toxic exposure, but their behavior certainly was affected. They were attacking and tearing each other apart. So I had hoped to study the behavior to see if it offered any insight into the toxicity."

While narrating, Graff had settled the crab twice more to the table, but no matter where he placed it, no matter which way he faced the creature, the determined crustacean would turn and make a beeline, hitting the same corner of the table before almost toppling off.

He demonstrated it a few more times.

Strange.

Graff explained his supposition. "The Christmas Island land crab has a finely attuned nervous system that guides its annual migration pattern. Most crustaceans do. But the toxic exposure seems to have rewired the crab's nervous system, turned it into the equivalent of a fixed compass. The crab always crawls in the same direction, the same compass heading."

Graff collected his crab and deposited it in a tank. "Once things calm down over at the island," he finished, "I'd like to test other crabs to see if they are similarly rewired to the same setting. It's a fascinating study. I would be happy to write up that grant proposal you mentioned earlier, Dr. Jennings."

"It certainly is an intriguing anomaly, Dr. Graff," Jennings said. "My colleague and I will consult and get back to you. I appreciate your time."

The call was disconnected, and the screen went blank. But Jennings continued typing at Painter's computer station.

A new image appeared on the plasma screen, fed from the computer, a globe of the world.

"When I heard about this anomaly," Jennings said, "I went ahead and collated Dr. Graff's data and tracked the crab's trajectory." A dotted line appeared encircling the globe. "I didn't think my results proved anything until you sent down the update from Commander Pierce."

The globe spun and zoomed large on the screen.

Painter leaned in close. The view swelled with the image of Southeast Asia. The dotted line traversed Indonesia, spanned the Gulf of Thailand, and ran straight across Cambodia.

Jennings tapped the screen, noting one spot crossed by the crab's trajectory. "Angkor Wat."

Painter straightened. "Are you suggesting—?"

"A rather odd coincidence. It makes me wonder if this crab had been rewired to march itself straight over there."

Painter stared at the screen, picturing Gray Pierce, reminded of the deadly bluff being played out there. "If you're right, then Marco's trail might not be such a dead end after all. Something must be there."

Jennings nodded, hands on his hips. "But what?"

5:32 A.M.
Siem Reap

VIGOR REMINDED HIMSELF never to play poker with Gray.

The commander sat in a rattan lounge chair in the hotel's bar. The facility was closed at this hour, but Nasser had rented the space out for privacy. The Elephant Bar gained its name from the pair of large curved tusks near the entrance. Continuing the motif, the lounge was appointed with bamboo furniture upholstered in zebra and tiger prints.

Gray sat across a glass coffee table from Nasser, playing a cautious game.

Seichan had sprawled herself across a sofa, ankles crossed.

Kowalski sat at the long bar, staring at the gemlike spread of bottles. But Vigor also noted how the large man continued to spy upon Gray and Nasser in the bar's mirror.

Not that there was much any of them could do.

Nasser's men stationed themselves at all the exits and lined both walls.

With a clank of metal on glass, Nasser returned one of the gold *paitzus* to the tabletop. Before he even entertained any discussion about cures, Nasser wanted to verify that the ruins of Angkor were indeed where Marco Polo had first encountered the Judas Strain. Gray had laid it all out, decoding the entire story as he had aboard the seaplane.

Vigor stood over the table, studying the angelic script, the star chart, the map of the ruins. He had again listened to the complete decipher.

Nasser finally accepted the truth. He leaned back. "And this cure?"

Vigor fought against flinching. On the flight here, Gray had explained his take on the last story of Marco Polo: his theory of vaccination through cannibalism. It was intriguing, but in the end, it offered no real cure.

Because of the risk of this bluff, Gray had attempted to shuffle Vigor onto a different flight when they changed planes in Bangkok.

"It's too dangerous," Gray had warned. "Go back to Italy."

But Vigor had refused. Besides the fact that Nasser had ordered *all* of them to Cambodia, Vigor had his own reasons for continuing. Somewhere among these ruins, Friar Agreer had vanished, a fellow brother of the cloth, sacrificing himself to save Marco and the others. Vigor could not turn his back on such selfless bravery. But he also had a more important argument to offer Gray.

"The natives who had offered the cure recognized something in Friar Agreer, some commonality," Vigor had explained. "Why did they seek him out? If there is some answer beyond where Marco left off, it might take another brother of the cloth to find it."

Gray had reluctantly agreed.

Still, Vigor had one last reason for continuing, one he left unvoiced. Something he had noted in the young man's eyes. Desperation. As these last cards were being played out, Gray was getting reckless. Like this risky bluff, walking into a trap with no secondary strategy. All Gray's hopes lay with Director Crowe, trusting that his boss would find some way to secure his parents in time, freeing Gray to act.

But was Gray up to the game being played here, especially plagued by the worry for his parents? Plainly some of the sharp edge of his mind had been dulled.

Vigor stared down at the spread of maps and angelic scripts.

For example, how had Gray missed seeing this earlier?

"The cure," Nasser persisted, pulling Vigor's attention up. "Tell me what you know."

Across the table, Gray remained cool and calm, not a bead of sweat on his brow. "I will give you an airport locker number. Back in Bangkok. Tell you where to find the key to confirm what I'm about to say. We stashed the third and final scroll in that locker. In that last document, Marco describes the cure. It is in two parts. I will tell you the first part, free of charge."

Nasser shifted, one eye narrowing.

"Once I'm done, as a mark of good faith, you'll release one of my parents. And I will expect satisfactory confirmation. With that, I will tell you the locker number and location of the key. You can verify my claim. Is that satisfactory?"

"It depends on what I hear."

Gray merely stared, not blinking.

Vigor knew it was all a stalling tactic, stretching out the reveal for as long as possible. The scroll had indeed been secured in an airport locker in Bangkok, but it was a wild-goose chase. There was no second half of the cure.

Gray sighed, as if relenting. "Here then is the story found within the third scroll. According to Marco . . ."

As Gray related what the embroidered scroll revealed, Vigor studied the documents on the table, only half listening.

The commander kept to the truth, knowing that more time would be bought with the facts than lies. After Gray was finished, Nasser would make the necessary calls, arrange to have the scroll recovered from the locker, then translated. All of it would take time. The discovered scroll would verify Gray's story and make it more likely Nasser would buy any fabrication to follow. And even if Gray's lies failed to convince, at least one of his parents would be saved by then.

That was the plan.

Gray finally finished his narration, laying out the science. "So clearly the cannibalism served some means of vaccinating against the disease. But exactly how that was achieved will wait until I know one of my parents is safe."

Gray folded his hands in his lap.

Nasser sat silent for a moment, then spoke slowly. "So we really just need someone who is cured of the Judas Strain, someone who survived. Then we can construct the vaccine from their white blood cells and antibodies."

Gray remained silent, offering only a slight shrug of his shoulders, quietly stating that any further answers would wait until one of his parents was free.

Nasser sighed, reached to a pocket, flipped open the phone, and pressed a button. "Annishen," he said. "Pick one of the hostages. Your choice."

Nasser listened.

"Yes, that's fine . . . go ahead and kill them."

5:45 P.M.

GRAY LUNGED ACROSS the table.

He had no plan, reacting on pure instinct.

But Nasser must have signaled one of the men. Gray's head exploded with pain, clubbed from behind, his vision blew away into brightness, then collapsed into momentary darkness. His body struck the cocktail table and rolled with a thump to the floor, jarring back his sight.

Five guns now pointed at Gray.

More at Seichan and Kowalski.

Vigor stood with his arms crossed.

Nasser had not moved, his phone still lifted to his ear. "Hold, Annishen. For the moment." He lowered the phone, half covering the receiver with a hand. "It seems this is the end, Commander Pierce. Of many trails. Polo's last scroll only confirms what I've heard from the Guild contingent in Indonesia. The scientific team has come to the same conclusion. A potential cure does reside within the body of a survivor. One who happens to *glow,* like revealed in Polo's story."

Gray shook his head. Not in denial, he just had difficulty comprehending what Nasser was saying. Blood pounded in his ears, deafening him. His plan had failed.

Nasser lifted his phone again. "So it seems our historical trail has run full circle back to the scientific trail. This is the end of the proverbial road. For you. For your mother and father."

Gray sensed the world closing in on him. Even his vision narrowed, voices sounded more hollow. Until Vigor stepped closer.

"Enough," the monsignor snapped out with the command of a professor in an auditorium.

All eyes turned to him. Even Nasser paused.

Vigor stared at their captor. "You make many assumptions, young man. Assumptions that will not serve you, or your associates."

"How so, Monsignor?" Nasser kept his tone civil.

"This cure. Have your scientists tested it yet?" Vigor stared at Nasser, then a small snort escaped him. "I wager not. All you've come up with are theoretical conjectures, supported perhaps by Marco's story. But that is a far cry from certainty. And I'm sorry to discount your statement that the historical trail has ended. It may indeed have run into the scientific trail, but rather than ending, I believe the more accurate description is that the two trails have *merged* here. Do not be too quick to ignore history. Not yet, young man. The historical trail continues."

Gray's mind sought to work through what the monsignor was saying. Was he lying, bluffing, or telling the truth?

Nasser sighed, apparently weighing the same. "I appreciate your attempt, Monsignor. But I see nothing here to warrant further investigation. The scientists can handle it from here."

Now Seichan snorted. "That is why you will never rise higher in the Guild hierarchy, Amen. Pawning off your responsibility to others. I suggest you listen to the monsignor."

Nasser glared, but he did glance back to Vigor. "Marco's map points here to the ruins. It ends here."

Vigor bent down and lifted the map of Angkor's extensive complex of ruins. "This covers over one hundred square miles. That's a lot of territory. Does this strike you as an *end*?"

Nasser's eyes narrowed. "Do you propose we search all one hundred square miles? To what end? We have the cure."

Vigor shook his head. "There is no need to search the entire complex. Marco pinpointed the most significant site for us."

Nasser turned to Gray, ready to threaten, his eyes dark on him.

Vigor stepped between them. "Commander Pierce has not held anything back. He does not have this answer. This I swear on my soul."

Nasser frowned. "Yet, you do."

Vigor bowed his head. "I do. And I will tell you. But only upon your sworn word that you'll allow Commander Pierce's parents to live."

Nasser's features hardened, suspicious.

Vigor lifted a hand. "I'm not asking for you to release them. Only to hear me out, and I think you'll understand the need to follow the trail to its end."

Gray noted the wavering uncertainty in Nasser's countenance.

Oh, please, God, let Vigor convince him.

Vigor continued. "Once you follow the trail to the end, *then* make your decision. About them, about us. It would be foolish to destroy hostages or resources until you discover what lies at the true end of that trail."

Nasser sank to his seat. "So then show me where it ends. Convince me, Monsignor."

"And if I do so, as a man of honor, will you keep Gray's parents alive?"

Nasser waved a hand. "Fine. For now. But if you are lying, Monsignor . . ."

"I'm not." Vigor lowered to one knee before the table.

Gray joined him.

Vigor shifted forward three sheets of paper: the map of Angkor, the obelisk's angelic code, and the line of three symbols from the keys. The monsignor lifted the sheet of angelic code.

"As Commander Pierce has already related, all the blacked-out diacritical marks—the circles that accent the script—actually represent temple sites that make up Angkor."

Nasser nodded.

"And here again are the three symbols from the keys.

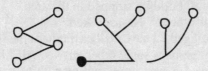

"Now compare these three symbols to the matching circled symbols on the obelisk. What do you see different?"

Nasser leaned forward, as did Gray.

"There're three blacked-out circles on the symbols on the obelisk," Nasser said.

"Representing three temples," Vigor said. "Now, how many blacked-out circles are there among the three key symbols."

"Only one," Gray said. He understood now. He had been so certain he had solved the puzzle earlier that he had failed to look one step further. "One temple. That blacked-out circle doesn't just represent the Portuguese castle—it represents one of the temples!"

Gray shifted the map to him and took a pen to circle the corresponding temple and connected them.

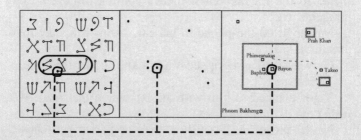

Nasser leaned closer to read the temple marked on the map of Angkor. "Bayon." He leaned back. "But how can you be sure it's significant?"

"The Bayon was the last temple ever built in Angkor," Vigor said. "Built about the time Marco came through the area. The strange thing about the temple is that after it was constructed, all building stopped in the area."

"But what's there?" Nasser asked.

Vigor shrugged. "I have no idea. Perhaps the source of the Judas Strain, perhaps some other answer. All I know is that Marco believed it was important enough to preserve. And even if I'm wrong, after following this trail halfway around the world, why stop when you are only steps from the very end?"

Nasser stared around the room.

Seichan stirred. "We can be there in half an hour, Amen. It's worth at least going there."

Gray feared to agree with them, lest he only stir up Nasser's wrath.

Vigor was not as bashful. "Marco went to much trouble to preserve the location of this temple. The Vatican mystics went through as much trouble to secure it in code. Even the locals here claim the temple still holds many hidden treasures. It bears investigation."

Kowalski raised his hand. "And I have to take a leak. Bad."

Nasser frowned, but he gained his feet. "We'll head over there. To the Bayon. But if there's nothing discovered by noon, it's over."

Nasser lifted the phone to his ear. "Annishen, stay that execution order."

Gray reached and gripped Vigor's knee under the table. *Thank you.*

Vigor glanced to him with an expression that read, *We aren't out of the woods yet.*

Nasser proved it. "Annishen, the one parent you chose. We'll spare their life as per my word to the monsignor. But we'll still need some incentive to encourage the commander's continued and heartfelt cooperation."

Nasser's eyes fixed to Gray. "For every hour in which we don't have satisfactory results, cut off one finger. And since we've stalled here for much longer than an hour due to Commander Pierce's futile attempts to barter, you may take that first finger now."

Nasser snapped his phone closed.

Gray knew silence would serve him better, but the words were out of his mouth before he could stop them. "You goddamn bastard. I will kill you."

Unperturbed, Nasser turned away. "By the way, Commander Pierce, the parent Annishen chose . . . it was your mother."

6:55 P.M.

As the hood was ripped from her head, Harriet knew something was wrong, dreadfully wrong.

She had been dragged from a closet where she'd been locked up and forced to sit on a steel chair. With the hood pulled away, she saw they were in an abandoned warehouse. The space was cavernous, with concrete floors and walls. Steel exposed beams and pipes ran across the ceiling, and chains hung from rusted pulleys. It smelled of motor oil and burned rubber.

Harriet glanced around.

No windows. The only light came from a few bare bulbs, pooling patches in the darkness. A steel staircase rose to one side. Beside it, an old freight elevator stood open.

It all appeared deserted—except for their captors.

A step away to the left Annishen leaned on a table, a cell phone at her ear, standing silent. It appeared she was listening in to some conversation. A pistol lay on the table, next to a pair of bolt cutters and a small blowtorch. Three other men patrolled the basement's darkness.

Directly across from her, Harriet's husband sat slumped in a similar chair. Like Harriet, his wrists were in handcuffs. One of the three men stood guard over him with a hand on a holstered pistol. But Jack was no threat. His head hung, trailing a rope of drool. They had stripped him of his pants. He had urinated on himself, soaking the front of his boxers. His left leg, from the knee down, was strapped into his prosthesis. The old industrial accident had stripped so much of Jack's pride. Nature had taken the rest.

And not just nature.

Harriet felt the weight of the unused pills in her sweater pocket.

Tears welled up and streamed down her face.

Annishen spoke, finishing her call with a snap of her cell phone. She faced Harriet and motioned to another of the guards. "Undo her cuffs."

Harriet did not object. She lifted her arms to allow the handcuffs to be keyed open. Their weight fell away. She rubbed her wrists.

What was going on?

Obeying a signal from Annishen, one of the men dragged her in her chair over to the table. The loud squeak of steel on cement drew up her husband's bleary face.

"Harriet . . ." he mumbled. "What time is it?"

"It's okay, Jack," she mumbled tenderly. "Go back to sleep."

Annishen stepped over to him. "I don't think so. He's done enough sleeping. Those little pills you gave him finally kicked in, really knocked him out. But now it's time to wakey-wake." She cupped his chin and pulled his face up. "Hold him like this," she instructed his guard. "He should watch the show."

Jack did not offer any fight as the man pinned his head.

Annishen returned to the table, wiping Jack's drool on her pant leg. She nodded to the guard beside Harriet's chair. He reached over, grabbed Harriet's left arm, and yanked it hard over the tabletop, pinning her wrist against the wood.

Instinctively, Harriet fought back, but the man just dragged her arm farther, stretching her limb until her armpit was jammed against the table's edge. She felt the cold muzzle of a pistol against her cheek, held by the third guardsman.

Annishen sauntered over. "It seems we must teach your son a little lesson, Mrs. Pierce."

She picked up the blowtorch and pulled the trigger on the self-igniter. A blue flame spat out the torch's muzzle with a sharp hiss. She settled it to the table near her hand. "For cauterizing the stump."

"What . . . what are you doing?"

Ignoring her the woman picked up the bolt cutters, pulling the handles wide. "Now which finger shall we cut off first?"

6:01 A.M.

GRAY RODE IN the backseat of a white van. Seichan sat pressed against his side, the pair of them pinned between two armed guards. Nasser faced them from the bench seat ahead, flanked by more guards.

Kowalski and Vigor rode in the vehicle behind theirs. Another two vans followed front and rear, piled in with more khaki-dressed gunmen.

Nasser was taking no chances.

Through the windshield, Gray dully watched the spires of Angkor Wat rise out of the mists ahead, five massive corncob-shaped towers, lit by the first rays of the rising sun. Angkor Wat was the first of many temples spread across a hundred square miles of ruins. It was also the largest and best preserved, considered a Cambodian icon, with its immense jumble of chambers, walls, scalloped towers, carvings, and statues. This temple alone covered five hundred acres, encircled by a wide moat.

But it was not their goal.

They were headed to Angkor Thom, another mile north.

And while not as large as Angkor Wat, the walled ruins of Thom housed the great Bayon temple, considered to be the heart of all of Angkor.

A resounding bump shook the van.

Gray caught his own reflection in the rearview mirror. His cheeks were sunken, shadowed, his lips cracked, the stubble over his jaw and chin looked like a black bruise. Only his eyes still shone flinty and hard, fueled by his anger and vengeance. But deeper in his chest, there remained only grief and guilt.

Seichan, perhaps sensing him sinking into a numbing despair, gripped his hand in her own. It was not a tender gesture. She squeezed hard, nails biting, refusing to let him slip away, dragging him from the edge of that well.

Nasser noted her gesture. A shadow of a sneer appeared, then vanished away again. "And I thought you were smarter than that, Commander," he muttered. "Is she fucking you yet?"

Gray focused back at him. "Shut the hell up."

Nasser laughed, once, sharp, amused. "No? Too bad. If you're being screwed over, you should at least get something out of it."

Seichan slipped her hand from Gray's. "Fuck you, Amen."

"Not anymore, Seichan. Not after I kicked you out of bed." Nasser's eyes turned to Gray. "Did you know? That we were once lovers?"

Gray snapped a glance toward Seichan. Surely Nasser was lying. How could she . . . with the bastard who had just ordered his mother's torture? Just the thought of his mother spilled more acid into his stomach.

But Seichan refused to meet Gray's eye, glaring instead at Nasser. Her fingers curled into a fist on her knee.

"But all that ended," Nasser said. "The ambitious bitch. We were both vying to rise to the next station in the Guild hierarchy. The last rung to the very top. But we came to a difference of opinion. About how to acquire you."

Gray swallowed. "What the hell are you talking about?"

"Seichan wanted to use her wiles to lure you into cooperating of your own volition, to help the Guild follow Marco's trail. I, on the other hand, believed in a more direct approach. Blood and coercion. A man's way. But when the Guild decided against her plan, Seichan sought to take matters into her own hands. She murdered the Venetian curator, stole the obelisk, and fled to the United States."

Seichan crossed her arms, glowering back in disgust. "And you're still piss-sore that I beat you to the prize. Again."

Gray studied Seichan.

All her talk of saving the world . . . could it have all been a lie?

"So I followed her to the States," Nasser continued. "I knew where she'd be going. It was easy enough to lay a trap."

"Where you missed killing me," she scoffed, "once again proving your incompetence."

He pinched his fingers up between them. "By a fraction of an inch." He lowered his arm. "Still, you kept to your original strategy, didn't you, Seichan? You still sought Commander Pierce out. Only perhaps as more of an ally now. You knew he'd come to your rescue. You and Gray against the world!" He laughed coarsely. "Or are you still playing him, Seichan?"

Seichan merely sniffed in derision.

Nasser turned back to Gray. "She is nothing if not ambitious. Ruthless. She'd step over her own dying grandmother to rise up in the hierarchy."

Seichan leaned forward, glaring. "But at least I didn't kneel quietly while my mother was murdered before my eyes."

Nasser's face clenched hard.

"Coward," Seichan mumbled, falling back into the seat with a satisfied sneer. "You even murdered your father while his back was turned. Still couldn't face him."

Nasser lunged at her, a hand going for her throat.

Gray instinctively knocked Nasser's arm away.

Maybe he shouldn't have.

Still, Nasser pulled back on his own, his eyes sharpened by hate. "Best you know who you're in bed with," he said savagely to Gray. "Should be careful what you tell that bitch."

The combatants settled silently to their corners. Gray eyed Seichan, realizing that for all her bluster she had never denied Nasser's statements. Gray reran the past days' events over in his skull, but it was hard to concentrate with his head pounding and fear wormed deep into his belly.

Still, there were some realities that were hard to dismiss. Seichan had murdered the Venetian curator to get the obelisk. In cold blood. And when they'd first met years ago, she had even tried to kill him.

Nasser's words echoed in his head.

Best to know who you're in bed with . . .

Gray didn't know.

Ultimately, he didn't know whom to believe, whom to trust.

Gray knew only one thing for certain. There could be no missteps from here. Any failure threatened more than just his life.

7:05 P.M.

HARRIET STRUGGLED, SOBBING in terror. "Please, no . . ."

Her wrist was clamped in the vise of the guard's grip, pinned to the table, her hand flattened under the same guard's fist. The blowtorch hissed a few inches away.

Annishen held the open jaws of the bolt cutter over Harriet's splayed fingers. "Eenie, meenie, minie, mo . . ."

She lowered the jaws toward Harriet's ring finger. The diamond on her wedding band glinted under the bare bulb.

"No . . ."

A loud *crack* echoed, startling them all.

Harriet turned her head as Annishen straightened. Two yards away, the guard who had been cradling Jack's chin, forcing her husband to watch the impending mutilation, cried out and stumbled back. Blood poured from the guard's nose.

Jack lunged out of the chair, twisting away from where he had just head-butted the guard. As he turned, he yanked the guard's pistol out of its holster and swung it around in his cuffed hands.

"Get down, Harriet!" he said, firing at the same time.

The guard who had been holding the pistol against Harriet's cheek took a round to his chest. He flew backward. His gun skittered into the darkness.

The second guard released Harriet's arm and went for his weapon.

—*BANG*—

From the corner of her eye, Harriet saw the man's cheek and ear vanish in a mist of blood and gore. But her full attention was on Annishen. The woman had already dropped the bolt cutters with a clatter and snatched her pistol from the tabletop. She was whip-fast, turning on Jack.

Harriet, her arm still on the table, lunged and grabbed the blowtorch. She flashed the flame over the woman's hand and wrist. Annishen screamed. Her gun fired. A wild shot struck the cement floor and ricocheted away. The woman's sleeve caught fire as she fell back, dropping her pistol.

Jack fired again, but pain only made Annishen faster.

The woman danced to the side, kicked the table over, and dove with a trail of flame out a back doorway.

Jack fired another two shots, chasing the woman off—then was at Harriet's side. He hauled her up, hugged her tight, then hurried with her toward the stairs. "Must get out of here. The shots—"

Already shouts rang above their heads. The blasts had been heard.

"The freight elevator," Jack said.

Together they rushed toward the open cage, Jack hopping a bit with his prosthesis. Once inside, Jack hauled the gate closed and punched the button for the sixth floor. The second from the top.

"They'll have the main floor guarded. We'll head up. Seek a fire escape . . . a telephone . . . or just find a place to hole up."

He pulled Harriet to the elevator's back corner as the cage climbed past the main floor. Shouts reached them. Flashlights bobbled through the darkness. At least twenty men. Jack was right. They'd have to find another way out or some way to call for help. Failing that, they would have to hide.

The elevator continued to climb.

Jack held her.

She clung to him. "Jack . . . how . . . you were so—?"

"Gorked?" Jack shook his head. "Jesus, Harriet, do you think I'm really that bad off yet? I know I had an episode at the hotel. I'm sorry I hit you."

His voice cracked a bit at the last.

She clutched to him, accepting his apology. "When they zapped you with the Taser, I thought something had gone worse neurologically." She squeezed him again. "Thank God."

"Stung like a son of a bitch. But later, when I realized you were only pretending to give me those damn pills, I figured you were trying to tell me to act up, to fake being worse off than I was, so they'd let their guard down."

She glanced up. "So you were faking all along?"

"Well, I really did piss myself," he said angrily. "But they wouldn't take me to the goddamn can."

The elevator stopped.

Jack opened the gates, waved her out, then closed them again. He reached through the slats of the wooden gate and pressed the basement button, sending the cage back down.

"Don't want them to know which floor we got off on," he explained.

Together they headed off into the gloom of the warehouse. It was full of old equipment. "An old canning plant, from the looks of it," Jack said. "There should be plenty of places to hide."

Somewhere far below, a new noise rose up.

Barking . . . agitated, excited.

"They have dogs," Harriet whispered.

15

Demons in the Deep

IT HAD TAKEN too long to cross the island's net.

While Monk and his army crept over the roof of the world, the storm's eye had passed over the island and was headed back out to sea. To the east, the typhoon rose like a mighty wave, ready to crash again onto the island.

The winds were already kicking up.

Monk clung to the bridge's slats as the net rattled. Thunder boomed like cannon fire, and lightning crackled in shattering displays across the black skies. As the clouds opened up, rain slashed down with whipping snaps.

Clinging white-knuckled, Monk stared below.

The *Mistress of the Seas* floated in the lagoon, bright and inviting.

Ropes slithered from the net's underside and snaked down to the helipad atop the sun deck. Monk wished the helicopters were still here, but the birds had flown the coop before the ship had entered the island's lagoon.

That left only Ryder's boat.

More ropes dropped, making an even dozen, swaying in the wind.

Ahead, Jessie yelled out orders in Malay. The young nurse was only thirty yards away, but the winds tore most of his words away. Jessie sat on the net, his legs wrapped tight. He motioned and waved down.

The closest tribesmen ducked headfirst through the net, dropping away, like diving pelicans into the sea. Monk spied under the net. The trio reappeared, clinging to ropes. They slid with practiced skill as more ropes were mounted.

Slowly the army began to crawl again, flowing toward the rigged lines and down. Monk followed along the bridge. He reached Jessie as Ryder grabbed a rope and leaped through the net. The billionaire did not hesitate.

Monk understood his hurry.

Lightning slammed into the net's far side. Thunder clapped, deafening. Blue energies shot outward along the canopy's skeleton, but it faded before it reached them. The smell of ozone hung in the air.

"Keep off anything metal!" Monk screamed.

Jessie nodded, repeating his warning in Malay.

In another minute, Monk had joined Jessie. "Get below!" he ordered, and pointed down.

Jessie nodded. As he rolled off the bridge, the storm crested the island and blew with a sudden and sharp gale, roaring like a freight train. Jessie, caught in midreach, unanchored, was shoved bodily off the slatted bridge. He rolled out onto the looser camouflaged netting. His weight tore through it.

Monk lunged and grabbed his ankle. His prosthetic hand clamped hard as Jessie fell away. Monk's shoulder wrenched with fire as he caught Jessie's weight. The young nurse hung upside down below him, screaming a string of Hindu curses . . . or maybe it was prayers.

"The rope!" Monk yelled down to him.

One of the rigged lines hung ten feet away.

Monk began swinging the man. Jessie understood, his arms out, hand clawing for the rope. It was still too far. But only by a foot.

"I'm going to throw you!"

"What? No!"

He had no choice.

Monk's shoulder burned as he swung Jessie one last time. "Here we go!" Monk tossed the nurse underhanded toward the line.

Jessie tangled into the rope, scrabbling for the wet line. His body began falling, sliding, kicking. Then he hooked a leg and found a grip. He braked and halted his plunge. He clung to the rope, his cheek against it. His lips moved in a silent prayer of thanks—or maybe a curse aimed at Monk.

With the boy safe, Monk rolled back atop the bridge and crawled with caution. The winds pounded him, but he reached the nest of rigged ropes.

Another lightning strike blasted behind him.

Monk flattened as thunder deafened. He stared back over a shoulder as the net jolted like a trampoline. The rear of the bridge shattered upward from the strike, the wooden slats on fire. One of the tribesmen flew high in the air, arms pinwheeling, while electric-blue current crackled through the netting to either side—but the acrobat landed safely among his brethren.

Lucky man, but there was no going back now.

Only one way to go.

Monk grabbed the nearest rope and dropped through the net.

He slid down toward the rain-swept helipad and landed cleanly.

The rest of the army followed.

Ducked low, Monk hurried to where the others had gathered near the staircase that led down from the helipad. Jessie was already directing the tribesmen, pointing toward Monk, toward Ryder. They would split up from here. Monk would go after Lisa. Ryder and Jessie would head down, clearing a path and readying the boat.

Behind Monk bare feet slapped the decking as the last of the army drained down from the sodden net.

Monk turned to Ryder and Jessie. "Ready?" he asked.

"As we'll ever be," Ryder answered.

Monk glanced over at the raiding party, armed with bone axes and AK-47s. Lightning flashed, limning the army with fire. Eyes glinted from ash-painted faces.

In that momentary flash Monk felt a twinge of misgiving, a moment of unease. He shook it away. It was just the storm feeding his fears.

"Let's go find my partner, and get the hell out of here."

5:02 A.M.

LISA LAY STRAPPED to a steel surgical table, tilted at a forty-five-degree angle. She hung from her arms, wrists snugged in plastic ties over her head. Her legs were loose, unable to touch the floor. She wore only her hospital gown. Cold sweat plastered the thin cotton to her skin, while the steel of the table chilled her back.

She had been tied here for over an hour.

Alone.

Hopefully, forgotten.

To one side a stainless-steel tray held a line of tools used for forensic autopsies: cartilage saws, dissecting hooks, snipping scissors, postmortem needles, spinal cord chisels.

Dr. Devesh Patanjali had removed the tools from a black leather satchel, held open by Surina. He had precisely lined each instrument atop a stretch of green surgical drape. A steel bucket hung from the foot of the inclined table, ready to catch the flow of blood.

While he laid out his tools Lisa had attempted everything to dissuade him from the torture to come. She had tried appealing to his reason, explaining that she could still be useful. That once Susan was recaptured, Lisa would lend her full support to derive a cure from the woman's blood and lymph. Hadn't Lisa already proven her ingenuity?

Despite her best arguments, Devesh had ignored her. He simply lined up each tool, one after the other, on the tray.

Eventually, her arguments turned to tears. "Please . . ." she had begged.

With Devesh's back turned, Lisa's attention had turned to Surina. But there was no hope to be found there, only a deadened disinterest, her face carved in cold marble. The only bit of color was the ruby *bindi* dot on her forehead, reminding Lisa of a drop of blood.

Then Devesh had received a call. He answered it and grew plainly excited, pleased with what he was hearing. He spoke rapidly in Arabic. All Lisa understood was the word *Angkor*. Devesh left, stalking out of the room, shadowed by Surina. Devesh hadn't even looked back.

So Lisa hung here, not knowing what was happening.

But she knew her fate.

The polished surgical instruments glistened. If she shifted, the blood pail rattled at the foot of the table. She teetered between exhaustion and a keening edge of terror. She almost welcomed the return of Devesh. The waiting, the anticipation, threatened to unhinge her.

Still, when the door finally did open, she cringed, gasping out slightly. She couldn't see who entered, but she heard the *click-clack* rattle of wheels.

A gurney appeared into view, pushed from behind.

A small figure was draped atop it, tied down, spread-eagled.

Devesh spoke, shoving the gurney so it came to rest directly in front of Lisa. "Sorry for the delay, Dr. Cummings. My call took longer than I anticipated. And it took me some time to track down our subject here."

"Dr. Patanjali," Lisa begged, staring at the gurney. "Please, no . . ."

Devesh stepped over to his tools. He wore a white apron over his clothes, having shed his jacket. "Now where were we?"

Off to the side, Surina glided into view, hands folded, demure. But her eyes held a rare flicker of fire. Angry.

Devesh continued to speak. "Dr. Cummings, you were quite correct earlier. Your expertise may prove of value as we finalize our study. Yet still, it seems some punishment is in order. Someone will have to settle the debt of blood that I can't collect from you."

Lisa stared down at the gurney, at the gagged and wide-eyed figure.

It was the girl, the same child whom Devesh had threatened earlier—then let go and murdered Dr. Lindholm instead. But there would be no scapegoat this time. Devesh intended to slaughter this little lamb, while making Lisa watch.

Devesh pulled on a pair of latex surgical gloves and picked up the cartilage knife. "The first cut is always the worst."

As Devesh turned, gunfire chattered, sounding distant but still loud.

He paused.

Another blast of a rifle erupted, echoing up from the floor below. "Not again," he sighed out in irritation. "Can't they keep these patients restrained?"

More blasts.

Devesh slammed his knife to the tabletop, rattling the other tools. He nicked himself and lifted a bloody finger to his lips. With a deep scowl, he headed again to the door.

"Surina, watch over our guests. I'll be right back."

The door slammed closed.

As if caught in the wind from the swing of the door, Surina flew to the table. She collected the cartilage knife and returned to the strapped child.

"Don't hurt her," Lisa warned, a threat in her voice, impotent though it might be.

Surina's eyes flicked with disinterest at Lisa. She swung her attention to the child, raised the knife, and slashed out in strokes of flashing steel—the child's bonds fell away. The strange woman scooped the child in her arms, to her shoulder, then glided to the door.

Lisa heard the quiet clicks as the door opened and closed, leaving her alone again.

Lisa frowned. She remembered Surina offering a candy to the same child earlier, a rare compassion. Lisa recalled Surina's eyes when she first came in here, feral and wild, like a lioness. Angry. It seemed this lioness retained some compassion for the most innocent. Perhaps this rescue was some bit of grace to compensate for her other cruelties.

Either way, she was gone.

Lisa imagined Devesh's rage when he returned, already inflamed by another breakout. There would remain only one person here upon whom he could vent his frustrations. Lisa struggled against her wrist ties. The pail bumped and clanked.

Gunfire continued, some blasts louder than others, coming from different directions. Lisa realized more than one firefight was under way. She searched around. What was happening?

Automatic fire exploded accompanied by crashes of glass, sounding just yards away. More gunshots followed, accompanied by shouts and a strange ululating war cry. The fighting went on for a long minute.

Behind her the door burst open.

Lisa froze.

A half-naked figure leaped into view, streaked in black, nose pierced by a sharpened tusk, crowned by a shock of emerald feathers. He hefted a sharpened blade, bloody to the elbow.

Lisa pressed back against the table, frozen in fear.

"In here!" a familiar voice yelled.

It was Henri.

Boots pounded behind her. A cold blade slipped between her wrists. Plastic ties snapped and popped away. Lisa slumped off the inclined table, scrabbling not to fall. A figure caught her.

He spoke in her ear. "So if you're done just hanging around, how about we kiss this Love Boat good-bye."

She sank into the man's arms, shaking and weak with relief. "Monk . . ."

5:19 A.M.

DEVESH KNEW SOMETHING was wrong when a flurry of rifle fire exploded above his head, two decks up. It rang out from the direction of the science wing.

Devesh stood halfway down the lower-deck passage, surrounded by a group of seven guards and their Somalian leader. Blood flooded the carpet here—but they had found no bodies.

Now the gunfire above.

Devesh craned up. Before he could react, klaxons erupted, ringing throughout the ship, sounding the general alarm.

What was going on?

More gunfire blasted above. Again from the science wing.

"Back up!" Devesh yelled, and pointed his cane at the stairwell.

Turning in unison, the guards headed back—but down the hall, a short figure flashed past an intersecting passageway: bare-legged, dressed in feathers and rattling bones, his body daubed in black.

One of the island's cannibals.

He'd had an assault rifle in his hands.

The guard leader swore.

Gunfire rattled behind them. Rounds tore into carpet and walls. One of the guards fell back as if punched. Blood coughed out his nose and mouth as he crashed to the floor. The other guards flattened to all sides, returning fire. The Somalian dragged Devesh behind him, crouching and blasting with a pistol in his other hand.

But no one was there.

A door to one side popped open. A bone ax chopped

down, cleaving deep into another guard's skull. Then the door slammed closed again. The guard crawled, an ax handle protruding from the back of his head, then dropped flat.

Another man fired into the door. Rounds pounded through it.

But Devesh read the door's sign: EMPLOYEES ONLY. It led to the cruise ship's inner passages. The killer had surely fled.

Another cannibal.

The ship was under attack, its defenses breached.

Flurries of gunfire erupted elsewhere on the ship, echoing hollowly down to them. They were losing control of the ship. The Somalian leader stepped to Devesh's side. The remaining guards stood ready, half facing forward, half backward, wary of all doors.

"Sir, we must get you somewhere safe," the Somalian growled.

"Where?" Devesh half moaned.

"Off the ship. We can take a tender over to the island town and secure you there. I'll gather another hundred men, along with stiffer armaments, and return to clean out the ship."

Devesh nodded. Until matters were settled, he wanted off this boat.

The Somalian led them swiftly back to the stairwell. Alarm bells and rattling blasts accompanied them. They hurried down. They passed four bodies, fellow pirates.

When they reached the level of the tender dock, Devesh paused.

"Sir?"

"Not yet." Devesh had grown angrier with each level he had descended. He would not abandon the ship without some reprisal. And he knew what to do. He headed down the stairs again.

Toward the ship's bowels.

To where he maintained a special set of locked wards.

Before he left, he would make matters more difficult for those who sought to take his ship. To fight fire with fire.

The island was not the only source of cannibals.

5:22 A.M.

SUSAN STOOD AT the fringe of the jungle, staring toward the *Mistress of the Seas*. Alarm bells rang across the water, along with muffled blasts.

The assault was under way.

She held her hands clenched to her belly, scared, praying.

She heard stealthy noises in the forest around her: the slip of a wet leaf, the squelch of mud. Her escorts closed around her, drawn to protect their queen, but also curious, coming to watch the fireworks.

Just ahead, pulled up on the beach, a dugout canoe rested in the sand, ready to ferry her swiftly to Ryder's boat.

If it should ever arrive.

The knuckles of Susan's fingers ached as she squeezed.

Please let them come . . .

5:23 A.M.

BURIED IN HIS poncho, Rakao waited in his hidden blind. He stared through his infrared goggles, watching his team cinch the snare tighter.

He no longer had to wonder where the other escaped prisoners had gone. Minutes ago, another of his guards had spotted suspicious movement atop the cruise ship. Rakao had diverted his attention on his target long enough to roll aside and survey the ship. While he failed to spot any movement atop the ship, he did make out what appeared to be storm-loosened strands of the net weeping down toward the helipad.

Ropes.

With a silent curse Rakao knew what had happened.

An assault over the canopy's bridge . . .

Rakao had lived on this island for a decade, rising through a series of bloody coups to assume the leadership of the pirate clan there, whose history stretched back a full century.

But he had larger ambitions. Beyond even the spoils of a cruise ship and black-market slaves. There was a wider world to plunder, and the doctor offered him access to it, through an organization that stretched back far longer than a century. Where ambition and ruthlessness were recognized and rewarded.

So when he had discovered he'd been outmaneuvered, Rakao seethed, but he knew better than to lash out. He had the dried tongues of his predecessors nailed to the lintel above the door to his village house. He hadn't climbed to his position by reckless actions.

Staying focused, Rakao had his radioman retreat thirty yards so as not to be heard, then contact the ship, to warn them of an impending attack. But as Rakao waited, shots rang out—followed by alarm bells. His warning had reached the ship too late.

So be it . . .

Rakao maintained his position.

If the sneak attack aboard the ship failed, his radioman would let him know. If not, Rakao knew where the victors would end up.

The true prize was here.

Rakao watched his target, standing at the edge of the jungle.

It should not be long.

5:33 A.M.

MONK RACED DOWN the last flight of stairs. Lisa followed with a pair of WHO scientists: a Dutch toxicologist and an American bacteriologist.

At the bottom of the stairs a pair of pirates lay tangled in a widening pool of blood. A cannibal stood a step away, motioning for them to leave the stairwell.

He was another of Ryder's bread crumbs, leading a safe path through the besieged ship. It was a circuitous route down flights of stairs, through a passenger hallway, along the outer deck, even trespassing across a kitchen. Gunfire continued in sporadic bursts of guerrilla fighting.

At least the alarms had finally gone silent.

But was that good news or bad?

Monk led the way across the bloody landing and out into the main starboard hallway. They had reached the lower deck that lay even with the waterline. Ryder's private launch was on this level. Monk took a breath to orient himself. This deck also housed the ship's tender dock, along with a theater, day-care center, video arcade, and the Midnight Blue disco. Ryder's launch was near the ship's bow.

"This way!" He headed to the right, stopped, turned around again. "No, this way!"

They headed off again, trailing tribesmen.

He spotted furtive movement ahead, rising from a mid-deck stairwell, not far from the opening to the tender dock. He recognized the shabby uniforms.

Pirates.

Both parties spotted each other at the same time.

Monk shoved Lisa into the arcade. "Get down!"

His group scattered into other doorways or behind support pillars. One of the cannibals took a round to the head, flying back. But Monk's party outnumbered the pirates. They laid down a continual swath of return fire, chewing down the passageway. Three pirates fell. The tallest shoved a slender man back into the stairwell and fled away.

Monk led a handful of the cannibals forward. One ripped a fresh weapon from one of the dead pirates' hands and tossed aside his smoking rifle. Another pinched one of the corpses' cheeks. Not in affection. Just testing for tenderness.

"That was Devesh hightailing it out of here," Lisa said, joining Monk and pointing down the stairwell as they passed it. "The Guild leader here."

Monk glanced toward the tender dock. "They must have been planning on crossing over to Pirate Town, to gather reinforcements."

The thought spurred him faster down the hall toward the ship's bow. Monk wondered if reinforcements weren't already headed there, radioed in.

The hallway curved ahead, following the shape of the ship's front end. As they rounded the bend, Monk spotted the open doorway to Ryder's private launch.

They'd made it.

Before he could continue, shrieking cries erupted from the hall behind him.

Monk turned.

From the middeck stairwell, a dozen figures tumbled out into the hallway, scrambling, fighting, agitated, half naked in ripped and soiled hospital gowns. Limbs were blistered and weeping. Bloody lips peeled back in savage snarls. Even from fifty yards away, Monk recognized the sheen of madness shining from eyes caked with pus.

"Patients," Lisa whispered, grabbing Monk's arm and drawing him back. "In a catatonic psychosis. They'll attack anyone. Devesh must have set them loose."

"Bastard." Monk waved the last of his party around the bend, out of sight. He hurried toward the open door to Ryder's launch. More cries arose from ahead, past the door, where the hallway curved around to the port side.

Feet pounded in that direction, running toward them.

Monk lifted his weapon—but a familiar figure raced into view, one hand along the outer wall, keeping him upright. Jessie spotted his group, face brightening with relief. He was followed by a clutch of seven cannibals. The last two supported a third, a man bleeding heavily from a rip to the neck. From his green surgical scrubs, he was one of the WHO doctors.

The two groups met at the open door to the launch bay.

"You made it," the young nurse gasped out.

Ryder, drawn by the commotion, appeared at the doorway with his own escort of cannibals. He smelled of gasoline, wiping oil from his hands on a rag. "What's happening?"

Monk nodded. "Is your boat gassed up?"

A nod. "She's ready to fly."

To the side, Jessie allowed Lisa to hug him briefly while nodding to the other two WHO doctors. "Dr. Barnhardt. Dr. Miller." He waved a hand to the man in the green scrub smock. "I need help with him."

The cannibals lowered the wounded man to the floor. Blood, dark and heavy, pumped from his neck wound.

Lisa knelt to one side, the other two doctors on the man's other side. Jessie already had his shirt off and passed it to Lisa. She bunched it and pressed it against the wound.

The man convulsed once, coughing blood. Then he lay still, unmoving, eyes open. Only his chest collapsed a bit deeper, sagging with death.

Still holding the bundled shirt to the wound, Lisa checked for a pulse on the other side of the man's neck. She shook her head. There was nothing they could do for the man.

As she had worked, Jessie had related his story, wiping his brow and smearing blood there. "We rescued him. He was being attacked by one of the patients. We had to shoot her. But others are rising up from below. They're already rampaging through the lower decks and moving up. Hundreds of them."

Punctuating his words, savage cries echoed amid more shooting.

"Time to abandon ship," Ryder said.

Monk turned to Ryder. "How many can your boat hold?"

"Six seats . . . but we can squeeze in one or two others." Ryder eyed the number of people gathered here.

Jessie shook his head and backed a step. "I'm not going."

Lisa took his elbow. "Jessie."

"Someone has to defend the people, the children, still on board. From the pirates, from the madness. The tribesmen are their only hope. And they know me. They'll listen to me."

Dr. Barnhardt stepped to the young nurse's side. "I'll help him. We'll attempt to set up some secure barricade. Gather as many as we can. To wait you all out."

Dr. Miller stared with reluctance toward the open

hatchway, then down to the dead doctor. He nodded. "These . . . these are our people. Our friends and colleagues. We can't leave them."

Lisa hugged each one in turn. "Henri . . ." she mumbled in a half plead to the last one.

The older man squeezed her and pushed her toward the open doorway. "Go get Susan. More than our lives, the cure must be taken beyond the Guild's reach."

Lisa nodded and allowed Monk to turn her.

They followed Ryder into the launch bay.

Monk's steps faltered as he cleared the doorway and spotted Ryder's boat.

"Holy Mother of Christ!"

5:43 A.M.

DEVESH DESCENDED TOWARD the darkened stage of the ship's musical theater. The glittering crimson curtain hung closed. He followed the broad back of the Somalian guard down the theater stairs. After being ambushed and driven away from the tender docks, Devesh and the guard had fled up.

Down was not an option.

Not any longer.

The screams and cries had chased them up the stairwell. Down in the ship's bowels, Devesh had opened all five storage holds, unleashing the horrors contained within. They'd been feeding on one another, the strongest preying on the weakest.

Over two hundred.

Kept for experimentation.

Devesh had sought to use the unleashed madness to combat the cleverness of the ship's attackers, to thwart them long enough for him to orchestrate a return to the ship with grenades and machine guns. He would then slaughter the whole lot of them.

He would retake his ship.

But for the moment, he was caught in his own trap.

It was his Somalian bodyguard who had come up with this plan to escape. To reach the tender docks, rather than descending any of the main stairs, the Somalian had led Devesh to the upper balcony entrance of the ship's three-story-tall theater. They used the theater's stairs to descend the three levels back down to the deck that housed the tender dock.

The theater's lower doors lay directly across the hallway from the dock. A short dash, and they'd be motoring away from this hellish battle.

Devesh used his cane to thump down the last few stairs.

The Somalian guard held up a hand and headed to the door. "Stay back. Let me make sure it's clear." He clutched a large pistol in his other fist.

He cracked open the door, checked the hall, covering it with his pistol. He waited a breath, then opened it farther. Turning, he announced with relief, "Hall's clear."

Devesh took a step toward him—but movement over the man's shoulder stopped him. One of the feathered tribesmen stepped out of hiding, sheltered within the hatchway that led down to the tender dock.

The cannibal held a drawn bow in his hands.

The large Somalian must have read something in Devesh's expression. Even before fully turning around, the man began firing blindly.

The cannibal took three shots to the chest, falling back with a sharp cry.

But the tribesman had already let loose his bowstring.

The arrow pierced the guard's throat, sprouting like some bloody tongue out the back of his neck. The large man stumbled, fell to his backside. Still, he kept his pistol pointed toward the door.

But the cannibal did not rise again, and the hall remained quiet.

Devesh knew he had to take the chance. He rushed to the guard.

"Help me," the man croaked out, eyes winced with pain, slipping back to one arm to support himself. The other arm trembled to hold the pistol up.

Devesh kicked the man's supporting arm out from under him. The Somalian fell back, startled. The arrow tip cracked against the polished wood floor. Devesh knelt on the man's shoulder and tossed his cane aside. He needed a better weapon. He wrestled the pistol from the man's grip.

But the large man refused to relent, fingers clenched with fury and pain.

"Let go!" Devesh shifted his knee to dig against the embedded arrow.

A loud wooden *crash* stopped their struggle.

The doors on the opposite side of the theater had banged open behind them. Devesh yanked the pistol free and turned. A figure flew into view, swift on tiny feet, swirling in silk, stained with swaths of blood.

"Surina!"

But she was not alone.

A roil of shapes pursued her, fueled by adrenaline and hunger. They poured in after her. Some slipped on the polished wood, down to knuckles, then up again, bestial in their hunt. But the tangled stumbling slowed them long enough for Surina to gain half the theater.

Devesh scrambled to his feet, both relieved and horrified at her arrival.

He didn't want to be alone.

Surina flew to his side, one arm sweeping down. Her fingers collected his abandoned cane, and in a breath, wood slipped off of steel. She brandished the sword.

Devesh headed toward the open door. "This way!"

Cradling the pistol in both hands, he leaped over the Somalian, who groaned, only half conscious, blood spreading over the dark wood. At least the man's body might distract the cannibals.

As Devesh landed, he felt two sharp bites at the backs of his knees.

He took a startled step, but suddenly his legs lacked any ability to hold him upright. He fell to a knee in the doorway, then harder to an elbow, knocking the pistol away. The pain rang up his arm to his skull. From the corner of an eye, he watched Surina rise from a low stance behind him, her sword held out to one side, blood spattered from its tip.

Devesh kicked to stand. But he had no ability to control his legs. He watched blood pouring through the knees of his pants. As Surina slipped past him, he realized what had happened. The bitch had sliced through the tendons at the back of his knees, hamstringing him.

She sailed across the hall and vanished into the darkness of the dock.

"Surina!"

Devesh tried to crawl, dragging his legs.

Toward his pistol.

But other hands fell upon him, drawn by the blood, digging into his flesh. He heard the guard's agonized scream from the depths of the dark theater. Devesh was dragged back to join him, his palms scrabbling through the smears of his own blood, fingers dug for some purchase, some last mercy.

He found none.

5:45 A.M.

AS SCREAMS AND gunshots echoed down to them, Lisa joined Monk at the bottom of the launch bay's stairs. She shivered in the damp breeze.

Ryder's private bay was small, arched in steel, reeking of gasoline and oil. In the center rested what looked like the aluminum tracks of a roller coaster, consisting of a pair of cushioned rails, tilted at an angle and aimed toward an open hatch in the ship's side. Beyond the hatch, the dark lagoon beckoned, brushed with sweeps of rain.

But it was what rested atop the tracks that continued to hold her partner's full attention. "That is no goddamn boat," Monk blurted out.

Ryder led them forward, hurrying. "It's a *flying* boat, mate. Half seaplane, half jet boat."

Monk gaped at the sight.

Lisa was no less awed.

Seated on the launch tracks, the craft looked like a diving hawk with its wings tucked back. The enclosed cabin ended in an aerodynamic point at the bow. Its stern supported two raised propeller engines. And over the top, two wings lay folded over the cabin, tips touching just in front of the upright tail section and propellers.

"She's built by Hamilton Jet out of New Zealand," Ryder said as he ran a hand along her hull and led them to the open side hatch. "I call her the *Sea Dart*. In the water, her twin V-12 petrol engines pump water from the front and shoot it out the stern's dual nozzles. Once you get her up to speed, all you have to do is explode the hydraulics to snap wide the folded wings, and she sails into the sky . . . where her rear props keep her aloft." Ryder patted its side. "She's quick on her legs, too. Sky or water. Clocked her airspeed up to three hundred miles per hour."

Ryder held out a hand toward Lisa. He helped her up the steps beside the launch track. She ducked into the cabin. It was not that much different from a Cessna: a pair of seats for a pilot and copilot in front and four more seats in the back.

Ryder climbed in behind her and scooted forward to settle into the pilot's seat. Monk clambered in last, closing the hatch.

"Strap in!" Ryder called out.

Monk took the seat nearest the side hatch, ready to haul Susan inside when they reached the beach. Lisa climbed forward and took the seat next to Ryder.

"Hold on," he said to her.

Ryder triggered an electronic release, and the *Sea Dart* rolled smoothly down the inclined tracks and dumped into the lagoon with a slight jar.

Water washed over the windshield as the boat's bow bobbed deep.

Lisa immediately heard the rumble of engines behind her, throaty and growling with horsepower. She felt it in the seat of her pants, too.

The *Dart* began to glide forward across the water with a gentle burbling from the stern. Rain rattled in fits and splashes over the top of the cabin.

"Here we go," Ryder mumbled, and throttled the speed.

The boat lived up to its name and shot like an arrow across the storm-swept water, throwing Lisa back into her seat.

Behind her an appreciative whistle flowed from Monk.

Ryder angled the boat, skimming over the water as if on ice. He sailed the boat around the cruise ship's bow, a gnat before a whale.

Lisa stared up at the mighty ship. Away from the gunshots and screams, the *Mistress of the Seas* looked peaceful, gently aglow in the storm's gloom.

But she knew the ship was anything but peaceful.

As she settled back, she could not escape a slight twinge of guilt. For Jessie, for Henri, and Dr. Miller. And for all the others. She still felt like she was running from a fight, abandoning the others for the sake of her own skin.

But she had no choice.

Ryder swung the boat and aimed for the island, where they were to rendezvous with Susan. The boat sped toward the expanse of dark jungle, trimmed by a narrow beach.

She silently repeated Henri's last words to her.

The cure must be taken beyond the Guild's reach.

Lisa watched the jungle swell ahead of her, the beach stretch wide.

They could not fail.

5:50 A.M.

RAKAO WATCHED THE strange craft sweep around the cruise ship and speed straight toward his location. Through his infrared binoculars, the boat was a hot crimson smear across the colder water.

He signaled his team to be ready. They were waiting for his first shot before launching the full assault.

Rakao lowered his binoculars and brought to his eye the telescopic sight on his rifle. He fixed again upon his target, the escaped woman. She had stepped out of the jungle, easily discernible now, and waited on the beach.

Rakao heard the rumbling of the approaching boat.

She lifted an arm. Her limb seemed to catch the moonlight as it was raised. But there was no moon.

Rakao felt a chill at the sight. Still, he did not let it distract him. He had a mission here. Answers would come later.

Out on the beach, one of the tribesmen shoved the lone dugout canoe off the beach and into the shallows. He beckoned the woman to come. She crossed to the water, climbed aboard, and sat awkwardly in the back.

Standing behind the stern, the tribesman bent down, ready to shove the woman out toward the coming boat. They did not have long to wait.

The craft swept up, turning smoothly to expose its starboard flank, idling about seven meters out.

The side hatch was already open.

Rakao spied a man inside, braced in the opening.

Perfect.

Rakao shifted his rifle, aimed, and fired.

5:51 A.M.

MONK JUMPED AT the crack of a rifle.

From his perch in the hatchway he watched the tribesman behind Susan collapse into the water. His falling body bumped the canoe, sending it drifting toward him.

A flurry of gunshots followed, tiny flashes of fire in the dark jungle.

Another tribesman stumbled out, bleeding from chest and shoulder. He held an arm out toward Susan in the water, hoping the witch queen could save him. But another crack of a rifle, and his head flew back and the lower half of his face exploded.

He fell to the sand.

This was all a trap . . . with Susan as bait.

A spat of rounds peppered the flank of the *Sea Dart,* driving Monk back inside. Ryder swore harshly. Monk scrambled to the assault rifle on the backseat, fumbling around with it.

But a barked shout stopped the strafing of the boat.

In the silence Monk warily crept back.

A man with a familiar tattooed face stood knee-deep in the water. Rakao held a spear in one hand and a Sig Sauer pistol in the other. With his arm extended, he aimed the pistol's muzzle at the back of Susan's head as she floated in the canoe, crouched low in the stern.

Susan's eyes, aglow in the darkness, stared back in terror toward Monk.

Rakao yelled across the water in English. "Cut your engines! Throw out any weapons! Then one at a time, you're going to jump and swim to me."

Monk turned. "Lisa, I need you here. Ryder, do not cut those engines. When I yell *go,* you blast the hell out of here."

Lisa struggled with her straps but finally freed herself.

Monk shifted his rifle to grip it by its stock and held it out the open hatchway. A single round pinged off the side of the *Sea Dart.* Rakao barked at the stray sniper, angry. No damaging the merchandise. Rakao must recognize a prize well worth preserving.

Monk climbed into view, exposing himself fully in the hatch. He held his rifle out to one side, his other hand open and high.

Lisa whispered to him. "What are you doing?"

"Just be ready," he murmured.

"For what?"

It would take too long to explain.

Rakao noted his appearance and stepped farther into the water, his muzzle only a foot from the back of Susan's head. The bow of the canoe pointed toward the *Sea Dart,* slightly tilted up from Susan's weight in the stern.

Monk called, "We're coming out!"

To demonstrate his sincerity he tossed his rifle to the left in a dramatic underhanded throw. It cartwheeled through the air. As he had hoped, Rakao's eyes flicked to follow it, the reflex of a hunter toward movement.

Monk leaped a fraction of a second after it. He jumped high, like he was planning on doing a cannonball into the lagoon. Instead, he landed on the tilted bow of the canoe. His weight and momentum slammed the bow deep. The stern of the canoe catapulted up like a seesaw.

Susan flew over Monk's head—thrown straight at the *Sea Dart.*

A shot rang out from Rakao, but the stern edge of the boat had clipped the Maori's hand, sending the pistol flying.

Monk heard a splash behind him as Susan landed.

Then the canoe crashed back to the water, throwing Monk into a sprawl on the dugout's bottom. He lifted himself up on an elbow. He caught sight of Susan's legs as Lisa dragged the woman through the side hatch.

Good girl.

Monk bellowed at the top of his lungs. "Ryder! Go!"

But the *Sea Dart* just idled.

Monk prepared to yell again, when the canoe jarred.

Rakao had hauled into the canoe, rising to his feet. The canoe spun, but he expertly kept his balance. He drove his spear at Monk with both arms.

Monk reacted instinctively. He tried to block the deadly plunge by grabbing its shaft. Prosthetic fingers locked onto it.

A mistake.

A fierce jolt of electricity ripped through his body. He remembered Rakao's earlier rescue of Lisa, striking out with his electric spear.

Monk's body clenched with agony. Muscles spasmed with a bone-breaking intensity. Still, he heard the fresh barrage of gunfire pelting at the *Sea Dart.*

Why was Ryder still here?

Monk fought the electrocution. He should have been killed at the outset as the volts fried through him. He only lived because of the dampening insulation of his prosthetic hand. But now he smelled plastic burning.

Ryder . . . get the hell out of here . . .

5:54 A.M.

"WAIT!" LISA SCREAMED over the rattle of bullets against the flank of the *Sea Dart.*

Lisa lay beside Susan on the floor. She had a view of Rakao, leaning his weight on the spear, trying to drive its electrified steel tip into Monk's chest. Monk fought. Black smoke rose from his prosthetic hand.

The canoe spun, close . . . or at least close enough.

"Now!" she yelled.

A loud explosive *pop* sounded over her head, detonating the hydraulics above. The *Sea Dart* snapped out its wings, chopping out like a pair of ax blades. One wing cracked into Rakao's shoulder, sending him flying from the canoe and dumping him in a sprawl into the lake.

The barrage of rifle fire momentarily stopped as the maneuver stunned the shooters.

Lisa yelled into the ringing silence, "Monk! Above your head!"

GROGGY, MONK HEARD Lisa's command.

It took him a moment to realize what she meant. Something was above his head. One of the wings of the *Sea Dart.*

Trembling in a continuous quake, he gathered his legs under him—and leaped.

He didn't trust the strength in his real hand. Smoking plastic fingers latched on to one of the wing struts. He clamped tight, twitching a signal to lock down.

Go . . .

"Go!" Lisa hollered, still on the floor, bracing herself against the seats.

Under her belly she felt the twin engines rev. The *Sea Dart* leaped away, swinging its stern toward the beach as the snipers again opened fire, finally shaken free of their momentary stun.

Lisa watched a stray round strike Monk's flailing right leg.

Blood burst from his calf. She read the twist of agony in his face. His lower leg hung crookedly as Monk shifted. The bullet must have shattered through his tibia, breaking it.

Thank God, he still held on . . .

Ryder aimed away from the beach, flying across the water, out of range.

Lisa wanted to weep.

They would make it.

5:55 A.M.

Rakao choked and sputtered his face out of the water. His toes, then heels, found rock and sand underfoot. He stood chest-deep in the lagoon. The roar of a motor drew him around.

The enemy's boat shot across the lagoon, dangling a figure from one wingtip. Furious, he waded toward the beach. His left arm was on fire, burning in the seawater. He fingered the upper arm on that side, felt the sharp point of bone protruding through his skin, broken by the blow that had sent him flying.

He clutched his spear in the other hand.

Luckily he had not lost the weapon, having clung to it.

He might need it.

Already Rakao noted the flashes of fire under the water, aiming for him, drawn by the blood. He turned his back on the beach and retreated step-by-step. He kept his weapon poised, ready to use it. The shock might sting him, but it should drive the squids away.

Reaching waist-deep water, Rakao allowed himself a breath of relief.

Once out, he would hunt the others down.

No matter where in the world they landed, he would find them.

This, he swore.

Lightning cracked overhead, momentarily lighting the black waters, bright enough to illuminate the depths. A tangle of arms spread wide around his legs. The longest arms winked with a yellow glow. The bulk of the monster rested quietly in the sand only a step away. Then the flash ended, turning the lake into a dark mirror, reflecting the terror in his face.

Rakao stabbed down with his spear, thumbing the charge to full.

Blue fire crackled across the water. He gasped at the pain, like a steel trap snapping closed over his midsection. But it lasted only a fraction of a second—then the spear popped in his hand. With a final zap of electricity and an acrid spurt of smoke, the weapon shorted out, overloaded by his battle with the American.

Rakao stumbled back, splashing, his broken arm screaming.

Had the charge been enough?

The answer came in a slash of fire across one thigh. Chitinous hooks tore into the meat of his leg. He fought as the creature tugged him toward the deeper waters. Its bulk surfaced, rolling an eye.

Rakao stabbed at it. The weapon might not have a charge—but it did have a sharp point. He felt the blade sink deep. The grip on his leg spasmed, then went slack.

With grim satisfaction, he retreated again.

But the waters suddenly erupted all around him with streaks of fire: blues and emeralds, but mostly a blaze of crimson. More of the pack had been lying in wait. Rakao read the fury in the flickers. They swirled like a luminous whirlpool around him.

Something bumped his leg. Teeth clamped to his ankle.

Rakao knew it was the end.

Too many.

His men would never reach him in time.

Rakao stared across the waters at the fleeing boat. He dropped his spear and clutched to a holster at his shoulder. He kept it with him at all times. It held no gun. Only insurance. He twisted the T-handle that protruded from the leather holster and pulled the plunger out.

A tentacle wrapped around his waist, ripping with teeth.

If he couldn't escape, no one would.

Rakao shoved the plunger as a tangle of tentacles lashed out of the water like flailing whips. From all directions, they fell upon him, ripping cloth and flesh, taking his legs out from under him. He felt his right ear torn away as he was dragged beneath the water.

Still, he heard the explosions, thunder from above, pounding through the water, reaching him as the monsters dragged him deep.

Boom, boom, boom . . .

5:57 A.M.

LISA WATCHED THE fiery explosions lighting up the island's highlands. At first, she thought it was lightning strikes—but they exploded sequentially, rimming around the top of the island.

"What the hell?" Ryder called from the pilot's seat.

Sections of the island's canopy began to fall in fiery ruin.

She yelled. "Someone's blowing up the net! It's all coming down!"

Ryder cursed.

Explosions continued. Fires lit the skies, speeding around the island's heights. Unless they fled faster, reached the lagoon's exit, they'd be smothered under the net when it all came down.

"I need to get airborne!" Ryder called back.

That would be a problem.

5:57 A.M.

CONCUSSIVE BLASTS LIT up the rim of the island.

Monk understood.

The net . . .

The *Sea Dart* suddenly sped faster, trying to outrun the explosions. The boat lifted out of the water a few inches as it surpassed takeoff speeds.

But Monk's swinging weight unbalanced the boat, tilting it. His toes skimmed the waters. Ryder corrected, slowing the speed. They struck the water, bounced, then settled again.

Pain shot up Monk's broken leg. Still he hung clamped to the strut.

Even if he had wanted to, he could not detach. His tussle with Rakao's spear had fried the electronics of his prosthetic hand. It had shut down after clamping to the wing strut. He was hooked like a slab of beef in a butcher's shop.

He twisted around, watching the explosions continue around the island. The entire back half of the net drifted down, raining fire amid the storm's downpour.

And more of the sky fell with each explosion.

Monk stared back toward the exit to the lagoon, the narrow crack in the volcanic caldera. The *Sea Dart* had to reach it before the explosions completed their circuit around the volcanic rim and dropped the net over the lake. Monk calculated their odds. Not good. And they'd never make it—not while dragging a side of beef from one wingtip.

"CAN YOU RETRACT the wings?" Lisa called to Ryder.

Maybe they could pull Monk in close, get him inside, then extend the wings out again. All without slowing.

Ryder dashed this thin hope. "Once extended, the wings are locked out! A built-in safety feature!"

Lisa understood. It would not be good to have the wings retract while in midair.

Lisa watched Monk struggling. He was digging at his prosthetic wrist with his good hand. What was he doing?

Then it dawned on her.

Monk must have realized the threat he posed.

"No!" she called to him. "Monk! No!"

She didn't know if he heard her past the explosions and wind.

Still, he did twist his head and faced her. He pointed toward the lagoon's distant beach. He yelled something, but one of the thunderous blasts battered away his words.

He returned to his efforts.

Monk . . . please, no . . .

DAMN IT ALL . . . why can't I let go . . . ?

His fingers dug at the plastic wrist. The toggle that manually released his hand from its wrist attachment had melted. His fingernails tore into the bubbled synthetics.

Finally the toggle snapped open.

Thank God . . .

He reached a finger inside.

"Monk!" Lisa called to him.

Relenting, he pointed again to the beach. He would make for shore. They had to go on without him.

Lisa knelt in the opening, wind whipping her hair. He read the defeat there, too. There was no alternative.

Monk reached through the open toggle and pressed the release button.

Wrist detached from hand.

He fell, tumbling to the water, skipping along, like a skimmed stone. Then he sank into the depths. He kicked his good leg to reach the surface; his other leg felt like someone had jabbed a burning poker through his calf.

Treading water, he watched the *Sea Dart* speed across the lagoon, heading for the crack in the caldera that led out to the open sea.

Ryder didn't hesitate. He understood the sacrifice.

As the last explosions ripped along the rim of the island, Monk stared up. The netting swamped down toward him. He glanced back. Across the lagoon, the canopy fell like a fiery shroud over the *Mistress of the Seas,* starting at the stern and working toward the bow.

In seconds the cruise ship was swamped under it, caught like a dolphin in a tuna net. And the collapse continued, sweeping toward Monk. He had no hope of reaching any beach. The closest lay five hundred yards away.

In the other direction, he watched the *Sea Dart* escape into the air, pulling up, lifting off the lake, and racing toward the opening in the caldera wall.

They would make it.

This thought helped settle his heart as the net fell atop him, heavy with cabling and sodden rope. It dragged him down, down, down . . .

Monk struggled for a way through it, to reach the surface again. But his broken leg confounded him. And the net had folded a bit on itself. He could find no way through.

He stared up at the lights of the cruise ship.

With only one regret . . . a broken promise . . .

He'd sworn to Kat that he would return from this mission, and he had kissed Penelope with the same silent promise.

I'm sorry . . .

He reached one arm up, praying for some rescue.

His hand found a hole in the tangled net. He used the stump of his other arm to force it wider. He kicked both legs, ignoring the pain from his right calf. He struggled to worm through the opening.

Then something snagged his broken leg, latching to his ankle, and tugged hard. Bone ground against bone. Agony lanced from leg to spine. Monk gasped out his last breath and stared down.

Lights in the water streaked up toward him.

Arms climbed his body, wrapped around his waist, over his chest. A rubbery limb clamped across his face, across the same lips that had once made a promise, once kissed a child.

Lights flashed around him as Monk was dragged down, down, down . . .

Still, he searched up one last time.

As the glow of the cruise ship faded and darkness closed over him, he sent his heart out to the two women who gave his life any meaning.

Kat.

Penelope.

I love you, love you, love you ...

6:05 A.M.

LISA SAT IN the backseat of the *Sea Dart,* bent over her knees, sobbing.

Susan sat next to her, resting a hand on her back.

No one spoke.

Ryder fought the winds as he flew the *Sea Dart* across the open water. The island of Pusat faded behind them.

The storm blew them like a leaf in a gale. There was no use fighting it. They simply fled with the wind, skimming north.

They had no radio. A stray round had punched through the unit.

"The sun's rising," Susan mumbled, staring out the window, ignoring the navigation map on her lap.

Her words broke some barrier.

Ryder spoke from the pilot's seat. "Maybe he made it to shore."

Lisa sat back. She knew Monk had not. Still, she wiped her eyes. Monk had sacrificed himself so they might escape. So that those left behind aboard the *Mistress of the Seas* had some chance of rescue, that the world had some hope of a cure.

Still, Lisa only felt numb and dead.

"The sun . . ." Susan said.

Ryder banked east, skirting around another island peak. Off near the horizon, there was some sign of an end to the night's storm. The black clouds split enough to allow sunlight to stream toward them. The first edge of the day's sun peeked above the horizon.

Through the windshield, light flooded the cabin with brilliance.

Lisa stared toward it, seeking some absolution, to bask in the brightness, to let it inside her, to chase away the darkness there, too.

And it seemed to work—until Susan let out a terrifying scream.

Lisa jumped and turned. Susan sat bolt upright in her seat, staring wide-eyed toward the sun. But something in her eyes shone even brighter.

Raw fear.

"Susan?"

The woman continued to stare. Her mouth moved, breathless. Lisa had to read her lips. "They must not go there."

"Who? Where?"

Susan didn't answer. Without looking down, she took a finger and placed it on the navigation map in her lap.

Lisa read the name under her finger.

"Angkor."

16

Bayon

GRAY MARCHED WITH the others toward the massive gates of the walled temple complex of Angkor Thom. The morning sun, low on the horizon, cast long shadows across the south causeway. Cicadas buzzed, along with the morning chorus of frogs.

Except for a handful of tourists and a pair of saffron-robed monks, they had the bridge to themselves at this early hour. The causeway stretched a full football field in length, framed along the edges by rows of statues: fifty-four gods on one side and fifty-four demons on the other. They overlooked a moat, mostly dry now, where once crocodiles swam, protecting the great city and the royal palace inside. The deep moat, bordered by earthen embankments, now languished in emerald expanses of algae-covered pools and swaths of grass and weeds.

As they marched, Vigor reached out to one of the bridge's demon statues and placed a palm upon its head. "Concrete," he said. "The original heads were mostly stolen, though some remain in Cambodian museums."

"Let's hope what we're looking for wasn't stolen," Seichan said dourly, plainly still upset after the conversation in the van with Nasser.

Gray kept his distance from her. He wasn't sure which of the two Guild agents was the more dangerous.

Nasser's team of forty men spread ahead of them and behind, an escort in khaki and black berets. Nasser kept a yard behind them, continually searching around warily. Some of the tourists showed interest in their large group, but mostly their party was ignored. The ruins ahead held everyone's attention.

At the end of the causeway, thirty-foot-tall walls of laterite stone blocks enclosed the four square miles of the ancient city. Their goal—the Bayon—lay within the enclosure. Dense forest still enveloped the city ruins. Giant palm trees shaded the walls, shrouding the massive eighty-foot-tall gate. Four giant faces had been carved into the stone tower, facing each cardinal direction.

Gray studied the faces, painted in lichen, worn by cracks. Despite the corruption of age, there remained a certain peacefulness in their expressions: broad foreheads shadowed downcast eyes, while thick lips curved gently, as enigmatic as any Mona Lisa.

"The Smile of Angkor," Vigor said, noting his attention. "The face is that of Lokesvara, the bodhisattva of compassion."

Gray stared a breath longer, praying for that compassion to spread to Nasser. Gray checked his watch. Twenty-five minutes until the next hour mark, when Nasser would order another of his mother's fingers chopped off.

To stop that they needed some bit of progress to appease the bastard, to hold him off longer. But what?

Gray's breathing became more pained at this thought. His objectives tugged between two extremes: a desire to hurry forward and discover those clues that would stay Nasser's hand *and* an equally strong need to delay Nasser for as long as possible, to give Director Crowe more time to find his mother and father.

Stretched between the two, Gray fought for focus, for his center.

"Look . . . elephants!" Kowalski said, and pointed a bit too excitedly toward the massive gateway. He took a few hurried steps forward, his long duster jacket billowing out behind his legs.

Past the entrance, Gray spotted a pair of whitish-gray Indian elephants, trunks hanging slack to the stones, eyes smattered with flies. One of the tourists, burdened by a massive camera around his neck, was being helped to mount the great animal's back, where a teetering colorful saddle, called a howdah, had been strapped. A hand-painted sign stood on a post cemented into a tire, announcing in a variety of languages: ELEPHANT RIDES TO THE BAYON.

"Only ten dollars," Kowalski read.

"I think we'll be walking," Gray responded, disappointing the man.

"Yeah, straight through elephant shit. Before long, you'll be wishing we paid that ten bucks."

Gray rolled his eyes and waved Kowalski to follow the trail of Nasser's men through the gate and into Angkor Thom.

Past the wall, a paved walkway shot straight ahead, shaded by towering silk-cotton trees, whose twisted roots snaked under and over stone blocks. Seedpods from the trees littered the way, crunching underfoot.

The forest grew denser ahead, obscuring the view.

"How much farther?" Nasser asked, joining them, but keeping a yard away, a hand in the pocket of his jacket.

Vigor pointed ahead. "The Bayon temple lies a mile into the jungle."

Nasser checked his watch, then glanced significantly toward Gray, the threat plain.

One of the ubiquitous tuk-tuks buzzed past them, the main means of transportation, basically a rickshaw hooked to a two-stroke motorbike. A pair of tourists snapped pictures of their legion in black berets, chattering away in German. Then they vanished ahead.

Gray followed its trail of exhaust, picking up the pace.

Kowalski stared into the dense forest of palms and bamboo. His face pinched with suspicion.

Vigor spoke as they walked. "Over one hundred thousand people once lived here in Angkor Thom."

"Lived where?" Kowalski asked. "In tree houses?"

Vigor waved an arm toward the forest. "Most of the homes, even the royal palace, were made of bamboo and wood, so they rotted away. The jungle consumed them. Only the temples were made of stone. But this once used to be a bustling metropolis, with markets selling fish and rice, fruit and spices, with homes crowded with pigs and chickens. The city planners had engineered a great irrigation and canal system to support the populace. It even had a royal zoo, where elaborate circuses were performed. Angkor Thom was a vibrant city, colorful and boisterous. Fireworks filled the skies during celebrations. Musicians outnumbered the warriors, ringing out with cymbals, hand bells, and barrel drums, playing harps and lutes, blowing trumpets made of horns or conches."

"A regular orchestra," Kowalski groused, unimpressed.

Gray tried to picture such a city as he studied the dense forest.

"So what happened to all these people?" Kowalski asked.

Vigor rubbed his chin. "Despite what we know of daily life, much of Angkorian history remains a mystery, or at least remains purely hypothetical. Their writings were in sacred palm-leaf books called *sastras*. Which, like the homes here, did not survive. So Angkorian history was gathered piecemeal from studying the carved bas-reliefs on the temples. As a consequence, much of its history remains a mystery. Like what happened to the populace. Their true fate remains cloudy."

Gray kept pace with the monsignor. "I thought they were invaded by the Thai, who trampled the ancient Khmer civilization?"

"Yes, but many historians and archaeologists believe

the Thai invasion was secondary, that the Khmer people had already been weakened in some manner. One theory is that the Khmer had become less militarized due to a religious conversion to a more peaceful form of Buddhism. Yet another theory holds that the massive irrigation and water-management system that sustained the empire fell into disrepair, silting up, weakening the city, leaving it susceptible to invasion. But there is also historical evidence of repeated and systematic outbreaks of plague."

Gray pictured Marco's City of the Dead. They were walking those same death fields, now overgrown with forest and jungle. Nature had returned, erasing the hand of man.

"We know that Angkor persisted after Marco," Vigor continued. "There is a brilliant account of the region by a Chinese explorer, Zhou Daguan, a full century after Marco passed through here. So the cure that was offered Marco must have eventually allowed the empire to survive, but the viral source must have persisted and continued in outbreaks of plague after plague, weakening the empire. Even the Thai invaders did not occupy Angkor. They left the vast infrastructure abandoned and fallow, letting the forest take it over. Makes you wonder why? Had they heard the stories? Had they purposefully shunned the region, believing it somehow cursed?"

Seichan had drawn closer during Vigor's account. "So you're suggesting that the source may still be here."

Vigor shrugged. "Answers await at the Bayon." He pointed through a break in the forest.

Ahead, framed by the jungle, a sandstone mountain appeared, climbing high, stippled by the morning sun into shining outcroppings of dew-damp rock and pockets of deep shadows. Smaller peaks surrounded it, clustered close, massed together into a single crag. The temple reminded Gray of something organic, like a termite mound, an ill-defined pile, as if the centuries of rain had melted the sandstone into this pocked and flowing mass.

Then a cloud passed over the sun, and shadows deepened, shifted. From out of the mass, giant stone faces appeared, pushing forth with their sphinxlike smiles, covering every surface, staring outward in all directions. The initial mass of peaks became discernible as scores of towers, rising in different levels, piled close and tight, each decorated with massive visages of Lokesvara.

Vigor mumbled, " 'Lit by the fullness of the moon, a great mountain towered above the forest, carved with a thousand faces of demons.' "

Gray's skin chilled. He recognized the words from Marco's text. It was where Polo's confessor, Friar Agreer, had last been seen heading, toward a mountain carved with faces. Gray was suddenly conscious of his own feet slowing with dread. He forced his pace back up.

They had followed Marco's trail here . . . now it was time to follow the last steps of Polo's confessor. But where did Friar Agreer go?

6:53 A.M.

AS THE TEMPLE grew before them, a heavy silence fell over the group. Most eyes were raised toward the ruins ahead, but Vigor took the moment to study his companions. Ever since had arrived at Angkor Thom, he had sensed an unspoken tension between Gray and Seichan. While the two had never been bosom companions, there had always been a strained intimacy between them. And though their arguments had remained heated, the physical distance between the pair had diminished over the past day, a narrowing of personal space.

Vigor doubted either one was aware of it.

But since they'd stepped out of the vans here, it was as if some internal polarity had reversed inside them, repelling them far apart. Not only did they keep well away, he noted a heaviness to Gray's study of Seichan when her back was turned, and Seichan had grown harder again, her eyes tighter, her lips thinner.

Seichan kept closer to Vigor, as if needing some reassurance from him, but was unable to ask for it. Her gaze remained fixed on the ruins. They were close enough that the true breadth of the Bayon was now discernible.

Fifty-four towers clustered on three rising levels.

But the most striking feature was the number of carved faces.

Well over two hundred.

The morning light shifted with the clouds, creating the illusion that the faces were alive, moving, observing those who approached.

"Why so many?" Seichan finally mumbled at his side.

Vigor knew she was asking about the stone visages. "No one knows," he answered. "Some say they represent vigilance, faces staring out from a secret heart, guarding inner mysteries. It is also said that the Bayon's foundations were built upon an even earlier structure. Archaeologists have discovered walled-up rooms, where more faces were hidden, forever locked in darkness."

Vigor waved ahead. "The Bayon was also the last temple ever built in Angkor, marking the end of a period of almost continuous construction that spanned centuries."

"So why did they stop building?" Gray asked, moving closer.

Vigor glanced to him. "Maybe they uncovered something that discouraged further excavations. When the Khmer engineers built the Bayon, they dug down. Deep. A quarter of the Bayon is buried."

"Buried?"

Vigor nodded. "Most of the Angkor temples are based on the design of mandalas. A series of stacked rectangles, that represent the physical universe, surround a circular tower in the center. The middle tower represents the magical mountain of Hindu mythology, Mount Meru, where the gods reside. By partially burying the temple, the central tower embodies Mount Meru, demonstrating the penetration of this magical mountain from the earth up to heaven. Stories persist of both treasures and horrors hidden in those lower levels of the Bayon."

By now they had reached the end of the pathway. It widened into an open stone plaza. The bulk of the temple rose ahead of them. Dozens of faces stared down. Tourists could be seen climbing about the temple's various levels.

They continued forward, crossing alongside a row of parked tuk-tuks. Ahead, a small line of roadside stands proffered fruits in all their variety: mangoes, jackfruit, tamarind, Chinese dates, even small softball-size watermelons. Thin-limbed children dashed among the stands, reviving a little of the ancient city's vibrancy with their laughter and calls. Off to another side, a more solemn group of six saffron-robed monks sat on woven mats, heads bowed, praying amid a cloud of incense.

Vigor added his own silent appeal as he passed, praying for strength, wisdom, and protection.

Ahead, their man Kowalski had stopped at one of the stands. A wrinkled old woman with a perfectly round face stood bent over an iron brazier, cooking breakfast on sticks. Chicken and beef roasted alongside turtle and lizard. The man sniffed at an appetizing skewer.

"Is that soft-shell crab?" he asked, leaning closer for a whiff. The skewer speared something meaty with jointed legs, blackened and curled by the fire.

The woman nodded her head vigorously, smiling broadly at his interest. She spoke rapidly in Khmer.

Seichan stepped to Kowalski's side, placing a hand on his shoulder. "It's fried tarantula. Very popular for breakfast in Cambodia."

Kowalski shuddered and backed away. "Thanks. I'll stick with an Egg McMuffin."

A less picky thief—a macaque monkey—bounded out of the ruins, grabbed an ear of corn from behind the woman, and dashed straight in front of Kowalski. The large man startled back, bumping into Gray, scrambling out of the way.

Kowalski's hand jerked back under his jacket.

Gray stopped him, pinching his elbow hard, too hard. Gray's eyes flicked back to Nasser, then away again. "It was only a monkey."

Kowalski shook free of Gray's hand. "Yeah, well, I don't like monkeys." The large man glowered and stormed ahead. "Had a bad experience with 'em once before. I don't want to talk about it."

Vigor shook his head and led them around to the eastern entrance to the Bayon. The stone causeway here was a ruin of jumbled blocks, studded with giant date palms and more of the silk-cotton trees with their snaking tangles of roots. They crossed in a crooked line through the entrance to the first level, passing under the watchful gaze of more bodhi-sattva faces.

They entered an inner courtyard, framed in galleries. The walls were carved in intricate bas-reliefs, covered from top to bottom in strips of story. Vigor glanced at the nearest. They depicted everyday scenes: a fisherman casting nets, a farmer harvesting rice, two cocks fighting amid a crowd, a woman cooking skewers over a charcoal. The last reminded Vigor of the old woman with the fried tarantulas, demonstrating how the past and present were still entwined.

"Where do we begin?" Gray asked, daunted at the ten acres of temple grounds to search.

Vigor understood his consternation. Even from here, it was evident that the temple was a veritable three-dimensional maze of stooped passages, squared archways, dark galleries, steep steps, sunlit courtyards, and cavelike rooms. And all around, towers or *gopuras* rose in giant spears and cones, decorated with the ubiquitous faces.

It would be easy to get lost in there.

Even Nasser seemed to sense this. He waved a portion of his men into a tighter clutch around Gray's group. He sent a few others running forward to take up key positions in the courtyard here, covering all the exits, setting another level of defense.

Vigor felt the noose around his neck, but there was only one way to go. He pointed ahead.

"From a map I studied, the next level from here is another square court, like this one. But I think we should continue directly to the third level. To where the central sanctuary lies. We can get to it by going this way."

Still, as they made their way around the first level, Vigor paused by a spectacular bas-relief on the north wall, larger than all the rest, covering an entire section all by itself. His feet slowed as he passed it.

It depicted two forces—gods and demons, the same as the statues along the causeway. They were playing tug-of-war with a great snake as a rope. Between them, the snake was wrapped around a mountain seated on the back of a turtle.

"What is it?" Gray asked.

"One of the main Hindu creation myths. The Churning of the Ocean of Milk." Vigor pointed out details. "On this side are the *devas* or gods . . . on the other are the demonic *asuras*. They are using the snake god Vasuki as a rope to turn the great magical mountain. Back and forth, back and forth. Stirring the cosmic ocean into a milky froth. It is from this froth that the elixir of immortality called *amrita* will be churned. The turtle underneath the mountain is an incarnation of the god Vishnu, who aids the gods and demons by holding up the mountain so it doesn't sink."

Vigor pointed to the central tower of the Bayon. "And supposedly there is that mountain. Or at least its representation here on Earth."

Gray glanced to the fifteen-story tower, then back to the bas-relief. He trailed a finger along the carved mountain, his brow furrowed. "So what happened? Did the elixir get made?"

Vigor shook his head. "According to the story, there were some complications. The snake Vasuki got sick from all the tugging and vomited a great poison. It sickened both gods and demons, threatening to kill them all. Vishnu saved them by drinking up the poison himself, but in the process of detoxifying it, he turned blue, which is why he is always depicted with a blue throat. And with his help, the churning continued that produced not only the elixir of immortality but also the dancing celestial spirits called *apsaras*. So all ended well."

Vigor tried to urge them onward, but Gray remained where he was, staring at the bas-relief, an odd expression on his face.

Nasser came up to him. "Time has run out," he said, tapping his wristwatch with his cell phone. His voice was thick with disdain. "Do you have any sudden insights?"

Vigor felt coldness flowing from the man amid a dark amusement. He was enjoying torturing Gray. Vigor started to step between them, fearing Gray might react badly and attack Nasser again.

But instead Gray only nodded. "I do."

Nasser's eyes widened, surprised.

Gray placed a palm on the bas-relief. "The story here. It's not a creation myth. It's the story of the Judas Strain."

"What are you talking about?" Nasser asked.

Vigor had the same question.

Gray explained. "From what you told us about the exposure over in Indonesia, the disease all started with seas in the area glowing with bacteria. Seas described as frothy and white. Like churned-up milk."

Vigor straightened, stepping around Gray to view the bas-relief with new eyes. He stood with his hands on his hips.

Seichan joined him. Off to the side, Kowalski remained where he was, studying a line of bare-breasted women, his nose close to the stone.

Gray continued, pointing to the snake. "Then a great poison was released that threatened all life, good and bad."

Seichan nodded. "Like the toxic bacteria, spewing poison and laying a swath of death."

Nasser looked unconvinced.

Gray pressed his point home. "And according to this

myth, *someone* survived the exposure and saved the world. Vishnu. He drank the poison, detoxified it, and turned blue . . ."

"As if he were glowing," Vigor mumbled.

"Like the survivors described in Marco's book," Gray added. "And like the patient you described, Nasser. All glowing blue."

Vigor slowly nodded. "It's too perfect to be coincidence. And many ancient myths grew out of true histories."

Gray turned to Nasser. "If I'm right, here is the first clue that we're on the right track. That perhaps there is more yet to learn."

Nasser's eyes narrowed, momentarily angry—but he slowly nodded. "I believe you may be right, Commander Pierce. Very good. You just reset the clock for another hour."

Gray attempted to hide his relief, letting out his breath with a slight rattle.

"So let us continue," Nasser said.

Vigor drew them toward a shadowed flight of steep stairs. Behind him, Gray lingered a moment more, studying the carving. He reached out and ran a finger along the carved mountain—then back to the central tower.

Gray's eyes met Vigor's. Vigor noted the barest shake of the commander's head when he turned away.

Did Gray know something more?

Vigor ducked into the narrow stairs. Before Gray had turned, Vigor had noted something else, something in the commander's face.

Fear.

7:32 A.M.
Island of Natuna Besar

"THEY MUST NOT go there . . ." Susan moaned again.

The woman lay sprawled across the rear seats of the *Sea*

Dart, slipping into and out of consciousness, close to rolling back into a full catatonic stupor. Susan fought to pull away the fire blanket that Lisa had spread over her.

"Lie still," Lisa urged. "Try to rest. Ryder will be back soon."

The *Sea Dart* rocked and bumped against the end of the fuel dock. They had landed in the sheltered bay of a small island, somewhere off the coast of Borneo. Rain continued to pour out of low clouds, but the dark anger of the typhoon had swept away. Thunder rumbled, but it sounded distant and fading.

Still leaden with grief over Monk, Lisa stared past the *Sea Dart*'s windshield. While she waited, her thoughts slipped easily into recriminations. She could have done more. Moved faster. Thought of something clever at the last moment. Instead, Monk's prosthetic hand still hung from the wing's strut. Ryder hadn't been able to pry it off.

Lisa glanced to the hatch, wishing Ryder would get back soon. He had topped off his boat's petrol tank and gone in search of a telephone with a fistful of emergency cash he had stored here.

But his chances looked doubtful. The nearby village lay dark along the beach, storm-damaged with stripped roofs, downed palm trees, and beaches littered with overturned skiffs and debris. There had been no power at the dock's fuel pumps. Ryder had to hand-crank the petrol, passing a wadful of cash to a wet dog of a man in flip-flops and knee-length shorts. The man had left with Ryder on a motorcycle, assuring him they could find a phone near the island's small inland airport.

The tropical island of Natuna Besar served the tourist trade with its abundant snorkeling reefs and excellent sport fishing. But it had been evacuated with the threat of the typhoon. The place looked deserted.

Most of the islands they had flown over had been in a similar state of shambles.

From the air, Ryder had spotted the airport on Natuna

Besar. "Surely someone down there has a sat-phone we could borrow," he had said. "Or a way to repair our radio."

Needing to fuel anyway, they had made a landing in the sheltered bay. Lisa now waited with Susan.

Worried, Lisa placed a hand on the woman's damp brow. In the dimness of the cabin, Susan's face shone with a deeper glow, seeming to rise more out of her underlying bones than her skin. Lisa felt a burn under her palm as she rested it on Susan's forehead.

But it was not a fever.

Lisa lifted away her hand. It still continued to burn.

What the hell?

Lisa frantically rinsed her palm with water from a canteen and dried it on the fire blanket. The smolder subsided.

Lisa stared at the sheen of Susan's skin, rubbing the sting from her fingertips. This was new. The cyanobacteria must be producing a caustic chemical. And while it burned Lisa's skin, Susan remained resistant or protected.

What was happening?

As if reading her thoughts, Susan squirmed an arm out from under the blanket. Her hand stretched toward the square of weak sunlight flowing through the hatch window. The glow in her flesh vanished in the brighter light.

The contact seemed to settle Susan. She let out a long sigh.

Sunlight.

Could it be?

Curious, Lisa reached to Susan's hand and brushed a fingertip across her sunlit skin. Lisa yanked her arm back, shaking her fingers. Like touching a hot iron. She again doused her skin with water, the fingertip already blistering.

"It's the sunlight," Lisa said aloud.

She pictured Susan's earlier outburst, when she'd first set eyes on the rising sun. Lisa also remembered one of the unique features of cyanobacteria. They were the precursors to modern plants. The bacteria contained rudimentary chloroplasts, microscopic engines to convert sunlight into energy. With the rise of the sun, the cyanobacteria were ramping up, energizing in some strange manner.

But to do what?

Lisa glanced to the navigation chart on the floor. She remembered Susan's earlier outburst, pointing down to a spot on the map.

"Angkor," Lisa mumbled.

Lisa had attempted to convince herself it was just a coincidence. But now she was less sure. She remembered eavesdropping on a conversation while strapped to a surgical table. Devesh had been on the phone, speaking in Arabic. She had made out only one word.

A name.

Angkor.

What if it wasn't a coincidence?

And if not, what else did Susan know?

Lisa suspected one way to find out. She shifted over and cradled Susan's shoulders in her arms, keeping the blanket between them. Lisa lifted Susan into the shaft of sunlight flowing through the front windshield.

Susan shuddered as soon as her face touched the brightness. Her eyes fluttered open, black pupils shifted toward the weak light. But rather than constricting in the brightness, Susan's pupils dilated, taking in more light.

Lisa remembered the bacterial invasion of the woman's retinas, centered around the optic nerve, direct conduits to the brain.

Susan stiffened under her. Her head lolled—then grew steadier.

"Lisa," she said, thick-tongued and slurred.

"I'm here."

"I have to . . . must get me there . . . before it's too late."

"Where?" But Lisa knew where.

Angkor.

"No more time," Susan mumbled, and swung her face toward Lisa. Her eyes twitched from the sunlight, shying from it. Frightened. And not just because of the danger to come.

Lisa saw it in her eyes. Susan was scared of what was happening to her body. She knew the truth, yet was unable to stop it.

Lisa lowered Susan out of the sunlight.

Susan's voice momentarily steadied. One hand clutched Lisa's wrist. Out of direct sunlight, the touch burned, but it was not blistering hot. "I'm . . . I'm *not* the cure," Susan said. "I know what you're all thinking. But I'm not . . . not yet."

Lisa frowned. "What do you mean?"

"I must get there. I can feel it, a pull at my bones. A certainty. Like a memory of something buried just beyond my ability to recall. I know I'm right. I just can't explain why."

Lisa recalled her discussion back aboard the ship. About junk DNA, about old viral sequences in our genes, collective genetic history in our code. Were the bacteria awakening something in Susan?

Lisa watched the woman withdraw her other hand from the square of sunlight and pull a corner of the blanket over her face. Did she know it, too?

As Susan burrowed into her blanket away from the sunlight, her voice grew fainter. "Not ready . . ."

Still one hand remained clamped to Lisa's wrist.

"Get me there . . . somehow." Susan sagged, slipping away again. "Or the world will be lost."

A loud knock startled Lisa.

Ryder's scruffy face appeared in the hatch window. Lisa leaned forward and unbolted the lock. Ryder climbed in, sopping wet, but wearing a huge smile.

"I found a sat-phone! It's only a quarter charged, and the bloody thing cost me the equivalent of a small beach house in Sydney Harbor."

Lisa accepted the large device. As Ryder returned to the pilot seat, Lisa joined him in front. Even soaked to the skin, he looked like he had just returned from a grand lark, eyes bright with the excitement of it all. But Lisa also noted a serious edge to the man, a hardness around the corner of his lips. Ryder might enjoy his wild adventures, but one didn't achieve his level of success without a steely core of practicality.

"Satellite signal will be stronger away from the cliffs," he said, and engaged the jet pumps. With a burbling of the engines, he idled them clear of the rocky heights.

As he did so, Lisa related what Susan had said.

I am not the cure . . . not yet.

The two came to a consensus together.

Ryder pulled the navigational chart and propped it open on the wheel of the craft. "Angkor lies four hundred and fifty miles due north. I can fly this little blowie there in about an hour and a half."

Lisa lifted the sat-phone and pinpointed a strong signal.

She had one last person to convince.

8:44 P.M.
Washington, D.C.

"LISA?" PAINTER SHOUTED into his headpiece's receiver. The signal was faint, but most of his boisterousness had nothing to do with a weak connection. It was pure elation and heady relief. He stood behind his desk, back straight. "Are you okay?"

"Yes . . . for now. I don't have much time, Painter. Not much charge left on the phone."

He heard the anxiousness in her voice. He kept his voice firm, pulling back from his elation. "Go ahead."

Lisa quickly related all that had happened, speaking tersely, as if reporting a terminal diagnosis to a patient, sticking to the facts. Still, Painter recognized a tremble behind her voice. He wanted to reach through the phone and hold her, to squeeze her fear away, to clutch her to him.

Still, as she related an account of disease, madness, and cannibalism, he sank into his seat. His back bowed. He asked questions, filled in some blanks. She gave coordinates to an island. Pusat. He slid the notes to his aide, to fax to his superior, Sean McKnight. A team of Aussie commandos from the Counterterrorism and Special Recovery Team were already awaiting a target, stationed in Darwin, ready to coordinate a rescue operation. Before Painter finished this conversation, jets would be in the air.

But the danger was larger than a single hijacked cruise ship.

"The Judas Strain?" Lisa asked. "Has the disease spread?"

Painter only had bad news there. Early word had cases already being reported in Perth, in London, in Bombay. More would surely come in.

"We need that woman," Painter finished. "Jennings in research believes such a survivor is the key to a cure."

Lisa agreed. "She is the key, but she's not the cure . . . not yet."

"What do you mean?"

Painter heard her sigh from halfway around the world.

"We're missing something. Something tied to a region in Cambodia."

Painter straightened again. "Are you talking about Angkor?"

A long pause followed. "Yes." He heard the surprise in her voice. "How did you—?"

Painter told her all about the Guild's search along the historical trail and where it ended.

"And Gray is already there?" Lisa asked, sounding suddenly frantic. He heard her mumble, as if quoting someone. *"They must not go there."* Her voice grew firmer. "Painter, is there any way to call Gray off?"

"Why?"

"I don't know." Her voice had begun to cut in and out. Her phone was losing power. "The bacteria are doing something to Susan's brain. Energizing it in some manner, using sunlight. She has this strong urge to get to Angkor."

Painter recognized what she was implying. "Like the crabs."

"What?"

Painter related what he knew about the Christmas Island crabs.

Lisa understood immediately. "Susan must have been rewired in the same way. A chemically induced migratory impulse."

"If that's so, then maybe she's mistaken about the necessity to go there. It might just be a blind drive. There's no reason to risk going there yourselves. Not until things quiet down. Let Gray play out his game."

Lisa was not convinced. "I think you're right about an underlying biological drive. And in a lower life-form, like a crab, it might be nothing more than blind instinct. Crabs, like all arthropods, have only rudimentary—"

She stopped talking. Painter feared he'd lost the connection. But sometimes Lisa did that when she had a sudden insight. She would just switch off, using her full faculties to pursue some angle of thought.

"Lisa?"

It took another moment for her to respond.

"Susan could be right," she mumbled—then louder, firmer: "I have to get her there."

Painter spoke rapidly, knowing that they were about to lose the connection. He heard the resolve in Lisa's voice and feared he would not have time to dissuade her. If she was going to Angkor, he wanted her somewhere out of harm's way.

"Then land at the large lake near the ruins," he said. "Tonle Sap Lake. There's a floating village there. Find a phone, contact me again, but stay hidden there. I have a campaign being organized in the area."

He barely made out her next words, something about doing her best.

Painter attempted one last exchange. "Lisa, what did you figure out?"

Her words cut in and out. "Not sure . . . liver flukes . . . virus must—"

Then the call fully died away. Painter called out a few more times, but he failed to raise her again.

A knock at his door drew his eyes up.

Kat rushed in, eyes sparkling, cheeks bright. "I heard! About Dr. Cummings! Is it true?"

Painter stared up at Kat. He read the question in Kat's expression, in her whole body, a yearning to know. Lisa had told him. First thing. She had spoken in a rush, needing to unburden herself. Afterward, Painter had compartmentalized it away.

But confronted by Kat, by her hope, by her love, the truth struck him hard.

He stood and stepped around the table.

Kat saw it in his face.

She backed away from him, as if she could escape what was coming.

"Oh, no . . ." She grabbed a chair arm, but it failed to hold her. She went down to a knee, then collapsed to the other, covering her face with her hands. "No . . ."

Painter joined her on the floor.

He had no words to offer her, only his arms.

It wasn't enough.

He pulled her against him, wondering how many more would die before this was over.

8:55 P.M.

THEY WERE RUNNING out of places to retreat.

Harriet waited for her husband at the foot of the stairs that led up to the top floor. She stood in the stairwell doorway. Jack had gone out to leave more false trails for the hunting dogs. She had already stripped her husband's shirt and helped him hide pieces of it across the lower two floors: tossed into boarded-up offices, shoved into piles of refuse, hung from the metal drawer in a maze of secretarial cubicles. They did their best to confound the pursuers.

Jack had been hunting all his life. Duck, pheasant, quail, deer. He'd had his share of retrievers before the oil-rig accident required amputating his leg below the knee. He knew dogs.

And he still had three rounds left in the pistol he had stolen from the guard. Harriet sought any measure of hope. But she heard the dogs barking below. Annishen had been systematically clearing each level. She knew they were up here, periodically calling out to them, taunting them.

All the exits were well guarded. Even the fire escapes. No neighboring buildings were close enough to reach. And the entire district looked long abandoned. Not a light shone, except far off in the distance. There was no one to hear a call for help. They'd tried a few dusty wall phones, but they were all dead.

Like the desperate fleeing a high-rise fire, they had nowhere to go but up. And only one last floor remained. That and the roof.

Harriet heard a scuffle, and her husband appeared out of the gloom, dressed only in his boxers, carrying the pistol. He limped up to her.

"What are you still doing here?" he whispered in a hard voice. His face shone with sweat. She recognized that his angry tone only masked his fear for her. "I told you to get up there."

"Not without you."

He sighed and hooked an arm around her. "Then let's go."

They headed up to the top floor, using one of the narrow back stairs. Below them in the stairwell, a waste-management Dumpster had been shoved down the steps long ago, blocking the way up from lower levels.

It should have been safe.

A low growl dismissed this conceit. A scuffling sounded on the lower landing, from beyond the Dumpster.

They both froze.

"Whatchu smell in there, girl?" a voice barked. Footsteps entered the lower stairwell. A flashlight's glow flowed up to them.

Harriet and Jack edged to the walls.

The snarling grew more intense.

"Get up there now. Go on. Squeeze on through there."

Jack pushed Harriet up the stairs. They moved quietly.

Below, the snarling had softened to a heavy snuffling, along with a frantic scrabbling of claws on tile.

"There you go," the voice said. "Flush 'em out. I'll go on around." The voice headed out of the lower stairwell, plainly seeking another way up. A crackle of radio trailed after him along with some mumbling as he reported in.

They were sending the dogs up to the next level.

As Harriet and Jack fled up toward the door at the next landing, a sharp bark echoed to them, half triumphant, half savage. Something large pounded up the steps.

"Run, Harriet," Jack urged.

She fled ahead and reached the next landing. The door to the top floor lay a yard away, closed. Behind her, Jack missed his footing in the dark and fell. He crashed two steps below. The pistol skated across the landing to Harriet's toes. She quickly gathered it up. As she straightened, lights through the tiny window in the stairwell door caught her eye.

Flashlights bobbled across the dark top floor.

Annishen called out. "We'll search through here and work down. Squeeze them out."

Harriet turned. Jack scrabbled up toward her. Beyond his form, a dark shape rounded the lower stairs and bounded toward her husband. A thick growl flowed.

Harriet lifted her pistol. If she fired, Annishen would hear the shot. Their captors would know where they were hiding and swarm here in seconds.

She hesitated too long.

Snarling savagely, the massive dog leaped at her husband.

7:58 a.m.
Angkor Thom

SEICHAN STOOD A step away as Gray circled the central altar.

It had taken them almost twenty minutes of backtracking and searching to discover the route up to the central sanctuary of the Bayon's third level. The ten-acre complex was a veritable maze of dark galleries, sudden sunlit courtyards, stooped passages, and precipitous drops. The low ceilings scraped heads, some walkways had to be traversed in single file, shuffling sideways, and many corridors merely dead-ended.

By the time they reached the small inner sanctuary, they were all dusty, covered in sweat. The morning had rapidly warmed, and humidity weighted the air down. But they had reached their destination.

"Nothing's here," Nasser said sourly.

Seichan recognized his attitude, read the hard stance to his posture. She doubted his patience would last until noon. Unless there was some real progress soon, she expected he would end things in the next hour. Order Gray's parents killed. Execute all of them here. And move on.

Ever practical.

No damn imagination.

It made him a dull lover.

Ahead, Gray circled the altar a third time. He was drawn thin, covered in dust and dirt, black hair plastered to his forehead, sticking out in damp tufts. Dried blood caked at his collar, where he'd been pistol-whipped behind the ear by one of Nasser's men back at the hotel.

He still refused to look at her.

It made her angry, mostly because it hurt, and she hated that even more. She sought that place of cold dispassion where she once easily lived, a dispassion that allowed her to sleep with Nasser to get what she needed, as she'd been trained to do.

Seichan turned her attention to the guards, going practical, strategizing some way out of here. The guards were

mostly locals, including many former Khmer Rouge soldiers, long recruited by the Guild, gathered after the fall of
the genocidal dictator Pol Pot. They would be fierce fight-
ers. They guarded the four exits to the chamber, heading
off in each cardinal direction. More men had taken posts
throughout the ruins, discouraging tourists from disturbing them.

"According to what I read about this place, a giant statue
of Buddha once rested here," the monsignor announced,
pacing Gray around the altar. Vigor waved an arm across
the two rectangular slabs, stair-stepped one atop the other.
"But when the religion changed to Hinduism, the Buddha
was torn down and tossed into that large well we passed
coming up here."

The only other bits of decoration in the stone room were
four more shadowy faces of the bodhisattva Lokesvara.
Only these were all gazing inward, toward the altar and its
missing Buddha. Kowalski leaned against one face, staring
upward.

The great central tower of the Bayon rose above the altar,
climbing forty meters. Cored through its center like a chimney, a square shaft cut straight up to the sky above. It was
the only source of light.

"This has to be the place," Gray said, finally stopping.
"There has to be a way down from here."

"Down to where?" Nasser asked.

Gray lifted a hand toward the monsignor. "Vigor mentioned how the foundations of this tower were buried underground. Deep. We need to find some access to those lower
rooms. And I wager under the altar would be a good place to
look."

Vigor stepped next to him. "Why do you think it's
important?"

Gray swiped the hair from his brow, plainly weighing
how much to say.

Nasser also read the man's hesitation. "We're past another hour mark." He tapped a finger on his wristwatch. "Tick tock, Commander."

Gray sighed. "The bas-relief we saw earlier. Of the Churning of the Milk. Every piece of the story was important. The snake, the frothing seas, the poison, the world threat, the glowing survivor. But one piece stood out as odd and unexplained. It didn't fit with the others."

"What's that?" Nasser asked.

Seichan saw it pained Gray to speak. Each word came out with a wincing reluctance.

"The turtle," Gray finally admitted.

Vigor scratched at his chin. "The turtle in the relief represents the god Vishnu, an incarnation of himself. In his turtle form, he supported Mount Meru as it was churned back and forth, to keep it from sinking."

Gray nodded. "On the bas-relief, the turtle was carved beneath the mountain. Why a turtle?" He leaned and drew in the dust on the altar. He sketched a crude doodle of a mountain with a domed shell beneath it.

He tapped the shell. "What does this look like to you?"

Vigor leaned down. "A cave. Buried beneath the roots of the mountain."

Gray stared up the shaft of light. "And the tower here represents that mountain."

Seichan drew closer. "You think there is a cavern beneath this tower. Beneath its buried foundations."

He answered her, his eyes flicking to her briefly, then

away. "The only way to find out is to get down into the foundations—then search for some access to that cavern."

Nasser scowled. "But what can be so important about the cavern?"

"It could be the source of the Judas Strain," Vigor said. "Maybe when they were excavating the temple, they broke into that cavern, released something that lay buried down there."

Gray sighed, tired. "Many disease vectors have appeared in the world as mankind spread into regions normally unpopulated. Yellow fever, malaria, sleeping sickness. Even AIDS appeared when a road was being built through a remote region of Africa, exposing the world to a virus found only in a few monkeys. So perhaps when the Khmer cultivated and populated this region, something was released."

Gray rubbed his neck. His eyes held a steady stare at Nasser.

Too steady.

Seichan sensed Gray was still holding something back. She studied again his stylized pictogram. The mountain and shell represented the tower and cave. So what else was here? Then she realized.

The turtle itself.

Of course . . .

Her eyes rose to Gray's.

He must have felt her attention. He turned to her, casually, but the weight of his gaze was heavy. He knew she had realized what he'd left unspoken. He willed her to be quiet.

She stepped back, folded her arms.

He stared another breath—then away again.

Seichan felt a measure of satisfaction. More than she had been expecting.

Nasser breathed deeply through his nose, nodding. "We must find a way down there."

Gray frowned. "I had hoped there would be some evidence of a secret passage."

"Doesn't matter," Nasser said. "We'll blow the entrance."

"I'm not sure that's wise," Vigor said, aghast. "If this is the source of the Judas Strain, it may be horribly toxic down there."

Nasser remained unperturbed. "That's why I'll be sending you all down first."

To be canaries in a coal mine.

Seichan again matched gazes with Gray. He raised no objections. Like Seichan, he knew that there was something larger than just the source of the Judas Strain down there.

The turtle's shell might represent the cavern—*but the turtle itself represented the god Vishnu*—suggesting more than just a cavern rested beneath the Bayon temple. Possibly something else waited for them down there, too.

Gray stepped toward Nasser. "Does that demonstrate enough cooperation to spare my mother for this hour?" he asked, his voice tight.

Nasser shrugged, agreeing. He moved to the shaft of light, seeking better reception for his cell phone.

"I should perhaps hurry, then," Nasser said, flipping open his phone. "It's already after the hour. Annishen has little patience. No telling what she might do."

9:20 P.M.
Washington, D.C.

HARRIET REMAINED FROZEN on the landing.

The slathering dog leaped at Jack's sprawled form on the stairs. It was impossible to tell the breed in the dark stairwell, only that it was large and muscled. Pit bull. Rottweiler. Jack rolled to his back and kicked out—but the dog was faster, attack-trained. With a growling snarl, it bit deep into his ankle.

Jack tugged at his knee and kicked out with his other leg, square in the dog's chest.

The dog went flying down the stairs, bouncing hard,

still latched on to her husband's prosthetic leg. Jack had unstrapped the limb, freeing himself.

Harriet helped Jack up to the landing.

Below, the dog struck the wall and scrambled back to its paws. It refused to let go of the prosthetic leg, ripe with her husband's scent. Angry, confused, it thrashed its head back and forth, tossing drool, shaking the captured limb.

Harriet drew Jack up the next set of stairs, passing the closed landing door. She glanced through its small window. Flashlights continued to search the top floor. That left Harriet and Jack only one way to go.

The roof.

Down the stairs, the dog continued savaging the captured limb, triumphant with its prize.

Jack leaned on her shoulder. He hopped and hauled his way to the roof door. They had already searched the exit and found it chained, but only loosely. At some point, someone had used a crowbar to bend back the lower corner of the steel door. There was just enough room to squirm under the loose chain and through the bend in the door.

Once out into the night, Jack used an abandoned length of pipe to prop the door closed. It wouldn't hold long. But it didn't much matter. There were a half-dozen other roof access points. They couldn't block them all.

"This way," Jack said, and pointed. He had scouted the roof and discovered an old heating-and-air-conditioning unit, half gutted of equipment. There was enough room inside to hide two people.

But neither held out much hope.

The dogs would scent them out before too long.

They crossed the roof to the unit, circled it to put its bulk between them and the door. Both sank to the tar paper roof, remaining outside the HVAC unit for the moment. The stars shone above, along with a sliver of a moon. A plane passed by far overhead, winking lights.

Jack put his arm around Harriet and drew her close to him.

"I love you," he said.

It was a rare admission, seldom spoken aloud. Not that Harriet ever doubted it. Even now, he said the words matter-of-factly. Like saying the earth was round. So simple a truth.

She leaned into him. "I love you, too, Jack."

Harriet clung to him. She didn't know how much time they had left. Eventually the search below would end. Annishen would turn her attention to the roof.

They waited together in silence, having spent a lifetime together, sharing joy and heartbreak, tragedies and victories. Though not a word was spoken, they both knew what they were doing, fingers entwined. They were saying good-bye to each other.

17

Where Angels Fear to Tread

GRAY LEANED AGAINST the brick wall of the cavelike cell.

Beyond the narrow opening, a half-dozen men stood guard. The closest had their weapons in plain sight. Nasser had ordered them in here while he set about arranging for munitions to blow the altar stone. Gray checked the illuminated dial of his dive watch.

They'd been here almost an hour.

He prayed Nasser was busy enough with his plans to skip his hourly threat against his parents. Something had certainly upset Nasser—beyond the delay in obtaining armaments. After sending them here, he had stormed off, phone to his ear. Gray had overheard the mention of a cruise ship. It had to concern the scientific leg of the Guild's operation. Painter had related the story of the hijacked ship and the unknown whereabouts of Monk and Lisa.

Something had plainly gone wrong.

But was that good news or bad regarding the fate of his friends?

Gray shoved off the wall and paced the length of the cell. Seichan sat on a stone bench next to Vigor.

Kowalski leaned near the opening. One of the guards had a rifle pointed at his stomach, but he ignored it. He spoke as Gray neared. "I just saw some guy climb past with a jackhammer."

"They must be about ready," Vigor said, and stood up.

"What's taking so long?" Gray asked.

Seichan answered, still seated. "Bribes take time."

Gray glanced back to her.

She explained, "I heard some shouting in Khmer. Nasser's men are clearing the ruins of tourists, chasing them off. It seems the Guild has rented the Bayon for the remainder of this private party. It's a poor region. It wouldn't take much to get the local officials to look the other way."

Gray had already guessed as much. The guards were no longer making any effort to hide their weapons.

Vigor leaned a palm on a column near the door. "Nasser must have convinced the Guild of the value in investigating the historical trail a bit longer."

Gray suspected it was something more than that. He remembered the agitation concerning the cruise ship. If something had befallen the scientific trail, the value of the historical trail would be that much more important.

He had confirmation a moment later.

Nasser shoved through the guards. The earlier fury of his manner had died back down to his usual cold cunning. "We're ready to proceed. But before we continue, it seems we've crossed another hour mark."

Gray's stomach muscles tightened.

Vigor came to his defense. "You've locked us up all this time. Surely you can't expect us to have any further insight."

Nasser cocked an eyebrow. "That's not my concern. And Annishen grows impatient. She certainly needs something to entertain her."

"Please," Gray said. The word slipped out before he could stop it.

Nasser's eyes sparked with amusement, allowing Gray to stew.

"Don't be an ass, Amen," Seichan said behind them. "If you're going to do it, then do it."

Gray's fist squeezed. He had to resist swinging on her, to shut her up. He didn't need Nasser antagonized. Not now.

The cool lines of Nasser's brow had knotted up in anger. He raised his fingers and smoothed them out, refusing to rise to her bait. He turned away and headed back through his guards. He didn't say a word.

"Nasser!" Gray called back to him, his voice cracking.

"If we skip this hour," Nasser answered without turning, "I'll expect even greater results once we penetrate the altar. Anything less, I'll take more than a finger from your mother. It's time we lit a larger fire under you, Commander Pierce."

Nasser raised an arm, and the guards brought them out of the cell.

Seichan crossed past Gray, bumping his shoulder. Her words were low, barely discernible. "I was testing him."

She continued past.

Gray, caught in her wake, followed—then edged next to her.

She spoke under her breath without looking at him. "He was bluffing . . . I could tell."

Gray bit back an angry retort. She was risking his parents' lives.

She glanced aside at him, perhaps sensing his anger. Even her words responded in kind, going harder. "What you must ask yourself, Gray, is *why?* Why is he bluffing?"

Gray relaxed his jaw. It was a good question. The back of her hand brushed his. He reached a finger toward her wrist, to acknowledge the merit. But she had already stepped beyond his reach.

Nasser led them back to the central sanctuary. The demolition team had been hard at work. Holes had been drilled into the massive, double slab of sandstone. Wires trailed out, winding together into a single braid. At the four exits, men stood with red fire extinguishers strapped to their backs.

Gray frowned. What did they expect to burn? It was all stone.

Nasser spoke to a dwarfish man wearing a vest full of tools and a coil of wire over one shoulder, plainly the demolition expert. Nasser got a nod from the man.

"We're ready," Nasser announced.

They were marched down the western exit and around the corner.

Vigor somewhat resisted. "An explosion could bring all this down on top of us."

"We know that, Monsignor," Nasser said, and lifted a radio to his lips. He gave the go order.

A moment later a sonorous thud as loud as a thunderclap thumped chest and ears. Once. Along with a fiery flash. Then a sharp acrid scent rolled over them, burning both nose and throat.

Vigor coughed. Gray waved a hand in front of his face.

"What the hell was that?" Kowalski asked, spitting into a corner to rid himself of the taste.

Nasser ignored him and led them forward.

He followed one of the men with the fire extinguishers. The man pulled down a face mask and triggered his hose. A foggy stream jetted out, spraying floors, walls, and ceilings. The narrow passageway filled with a cloud of fine powder, coating every surface.

Nasser led them back to the sanctuary.

Through the fog Gray noted other men with extinguishers converging on the chamber ahead. Under their combined spray, the view into the sanctuary momentarily clouded over. Gray could barely discern the four men spraying.

Nasser held them up.

After another half minute the spraying stopped, and the dust literally settled. The room, still foggy, reappeared. Sunlight streamed from the tower's chimney.

Nasser took them forward. "Neutralizing base," he explained, waving the residual dust from his face.

"Neutralizing what?" Gray asked.

"Acid. The demolition holds an incendiary charge paired

with a corrosive acid. Engineered by the Chinese during the building of the Three Gorges Dam. Minimum concussion, maximum damage."

Gray entered the chamber behind Nasser and gaped at the sight.

The walls were covered in white powder, but the change was dramatic. The four bodhisattva faces looked like someone had melted their features away. What once had been beatific visages were now ruins of slag. The floors were equally scoured, as if someone had taken a sandblaster to them.

The altar in the center, lit from above, was a cracked ruin. One corner section had fallen through into a lower chamber.

Some space was definitely under there.

Most of the slab still held.

Another demolition-team member stepped into the chamber, bearing aloft a sledge. Nasser signaled him forward. Another man followed, dragging a jackhammer.

Just in case.

The first man swung his sledge, smashing square in the center. Fiery sparks blasted out from around the hammer's head, and the great mass of sandstone gave way.

The altar tumbled into the pit.

10:20 A.M.

SUSAN SCREAMED, ARCHING up out of the backseat.

Lisa, strapped in the copilot's seat, jarred around. She had been staring down at the expanse of the great inland lake as the *Sea Dart* circled, readying to land. Below, a floating village drifted from the shoreline, a tangled accumulation of Vietnamese junks and houseboats.

It was where Painter had told her to go into hiding. The fishing village lay twenty miles from Angkor. Out of harm's way.

Lisa fumbled with her seat harness as Susan wailed. Freeing herself, she stumbled to the back of the plane.

Susan thrashed out of the fire blanket, gasping. "Too late! We're too late!"

Lisa gathered the blanket and urged her to lie down. She had been sleeping quietly for the whole ride here. What had happened?

Susan clawed out a hand and grabbed Lisa's forearm. The grip seared her skin, burning away the fine hairs.

Lisa yanked her arm away. "Susan, what's wrong?"

Susan pulled herself up in the seat. The wildness in her eyes ebbed slightly, but she continued to quake all over. She swallowed hard.

"We must get there." She mumbled her usual mantra.

"We're landing now," Lisa said, trying to calm her. She even felt the *Sea Dart* bank downward.

"No!" Susan reached again for her, but then withdrew her hand, noting Lisa shying away. Her fingers curled and slipped back under the fire blanket. She took a shuddering breath. Her eyes rose to Lisa's. "We're too far. Lisa, I know how this sounds. But we have only minutes left. Ten or fifteen at most."

"Left for what?"

Lisa remembered her earlier conversation with Painter, about the Christmas Island crabs, about chemically induced neurological changes, triggering manic migratory urges. But in the sophisticated mind of a human, what did those same chemicals do? What other changes were wrought? Could Susan's urges be trusted?

"If I don't get there . . ." Susan said, shaking her head as if trying to jar a memory loose. "They've opened something. I can feel the sunlight. Like fiery eyes burning into me. All I know . . . and I know it in my bones . . . if I'm not there in time, there will be no cure."

Lisa hesitated, glancing back to Ryder.

The lake rose up as the *Sea Dart* swept downward.

Susan moaned. "I didn't ask for this."

Lisa heard the grief in her words, sensing that the pain encompassed more than the biological burden. Susan had lost her husband, her world.

She turned back to the woman.

Susan's face shone with a blur of emotions: fear, grief, desperation, and a deep loneliness.

Susan placed her palms together. "I'm not a crab. Can't you see that?"

Lisa did.

She swung around and called to Ryder. "Pull up!"

"What?" Ryder glanced back.

Lisa motioned her thumb in the air. "Don't land! We have to get closer to the ruins." She clambered up and used the seat backs to pull herself up to the copilot seat. "There's a river that runs through the town of Siem Reap."

She sank into the seat. She had studied the navigational maps of the region. The town still lay six miles or so away. She remembered Susan's warning.

Ten or fifteen minutes at most.

Would that be close enough? Her own blood was now ignited by the urgency. It took her another breath to realize why. Susan's last words.

I'm not a crab.

Susan didn't know anything about the Christmas Island land crabs. Lisa hadn't spoken aloud about Painter's conversation, not even with Ryder. Maybe in her stupor, Susan had overheard her end of the discussion. But Lisa couldn't recall if she'd used the word *crab*.

Either way, she flipped open the nav-chart and searched.

They needed somewhere closer to land.

Another lake or river . . .

"Or here," she said aloud, pulling the chart closer.

"What's that, lass?" Ryder asked. He dragged up the *Sea Dart*'s nose and sent them sailing high over the lake.

Lisa flipped the chart toward him and tapped at it. "Can you land here?"

Ryder's eyes widened. "Are you bloody crazy?"

She didn't answer. Mostly because she didn't know the answer.

Ryder's face split into the wide grin. "What the hell! Let's give it a try!" Ever up for a thrill, he reached and patted her thigh. "I like the way you think. How firm is that relationship of yours back home?"

Lisa leaned back into the seat. After Painter heard about this . . .

She shook her head. "We'll see."

11:22 P.M.
Washington, D.C.

"Sir, that GPS lock that you had me tracking, it's moving off course."

Painter swung around. He had been coordinating with the Australian Counterterrorism and Special Recovery Team. They had arrived on-site at the island of Pusat fifteen minutes ago, proceeding to the coordinates Lisa had left. Early intel from the island remained confusing. The *Mistress of the Seas* was found burning, wrapped in a tangle of netting and steel cable. It listed almost forty-five degrees. A major firefight was under way aboard ship.

Kat sat on his other side, earphones in place, holding them with both hands. She had refused to go home. Not until she knew for sure. Her eyes were red and swollen, but she remained focused, surviving on a thin hope. Maybe, somehow, Monk was still alive.

"Sir," the technician said, pointing to another screen. It showed a map of Cambodia's central plateau. A large lake spread in the middle. A small blip crept in tiny pixilated jumps across the screen, tracking the *Sea Dart*.

While the seaplane had been circling near the shoreline a moment ago, it now headed away from the lake.

"Where are they going?" Painter asked. He watched a few seconds more, getting a trajectory. He extended it with a finger. Their air path led in a beeline straight toward Angkor.

What are they doing?

Motion at the door drew Painter's eye. His aid, Brant, flew into the room, braking his wheelchair with a squeal of rubber on linoleum.

"Director Crowe, I tried to reach you," he gasped out. "Couldn't. Figured you were still conferencing with Australia."

Painter nodded. He had been.

Brant grabbed a fax crumpled in his lap and held it out.

Painter took it and scanned it once quickly, then a second time more carefully. *Oh God . . .*

He headed to the door, bumping past Brant. He paused, turned. "Kat?"

"Go. I've got it covered."

He glanced back to the screen map of Cambodia, to the tiny blip edging toward the ruins of Angkor.

Lisa, I hope you know what you're doing.

He fled out of the room and ran for his office.

For the moment, she was on her own.

10:25 A.M.
Angkor

"HANG ON!" RYDER warned—though it sounded more like a war cry.

Lisa clutched tight to the arms of her seat.

Ahead, the giant beehive-shaped black towers of Angkor Wat rose into the sky. But the spectacular temple, sprawled over a square mile, was not their goal.

Ryder dipped the *Sea Dart* toward the man-made stretch of green water off to one side. The moat of Angkor Wat. Unlike Angkor Thom, it still held water. Its entire length around the temple stretched four miles, leaving a mile of straight water on each side. The only problem—

"Bridge!" Lisa yelled.

"Is that what you call it?" Ryder commented sarcastically. He had a cigar clamped in his teeth. He blew a stream of smoke out the corner of his lips.

It was his only cigar, kept stashed for emergencies like this. As Ryder had said before he lit up, "even a condemned man is allowed one last smoke."

The billionaire soared over the moat, shifting their flight path's elevation up and down a bit, just enough to clear the bridge.

Lisa held her breath as they swept over. Tourists parted to either side.

Then they were over, and Ryder dropped the *Sea Dart* fast, skimming the moat and trailing a plume of water. Then they settled deeper, still going fast as the plane became a boat. Their momentum propelled them toward the far corner, too fast to make the turn.

The earthen embankment at the end swept toward them.

Ryder pulled a crank in the floor. "This is called a Hamilton Turn! Hold tight!"

With a puff of smoke, he yanked and twisted the wheel.

The *Sea Dart* spun, as if on ice, throwing its back end fully around. The twin engines roared as its rear jets braked them. The craft slowed.

Lisa cringed, still expecting to slam into the embankment.

Instead, Ryder turned the wheel and slipped the boat sideways. The *Sea Dart* plowed a wave right to the edge of the sloped embankment and bumped to a gentle stop.

Ryder sighed out a stream of smoke and cut the engines. "Lord, that was bloody fun."

Lisa immediately unbuckled and went to Susan.

"Hurry," Susan said, struggling.

Lisa helped the woman undo her belt. Ryder followed and cranked the hatch open.

"You know what you need to do?" Lisa asked him as they tumbled out into the shallow water and waded the few steps to the embankment.

Already shouts arose all around.

"You told me sixteen times," Ryder said. "Find a phone, call your director, let him know what you're doing, where you're going."

They clambered up the slope to a road that crossed alongside the moat. Susan remained wrapped in the blanket, holding it clutched shut, wearing sunglasses, attempting to keep as much of the sun's power away from her.

People pointed and called out.

Ryder hailed a passing vehicle. It was nothing more than a motorcycle hauling a small roofed cart. Ryder held up a fistful of cash, the universal language for *stop*. The vehicle's driver was fluent in that language. He jerked his motorcycle around and swerved straight to them.

Once it had stopped Ryder helped Lisa and Susan inside the rear cart and closed the tiny door. "The tuk-tuk will take you straight to that temple. Be careful."

"Just reach Painter," Lisa said.

He waved them off, like signaling the start of a race.

Obeying, the motorcycle sped away, dragging them behind it.

Lisa craned back. Already, uniformed police converged on Ryder, zipping up on their own motorcycles. Ryder waved his cigar, making a scene.

No one paid attention to their little tuk-tuk.

Lisa settled back.

Beside her, Susan remained cocooned in her blanket. A single word flowed out. "Hurry."

10:35 A.M.

ON HIS KNEES, Gray stared over the rim and down the circular stone shaft. Forty feet below, a face stared back up at him. Another of the stone bodhisattvas. It rose from the floor's surface, carved out of a single giant block of sandstone. The sunlight from the tower chimney shot a square shaft of light, sparkling with dust motes, down into the pit and bathed the dark stone face in warm sunlight.

The enigmatic smile welcomed.

To the side, a rolled-up caving ladder made of steel cable and aluminum rungs was dumped off the lip of the shattered altar. It unreeled with a rattle into the depths and struck the foundation floor. The upper end was bolted with carabiners to the stone roof of the sanctuary.

Nasser walked over to Gray. "You'll go down first. Followed by one of my men. We'll keep your friends up here for now."

Gray wiped the powder from his hands and stood. He crossed to mount the ladder. Vigor stood against the wall, his face dour. Gray imagined the monsignor's dark countenance was not solely from their situation. As an archaeologist, Vigor had to find the desecration here professionally abhorrent.

On Vigor's other side, Kowalski and Seichan simply awaited their fate.

Gray nodded to the three of them and began the long climb down. Rather than dusty, the pit smelled dank. The first thirty feet was a narrow stone shaft about seven feet wide, lined by blocks, not unlike a large well. But in the last ten feet, the walls angled away, creating a barrel-shaped vault, forty feet across and perfectly circular.

"Stay in sight!" Nasser called down.

Gray glanced up at the ring of rifles pointed at him. One of the soldiers was already on the ladder heading down. Gray jumped to the floor, landing near the bodhisattva's stone face.

He stared around. Four massive pillars studded the vault, equally spaced. Possibly load-bearing pylons for the tower above. Supporting this, the floor underfoot was not stone blocks. It was solid limestone. They'd hit bedrock. Here was definitely the structural foundation for the Bayon.

The clanking of the ladder drew his attention back up as the soldier approached. Gray considered jumping him and grabbing his rifle. But then what? His friends were still above; his parents were still under Nasser's fist. So instead, he stepped over to the carved face. He circled it. It was carved sandstone like all the others. It rested flat on its back, staring up, sculpted out of a single waist-high block.

The face appeared no different from the others: same upturned corners of the lips, same wide nose and fore-head, and those shadowed, brooding eyes.

The guard dropped to the floor, landing hard on his boots.

Gray straightened—then caught it out of the corner of his eye.

He turned back, noting something odd about the face, about those brooding eyes. Dark circles lay in the center of each, like pupils. Even the sunlight could not dispel them.

Gray had to lean atop the stone cheek to investigate. He reached a hand across and probed the dark pupil with a finger.

"What are you doing?" Nasser called down.

"There are holes! Drilled into the eyes, where pupils should be. I think they may pass clean through the face."

Gray searched up. Sunlight flowed down the tower's chimney, and with the altar removed, the beam struck the face hidden here.

But did the light travel even deeper?

He climbed higher onto the face, sprawling across it. He leaned his own eye to peer into the pupil of the stone god. Closing his other eye, he cupped around the sandstone eye-ball. It took a moment for his vision to adjust.

Far below, lit by the sunlight passing through the other pupil, he could see a shimmer of water. A pool at the bottom of a cavern. Gray could almost imagine the vaulted space, domed like the shell of a turtle.

"What do you see?" Nasser called down.

Gray rolled away, onto his back, staring up from the bot-tom of the well.

"It's here! The cavern! Under the stone face!"

Like the altar stone above, the bodhisattva guarded a hidden doorway.

Gray remembered Vigor's explanation for the hundreds of stone faces. *Some say they represent vigilance, faces staring out from a secret heart, guarding inner mysteries.* But as Gray lay there, he also remembered another man's words, much older and more forbidding, from Marco's text, the very *last* line of his story.

The words chilled through him.

The gateway to Hell was opened in that city; but I know not if it was ever closed.

Gray stared up at the shattered altar and knew the truth.

It had been closed, Marco.

But now they were opening it again.

10:36 A.M.

THE TUK-TUK STOPPED at the end of a paved road.

Lisa climbed out.

The way ahead was a jumbled stone plaza, half uprooted by giant trees. Beyond the plaza, the Bayon rose, framed in jungle, a jagged cluster of sandstone towers, covered with crumbling faces, etched with lichen, riddled with cracks.

A few tourists gathered on the plaza, taking pictures. A pair of Japanese men approached their tuk-tuk, plainly wanting to commandeer their vehicle once Lisa and Susan had vacated it. One man bowed his head toward Lisa. He lifted an arm toward the temple and spoke in Japanese.

Lisa shook her head, not understanding.

He smiled shyly, bowed his head again, and struggled out one word of English. "Closed."

Closed?

Lisa helped Susan out of the tuk-tuk, still wrapped head to toe in the blanket. Only a pair of sunglasses stared out. Lisa felt the tremble through the blanket as she supported Susan's elbow.

The tourist motioned to the tuk-tuk, silently requesting if they might take it. Lisa nodded and hobbled away with Susan across the uneven plaza of stone blocks. Ahead, Lisa spotted men inside the temple: leaning on towers, standing above gateways, patrolling atop walls. They all wore khaki and black berets.

Was it the Cambodian army?

Susan dragged her forward, plodding purposefully toward the eastern gate. A pair of men in berets stood guard. They had rifles on their shoulders. Lisa saw no insignias. The man on the left, plainly Cambodian, bore a set of raked scars down one side of his face. The other, similarly attired, was Caucasian, leather-skinned with a scruffy growth of beard. Both men's eyes were diamond hard.

These were not members of the Cambodian army.

Mercenaries.

"The Guild," Lisa whispered, remembering the intelligence Painter had passed to her regarding Gray's capture. *They're already here.*

Lisa tugged Susan to a stop, but the woman struggled to pull away, to continue on.

"Susan, we can't hand you back over to the Guild," Lisa said.

Especially not after Monk gave his life to free you.

Susan's voice was muffled through her blanket, but it sounded firm. "No choice . . . I must . . . without the cure, *all* will be lost . . ." Susan shook her head. ". . . one chance. The cure must be forged."

Lisa understood. She remembered Devesh's warning and Painter's confirmation. The pandemic was already spreading. The world needed the cure before it was too late. Even if it landed in the hands of the Guild, it had to be brought forth. They'd deal with the consequences after that.

Still . . .

"Are you sure there's no other way?" Lisa asked.

Susan's words trembled with fear and grief. "I wish to God there was. We may already be too late." She gently removed Lisa's hand from her sleeve and stumbled forward, plainly intending to go alone.

Lisa followed. She also had no choice.

They approached the guarded gateway. Lisa did not know how they would talk themselves through the barricade.

But apparently Susan had a plan.

She shed her blanket, letting it drop away at her heels. In the brightness of the sun, she looked no different from anyone else, only perhaps more pale, her skin thin and wan. She clawed away the sunglasses and turned to stare into the full face of the sun.

Lisa watched Susan's body quake, imagining the blinding brunt striking through the woman's pupils, to the optic nerve, to her brain.

But apparently it still was not enough.

Susan ripped away her blouse, exposing more skin to the sunlight. She unbuttoned her pants, and as gaunt as she was from her weeks in stupor, they fell away. In only her bra and panties, Susan approached the gate.

The guards did not know what to make of the near-naked woman. Still, they stepped forward to block the way. The Cambodian soldier waved them off in sharp, piercing words. *"D'tay! Bpel k'raowee!"*

Susan ignored him and continued, intending to pass between them.

The other guard grabbed the woman's shoulder, half turning her. His stoic expression clenched, agonized. He whipped his hand back. His palm was seared a beet red; his fingertips trailed blood as he fell back and collapsed against the wall.

The Cambodian hauled up his rifle, pointing it at the back of Susan's head as she continued past.

"Don't!" Lisa shouted.

The rifleman glanced back at her.

"Take us!" she said, struggling for the name Painter had used in relating Gray's story. Then she remembered. "Take us to Amen Nasser!"

10:48 A.M.

"COME SEE THIS!" Vigor called, unable to keep the amazement from his voice. He glanced back, searching for the others.

Gray stood a few yards away, examining one of the foundation pillars. The pylons were stacks of unmortared sandstone disks, a foot thick and a full three feet across. Gray fingered several deep cracks, stress fractures of an aging spine.

Off in the room's center, Seichan and Kowalski stood by the stone face, watching Nasser's demolition team prepare the carved block.

Again the sharp, grinding whine of a diamond drill bit rang out, echoing loudly in the barrel vault. Another inch-thin bore was cored a foot into the face. Already charges were being packed into the other holes and wired up, twice as many as they had used for the altar. Ropes hung down to ferry equipment and explosives up and down the well.

A shaft of bright sunlight illuminated their labors.

Unlike Seichan and Kowalski, Vigor had not been able to watch the mutilation. Even now he swung away and returned his attention to the wall he had been studying. Away from the central shaft, the vault here lay in deep shadow. Vigor had been allowed a flashlight so he could hunt for another entrance to the subterranean cavern. And while he hated to help Nasser, if he could find another way down, then he could perhaps limit the degree of defilement to these ancient ruins.

But Vigor hadn't been granted much time.

Ten minutes.

With preparations under way, Nasser had climbed out of the vault. Vigor had noted him checking his cell phone, searching for a signal. Apparently unsuccessful, he had climbed out, ordering them to be ready by the time he returned.

Gray joined Vigor. "What is it? Did you find that doorway you were looking for?"

"No," Vigor admitted. He had walked the entire circumference of the vault. There was no other door. It seemed the only way down was through the stone face of bodhisattva Lokesvara. "But I did find this."

Vigor waited for one of the patrolling guards to pass, then shifted his flashlight flat against the wall, casting the beam up the surface. Lit by shadow and light, an expanse of wall etchings appeared, reminiscent of the bas-reliefs above. But it depicted no figures, just cascading tangles.

"What is it?" Gray said, reaching his fingers out to examine what the light revealed.

By now, Seichan and Kowalski had joined them.

Vigor shifted the light, widening the beam to illustrate. "At first, I thought it was just decorative scrollwork. It covers all the walls." He waved an arm to encompass the breadth of the chamber. "Every surface."

"Then what the hell is it?" Kowalski muttered.

"Not *hell*, Mr. Kowalski," Vigor said. "This is angelic."

Vigor took the light and cupped it over a small fraction of the carved tapestry. "Look closer."

Gray leaned to the wall, tracing with his fingers. Understanding dawned in the commander's face. "It's made up of angelic symbols, all jumbled together."

Seichan joined Gray, following his fingers, nose to nose. "This is impossible. Didn't you say angelic script was devised by someone in the sixteen-hundreds?"

Vigor nodded. "Johannes Trithemius."

"How could it be here?" Gray asked.

"I don't know," Vigor said. "Maybe at some point the Vatican did send someone all the way to Cambodia to follow Marco's trail like we did. Maybe they returned with etchings of this script, and Trithemius somehow got ahold of it. Devised his script from it. And if he knew Marco's story of glowing angelic beings, it might be why he claimed the script was angelic."

Gray turned to Vigor. "But you don't believe that, do you?"

Vigor watched Gray step back, retreat a few more steps, his gaze fixed to the wall.

He sees it, too.

Vigor took a deep shuddering breath, trying to restrain what he suspected. "Trithemius claimed he gained knowledge of the script after weeks of fasting and deep meditative study. I think that's exactly what happened."

Seichan scoffed. "He just happened to dream all this up, a match to the ancient script here."

Vigor nodded. "That's exactly what I'm saying. Remember what I told you before, about how angelic script bears a striking resemblance to Hebrew. Trithemius even claimed his script was the purest distillation of the Hebrew alphabet."

Seichan shrugged.

"What do you know about Jewish Kabbalah?" Vigor asked.

"Just that it's some Jewish mystical study."

"Exactly. Practitioners of Kabbalah search for mystical insight into the divine nature of the universe by studying the Hebrew Bible. They believe that divine wisdom lies buried in the very shapes and curves of the Hebrew alphabet. And that by meditating upon them, one can gain great insight into the universe, into who we are at the most basic level."

Seichan shook her head. "Are you saying that this Trithemius fellow meditated and came up with this purer form of Hebrew? Stumbled upon a language—this same language—" She patted the wall. "A language that links to some great inner wisdom?"

Gray cleared his throat. "And I think *inner* is the key word here." He waved Seichan to step back, to join him. "What do you see? Look at the whole pattern. Does it look familiar to you?"

Seichan stared for a single breath, then snapped, "I don't know. What am I looking for?"

Gray sighed and stepped to the wall. He ran a finger along one of the cascades. "Look at the way it swirls down in spirals of broken helixes. Picture this section all by itself."

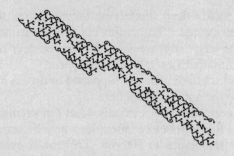

Seichan squinted. "It looks almost biological."

Gray nodded. "Follow the strands. Don't they look like double helixes of DNA? Like a genetic map?"

Seichan remained doubtful. "Written in an angelic language?"

Gray stepped away, his eyes still on the wall. "Maybe. In fact, there was a scientific study that compared patterns in DNA code with patterns found in human languages. According to a Zipf's law—a statistical tool—all human languages show a specific pattern of repetitive word usage. Such as the frequency of the word *the* or *a*. Or the rarity of other words, like *aardvark* or *elliptical*. When you plot a graph comparing the popularity of words against the frequency of their usage, you get a straight line. And it's the same whether English, Russian, or Chinese. All human languages produce the same linear pattern."

"And DNA code?" Vigor asked, intrigued.

"It produced *exactly* the same pattern. Even in our junk DNA, which most scientists consider to be biological garbage. The study has been repeated and verified. For some reason, there is a language buried in our genetic code. We don't know what it says. But—" Gray pointed at the wall. "That may be the written form of the language."

Vigor ran a hand along the carving, breathless with awe. "It makes you wonder. Could Trithemius have tapped into that language during his meditations?" He straightened as another thought struck him. "And consider ancient Hebrew, how its characters are similar to angelic script. Could early written languages have somehow been derived from this, arising out of some inherent genetic memory? In fact, it makes you wonder if this language isn't the Word of God, mapping out something greater in all of us."

Vigor shifted his light, sweeping it to cover the breadth of the vast chamber. "But either way, all of this. All this angelic language. What is it telling us?"

"I think it's a genetic blueprint," Gray said.

"But a blueprint to what?" Seichan said.

"Probably a turtle," Kowalski mumbled.

Vigor snorted at the man's joke, but both Seichan and Gray reacted with surprise, glancing to the man with matching expressions of incredulity.

"What?" Vigor asked, sensing something important.

Gray stepped closer, dropping his voice. "I think he may be right."

"I am?" Kowalski asked.

Gray expanded upon his theory of the cavern below. "The turtle's shell represents the cave. But what about the turtle itself? According to the story, it represents an incarnation of Vishnu, an angelic being." Gray waved to the wall. "And here is evidence of some strange biological process, some secret knowledge. Beyond merely a viral disease. I think the coding on the walls is some diary of that process. Possibly still incomplete."

Vigor studied the wall, the blueprint.

Before they could contemplate it further, a commotion arose from above.

They shifted in a group back to the center. It looked as if the demolition team were close to finishing. Their leader had coiled all his charge wires and cinched them into an electronic detonator so they could blow it all from above.

Overhead, Vigor spotted a woman climbing down the ladder. It was difficult to discern her features through the glare of the sunlit shaft.

Still, Gray recognized her, stepping forward. "Lisa . . . ?"

Farther above, near the lip to the shaft, Nasser appeared, accompanied by a frantic, half-naked woman. She fought forward, as if to throw herself into the pit, but she was restrained by the barrels of four rifles, kept at bay.

Vigor gaped up at her.

Dear God . . .

She *glowed*.

Her skin shone out from the shadows.

Impossible.

"Cover the eyes!" she screamed below, pointing an arm down into the pit. "Cover the eyes!"

Vigor could not comprehend what she was talking about.

Gray did. The commander swept from Vigor's side, dragged up a tarp used by the demolition team, and tossed it over the sculpture's eyes like a blindfold, cutting the flow of sunlight to the cavern below.

Up top, the woman collapsed as if the strings suspending her had been cut. She dropped to a slab of the broken altar.

Nasser frowned back at her.

Lisa stepped from the ladder and joined them. Her gaze remained above, but her words were for them all. "I'm sorry."

11:05 A.M.

TEN MINUTES LATER, Gray watched the last of Nasser's men mount the ladder and climb up. Above, a ring of rifles pointed down at their group. The last satchel of demolition equipment vanished over the lip, hauled up on one of the two ropes. The other rope still dangled, taunting.

"Why are they leaving us down here?" Lisa asked.

Gray eyed the rigged sandstone face. "I think we've just become obsolete," he mumbled.

Lisa remained quiet, then mumbled an apology. "I had no choice."

She'd already explained her sudden, unexpected appearance. A desperate act, born out of the necessity for a cure. The attempt had to be risked . . . even if it meant delivering the cure into the hands of the Guild.

"And Monk," Lisa said with a choke. "He gave his life . . . for this."

"No." Gray put an arm around Lisa's shoulders. He couldn't even acknowledge that reality. Not yet. "No. Monk got you all here. And as long as we're alive, there's still hope."

Nasser returned to the edge of the pit. "We're just about finished here," he announced, not so much gloating as simply stating a matter of fact. With all the cards in his hand, he kept his tone cold and civil. "Monsignor, you mentioned earlier how the scientific trail and historical trail merged at these ruins. It appears you were most astute. Here we have the two halves of Sigma joined." He waved below—then turned to Susan, who still sat in a stupefied slump, head hanging to her chest. "And it seems the Guild's efforts have also joined. The survivor from the scientific trail here . . . and the source of the Judas Strain below."

Gray slipped his arm from Lisa and stepped forward. "You may still need our help!" he called up, knowing it was a wasted breath.

"I'm sure we'll manage. The Guild has abundant resources to fit these last pieces together. We've managed to reach this point, starting with only a few words in an ancient text. A text, I understand, that came into our possession because of your actions, Commander."

Gray's fist tightened. He should have burned the Dragon Court's library when he'd had the chance.

"Of course, it was the Guild's efforts afterward—through the employment of marine archaeologists and satellite imagery—that uncovered one of Marco's sunken ships off the coast of Sumatra."

It took Gray a moment to realize what Nasser was implying. "You found one of Polo's ships?"

"And we were lucky. One of the keel beams, encased in insulating clay, still contained biological activity. But we couldn't understand its full capacity without an in vitro trial, a real-world scenario."

Gray felt his blood go cold. If Nasser was telling the truth, the outbreak at Christmas Island hadn't been a matter of chance exposure. "You . . . you purposely contaminated Christmas Island."

He glanced to Seichan for confirmation.

She would not meet his eyes.

Nasser continued. "From the study of sea currents and tidal patterns, it required just planting the beam off the coast and observing what happened. In fact, we were monitoring and collecting samples when our patient here stumbled onto the scene. She and her party. The first human subjects. Of course, the currents eventually carried the tide to the island. As planned. A perfect localized and contained scenario."

Lisa mumbled, "Then with the cruise ship, the Guild saw the opportunity to reap what they'd sown."

Gray sank back.

Seichan mumbled behind him. "Now you know why I had to stop them."

Gray glanced to her.

But she had failed . . . they'd all failed.

II:II A.M.

SUSAN DRIFTED IN a haze, as if in a waking dream.

Fire danced across her brain.

Since baring herself to the raw sunlight, she had passed beyond an edge. She felt it inside her skull. She was no longer fully herself—or maybe more herself than ever before.

She had become unmoored as a lifetime of memories rebuilt inside her. Her past swelled up out of recesses long thought lost and inaccessible. They knit together, one day to another, one hour to the next, blending into a seamless whole. Her past came alive again, not just bits and pieces, but the full spread and panorama of it all.

And she could remember it all as a single moment: from the crush of her skull as she was squeezed out of her mother's womb . . . to the beat of her heart now. She sensed the traces of air over her naked skin, every current, scribed into memory, indelible, adding to the whole.

It was all held in a suspended, shimmering bubble.

And beyond that thin surface . . . more.

But she wasn't ready to venture there.

She knew there were steps still to be taken.

Below.

With the fiery eyes closed, the panic inside her subsided to a dull glow.

Floating between past and present, adding moments with every breath, new words slowly dropped into the pool that was her life, overheard from a step away.

. . . it required just planting the beam off the coast and observing what happened . . . when our patient here stumbled onto the scene. She and her party. The first human subjects . . .

NO.

The single note rang through her.

With her life held in that endless moment between one breath and the next, she was again underwater, weightless. She saw the finger of age-blackened wood protruding from the sand. Her thoughts from then returned, as if she were still in those waters. At the time, she had supposed earthquakes had shaken the keel beam free, or perhaps the recent tsunami had stripped away the sand, exposing it.

Now she knew the truth.

The beam had been planted there.

Purposefully.

To kill.

She remembered how excited she had been to tell her husband, who loved diving wrecks. Just the memory of him filled her senses.

Gregg.

Now she knew the truth.

Why he had died.

And the truth was fire.

11:12 A.M.

LISA LEANED AGAINST Gray, his arm over her shoulders. She stared up at the rifles. Nasser was saying something, but she didn't hear, lost in her own guilt.

Gray suddenly flinched.

Though she hadn't moved, she snapped back to the moment.

At the rim of the well, Susan's head slowly lifted, her blond hair parting from a face lost in fury. The guards' attentions remained focused on Nasser. Past Nasser's shoulder, Lisa watched the soft glow of Susan's skin flush fiercer.

Her eyes burned with an inner fire.

Nasser must have sensed something and had begun to turn.

Lisa did not see Susan move.

One moment the woman was seated on the crumbled bit of altar—the next she was latched around Nasser, hugging tight to him, cheek to cheek in an intimate embrace.

He screamed—a wail that tore from his throat.

Smoke curled between them.

One of the guards reacted, clubbing Susan from behind.

She dropped loose, head lolling.

Still screaming, Nasser shoved her away.

Over the edge of the pit.

"Susan!" Lisa called up.

She tumbled in a tangle with one of the loading ropes used by the demolition team. A hand snatched out, instinctively catching herself. But she had no strength. She slid down the rope, too fast. The caustic acid of her skin flared in the shaft's direct sunlight, triggering some chemical reaction in the synthetic rope. It smoked and melted as she slid along it. Susan twirled as she plummeted, almost in free fall.

No one dared catch her.

Gray swung to the side and dragged the cloth tarp from the stone face. He whipped one end to Kowalski. His partner understood.

Overhead, the rope snapped, burned through where Susan had grabbed.

She dropped in a limp, boneless fall.

Unconscious.

Gray and his partner caught her, but her weight still ripped the tarp from their hands and she struck the floor hard. Using the tarp, Gray swung her out of direct sight, only her legs visible from above. He dropped beside her.

Nasser screamed down to them. On hands and knees. His cheek still smoked, flesh blackened. His bare arms looked like seared steak, weeping and bleeding. "I want that bitch!"

Gray stumbled back into view. "Neck's broken! She's dead!"

A war of emotions played across Nasser's face. It settled on a near-mindless rage. "Then you'll all burn!" He rolled back. "Blow it all up!"

Gray waved to everyone. "Back . . . out of sight."

Lisa obeyed, stumbling from the light and into the shadows.

A few bullets sparked, chasing them.

Lisa stared toward the rigged explosives. The electronic detonator was beyond their reach, out in the open. They would be shot if they dared approach.

Gray dragged the tarp, hauling Susan's limp form. "Behind the foundation pillars! They may offer some protection. Crouch low, find anything to cover your head and face!"

They scattered.

Four pillars, six of them.

Gray took Susan with him.

Lisa found herself huddled with the monsignor behind one of the sandstone pillars. He pulled her down, shielding her with his body.

Lisa placed her palm on the pillar. It was three feet across. She had no idea of the strength of the blast to come. She turned to Vigor.

"Father, will this protect us?"

Vigor stared down at her face and didn't answer.

For once Lisa wished a priest would lie to her.

18

The Gateway to Hell

GRAY CRADLED SUSAN, keeping her wrapped in the tarp.

She moaned and stirred. She had taken a good crack to the head when she struck the ground, but Gray had lied to Nasser about her neck being broken. The bastard, in his agony, had not questioned it, maybe had even hoped for it.

Gray had hoped to use the woman's body as a bargaining chip.

But that was not going well.

Up above, Nasser shouted, maddened by the pain. From the look of his blackened skin, he had sustained third-degree burns across large swaths of his body. And now he wanted them to suffer in kind. An eye for an eye. But apparently the demolition team hadn't been prepared for such a sudden order. They were scrambling, giving Gray's party a minute or so of a reprieve.

Taking advantage of it, Gray shifted Susan's weight, seeking to better protect her behind the pillar. If she was the potential cure, she had to be preserved. He tugged the tarp more thoroughly over her head. It parted briefly, revealing the soft glow of her naked skin beneath. Away from the bright sunlight, the sheen to her skin had begun to dim. He paused for a beat, amazed at the strangeness. As he drew the drape closed again, he noted the wall ahead of him.

The scrollwork of angelic script shone with an exceptional brilliance, fluorescing under the weak glow. The light emanating from the cyanobacteria in her skin must shed wavelengths in the ultraviolet range, igniting a fluorescent compound etched into the carvings.

It reminded Gray of the Egyptian obelisk, glowing with angelic script, a miniature and rudimentary version of this display. Had Johannes Trithemius had deeper revelations during his meditations? A vision of all this?

Gray opened the tarp wider, casting a broader beam of her glow. More of the script ignited, swirling off through the darkness in either direction, as if he had set flame to oil.

Gray sat higher. He noted a spot of darkness off to the far left, barely discernible, at the edge of the glow's reach, a dark rock in the shining stream of glowing script. The angularity of it caught his eye.

Could that be . . .

He turned Susan in his arms, letting more of the tarp fall away, keeping enough between the woman's skin and his own. The glow was still not strong enough to reach that far. He had to move Susan closer. He struggled with her weight, tangling the tarp, sensing the seconds ticking away.

He needed help.

"Kowalski! Where are you?"

A voice answered out from the pillar to his right. "I'm hiding! Like you said to!"

Gray hauled up. "I need you over here!"

"What about the bomb?"

"Forget about the bomb. Get your ass over here!"

Kowalski swore sharply, then headed over, grumbling under his breath. "Why is it always a goddamn bomb . . ."

The large man ran up to him, practically sliding behind the pillar, like he was stealing from third to home.

Gray motioned with his chin to the left. "Help me move Susan down that way."

Kowalski sighed heavily. Using the tarp like a stretcher, they slung her form between them and rushed off along the wall. As they hurried, the curve of script ignited along with them, brightening as they neared, fading again after they passed.

Seichan had been hiding behind the next pillar. She crossed toward them, drawn by the brilliant display and their frantic actions. "What are you—oh my God!"

Gray lowered Susan to the floor, keeping her uncovered, basking her glow on the wall, setting fire to the script. All except for a recognizable patch of darkness.

"Vigor!" Gray called out.

"I'm coming!" he answered. Plainly the monsignor had seen the sight all the way across the chamber. Gray heard the double tramp of steps as Lisa trailed Vigor.

They all stood before the wall, gaping at the sight.

Not at what was glowing—but what *wasn't*.

"Friar Agreer," Vigor said. "He must have left this marker, by washing down the wall. Cleaned the patch here as a sign."

"A sign of what?" Seichan asked.

"A clue to a hidden doorway," Gray said. "There must be another way down to the cavern."

"But what does the clue mean?" Vigor asked.

Gray shook his head, knowing they were running out of time. If they didn't find the door, get Susan somewhere safe and away from the Guild, it wasn't just their lives. According to Lisa, a pandemic was already spreading.

Nasser called down to them. "Say your last prayers!"

"Jesus H. Christ!" Kowalski blurted out, though it wasn't meant as a prayer. He knocked Gray and Vigor aside, crossed to the wall, and shoved hard in the center of the cross.

The stone door swiveled on a central pivot, revealing a passage beyond.

Kowalski turned. "It's not always rocket science, guys. Sometimes a door is just a door."

They piled through the exit. Gray and Kowalski again slung Susan between them. Once through, Seichan and Lisa shouldered the door back closed behind them.

Ahead, a stairway led down, cut out of the limestone bedrock.

No one doubted where it led.

As they started down, a muffled explosion echoed to them, a single boom of thunder. Gray sent a silent prayer of thanks to Friar Agreer.

He had saved Marco in the past.

And now he had saved all their lives.

Though relieved, Gray could still not escape a horrible dread. While he might be free, his parents were not. When Nasser found his prisoners gone, Gray knew who would be made to suffer for it.

12:18 A.M.

SEATED ON THE warehouse rooftop, Harriet drowsed in her husband's arms. It was a warm evening. Overhead, the moon moved imperceptibly across the night sky. Despite the terror, exhaustion had taken its toll. For the first hour, she had listened to the ebb and flow of shouts and barks. Then she stopped caring. Time stretched, long enough that Harriet was startled to find herself dozing when the first shout rose from the other side of the roof.

"They're here," Jack said, sounding almost relieved.

He shifted and motioned for Harriet to retreat inside the hollowed out HVAC unit behind them. There was barely room for two. Once Harriet was inside, she held out her hand toward her husband.

Instead, he collected the door grate from the tar paper.

"Jack?" she whispered out to him.

He lifted the grate between them, pushing it in place.

"No . . ." she moaned.

His lips were at the grate's slats as he snugged it closed over her. "Please, Harriet, let me do this. I can lead them away. Buy you more time. Give me at least this."

Their eyes met through the thin slats.

She understood. For too long, Jack had believed himself only half a man. He didn't intend to die that way. But to Harriet, Jack had never been half a man.

Still, she could not take this from him.

It was her last gift to him.

She reached her fingers through the slats, tears streaming. His fingers touched hers, thanking her, loving her.

Shouts drew closer.

They had no more time.

Jack turned and half crawled over to the roof's raised wall, his pistol clutched in a fist. When he reached the wall, he used its support to hobble away to the left.

Harriet tried to follow where he went, but he was soon out of sight.

She covered her face.

A sharp cry of discovery rose in that direction. She heard the retort of a pistol blast, coming from closer to the left.

Jack.

Harriet counted his shots, knowing he only had the three rounds left in his gun.

Return fire strafed her husband's position, pinging off metal. Jack must have found some cover. Another shot blasted from his spot.

One bullet left.

In the ringing lull of the brief firefight, Jack called out. "You'll never find my wife. I hid her beyond your goddamn reach."

A voice barked back, only steps behind Harriet's hiding spot, startling her.

Annishen.

"If the dogs don't find her," the woman called back to Jack, "I'll make sure your screams draw her out."

Annishen's legs stepped into view beyond the grate. The woman whispered into a radio, ordering her men to sweep wide and pin Jack down.

Then the woman stiffened, turning slightly.

Another noise intruded.

It sounded like the rush of a strong wind.

Across the roof, a black helicopter shot into view from below, angular, waspish in shape. Plainly military. A ripping chatter of automatic fire chewed across the roof. Men screamed. Feet pounded. One man ran past and had his legs cut out from under him, sprawling face-first.

Sirens erupted from the dark streets leading toward the warehouse.

A bellow of a megaphone from the helicopter ordered weapons to be dropped.

Annishen lowered into a crouch beside the HVAC grate, preparing for the short dash to the nearby roof exit. Harriet instinctively crouched away from her; her elbow bumped the unit's side with a hollow thud.

Annishen flinched—then cocked her head, peering inside. "Ah, Mrs. Pierce." She shifted, poking her pistol through the grate, in point-blank range. "Time to say good—"

The gunshot jolted through Harriet.

Annishen's body crashed against the grate, then sank to the tar paper.

Harriet caught a glimpse of a blasted eye socket.

As the woman collapsed, Jack hopped into view. He tossed aside his smoking pistol.

His last shot.

Harriet shoved the grate open. She scrambled over Annishen's legs, across the roof, and back into Jack's arms, sobbing. The two of them sank in a grateful huddle on the tar paper.

"Don't ever leave me again, Jack."

He hugged her tight. "Never," he promised.

Men in military uniforms dropped to the roof from the helicopter on snaking lines. Harriet and Jack were guarded as the roof was cleared. Sirens pulled up below. More gunshots and cries rose from the warehouse.

A figure stepped over to them, strapped in rappelling gear. He dropped to a knee.

Harriet glanced up, surprised to find the familiar face. "Director Crowe?"

"When will you start calling me Painter, Mrs. Pierce?" he asked.

"How did you find—?"

"It seems someone made quite a commotion on the street outside the butcher shop," he explained with a tired smile. "Vigorous enough to be remembered."

Harriet squeezed her husband's hand, thanking him for his earlier acting.

Painter continued. "We've been canvassing the street since this morning, and then forty-five minutes ago, one of the patrolling officers discovered a nice gentleman with a shopping cart. He recognized your picture and had been suspicious enough—or maybe paranoid enough—that he wrote down the van's license number, along with make and model. It didn't take long to track the van's GPS. I'm sorry we couldn't get here sooner."

Jack wiped at one eye, keeping his face turned away so no one could see his tears. "Your timing couldn't be better. I owe you a big bottle of that fancy single-malt whiskey you like."

Harriet hugged her husband. Jack might have trouble remembering people's names, but he never forgot what they liked to drink.

Painter stood up. "I'll take you up on that sometime, but right now I have an important call to make." He turned away and mumbled under his breath, but Harriet heard him.

"That is, if I'm not already too late."

11:22 A.M.

LISA STUMBLED DOWN the dark stairs, following the monsignor. She had to stay ducked low, running a hand along the damp wall. The air smelled of mulch, like decaying leaves in a wet forest. It was not unpleasant, except for a slight burn to the nostrils.

Ahead, a weak light drew them onward, flowing up from below.

Their goal.

The stairs finally ended, dumping them out into a wide cavern. Their footsteps echoed. Overhead, the dome of the cavern arched up five stories, dripping with a few blunt stalactites. The space was ovoid in shape, seventy yards across at the widest point. Where they entered, the roof spread up into a natural flowstone archway. A matching arch could be discerned across the cavern.

"It does look like a turtle shell," Vigor mumbled, his voice echoing hollowly. "Even the way it flares here and across the way. Like the front and back end of a turtle shell."

Kowalski grumbled, hauling Susan inside with Gray's help. "So which is it? Are we're climbing down the turtle's throat or up his ass?" But as he straightened, the large man whistled softly between his teeth.

Lisa understood his reaction.

Ahead, a circular lake of black water rested as still as a mirror, edged around by a stone rim. From the roof above, two straight beams of sunlight shot down and struck the center of the water, coming through the eyes of the stone idol above.

But where the sunlight struck the black water, a milky pool spilled outward, glowing, as if the sun had turned to liquid and poured down from above.

The milky glow shimmered and streamed, ebbing and flowing.

Looking alive.

Which it was.

"The sunlight is energizing the cyanobacteria in the water," Lisa said.

A few trickles from the idol's eyes struck the pool, hissing slightly. Where they splashed, the milky glow darkened.

"Acid," Gray said, reminding everyone of the danger above. "From the bomb. It's dripping through the eyes. I don't know how long it will take to neutralize the vault, but at least the stone block is holding for now. Still, they'll come down with sledges and jackhammers and finish breaking through here soon."

"So what do we do?" Seichan asked.

Kowalski scoffed. "We get the hell out of here."

Gray turned to Lisa. "Can you run ahead, check the far archway? See if there is another way out. Like Vigor said, a turtle shell has an opening for the head and one for a tail. It's our only hope."

Lisa balked. "Gray, I think I should stay with Susan. My medical background—"

A groan rose from the tarp. An arm lifted weakly.

Lisa stepped to Susan's side, careful not to touch her. "She's still the only hope for a cure."

"I can go," Seichan volunteered.

Lisa glanced up, noting a flash of suspicion on Gray's face, as if he didn't trust the woman.

Still, he nodded. "Find a way out."

She set off without a word.

The group followed along the stone bank.

Gray studied the space. "This looks like an old sinkhole. Like in Florida, or the cenotes of Mexico. The sandstone block must be plugging the original hole that once stood open."

Lisa bent near the wall and pinched up a bit of dried matter. It crumbled in her fingers. "Petrified bat guano," she said, confirming Gray's assessment. "This cavern must have been open to the air at one time."

Lisa wiped her fingers and glanced to Susan, beginning to put together what she had already suspected.

Vigor waved an arm to encompass the lake. "The ancient Khmers must have come upon the sinkhole, noted how it glowed, imagined it was the home of some god, and attempted to incorporate it into the temple here."

"But they didn't know what they were doing," Lisa added. "They trespassed where they shouldn't have. Interfered with a fragile biosystem and released the virus. If mankind pushes, nature sometimes pushes back."

They continued alongside the lake.

Ahead, a small spit of stone projected into the water, barely discernible in the darkness. Only the encroaching tide of milky water revealed the small peninsula.

Along with something more.

"Are those bones?" Kowalski asked, staring down into the water alongside their path.

The party stopped.

Lisa crossed to the pool's edge. The soft light penetrated deep into the crystalline water. The stone bank fell away at a gentle angle through the water, then vanished over a steep lip ten yards out.

All across the shallow bottom of the lake, bones lay in mounds and piles: fragile bird skulls, tiny rib cages of monkeys, something with a pair of curled horns, and not far from shore, the massive skull of an elephant, resting like a white boulder below, one ivory tusk broken to a nub. But there was more: broken femurs, longer tibias, larger cages of ribs, and like a scattering of acorns, skull after skull.

All human.

The lake was a massive boneyard.

Stunned to silence, they continued onward.

As they hiked along the stone bank, the glow slowly grew in the lake. The burn to the nostrils that Lisa had noted before grew more intense. She remembered Christmas Island, the tidal dead pool on the windward side.

Biotoxins.

Kowalski wrinkled his whole face.

And like smelling salts, the sting also stirred Susan. Her eyes fluttered open, glowing in the dark, a match to the shine in the lake. She remained dazed, but she recognized Lisa.

Susan tried to sit up.

Gray and Kowalski lowered her to the floor, needing to rest anyway, stretching their shoulders and kneading their hands.

Lisa sank beside Susan, modestly draping the tarp over her shoulders as she helped the woman sit up.

Susan shied back as Kowalski stepped near.

"It's all right," Lisa assured her. "They're all friends."

Lisa introduced the others to help reassure Susan. Slowly the panicky daze cleared. She seemed to collect herself—until she stared past Lisa's shoulders and spotted the glowing lake.

Susan surged away, hitting the wall with her back and propelling herself up into a teetering crouch.

"You must not be here," she keened, voice rising.

"No fucking kidding," Kowalski griped.

Susan ignored him, her eyes on the lake. Her voice lowered. "It will be like Christmas Island. Only a hundredfold worse . . . trapped inside the cavern. And you'll all be exposed."

Lisa did not doubt it. Already her skin itched.

"You must go." Susan steadied enough to gain her feet, leaning a hand on the wall. "Only I can be here. I must be here."

Lisa saw the fear shining in her eyes, but also the dead certainty.

"For the cure?" Lisa said.

Susan nodded. "I must be exposed one more time, by the source here. I can't say how I know, but I do." She lifted a palm to the side of her head. "It's . . . it's like I'm living one foot in the past, one foot here. It's hard to stay here. Everything is filling me up, every thought, sensation. I can't turn it off. And I . . . I feel it expanding."

Again the fear shone brighter in her eyes.

Susan's description reminded Lisa of *autism*, a neurological inability to shut off the flow of sensory input. But a few autistic patients were also *idiot savants*, geniuses in narrow fields, their brilliance born out of their rewiring. Lisa tried to imagine the pathophysiology that must be occurring inside Susan's brain, awash in strange biotoxins, energized by the bacteria that produced the toxins. Humans only used a small fraction of their brain's neural capacity. Lisa could almost picture Susan's EEG of her brain, afire, energized.

Susan stumbled to the water's edge. "We only have this one chance."

"Why?" Gray asked, stepping alongside her.

"After the lake reaches critical mass and erupts with its full toxic load, it will exhaust itself. It will take three years before the lake will be ready again."

"How do you know that?" Gray asked.

Susan glanced to Lisa for help.

"She just knows," Lisa answered. "She's somehow connected to this place. Susan, is that why you were so urgent about getting here?"

Susan nodded. "Once opened to sunlight, the lake will build to a blow. If I missed it . . ."

"Then the world would be defenseless for three years. No cure. The pandemic would spread around the world." Lisa imagined the microcosm aboard the cruise ship expanded across the globe.

The horror was interrupted by Seichan's return, pounding up to them, breathless, her face shining damply. "I found a door."

"Then go," Susan urged. "Now."

Seichan shook her head. "Couldn't open it."

Kowalski pantomimed. "Did you try giving it a hard shove?"

Seichan rolled her eyes, but she did nod her head. "Yes, I tried shoving it."

Kowalski threw his hands high, surrendering. "Well, that's all I got."

"But there was a cross carved above the stone archway," Seichan continued. "And an inscription, but it's too dark to read. The words might offer some clue."

Gray turned to the monsignor.

"I still have my flashlight," Vigor said. "I'll go with her."

"Hurry," Gray urged.

Already the air was getting difficult to breathe. The glow in the lake had spread far, sliding along the length of the spar toward shore.

Susan pointed to it. "I must be out on the lake."

They headed toward the peninsula of rock.

Gray paced Lisa. "You mentioned a trespassed biosystem earlier. Mind telling me what the hell you think is really going on here?" He waved to the glowing lake, to Susan.

"I don't know everything, but I'm pretty sure I know who all the key players are."

Gray nodded for her to continue.

Lisa pointed to the glow. "It all started here, the oldest

organism in the story. Cyanobacteria. Precursors to modern plants. They've penetrated every environmental niche: rock, sand, water, even other organisms." She nodded to Susan. "But that's getting ahead of the story. Let's start here."

"This cavern."

She nodded. "The cyanobacteria invaded this sinkhole, but remember they needed sunlight, and the cavern is mostly dark. The hole above was probably even smaller originally. To thrive here, they needed another source of energy, a food source. And cyanobacteria are innovative little adapters. They had a ready source of food above in the jungle . . . they just needed a way to get to it. And nature is anything if not ingenious at building strange interrelationships."

Lisa related the story she had once told Dr. Devesh Patanjali, about the Lancet liver fluke, how its life cycle utilized *three* hosts: cattle, snail, and ant.

"At one point, the liver fluke even hijacks its ant host. It compels the ant to climb a blade of grass, lock its mandible, and wait to be eaten by a grazing cow. That's how strange nature is. And what happened here is no less strange."

As Lisa continued, she appreciated being able to talk through her theories. She took a moment to explain Henri Barnhardt's assessment of the Judas Strain, how he classified the virus into a member of the *Bunyavirus* family. She remembered Henri's diagram, describing a linear relationship from human to arthropod to human.

Human ⟶ *Insect (arthropod)* ⟶ *Human*

"But we were wrong," Lisa said. "The virus took a page out of the fluke's handbook. *Three* hosts come into play here."

"If cyanobacteria are the first hosts," Gray asked, "what's the second host in this life cycle?"

Lisa stared toward the plugged opening in the roof and kicked some of the dried bat guano. "The cyanobacteria needed a way to fly the coop. And since they were already sharing this cavern with some bats, they took advantage of those wings."

"Wait. How do you know they used the bats?"

"The *Bunyavirus*. It loves arthropods, which include insects and crustaceans. But strains of *Bunyavirus* can also be found in mice and *bats*."

"So you think the Judas Strain is a mutated bat virus?"

"Yes. Mutated by the cyanobacteria's neurotoxins."

"But why?"

"To drive the bats crazy, to scatter them out into the world, carrying a virus that invades the local biosphere through its bacteria. Basically turning each bat into a little biological bomb. Laying waste wherever it lands. If Susan is correct, the pool would send out these bio-bombs every *three* years, allowing the environment to replenish itself in between."

"But how does that serve the cyanobacteria if the disease kills birds and animals *outside* the cavern?"

"Ah, because it utilizes a third host, another accomplice. *Arthropods*. Remember, arthropods are already the preferred host for *Bunyaviruses*. Insects and crustaceans. They also happen to be nature's best scavengers. Cleaning up the dead. Which is what the virus compelled them to do. By first making them ravenously hungry . . ."

Lisa's words stumbled as she remembered the cannibalism aboard the ship. She fought to stay clinical, to be understood. "After stimulating this hunger, ensuring a thorough cleanup, the virus rewired the host to return here, to this cavern, to haul their catch and bring it to the pit, to feed the bacterial pool. They had no choice. Similar to the fluke and the ant. A neurological compulsion, a migratory urge."

"Like Susan," Gray said.

Lisa grew grim at the comparison. She pictured in her head the life cycle she had just described. Triangular rather than linear: cyanobacteria, bats, and arthropods. All joined together by the Judas Strain.

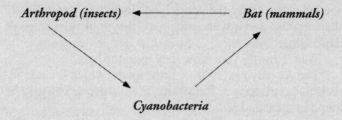

Arthropod (insects) ◄————————— *Bat (mammals)*

Cyanobacteria

"Susan is different," Lisa said. "Man was never supposed to be part of this life cycle. But being mammalian, like the bat, we're susceptible to the toxins, to the virus. So when the Khmer discovered this cavern, we inadvertently became a part of that life cycle, taking the place of the bats. Spreading via our two legs instead of wings. Sickening the population every three years, triggering epidemics of varying severity."

Gray stared toward Susan. "But what about her? Why did she survive?"

"Like I said, I don't have all the answers." She remembered her earlier discussions about Black Plague survivors, about viral code in human DNA. "Our neurological systems are a thousandfold more complex than any bat or crab. And like the cyanobacteria, humans also have a great capacity to adapt. Throw these toxins into our more advanced neurological system, and who knows what miracle might churn out?"

Lisa sighed as they reached the spit of land.

As she turned, she noted a strange sight above. Puffs of smoke streamed out of the pair of the idol's eyeholes, brightly lit by the sun's fire.

"The neutralizing powder," Gray said, spotting the same and hurrying them along. "Nasser must be finalizing the upper vault's decontamination. We have no more time."

11:39 A.M.

AT THE TOP of the stairs Vigor knelt beside the low stone door. Seichan held the flashlight behind him. An archway of limestone framed a slab of hewn sandstone, a mix of natural and man-made.

Above the door, set into the limestone's arched lintel, was a bronze medallion, impressed into it was a perfect crucifix. Vigor had examined it, sensing Friar Agreer's hand here.

And it was confirmed below.

Vigor ran his fingers over the stone door. The solid slab had been inscribed with writing. Not angelic. Italian. It was the last testament of Friar Agreer.

In the year of the incarnation of the Son of God 1296, I set to stone this final prayer. The curse was set upon me when I first arrived and caused me great suffering, but I arose like Lazarus from a deadly slumber. I do not understand what bedevilment has befallen me, but I was preserved, marked in some strange manner, feverish bright of skin. For such succor, I ministered to those few who survived the great pestilence. But now a strange compunction has come over me. The waters below already begin to boil with the fires from Hell. I know it is to my death that I am driven. With great effort I did convince and oversee the construction of this seal. And I go with only one prayer on my lips. More than my own soul's salvation, I pray this door to be forever sealed with the Lord's Cross. Let only one strong in the spirit of the Lord dare open it.

Vigor touched the carved signature at the bottom.

Friar Antonio Agreer.

Seichan spoke behind him. "So after Marco left, they exposed the friar to the disease, but rather than dying, he survived. Like the woman below."

"Maybe the other glowing pagans who offered the cure to Marco's party could tell Friar Agreer would survive. That is why they picked him. But the date, 1296. He lived here for three years. The same time span Susan described between eruptions." Vigor glanced behind him. "She was right."

Seichan waved to the door. "There's more writing under the name."

Vigor nodded. "A quote from the Bible, book of Matthew, chapter twenty-eight, concerning the resurrection of Jesus from his tomb." Vigor read the quote aloud. " 'Behold, there was a great earthquake, for an angel of the Lord descended from the sky, and came and rolled away the stone from the door, and sat on it.' "

"That's a lot of help."

It was.

Vigor stared up at the crucifix carved into a bronze medallion above the door. He said a silent prayer and made the sign of the cross.

Before he could finish, he felt the ground shake under his knees. A great crash of rock echoed behind him, sounding as if the cavern had collapsed.

Seichan retreated, taking the light, off to investigate. "Stay here!"

Darkness descended, chilling him. Though he could no longer read the words, they blazed in his mind.

Behold, there was a great earthquake . . .

11:52 P.M.

GRAY KNELT OVER Lisa as the resounding shock rattled through the cavern. Kowalski sheltered her other side. One of the stalactites broke away from the roof and plunged into the pool's depth. From where it had broken off, a scatter of deep cracks radiated outward, spanning the limestone roof.

Susan crouched halfway down the spar of rock as it thrust out into the glowing lake. All around the waters trembled with vibrations, sloshing back and forth. The stirring churned up more acidic wash, choking the air.

Rich with the Judas Strain.

Smaller concussions struck above, pounding like cannonballs against the roof of the cavern.

"What's happening?" Lisa yelled.

"Nasser's bomb," he gasped out, ears ringing.

Earlier, Gray had examined the foundation pillars of the Bayon. He had found the columns riddled with fissures and cracks, pressure fractures from old age and from periodic shifts in the earth. Gray imagined that the concussion of the double-strength bomb had widened the fissures even more. And then the wash of acid—splashing outward and flowing into all those cracks—had dissolved the hearts out of the pylons.

"One of the foundation pillars must have collapsed," he said. "Taking down a section of the temple with it."

Gray stared up.

The tumbling of stone blocks had stopped—but for how long? He swung around to Susan. She stood up, slowly, warily. She glanced back, plainly wanting to return to shore. But instead, she turned and continued onward.

Past her shoulders the twin beams of sunlight glowed even brighter as the noon hour struck, the full face of the sun baking down atop the ruins.

"Will it hold long enough?" Lisa asked, staring out at Susan.

"It'll have to."

Gray had no doubt that if another foundation pillar collapsed, the temple's weight would flatten this limestone bubble like a pancake. He pulled Lisa to her feet. They couldn't stay. Even if the pillars held, the lake was near to erupting.

The entire pool now glowed, from shore to shore. Where the twin beams of sunlight struck, the waters had begun to bubble, gasping out more toxin into the air, more of the Judas Strain.

They had to leave.

Down the spur of rock, Susan reached its end and sat down, hugging one knee. She kept her back to them, perhaps fearful if she saw them she would lose her nerve and come running back. She looked so alone, so frightened.

A racking cough shook through Gray. His lungs burned. He could taste the caustic toxin on his tongue. They could wait no longer.

Lisa knew it, too. Her eyes were bloodshot, weeping heavily from both the sting of the air and from the fear for her friend.

Susan had no choice. Neither did they.

They headed toward the distant archway. A flickering light halfway ahead revealed Seichan running back. Alone. Where was Vigor?

Another crack of rock blasted above.

Gray cringed, fearing another avalanche.

The reality was worse.

The stone plug shattered out of the rooftop, raining down chunks of the block. Sunlight blazed down. A large slab bearing a corner of an upturned lip splashed leadenly into the water, swamping Susan. More pieces struck like depth charges.

Triumphant voices echoed from above.

Gray heard Nasser's voice call out. "They have to be down there!"

But Nasser wasn't the worst danger at the moment.

The full face of the sun blazed unfiltered upon the lake, combusting the pool. Already primed, close to critical mass, the bubbling became an instant boil, erupting in vast expulsions, coughing up gouts of gas and water.

The pool was blowing.

They'd never make it to the stairs.

Gray backpedaled, dragging Kowalski and Lisa with him a few steps. He yelled at Seichan. "Drop flat! Now!"

He obeyed his own advice, waving Lisa and Kowalski down. Gray grabbed the abandoned tarp they'd used to transport Susan. He dragged it over all three of them, trying to trap as much air as possible.

"Pin your edges close to the stone!" he ordered the others.

Beyond the tarp he heard the crackles of boiling water, furious, hissing angry—then a deep sonorous whoop, as if the entire lake had jumped a foot then dropped. Water washed his ankles, then swept away.

The air under the tarp turned to liquid fire.

The three of them huddled, gasping, coughing, choking.

"Susan," Lisa finally croaked out.

12:00 P.M.

SUSAN SCREAMED.

She didn't cry with mere lungs, or the flutter of vocal cords. She howled out of the core of her being.

She could not escape the agony. Her mind, still attuned by sunlight, continued its detailed recording of every sensation. Forbidden from oblivion, her being scribed every detail: the sear of her lungs, the fire in her eyes, the flaying of her skin. She burned from the inside out, propelling her cry to the heavens.

But was there anyone to hear?

As she expelled all of herself upward, she finally found her release.

She fell back to the stone.

Her heart clenched one last time, squeezing out the last of her.

Then nothing.

12:01 P.M.

"WHAT ABOUT SUSAN?" Lisa gasped.

Gray risked a peek from under a flap of tarp, craning

back toward the rocky spar. The lake still boiled, burning under the fiery sun. The air above the lake shimmered with an oily miasma.

But the worst flow of gasses spiraled upward, through the opening, drafting up the flue of the Bayon's central spire, turning tower into chimney.

Gray knew it was the only reason they lived.

If the cavern had still been sealed . . .

Out on the spar another of their party had not fared as well. Susan lay sprawled on her back, as still as a statue. Gray could not tell if she was breathing. In fact, it was hard to see her shape against the glare of the sunlight.

And that's when he realized it.

The rocky spar did not extend fully into the stream of sunlight.

Susan still lay in shadow—but she no longer glowed. The brightness in her had blown out like a candle.

What did that mean?

Overhead, screams echoed down from the temple, now awash with the pool's toxic expulsion. Gray also heard more stones striking the roof of the cavern. The caustic gas had further weakened the precarious balance of stone above their heads.

"We have to get out of the cavern," Gray said.

"What about Susan?" Lisa asked.

"We'll have to trust she had enough exposure. Whatever she needed to happen, hopefully happened." Gray rolled to his knees, coughing hard. They all needed the cure now. He stared over to Kowalski. "Get Lisa to the stairs."

Kowalski pushed up. "Don't have to tell me twice."

Lisa clutched Gray's wrist as he stood, keeping the tarp over their heads. "What are you going to do?"

"I have to get Susan."

Lisa pinched around to see—then covered her mouth. The lake still roiled heavily, popping with gas. "Gray, you'll never make it."

"I'll have to."

"But I don't see her moving. I think the sudden explosion was too much."

Gray remembered Marco's story, of his forced cannibalism, drinking the blood and eating the flesh of another man to live. "I don't think it matters if she's alive or dead. We just need her body."

Lisa flinched at the callousness of his words, but she did not object.

"I'm going to need the tarp," Gray said.

Kowalski nodded, clutching Lisa by the arm. "Fine by me. I'm taking the girl."

Gray whisked away from them, cocooning himself in the tarp. He wrapped his head, leaving only a slit to peer out. He heard Kowalski and Lisa running down the strand.

Another boulder crashed onto the cavern roof from the temple above.

As good as a starter's pistol.

Keeping his head low, Gray sprinted down the causeway.

Thirty yards.

That's all.

There and back.

Steps from the shore, Gray bulled into the rising miasma of toxin. He held his breath. Still, it was like hitting a wall of fire. His eyes immediately burned, squeezing his vision to a pinpoint, while tears turned the rest of his sight into a watery blur. Barely able to see, he closed his lids, pulled the slit shut, and ran blind, counting his steps.

At thirty he risked a fast peek. An inferno greeted him.

But through the pain he spied an outflung arm. A step away. He took that step, bent down, and grabbed the arm. Luckily she no longer glowed, no longer burned. Still, he could not pick her up. He retreated, dragging her. The tarp tangled his feet, slowing him down. He finally tossed it aside, taking one breath before he did so.

It dropped him to a knee.

His chest clenched, his throat closed in protest.

Swallowing flames.

He pushed up, dragging blind, stumbling, hurrying.

His skin ran with fire, as if lashed with steel-studded whips.

Not going to make it.

Fire.

Flame.

Burn.

He tripped, went down to a knee.

No.

Then he was rising again—but not on his own.

"I've got you," she said in his ear.

Seichan.

She had an arm under him, dragging him bodily. His toes scraped the stones as he struggled to gain his footing.

He croaked at her, coughing.

She understood.

"Kowalski's got her."

"Right here, boss," the man said behind him. "That was some run. Made it to three steps shy of the goal line. Not a touchdown, but that's why you have a goddamn team."

As they fled around the lake, away from the central tempest, Gray's vision cleared. He finally found his feet.

Seichan still supported half his weight.

"Thank you," he whispered coarsely in her ear.

Her cheek was badly blistered, one eye swollen shut.

"Let's just get the hell out of here," Seichan said, sounding more irritated than relieved.

"Amen, sister," Kowalski said.

Gray glanced back to the pool. He watched something drop through the hole in the roof, dangling from a line like a baited hook. It swung back and forth a bit.

A thick, heavy satchel.

"Bomb . . ." Gray whispered.

"What?" Kowalski asked, incredulous.

"Bomb," he said louder.

Nasser was not done with them yet.

"Aw, hell, no . . ." Kowalski scrambled closer with Susan

over one shoulder, plainly trying to outrun them. "Why do people keep trying to blow me up?"

12:10 P.M.

SHOUTING ERUPTED BELOW, flowing up the stairs from the cavern.

Lisa wanted to go down. She had hated abandoning the others, but Vigor needed her help, too.

"Keep turning!" Vigor said, sweat pouring down the sides of his face. He glanced to the stairs—then back to Lisa. "From their shouting, I think we'd better hurry."

Between their palms, they had been unscrewing a large bronze bolt. Its platter-size head bore a crucifix, presently twirling as they spun the screw. By now, the greased bore protruded a full two feet from the arched top of the door.

How much more did they have to go?

They turned faster.

Vigor quoted the bottom inscription on the door, huffing as he labored.

" 'An angel of the Lord descended from the sky, and came and rolled away the stone from the door.' At first, I tried rolling the door itself, and gave that up pretty quickly. Then I remembered the last line. 'Let only one strong in the spirit of the Lord dare open it.' Plainly a nod toward the crucifix. I should've picked up on that from the outset."

Feet pounded on the lower stairs, coming up.

Kowalski yelled to them. "Bomb . . . door . . . hurry!"

"A man of few words, our Mr. Kowalski."

With a final twist, the bronze screw fell free of its socket. The weight caught them both by surprise, and the screw tumbled to the steps with a ringing clatter.

Kowalski came barreling up from below, carrying Susan. She hung limp. Kowalski's face sank when he saw the door still closed. "What have you been doing?"

"Waiting for you," Vigor said, and shoved the slab.

No longer screwed tight, the door toppled outward, crashing to the stone. Sunlight burst forth, reflecting off the stone all around. Lisa could barely see as she stumbled out with Vigor, making room for Kowalski and Susan.

Kowalski groused as he ducked through. "I thought Seichan said she tried pushing. Damn those scrawny arms of hers."

Straightening, Lisa blinked away the glare, realizing that they were at the bottom of a deep stone well, ten feet wide. The sheer walls stretched two stories high. No way up.

Kowalski lowered Susan to one side of the door. "Doc, I don't think she's breathing."

Reminded of her duty, Lisa rushed to his side. She'd had her fill of death for one day. She dropped beside Susan and checked for a pulse. She didn't find one. Still, Lisa refused to give up.

"Someone help me," she called.

Gray and Seichan fell through the door next, hobbling together. Gray noted her examination. "Lisa . . . she's dead."

"No. Not without a fight first."

"I'll help you," Seichan mumbled.

As she hobbled over, Lisa noticed blood seeping through the woman's blouse, through her pants, fresh and wet.

Seichan noted her attention. "I'm fine."

Gray warned them to keep as quiet as possible—in case any of Nasser's men were nearby. He also waved everyone away from the doorway. His face and arms were blistered and raw. The whites of his eyes were a solid blood red.

On the other side of the doorway, Lisa began cardiac compressions while Seichan performed mouth-to-mouth. Vigor stood nearby, crossing a blessing over Susan.

"Those better not be last rites," Lisa whispered, keeping her elbows locked as she compressed.

Vigor shook his head. "Just a prayer for—"

The bomb blasted with a clap of thunder, shuddering the ground underfoot. A wash of foul air shot out from below, a poisonous exhalation still ripe with caustic fumes and a blast of heat.

Lisa leaned over Susan.

The worst of it all plumed up the shaft and away.

"That wasn't too bad," Kowalski said.

Gray continued staring high. "Everybody hold tight."

Lisa glanced up as she pumped her arms on Susan's chest.

To the left, the top half of the Bayon's center spire could be seen. Stone faces gazed back down at them. All of them were shaking.

"It's coming down!" Gray said.

12:16 P.M.

NASSER FLED WITH six of his men, racing across the second tier's courtyard. Every step was agony. His entire body continued to burn, as if the hellish woman were still clutched to him. But he had a more immediate concern.

He glanced back as he ducked behind a gallery wall.

The Bayon tower trembled—then in an oddly slow fashion, it collapsed in on itself, imploding and dropping a quarter of its height with a rumble of stone. The death rattle of a hundred bodhisattvas. Stone dust flumed around the collapsed pile, shooting high. More rocks continued to bounce and roll, chattering down the mountainside.

His demolition expert had warned against the size of the charge, warned this might happen. But Nasser could not risk Commander Pierce escaping with the prize.

As he turned away he noted a second plume of smoky dust, rising off to the side. It twisted up like a gray smoke signal.

Nasser's eyes narrowed.

Did it mark another exit to the cavern?

12:17 P.M.

GRAY CHOKED ON the dust, barely able to see anyone else in the confined space of the well. The tower had crashed, collapsing into its foundations and crushing the cavern below. An acidic wash of smoke and dust jetted outward, spiraling up the well's throat.

Gray wiped his eyes and twisted around. He searched back through the doorway. Boulders filled the steep stairway, its ceiling collapsed.

Gray leaned his shoulder against the wall and stared up. The north wall of the well leaned precariously outward. They'd been lucky it hadn't collapsed and crushed them all. A few of the blocks stuck out like buckteeth.

More coughing echoed around the well.

The dust cleared enough to reveal one of the sufferers.

Lisa helped Susan sit up. The woman covered her mouth with a fist and continued a racking jag.

Welcome back to the world.

Maybe their luck was turning.

A voice, calling down from above, dismissed that possibility.

"Who do we have here?" Nasser yelled down. "To use a quaint American colloquialism, I'd say we've found a bunch of fish in a barrel."

Rifles circled the well on all sides, pointing down at them.

Gray slid along the wall, bumping into Kowalski.

"What now, boss?" he asked.

Before Gray could answer, a cell phone rang out sharply. It came from above, but the ring tone was familiar. Nasser reached to a pocket and removed Vigor's phone. He had confiscated it from the monsignor after they had been captured at the hotel. They'd all been thoroughly searched before their sit-down at the Elephant Bar.

Nasser checked the caller ID. "Rachel Verona." He held the phone over the pit, leaning out. "Your niece, Monsignor. Would you care to say good-bye?"

The phone rang a third time, then went silent.

"I guess not," Nasser said. "A shame."

Gray closed his eyes and held his breath.

Nasser continued. "Or maybe, Commander Pierce, you'd like to call my partner, Annishen. I did promise you'd hear your parents' screams before you died."

Gray ignored him. His hand slipped behind Kowalski's back and under the man's long duster jacket. The interrupted call from Vigor's niece was a prearranged signal, from Painter, to let Gray know when his mother and father were safe.

Or dead.

Either way . . . beyond Nasser's control.

Gray's fingers wrapped around the butt of the pistol lodged at the base of Kowalski's back. The large man had almost yanked the gun out earlier, startled by a monkey. Luckily Gray had stopped him.

Gray pulled the pistol free and lowered it to his side.

Nasser continued. "Or maybe I'll just leave your parents' fate a mystery . . . leave you forever wondering, something to take to your grave."

"Why don't you go first . . ." Gray stepped forward, snapped his weapon up, and fired twice.

He clipped the man in the shoulder and the chest. The impacts spun Nasser sideways. He fell into the well, arms flailing, spraying blood against the stone walls.

Gray twisted on a heel, strafing along the well's rim. He struck three more men while the others fled back. Behind him, Nasser crashed to the stone floor, with a snap of bones and a cry.

Gray scanned above, his weapon ready. The 9mm Metal Storm pistol was an Australian design, the ultimate in power, firing off multiple rounds in fractions of a second. Propellant-driven, no moving parts, all electronic.

"Lisa, check Nasser for Vigor's phone! Get Painter on the line!"

She shuffled behind him.

As he slowly turned, guarding the well, Gray noted Nasser out of the corner of an eye. He lay on his back, one arm twisted under him, broken at the shoulder. Blood bubbled from his lips. Shattered ribs. But he still lived. Eyes tracking Gray, full of dismay and confusion.

Die wondering, you bastard.

Nasser finally obeyed, sighing out his last breath, eyes going blank.

Seichan voiced Nasser's question. "So where did you get the gun?"

"I arranged it with Painter. Back in Hormuz. I didn't want him to mobilize any local teams here. But I did ask for one small concession. A single gun, smuggled into the Elephant Bar bathroom before we ever got there, taped behind a toilet. I knew Nasser might still be suspicious of me, even search me multiple times. But Kowalski . . ."

Gray shrugged.

"At the bar, I remember," Seichan said. "Before we left. Kowalski said he had to 'take a leak.' "

"I knew we'd be searched before the meeting at the bar. It was the easiest way to get a gun to us afterward. To keep it close until my parents were safe."

Kowalski grunted. "Jackass should've watched the goddamn *Godfather* a few more times."

Lisa called behind him. "I have Painter on the line."

Gray's fingers tightened on his pistol. "My parents? Are they—?"

"I already asked. They're safe. And unharmed."

Gray let out a long breath of relief.

Thank God.

He cleared his throat. "You'd better tell Painter to set up a quarantine perimeter, at least a ten mile radius around the ruins."

Gray pictured the cloud of toxic gases, surely rich with the Judas Strain. The gateway had been open for only twelve minutes, slammed closed and bleached by Nasser's bomb.

A small blessing there. But how much of the Judas Strain had gotten loose?

Gray glanced at Susan. She huddled in the doorway. Kowalski guarded her. Had she succeeded? Gray was aware of everyone who shared the well with him. Each had contributed in no small measure to get them here. But had it all been in vain?

Lisa spoke up. "Quarantine's under way."

Gray searched the top of the well, weapon high. There was still a Guild army out there. "Then tell Painter we could use some help here, too."

She relayed the message—then lowered the phone. "He says it's already on the way. He said *look up*."

Gray glanced skyward. The rich blue of the afternoon sky swirled with stiff-looking hawks, wings wide. Scores of them, converging from all directions. But these hawks carried assault rifles.

Reaching a hand back, Gray asked for the phone.

Lisa slapped it into his palm.

Gray put the receiver to his ear. "I thought we agreed *not* to mobilize a local response."

"Commander, I don't exactly classify forty thousand feet in the air as *local*. And besides, I'm your boss. Not the other way around."

Gray continued to watch the skies.

The strike team plummeted toward the ruins, spreading out in an attack pattern. Each soldier had a fixed-wing glider harnessed to his back, like miniature wings of a jet fighter, allowing for high-altitude deployment.

They dove downward.

Spiraling and spiraling.

Then on one signal, each man pulled his ripcord, all shedding wings in unison. Glide chutes deployed, snapping wide for the last stretch of their descent. Like a choreographed dance, they swooped in from all directions.

Others noted the dramatic approach. Gray heard boots

pounding on stone, most heading away. Gray imagined black berets were being stuffed into garbage cans as the Guild's mercenaries hightailed it out of here.

But not all were so craven.

A few spats of rifle fire echoed. Slow at first, then furiously. A firefight raged for a full, tense minute. A glide chute swept overhead, the pilot firing on the fly. Then another, his legs lifted high as he prepared to alight on the ruins. Bodies thudded, landing all around the well, probably zeroed in on the phone in Gray's hand.

A man suddenly lunged over the well's low wall, a bit too quickly.

Gray came close to shooting him until he recognized the jumpsuit.

U.S. Air Force.

"You blokes all okay?" he called down in an Aussie accent, unhooking his chute.

Lisa shoved past Vigor, her voice full of amazement. "Ryder?"

The man grinned down at her. "That man of yours . . . Painter . . . bonzer bloke! Let me come along for the ride. It's not climbing over electrified nets with cannibals . . . but then what is?"

Someone called out.

Ryder lifted an arm, acknowledging, then glanced back down. "Hold fast! Ladders on their way!" He rolled away and vanished.

Gray continued to keep guard over those here, his weapon ready.

It was all he could do.

That, and one last thing.

He lifted the phone to his ear again. "Director?"

"Yes?"

"Thank you for not listening to me, sir."

"That's what I'm here for."

19

Traitor

A WEEK LATER Lisa stood at the window to her room in a private hospital outside of Bangkok. Tall walls surrounded the small two-story facility and its lush gardens of papaya trees, flowering lotus, sparkling fountains, along with a few quiet statues of Buddha wrapped in saffron robes, trailing thin spikes of smoke from morning prayer sticks.

She had said her own prayers at dawn this morning.

Alone.

For Monk.

The window stood open, the shutters thrown back for the first time in a week. Their quarantine was over. She took a deep breath, inhaling the scent of jasmine and orange blossoms. Beyond the wall she heard the slow bustle of village life: the lowing of oxen, the chatter of a pair of elderly women passing the gates, the heavy tread of an elephant dragging a log, and best of all, unseen, but as vibrant as sunshine, the laughter of children.

Life.

How close had they come to losing it all?

"Did you know," a voice said behind her, "that standing in front of the window, the sun shines right through that hospital gown? Leaves very little to the imagination. Not that I'm complaining."

She turned, swelling with joy.

Painter leaned against the door frame, holding a paper-wrapped bundle of yellow roses, her favorite. He was dressed in a suit, no tie, clean-shaven and scrubbed. He had a slight tan after a week in the tropics, out of Sigma's subterranean lair, setting off the spark to his blue eyes and dark hair.

"I thought you weren't going to be back here until late tonight," she said, stepping away.

He entered the room. Unlike the sterility of most hospital accommodations, the private facility had rooms lavishly appointed in teak. It was also adorned with vases of flowers, even a pair of fishbowls, swimming with tiny, orange-and-crimson goldfish.

"The meeting with the Cambodian prime minister was postponed until next week. And is probably unnecessary. Even the quarantine there will be ending within the next few days."

Lisa nodded. Crop dusters had spread a weak solution of disinfectant over the outlying areas. The ruins of Angkor Thom had been soaked thoroughly. The refugee quarantine camps had revealed some cases, but they were responding to treatment.

The cure had worked.

Susan was in another wing of the hospital, under the strictest guard, but even that was proving an unnecessary caution. She had indeed come forth with the cure, walking through fire to do it. Afterward, there remained no trace of the virus—*cis* or *trans*—inside her. It was all gone.

Except for the cure.

It proved not to be an antibody, or an enzyme, or even a white blood cell. It was bacteria. The same cyanobacteria that had made her glow.

The second toxic exposure had altered the bacteria yet again, churning the life cycle fully around. Like healthy lactobacillus in yogurt, the bacteria, when ingested or inoculated, produced beneficial compounds that destroyed any toxic bacteria generated by the Judas Strain and scavenged away all trace of the virus itself, digesting it.

The cure produced symptoms equivalent to a mild flu, then you were immune from further reinfection. The bacteria also appeared to act as a vaccine in healthy subjects, offering immunity against exposure, similar to the Salk's vaccine against polio. But best of all, the bacteria also proved easy to culture. Samples had been passed to laboratories around the world. Vast quantities were already being generated, a global storehouse to stamp out the early pandemic and protect the world from any future recurrence.

Health organizations continued to remain vigilant against such an event.

"What about Christmas Island, where it all started?" Lisa asked, sitting at the edge of her bed.

Painter replaced some wilting flowers with his roses. "Looking good. By the way, I read some of the papers your friend Jessie stole from the cruise ship before it sank. Apparently, as the Guild departed Christmas Island, they had dumped a tanker load of bleach along the windward shoreline. Not out of any altruism, mind you. Just trying to wipe out the major bloom, to confound any competitors to their discovery."

"Do you think that will keep the bloom from reappearing?"

Painter shrugged, stepped to the bed, and sat down. He took her hand—not in any purposeful way, just reflex, which was why she loved him so much.

"Hard to say," he answered. "The typhoon swept over the island. International teams of marine scientists are monitoring the waters—led by Dr. Richard Graff. After his help with the crab situation . . . figured he deserved the assignment."

Lisa squeezed Painter's hand. The mention of Graff only reminded Lisa of Monk. She sighed, watching the twirl of goldfish in the bedside bowl.

Painter freed his hand, put his arm around her shoulders, and pulled her close. His other hand found hers again. He knew where her heart lay at the moment. His voice dropped to a soft rumble, setting aside some of his playfulness.

"You heard we were interviewing all the survivors of the *Mistress of the Seas.*"

She didn't answer, just slid her arm around his waist. She knew the news to come was bad.

The island was still under quarantine, a joint venture between Australia and the United States. Australian commandos had been able to orchestrate a massive evacuation of the ship as it burned and sank. Most of the Guild's work now rested a thousand feet underwater, a new addition to the deepwater home of the predatory squids. It made diving on the wreck extremely dangerous. The squids had been classified as a new species of *Taningia,* granted the name *Taningia tunis* in the memory of Susan's husband.

Yesterday Lisa had spoken over the phone with Henri and Jessie at the refugee camp on Pusat. They had survived, managing to protect most of the patients and WHO staff, aided by the cannibals during the chaos. Everyone was now undergoing treatment, and so far, faring well. The only exceptions were those few who had passed into a full maddened rave. The brain damage appeared permanent. Most of the afflicted had died when the ship sank. Not a single member of the Guild team made it off the ship alive.

Except perhaps one.

Jessie had told Lisa a story of the evacuation. He had come upon a padlocked hold. He heard children crying inside. He had broken through in time to rescue the children, who told the story of a strange angel who came and gathered them all together, locking them up out of harm's way. This angel had then led a group of the ravening patients away from the hold, using herself as bait.

The children had described their angel.

Flowing black hair, dressed in silk, silent as the grave.

Surina.

She had vanished away.

Painter continued. "We interviewed everyone in camp."

"About Monk," she whispered.

"One of the WHO doctors had been hiding out on the ship's deck. He had binoculars. He watched your escape in the *Sea Dart*. Through binoculars, he saw Monk fall, witnessed the net dropping over him, dragging him down." Painter paused to take a tired breath. "He never resurfaced."

Lisa closed her eyes. She felt something burst inside, spreading a burning acid through her veins, weakening her. A part of her still had been hoping . . . some thin chance . . . It was why she had knelt outside before one of the Buddhas.

She had been praying he was still alive.

"He's gone," she murmured, fully admitting it to herself. *Oh, Monk . . .*

Lisa hugged tight to Painter. Her tears soaked through his shirt. Fingers clenched to him as she assured herself with his physicality. "Have you told Kat yet?" she mumbled, resting her cheek against his chest.

Painter remained silent.

Lisa felt him tremble.

He had.

She pulled his hand from her shoulder and kissed his palm.

He spoke in a whisper, coarse and deep. "Don't you ever leave me."

Lisa remembered why she had gone on this mission. To evaluate her life outside of Painter's shadow. To get some perspective as their lives merged together, professionally and personally.

She had learned her answer.

From cannibal attacks to the tortures of madmen.

She knew she was strong enough to stand alone.

But . . .

She leaned up, kissing his lips, whispering.
"This is where I belong."

12:02 P.M.

GRAY CROSSED DOWN the hospital's garden path. He had
changed into jeans, boots, and an untucked shirt with a
tropical print. It was good to be in regular clothes, to shed
the hospital gowns. It also felt good to be outside, under the
sun, though his lungs still felt heavy and the bright light
stung his sensitive eyes. He was still healing, but his rest-
less energy after a week indoors had built to an edgy
irritation.

His pace quickened, his stride lengthening. He had circled the entire garden, full around the building. He wanted
no surprises.

He had been plotting this for the past three days, and now
the timetable had been moved up. The gate to the hospital
appeared ahead.

They were allowed to leave, but only as far as the surrounding village.

Rounding a corner of a tall hedgerow, Gray came upon a
small alcove, a private altar with a fat Buddha draped in red
silk. A few smudge sticks lay on the ground, but currently
the smoke came from another source.

Kowalski leaned on the Buddha, a palm atop the stone
head. He removed the cigar from his mouth, puffing a long
thick cloud.

"Oh, yeah . . ." he moaned in grudging contentment.

"Where did you get a—oh, never mind." Gray held out a
hand. "Were you able to find what I asked for?"

Kowalski stubbed out his cigar on the Buddha's
shoulder.

Even Gray cringed a bit at the casual sacrilege.

"Yeah, but what do you want with all this?" he asked, and

lifted a paper-wrapped bundle from behind his back. "I bribed my nurse while getting a sponge bath. Of course it was a guy. Took all the fun out of it. But he was able to buy what you wanted."

Gray took the package and turned to head off.

Kowalski crossed his arms, his brows heavy with disappointment, even heaving out an irritated sigh.

Gray stepped back. "What's the matter?"

Kowalski opened his mouth—then closed it.

"What?" Gray pressed.

Kowalski flipped his hands in the air. "First . . . well, all this time, I didn't get to shoot a single goddamn gun. Not a rifle, not a pistol, not a popgun! I mean I might as well have been on guard duty back home. All I got for my troubles was a bunch of needles stuck in my ass."

Gray stood a moment, staring. It was the longest speech Kowalski had ever given. He was plainly passionate on the subject.

"I'm just saying . . ." Kowalski blurted, suddenly mildly chagrined.

Gray sighed. "Come with me." He stalked off and headed toward the gate. He did owe the guy.

Kowalski followed. "Where we going?"

Gray led him to the gate. The guards on duty nodded to them. Gray tucked the package under his arm and fished out his wallet. He stripped out a bill and passed it to Kowalski as they stepped through the gate.

"What am I supposed to do with ten dollars?" he asked.

Gray stepped farther out and pointed down the road to where a work crew labored. Thailand-style. Four men and their two work animals.

"Look . . . elephants," Gray said.

Kowalski stared down the dirt track, down to the bill in his hands, then back out to the elephants. A giant grin split his face. He strode off, turned back, struggled to express his thanks, failed, then headed down the road again.

"Oh, yeah, I'm all over this elephant ride . . ." He lifted his arm. "Hey, you! Gunga Din!"

Gray turned around and headed back inside.

Poor elephant.

12:15 P.M.

VIGOR RESTED IN his bed. He had a pair of reading glasses perched on his nose. He had books piled on his nightstand, crowding his goldfish bowl. He had articles printed out and stacked on the other side of the hospital bed: on angelic script, on Marco Polo, on the history of the Khmers, on the ruins of Angkor.

He was presently rereading for the fourth time the scientific report Gray had cited, an article in *Science* magazine from 1994, relating the study of human language to DNA code.

Fascinating . . .

Motion at his open door drew his attention from the paper. He spotted Gray. "Commander Pierce!" he called out.

Gray paused at the door, checked his watch, then leaned in. "Yes, Monsignor."

Vigor was surprised at the formality. Something had set Gray on edge. He waved the man inside. "Come in for a moment."

"I have just that . . . a moment." He stepped inside. "How are you feeling?"

"Fine." Vigor waved away such matters. "I read this article. I didn't realize that only three percent of our genome is active. That a full *ninety-seven percent* is junk and codes for nothing. Yet, when this junk is run through the cryptography program testing for language, even such random garbage also reveals a language. Amazing." Vigor took off his glasses. "Gray, what if we could understand that language?"

Gray nodded. "Some things may be forever beyond us."

Vigor scowled gently. "Now I certainly don't believe that.

God didn't give us these big brains and not want us to use them. We were born to question, to search, to strive for a fuller understanding of the universe, both external and internal."

Gray checked his watch again, subtly, a flick of his eyes down to his wrist, not wanting to appear rude.

Vigor decided to quit torturing the young man. He plainly was busy. "I'll get to my point. Remember back in the barrel vault beneath the Bayon, I mentioned how the angelic script—the possible written form of this unknown genetic language—could be the Word of God mapping out something greater in us, maybe something buried in that ninety-seven percent of our genetic code that is considered *junk*. What if it's not junk? Maybe we even caught a glimpse of that greater part of us."

"How do you mean?"

"The woman Susan. Maybe her transformation was a peek into the true translation of the angelic script?"

Vigor read the disbelief in the commander's face and held up a hand. "I talked to Lisa earlier this morning. She mentioned how she believed Susan's brain was fully excited by the energies of the bacteria when exposed to sunlight, awakening those parts of the human brain that are otherwise dormant. I find it interesting that only a tiny fraction of our genetic code is active, and at the same time, we only utilize a small portion of our brain. Don't you find that odd?"

Gray shrugged, noncommittal. "I suppose."

Vigor continued. "What if all that angelic script maps out our *full* potential, that which still remains hidden in all of us, waiting to be awakened? According to the book of Genesis, God made us in his image. What if that image is yet to be fully realized, buried in dormant sections of our brain, hidden within the angelic language of our junk DNA? Maybe all that script written on the walls under the Bayon, glowing in the dark, maybe the ancient writer was attempting to understand that potential, too. You mentioned yourself how it was incomplete, sections missing."

"That's true," Gray conceded. "And you raise some interesting conjectures worth exploring, but I don't know if we'll ever know the truth. Susan is back to normal, and I heard from Painter that an excavation team was able to breach the foundation vault beneath the Bayon. Some of the walls were found intact, but Nasser's acid bomb had stripped the surfaces clean. Nothing remains of the script."

Vigor felt his heart sink. "A shame. Still, I wonder about something that we never found down in the cavern."

"What's that?"

"Your turtle," Vigor said. "You thought that the vault might contain a deeper mystery, something that represents the incarnation of Vishnu."

"Maybe it was just the Judas Strain. The glowing pool. Even you mentioned how the ancient Khmer probably stumbled upon the glowing cavern and attributed it to some god's home. Maybe Vishnu's."

Vigor stared at the commander. "Or maybe Susan was a glimpse of that greater mystery, a peek at the godlike or angelic potential hidden inside all of us."

Gray finally shrugged, plainly ready to dismiss it. But as Vigor had hoped, he noted a slight pinch to the man's brows. Curiosity. He wanted Gray to keep his mind open.

Still, Vigor also saw that something more urgently pressed upon the man's mind and attention. He waved Gray out.

Vigor called to him as he stepped out the door. "Give my best to Seichan."

Gray stumbled a step, frowned a bit, and headed away.

Vigor replaced his reading glasses.

Ah, sweet youth . . .

12:20 P.M.

GRAY HANDED THE cup of coffee to the guard outside Seichan's door. "Is she awake?"

He shrugged, a young sandy-haired ensign from Peoria. "Don't know."

Gray pushed through the door. It was a dull assignment for the ensign. The patient was almost continuously sedated after going through a second operation for her gunshot wound. Seichan had retorn her injury and had been bleeding internally.

All because she had saved Gray's life.

He remembered Seichan's arms carrying him, the pain in her blistered face, her swollen eye. But he hadn't known that by coming back for him she had almost died.

Gray entered her room.

She lay handcuffed to her bed, arms spread to either side.

She wore a hospital gown and was covered with a clean sheet.

The room, built for mental patients, was sterile and cold. The only furniture was the bed and a rolling stand shoved against the wall. A high, narrow window had steel shutters over it.

Seichan stirred as he entered. She turned her head. Her face hardened with a slight downcast to her eyes, ashamed at her immobilization. Then anger flared up and burned all else away. She tugged at one of her handcuffed wrists.

Gray came and sat on the bed.

"Even though my parents are alive," he started right in, "that doesn't mean I forgive you. That I'll ever forgive you. But I do owe you. I won't let you die. Not this way."

Gray pulled the handcuff keys from his pocket. He reached out and lifted her wrist. He felt her pulse quicken under his fingertips.

"They're sending you to Guantánamo Bay in the morning," he said.

"I know."

And like Gray, she also knew it was a death sentence. If she wasn't immediately executed, the Guild would assassinate her to silence her, or one of the other intelligence agencies would. The Israeli Mossad still had an open kill order on her.

He slipped in the key and turned the lock. Her cuff snapped open.

Seichan sat up, still wearing a glint of suspicion.

She held out her palm for the key, testing him.

He gave it to her. As she undid her second cuff, Gray placed the package Kowalski had obtained on the bed.

"I have three sets of clothes: a nurse's uniform, local attire, and something in camouflage. There's also local currency. I couldn't do anything about ID, not on this short notice."

Seichan's other handcuff snapped free. Turning, she rubbed her wrists.

The soft sound of a body hitting the floor sounded past the door.

"Oh, and I drugged the guard."

She glanced to the door, then back to him. Her eyes sparked. Before he could move, she lunged, grabbed his collar, and pulled him to her. She kissed him hard, her mouth parting, tasting sweetly medicinal.

Gray instinctively pulled back. He hadn't come here to—

Oh, screw it . . .

He reached to the small of her back and cupped her tightly to him. Never releasing, she climbed into him, onto him, over him. Her feet lowered to the floor. He twisted, falling back.

He heard the *snick* of shackles.

She pushed off of him.

His right wrist had been handcuffed to the bed.

He glanced up in time to see her elbow swinging toward his face.

His head cracked back. He tasted blood on his lips.

She leaped on him, pinning him to the bed, sitting on his chest. She raised her fist. He lifted his free arm to block. She cocked her head. "This has to look convincing, or you'll be the one sitting in Guantánamo for treason."

She was right.

Gray lowered his arm.

She struck him hard, splitting his lip. His head rang with the blow. She shook the sting from her hand—then raised her fist again.

"And this is for not trusting me," she said, and lashed out again.

Blood spurted from his nose. He felt himself drift away, then back again.

She leaned down, near his ear. "Do you remember that little promise I made to you at the very beginning?"

"What's that?" He turned to the side and spat.

"That I'd reveal the mole to you after this was all over."

"But there was no mole."

"Are you certain of that?"

Her eyes hovered over his. Suddenly he wasn't so sure.

She sat back and whipped out with her elbow, a glancing blow to his eye.

"Christ!"

"That'll swell fine." She rubbed her lips, studying him, like an artist over an oil painting in progress. Then said, "I'm the mole, Gray."

"What—?"

"A mole planted inside the Guild."

She slammed a fist into his other eye. His vision went black for a breath.

"I'm one of the good guys, Gray. Haven't you figured that out yet?"

Gray lay there dazed, from her words, from her blows.

"A double agent?" he coughed out, incredulous. "Two years ago, you shot me! Point-blank in the chest."

She cocked her fist again. "I knew you had on liquid body armor. Didn't you ever wonder why I was wearing the same? Catch a clue, Gray."

Her fist hammered down, rocking his head back. She then pinched the bridge of his nose, plainly wondering if she should break it.

"And the anthrax bomb," he said. "At Fort Detrick?"

"Already sterilized. A dud. I was planning on blaming the bomb's designer."

"But . . . the curator in Venice?" he sputtered out. "You killed him in cold blood."

She slashed her fingernails down his left cheek, digging deep furrows of fire. "If I hadn't, his whole family would have been slaughtered. Including wife and daughter."

Wincing, Gray stared up. She had an answer for everything.

Seichan leaned back, cranking the heel of her hand up to her ear, eyeing his nose. "And I'm not stopping . . . not after five years, not when I'm this damn close to discovering who leads the Guild."

She punched down, but he caught her wrist this time.

She leaned her weight, pressing down on him.

"Seichan . . ."

She stared down at him, muscles straining, eyes fiery, as if in pain. Their eyes met. She searched his face, looking for something. She didn't seem to find it. For a flash, he saw disappointment in her eyes. Also regret . . . maybe loneliness. Then it was gone.

She slammed him with her other elbow, a blow to the ear, scattering stars across his vision. He released her. She fell back, scrambling off of him.

"That'll do," she mumbled, turning away.

She crossed to the clothes, shed her hospital gown, and quickly donned the nurse's uniform, including a demure silk scarf to hide her healing face. She kept her back to him.

"Seichan?"

Once dressed, she didn't say a word, only stepped to the door. She wouldn't even turn, only asked one last thing of him, spoken softly, a lifeline thrown back toward him.

"Trust me, Gray. If only a little. I've earned that much."

Before he could answer, she left. The door swung closed behind her.

Trust me . . .

Heaven help him, he did.

He shoved up in the bed, his face throbbing, his one eye swelling.

Fifteen minutes passed. Long enough to ensure that she escaped.

Finally Painter appeared at the door, pushing inside.

"Did you get all that?" Gray asked.

"The wire picked up everything."

"Could she be telling the truth?"

Painter frowned, staring back at the door. "She is a consummate liar."

"Maybe she had to be. To survive inside the Guild."

Painter undid the handcuffs. "Either way, the passive tracer we planted in her belly during the operation will allow us to track her whereabouts."

"And what if the Guild finds it?"

"It's a plastic polymer, invisible to X-ray. They'll never detect it."

Unless they cut her open.

Gray stood up. "This is wrong. You know it."

"It was the only way the government would allow us to free her."

Gray remembered Seichan's eyes, staring down at him.

He knew two truths.

She had not been lying.

And even now, she was certainly far from free.

Epilogue

AUGUST 11, 8:32 A.M.
Takoma Park, Maryland

"THE RESTORATION JOB looks great," Gray said.

His father slid a cloth moist with Turtle Wax over the hood of the Thunderbird. They had rescued the convertible out of impound, towing it away on a flatbed. Painter had arranged to have the T-bird repaired at the best classic restoration shop in the D.C. area. His father had gotten it back last week, but this was the first time Gray had seen it.

His father stepped back, hands on his hips. He wore an oil-stained undershirt and long shorts, showing off his new leg, another courtesy of Sigma, DARPA-designed, exceptionally realistic. But it wasn't the leg that concerned his father at the moment.

"Gray, what do you think of these new rims? Not as nice as my old Kelsey wire wheels."

Gray came around to stand next to his dad. They looked the same to him. "You're right," he said anyway. "These suck."

"Hmm," his father said noncommittally. "But they were free. That Painter fellow was pretty generous."

Gray could get a sense of where this was leading. "Dad . . ."

"Your mother and I talked it over," he said, still staring at the wheels. "We think you should stay with Sigma."

Gray scratched his head. He already had his letter of resignation in his pocket. When he had returned from Cambodia, he had found his father in the hospital, his chest burned from Taser strikes. His mother's arm was in a sling from a minor fracture to her wrist. The worst was his mother's black eye.

All because of him.

He had almost lost it in the hospital.

What security could he offer his parents if he continued? The Guild certainly knew who he was, where to find his folks. The only way to keep them safe was to resign. Painter tried to assure him that the Guild would back off. That retribution and retaliation were not their methods. In future missions, Painter had assured Gray his parents would be secured before he left.

But some missions came crashing up your driveway in a motorcycle.

There was no way to plan against that.

"Gray," his father pressed, "what you do is important. You can't let worries about us stop you."

"Dad . . ."

He lifted his hand. "I've said my piece. You make your own decision. I have to figure out if I like these rims or not."

Gray started to turn away.

His father reached out, grabbed his shoulder, and pulled him into a one-armed hug. He gave him one squeeze—then pushed him away a bit. "Go see what your mother is burning for breakfast."

Gray crossed to the back door and met his mother coming out.

"Oh, Gray, I just got off the phone with Kat. She said you were heading over there this morning."

"Before I go to the office. I have some of Monk's stuff on the front porch. Dad's letting me borrow the T-bird so I can run some errands for Kat this afternoon, too."

"I know the funeral isn't for another two days, but I have some pies. Could you take those over, too?"

"Pies?" Gray asked doubtfully.

"Don't worry. I bought them from the bakery down the street. Oh, and I have some toys for Penelope. I found this cute jumper with elephants and . . ."

He just kept nodding, knowing eventually his mother would stop.

"How is Kat holding up?" she finally finished.

Gray shook his head. "Good days and bad."

Mostly bad.

His mother sighed. "Let me get those pies. Last time I saw Kat she was thin as a rail, that poor girl."

Gray soon had a paper grocery bag stacked with boxed pies. He headed through the house to the front porch. He pushed outside and crossed to the stack of boxes. They contained everything from Monk's locker and a few things kept at Gray's apartment.

Gray also had a box to take to the funeral home. Ryder Blunt, the billionaire, had returned Monk's prosthetic hand, having to cut through the wing strut of his seaplane to free it. Kat had refused to even look at it. And Gray didn't blame her. But she did ask that the hand be added to the empty casket that would be lowered into Arlington National Cemetery. They were each supposed to also bring tokens of remembrances to include in the casket.

Gray had found a copy of Monk's favorite movie. The man had left it at Gray's apartment after a pizza-and-popcorn night. *Sound of Music*. Monk knew all the words, singing along as he bounced Penelope on his knee. Monk had the biggest heart of any man he knew.

He would've made a great father.

Gray crossed to the porch swing. He pulled out his letter of resignation folded into threes, crumpled a bit. He straightened the crinkles between his thumb and forefinger. He wished he could talk to Monk about this.

As he sat, he heard something scratching among the boxes.

The neighborhood squirrels were fearless.

Oh, damn, the pies . . .

Gray got up and crossed to the stack. But the noise wasn't coming from the bag of pies. He frowned. He shifted around until he found the right box.

What the hell?

Gray removed the top.

Painter hadn't only commissioned the repair to his father's leg and trashed T-bird. He had not wanted to send Monk's hand into the ground all charred. So he had the prosthesis meticulously restored. It rested in a foam mold.

Only now one of the fingers was digging at the foam.

Gray lifted the hand. The index finger wiggled in the air. Gray felt a shudder pass through him. What if Kat had seen this?

Must be a short in the wiring.

He set the hand down on the porch chair. The finger continued to move, tapping at the wooden seat. Gray turned away in disgust. He tugged out his cell phone, ready to blast whoever messed up at Sigma.

But as he dialed, his ear stayed morbidly attuned to the tapping. As he listened, Gray realized it drummed out a pattern.

In Morse code.

A familiar distress call.

S.O.S.

Gray swung around, staring down at the hand.

It couldn't be.

"Monk . . . ?"

2:45 P.M.
Cardamom Mountains, Cambodia

SUSAN TUNIS CLIMBED the steep ravine of the jungle-shrouded mountains, following the brilliant cascade of a waterfall. A fine mist hung in the air, scintillating in the dappled sunlight. A pileated gibbon chattered in protest at her passage, hanging from a vine by one arm, its black face framed by gray fur.

She continued onward, moving purposefully through the rain forest. The Cardamom Mountains formed the border between Cambodia and Thailand, an inhospitable land of dense forests and inaccessible hills. On her fourth day into the mountains, sleeping in a hammock under mosquito netting, she had spotted an endangered Indochinese tiger, with its stocky body and tightly drawn stripes. It slipped through the forest, uttering a low growl.

Otherwise, she hadn't seen anything larger than the howling gibbon.

Certainly no people.

Due to the isolation and difficult terrain, the mountains had once been the last refuge of the Khmer Rouge guerrillas, who retreated here because of the harsh terrain. Land mines were still a great risk.

But Susan suspected she was days past where even the guerrillas dared to tread. She reached the crest of a ridge and followed the stream across a forested plateau. Ahead, a few small shapes slipped into the water, from perches on logs.

Batagur baska.

Asian river terrapin. One of the most endangered species on the planet.

Also known as the Royal Turtle, revered as guardians of the gods.

Here they made their home.

Just past their mud nests and hibernating burrows, Susan came upon a collection of jars by the river, cylindrical clay pots standing three feet tall, scribed with lichen, carved with intricate designs. Ancient burial jars. They contained the bones of kings and queens. There were such sites scattered throughout the mountains, considered very sacred.

But no one visited this particular site, the most ancient of them all.

Susan left the river and passed through the cemetery. The

burial jars eventually thinned as the forest abutted against a cracked cliff face.

She knew where she had to go, knew from the moment she had been revived by Dr. Cummings. She had gained more than just the cure for the world—but she had told no one.

It was not the time.

Susan reached the cliff and crossed to a lightning-bolt-shaped crack, gaping two feet wide at the base. She wiggled out of her pack and turned sideways to push into the fissure. She took tiny steps, sliding deeper and deeper. Behind her, the sunlight faded, growing thinner and thinner.

Soon she was in total darkness.

Susan stretched out a hand, reaching her arm forward. A glowing fire, willed from within, ignited at her fingertips and spread down to her shoulder. She raised her arm like a lamp.

Here was another secret she had kept.

But not her greatest.

Lighting her own path, she headed deeper.

She didn't know how far she traveled, losing the firm passage of time. But it was certainly well into the night.

Eventually a glow appeared, flowing back to her.

Welcoming her.

A match to her own.

She continued at her same pace, sensing no need to hurry.

At last, she entered a great vaulted space. The source of the light became clear. Spreading far into the distance, small fires shone like a scatter of stars across the bowled floor. Hundreds and hundreds. She walked out into the cavern, passing the fires.

Each was a figure, spread-eagled on the floor, ablaze with an inner fire, burning flesh to a crystalline translucency. She stared down into one. All that remained visible was the nervous system: brain, spinal cord, and the vast tangle of peripheral nerves. The open arms, flowing with filamentous fibers, looked like unfurled wings, feathered with tufts of fine nerve bundles.

Angels in the dark.

Slumbering. Waiting.

Susan marched onward. She reached a figure who wasn't as consumed, who still showed the beat of a heart and the flow of blood, where bones still hinted at form and function.

Susan found an open spot at his side and lay down. She stretched her arms. Her fingertips brushed her neighbor.

The words reached her in an old Italian dialect, but she understood.

Is it done?

She sighed. *Yes. I am the last. The source has been destroyed.*

Then rest, child.

For how long? When will the world be ready?

He answered her. It would be a very long sleep.

What am I to do?

Go home, my child . . . for now, go home.

Susan closed her eyes and let that which needed to sleep drop away. All else, she slipped into the bubble that composed the entirety of her life and stepped through it to what lay beyond.

Light blinded as if she stared into the full face of the sun. She lowered her gaze, blinking away the glare. The world filled back in around her. The gentle rock of the boat under her bare feet. The cry of a lone gull, the hush of waves against the hull, and the sweep of wind over her skin.

Was this a dream, a memory . . . or something more?

She inhaled the salt air. A beautiful day.

She crossed to the ship's rail and stared out at the blue expanse. Green islands dotted the distance. A few clouds drifted. She heard the tread of feet on the stairs leading up from the cabin.

As she turned, he climbed into view, pulling up with his arms, dressed in shorts and an Ocean Pacific T-shirt. He spotted her, with a startled expression.

Then he smiled. "Oh, there you are."

Susan rushed to Gregg, wrapping her arms around her husband.

Downstairs, Oscar barked. A grumpy voice yelled back at the old dog.

Susan snugged against her husband, listening to the beat of his heart.

He hugged her back. "What is it, Susan?"

She stared up into Gregg's face, raised a finger to the three-day stubble on his chin. Then tipped up on her toes to reach his lips.

He bent down to meet her.

And she knew she was home.

AUTHOR'S NOTE

Truth or Fiction

ONCE AGAIN, THANKS for accompanying me on this journey! As usual, I thought I'd use these last pages to perform a postmortem on the novel, to separate fact from fiction. I've divided the postmortem by general topics:

MARCO POLO: The forward to this novel raised the central mystery concerning the fate of Polo's fleet during his return trip to Venice. What happened to the ships and men still remains a mystery. As to Marco's potential love affair with Princess Kokejin, rumors persist, especially as he died with the princess's headpiece in his possession. As to Marco's body after his death, it did indeed vanish out of the Church of San Lorenzo, its whereabouts still unknown.

ANGELIC SCRIPT AND OTHER LANGUAGE ISSUES: Angelic script was first developed by Johannes Trithemius and Heinrich Agrippa, who claimed that by studying these symbols, it was possible to communicate with angels. The script was derived from ancient Hebrew characters. Similarly, adepts of Jewish Kabbalah believe that pathways to inner wisdom can be opened by studying the shapes and curves of its characters. Finally, moving to modern times, we ask the question: Is there a hidden language buried in our genetic code? According to an article in *Science* magazine (1994), the answer is a resounding yes. Though what might be written there remains unknown.

PLAGUES: Eyam, a village in England, did indeed have an unusual survival rate during the Black Plague, a result of a genetic abnormality in half its populace. Strange but true. As to anthrax, the only difference between the deadly form of this bacterium and its peaceful garden-dwelling cousin are two rings of genetic code called *plasmids*. Which begs the question, where did those *plasmids* come from?

FAUNA: Christmas Island red land crabs do indeed have a spectacular migration each year, during which millions of the large crabs journey to the sea. Their claws have also been known to puncture tires. Moving on to those pesky liver flukes, the descriptions of their strange and disturbing life cycles are accurate. As to our predatory squids, I based them on the species *Taningia danae,* which grow to six feet in length, hunt in packs, have brilliant light displays, and bear claws on their suckers. Definitely tough calamari.

CANNIBALS AND PIRATES: Indonesian piracy is still a booming growth industry. Pick up applications at the back of the room. As to cannibals, tribes can still be found among the Indonesian islands, but you'll have to bring your own seasonings. As to the genetic condition known as Prader-Willi (resulting in insatiable appetites), it is a real and horrible condition, but is in no way related to cannibalism. Were we all once cannibals? Current research into genetics reveals humans carry a specific set of genes against diseases that can be acquired only by eating human flesh.

ANGKOR: All the details of the ruins—from the Churning of the Milk mythology to the two hundred stone bodhisattva faces—are accurate, including how the temples were laid out to mimic star patterns, specifically the constellation of Draco. For more details on this, check out *Heaven's Mirror* by Graham Hancock and Santha Faiia.

ALL THINGS BACTERIA: There are indeed milky seas of glowing algae that bloom up periodically. And according to a series of disturbing articles in the *Los Angeles Times,* our seas are increasingly threatened with the resurgence of ancient slimes, poisonous jellyfish, burning seaweeds, and toxic clouds bursting from algal blooms. As to the strangest claim in the novel: that only 10 percent of the cells in our body are human (and the rest are bacteria and parasites). This is true! There is a wonderful book exploring this topic that is as horrific as it is humorous, *Human Wildlife* by Dr. Robert Buckman. Just don't read it before you eat.

The ancient Greek Oracle of Delphi
foretold of divine purpose.

Did she predict the arrival of a gifted world prophet?

Or the destruction of mankind . . . ?

THE LAST ORACLE

**Available now
wherever books are sold**

What if you could bioengineer the next great world prophet to scientifically produce the next Buddha, the next Mohammed, or even the next Jesus?

A think tank of world scientists known as the JASONS formed during the Cold War discovered a way to enhance autistic children who show savant talents—yet a strange side effect begins to arise. Before it can be analyzed fully, a rogue group of the JASONS begins their own secret experimentation with a cadre of the best children. They seek to create a world prophet for the new millennium, one to be manipulated to craft a new era of global peace . . . a peace on their own terms. But such manipulation has grim consequences.

To stop the JASONS before they engineer the extinction of mankind, Commander Gray Pierce of SIGMA Force races against time to solve a mystery that dates back to the first famous oracle of history—the Greek Oracle of Delphi. But can the past save the future?

James Rollins—for the thrill of it!

393 A.D.
Mount Parnassus
Greece

THEY HAD COME TO SLAY HER.

Still, the woman stood at the temple's portico. She shivered in her thin garment, a simple shift of white linen belted at the waist, but it was not the cold of pre-dawn that iced her bones.

Below, a torchlight procession flowed up the slopes of Mount Parnassus like a river of fire, following the paved-stone road of the Sacred Way as it climbed in switchbacks up toward the temple of Apollo. The beat of sword on shield accompanied their progress, a full cohort of the Roman legion, five hundred strong. The road wound through broken monuments and long ransacked treasuries. Whatever could burn had been set to torch.

As the firelight danced over the ruins, the flames cast a shimmering illusion of better times, a fiery restoration of former glory: treasuries overflowing with gold and jewels, legions of statues carved by the finest artisans, milling crowds gathered to hear the prophetic words of the Oracle.

But no more.

Over the past century, Delphi had been brought low by invading Gauls, by plundering Thracians, but most of all, by neglect. Few now came to seek the words of the Oracle: a goat herder questioning a wife's fidelity, or a sailor seeking good omens for a voyage across the Gulf of Corinth. Even Emperor Julian's attempt to revive the old gods had died away.

It was the end of times, the end of the Oracle of Delphi. After prophesizing for thirty years, she would be the last to bear the name Pythia.

The last Oracle of Delphi.

But with this burden came one last great challenge.

Behind Pythia, the limestone cliffs known as the Phraedriades, the "Shining Ones," now danced with the approaching flames, reflecting the torchlight. She turned toward the east, where the sky had begun to lighten.

Oh, that rosy Eos, goddess of dawn, would hurry Apollo to tether his four horses to his Sun chariot.

One of Pythia's sisters, a young acolyte, stepped out of the temple behind her. "Mistress, come away with us," the younger woman begged. "It is not too late. We can still escape with the others to the high caves."

Pythia placed a reassuring hand on the woman's shoulder, then smoothed the long white alb that draped to her ankles. Over the past night, the other women had fled to the rugged heights where the caves of Dionysus would keep them safe. But Pythia had a final duty here.

"Mistress, surely there is no time to perform this last prophecy."

"I must."

"Then do it now. Before it is too late."

Pythia turned away. "We must wait for dawn of the seventh day. That is our way."

As the sun had set last night, Pythia had begun her preparations. She had bathed in Castilia's silver spring and had drunk from the sacred waters of Kassotis. While fasting through the night, she had burned bay leaves and barley meal on an altar of black marble outside the temple. She had followed the ritual precisely, the same as the first Pythia thousands of years ago.

Only this time, the Oracle had not been alone in her purifications.

At her side had been a girl, barely past her twelfth summer.

Such a small creature and of such strange manner.

The child had simply stood naked in the spring waters while the older woman had washed and anointed her. She'd said not a word, merely stood with an arm out, opening and closing her fingers as if grasping for something only she could see. What god so suffered the child, yet blessed her just the same? Surely not even Apollo. Yet the child's words thirty days ago could only come from the gods. Words that had plainly spread and stoked the fires that now climbed toward Delphi.

Oh, that the child had never been brought here.

Pythia had been content to allow Delphi to fade into obscurity. She remembered the words spoken by one of her predecessors, long dead for centuries, an ominous portent.

Emperor Augustus had asked of her dead sister, "Why has the Oracle grown so silent?"

Her sister had responded, "A Hebrew boy, a god who rules among the blessed, bids me leave this house . . ."

Those words proved to be a true prophecy. The cult of Christ rose to consume the empire and destroyed any hope for a return to the old ways.

Even she repeated such a doom a year ago.

Tell the emperor that my hall has fallen to the ground. Apollo no longer has his house . . . nor his prophetic spring. The water has dried up.

And so she had believed.

Then a moon ago, the strange girl had been brought to her steps.

Pythia glanced away from the flames and toward the *adyton*, the inner sanctum of Apollo's temple. The girl waited inside.

She was an orphan from the distant township of Chios. Her mother had died in childbirth; her father had been drowned at sea. Over the ages, many had hauled such orphans here, seeking to abandon such burdens upon the sisterhood. Most were turned away. Only the most ideal girls were allowed to stay: smooth and straight of limb, clear of eye and unspoiled of body, fierce and noble of constitution. Apollo would never accept a vessel of lesser quality for his prophetic spirit. In the past, Pythia had witnessed the god's *pneuma*, his prophetic vapors, slay those found wanting, proving them too weak a vessel to contain Apollo's spirit.

So when this willow branch of a girl had been presented naked to the steps of Apollo's temple, Pythia had given her hardly a glance. The child was unkempt, dirty, her dark hair knotted and tangled, her skin marked with pox scars and burnt by the sun to a dark copper. But deeper, Pythia had sensed something *wrong* with the child. The way she rocked back and forth. Even her eyes stared without truly seeing. At first, Pythia had thought the child was blind. But then those sky-blue eyes had found hers.

Her patrons had claimed the child was touched by the gods. That she could tell the number of olives in a tree with merely a glance, that she could declare when a sheep would lamb with but a touch of her hand, that she could predict which stage of the moon would appear for any night, even hundreds of years in the future.

Upon hearing such stories, Pythia's interest had stirred. She called the girl to join her at the entrance to the temple. The child obeyed, but she moved as if disconnected, as if the winds themselves propelled her upward. Pythia had to draw her by hand to sit on the top step.

"Can you tell me your name?" she asked the thin child.

The girl dug a fingernail into the marble.

"Her name is Anthea," one of her patrons declared from below.

Pythia kept her gaze focused on the child. "Anthea, do you know why you've been brought here?" she tried again.

"Your house is empty," the child finally mumbled to the floor.

So at least she could speak. Pythia glanced to the temple's interior. The hearth fire burned in the center of the main hall. It was indeed empty at the moment, but the child's words seemed to echo Pythia's own prophecy.

. . . My hall has fallen to the ground. Apollo no longer has his house . . .

Without looking up from the steps, the girl whispered in a reed-thin voice. "I can see far from here."

"That is indeed true."

From this perch, all of Delphi spread below, but Pythia sensed the child was not commenting on the view, but on something more significant. And then there was her manner. So strange, so *distant*, as if she stood with one leg in this world and the other beyond this realm.

The child glanced up with those clear blue eyes, so full of innocence, so in contrast from what spilled next from her lips.

"You are old. You will die soon."

From below, her patron attempted to scold her, but Pythia kept her words soft. "We all die eventually, Anthea. It is the order of the world."

She shook her head. "Not the Hebrew boy."

Those strange eyes bored into her. The hairs along Pythia's arms shivered. Plainly the girl had been taught the catechism of the cult of Christ and his bloody cross. But her words again. Such strange cadence.

The Hebrew boy . . .

Another echo, this time of her long-dead sister's prophecy of doom. "But another will come," the girl continued. "Another boy."

"Another boy?" Pythia leaned closer. "Who? From where?"

"From my dreams." The girl rubbed the heel of one hand at her ear.

Sensing there were depths to the girl that remained untapped, Pythia plumbed them. "This boy?" she had asked. "Who is he?"

What the child said next drew a gasp from the gathered crowd—even they recognized blasphemy when they heard it.

"He is the brother of the Hebrew boy." The child then clasped tight to the hem of Pythia's skirt. "He burns in my dreams . . . and he will burn everything. Nothing will last. Not even Rome."

For the past month, Pythia had attempted to learn more of this doom, even taking the girl into the sisterhood's fold. But the child had seemed only to retreat into herself, going mute. Still, there was one way to learn more.

The power of the Apollo's breath, his prophetic vapors.

If the girl were truly blessed, the vapors would fill her with Apollo's fire. It would burn free what was locked within the girl's strangeness.

But was there enough time?

A touch to her elbow interrupted her reverie and drew her back to the present. "Mistress, the sun . . ." her younger sister urged.

Pythia focused to the east. The eastern skies blazed, heralding the coming sunrise. Below, shouts rose from the Roman legion. Over the past turn of the moon, word of the girl had spread. Prophecies of doom had traveled far . . . even to the ears of the emperor. An Imperial courier had demanded the child be delivered to Rome, declaring her demon-plagued.

Pythia had refused. The gods had sent this child to her threshold, to Apollo's temple. There had to be a reason. Pythia would not relinquish the girl without first testing her, putting her to the question.

To the east, the first rays of the sun etched the morning skies.

They had waited long enough.

Pythia turned her back on the fiery legion. "Come. We must hurry."

She swept into the temple's interior. Flames greeted her here, too, but they were the welcoming warmth from the temple's sacred hearth. The fire had been stoked all night. Two of her elder sisters still tended the hearth. They were too old to make the harsh climb to the caves. So they had volunteered to remain behind, to aid Pythia in this last duty.

She nodded her gratitude to each in turn, then hurried past the hearth, followed by her younger sister.

At the back of the temple, stairs led down toward the private sanctum. Only those who served the Oracle were allowed to enter the subterranean *adyton*. As she descended, marble turned to raw limestone. The stairs emptied into a small cavern. The cave had been discovered ages ago by a goat herder, who upon nearing the cavern opening, fell under the sway of Apollo's sweet-smelling vapors and succumbed to strange visions.

Would that such gifts would last one more sunrise.

Pythia found the child waiting inside the cave. The girl was dressed in an alb too large for her and sat cross-legged beside the bronze tripod that supported the sacred *omphalos*, a waist-high domed rock that represented the navel of the world. The hollow stone marked the center of the world. Once, a pair of gold eagles had flanked the stone, representing the eagles of Zeus, but they had been stolen long ago. Even the statue of Apollo that once graced the chamber lay in a crumpled pile of broken marble.

The only other decoration in the cave was a single raised seat, resting on three legs. It stood over a natural crack in the floor. Pythia, long accustomed to Apollo's vapor, was still struck by the scent rising from below, smelling of almond blossoms.

The god's *pneuma,* his prophetic exhalation.

"It is time," she said to the younger sister. "Bring the child to me."

Pythia crossed to the tripod and mounted the seat. Positioned over the crack in the floor, the rising vapors bathed her. She felt Apollo's breath swell over her as she sat. "Hurry."

The younger sister gathered up the child. The girl did not resist. The woman carried her to Pythia and lifted the girl into her lap. Pythia cradled her gently, like a mother with a babe, but the child did not respond to such affection. The only acknowledgment of Pythia's touch was a stiffening of the girl's limbs.

Pythia rocked her. She already felt the effect of the *pneuma* rising from the earth below her. A familiar tingle ran along her limbs. Her throat burned warmly as Apollo entered her. Her vision began to close.

But the child was smaller, more susceptible to the *pneuma*.

The stiff resistance in her limbs relaxed. The girl's head rolled back; her eyelids drooped. Surely she would not survive Apollo's penetration for long. Still, if there was to be any hope, the girl had to be put to the question.

"Child," Pythia rang out, "tell us more of this boy and the doom he whispered to you. Where will he rise?"

The small lips moved in a whisper. "From me. From my dreams."

Small fingers found her hand and squeezed with more strength than Pythia thought remained in the girl.

Words continued to spill from the girl's lips. "Your house is empty . . . your springs have dried up."

Again she was repeating Pythia's own words of doom.

"But a new spring will flow."

Pythia's arms tightened on the girl. For too long, ruin had lingered over the temple. "A new spring at Delphi?"

"No . . ."

Pythia's breath grew more rapid. "Then from where will it spring?"

The girl's lips moved but no words came out.

She shook the girl. "Where?"

The girl lifted a boneless arm and placed a hand on her own belly.

With that touch, a vision swelled through Pythia, of silver waters gushing from the girl's navel. A new spring. But was it a vision from Apollo? Or was it born from her own hope?

A scream pierced her daze. Hard voices echoed down. From the stairs a figure stumbled into view. It was one of the elders who had tended the fire. She clutched a hand to her shoulder. A crimson bloom spread from under her palm. A black head of an arrow protruded between her fingers.

"Too late," the old woman cried out and collapsed to her knees. "The Romans are here."

Pythia heard the woman's words but remained lost in the vapors. Behind her eyes, she still pictured the silver spring flowing from the girl, a new font of prophetic power. But Pythia also smelled the smoke from the Roman torches. Blood and smoke leaked into her vision. The silver spring now ran with a thin stream of black crimson and swept into the future.

The child suddenly sagged in her arms, completely lost to the *pneuma*'s vapors. Still, as Pythia studied the vision, she watched the dark stream form a black figure . . . the shadow of a boy. Flames rose behind him.

The child's words from a moon ago echoed to her.

The brother of the Hebrew boy . . . he who would set fire to the world.

Pythia held the limp girl. The child's prophecy hinted at both doom and salvation. Perhaps it would be best to leave her to the Imperial legion, to end such an uncertain future here. From overhead, the tromp of heavy tread echoed down. There was already no escape. Except in death.

Still, the vision swelled in her.

Apollo had sent the child. To Pythia.

A new spring will flow.

She took a deep breath, drawing Apollo fully into her.

What must I do?

THE ROMAN CENTURION crossed the hall. He had his orders. To slay the girl who spoke of the Empire's doom. Last night, they had captured one of the temple's servants, a maid. Under the lash—and before he gave her to his men— she let it be known that the child still remained at the temple.

"Bring the torches!" he yelled. "Search every corner!"

Movement near the back of the hall drew his eye—and his sword.

A woman appeared from the shadows of a lower stair.

She stumbled forward, weaving two steps into view, unsteady, dazed. Dressed all in white, she bore a crown of laurel branches.

He knew who stood before him.

The Oracle of Delphi.

The centurion fought back a tremble of fear. Like many of the legion, he still secretly practiced the old ways. Even slaughtered bulls to Mithra and bathed in their blood.

Still, a new sun was on the rise.

There was no stopping it.

"Who dares violate Apollo's temple?" she called out to them.

With the stony weight of his men's eyes upon him, the centurion marched to face the woman. "Bring forth the girl!" he demanded. "She who speaks the empire's doom."

The Oracle met his gaze unblinking. He saw her eyes swimming somewhere beyond the moment. "She is gone. Beyond even your reach."

The centurion knew that was impossible. The temple was surrounded.

Unless the maid had lied.

Worry pushed him forward, but the Oracle stepped to block him from the stairs. She held a palm against his breastplate. "The *adyton* below is forbidden to all men."

"But not to the emperor. And I am under his edict."

She refused to move. "You will not pass."

The centurion had his orders under the seal of Emperor Theodosius. The old gods were to be silenced, their old temples torn down. All across the empire, including Delphi. The centurion had been given one additional command.

He would obey.

He thrust his sword deep into the Oracle's belly and drove it full to the hilt. A gasp escaped her. She fell against his shoulder like in a lover's embrace. He shouldered her away from him, roughly, mostly in shame, then yanked his sword back.

Blood splashed across his armor, across the floor.

The Oracle slumped to the marble, then to her side. A trembling arm reached to the pool of her own blood. Her palm settled into it. "A new spring . . ." she whispered as if it were a promise.

Then her body went slack with death.

The centurion stepped over her form and let his sword lead him down the stairs. Careful of any traps, he entered a small blind cave. To one side, an old woman's corpse, arrow-bit, lay in a black pool of blood. A three-legged chair lay toppled beside a riven crack in the floor. He searched the rest of the room as the air burned his nose.

A frown creased his face. He turned full circle, his sword outstretched. Impossible.

The chamber was empty.